UNLEASH
the
Night

Sherrilyn Kenyon

St. Martin's Paperbacks

This is a work of fiction. All of the characters, organizations, and events portrayed in this novel are either products of the author's imagination or are used fictitiously.

UNLEASH THE NIGHT

ISBN: 0-312-93433-5
EAN: 9780312-93433-0

Printed in the United States of America

St. Martin's Paperbacks edition / January 2006

St. Martin's Paperbacks are published by St. Martin's Press, 175 Fifth Avenue, New York, NY 10010.

10 9 8 7 6 5

"Thoughtful and provocative . . . *Kiss of the Night* is a perfect 10 and a strong contender for Best Paranormal of the Year. Long live the Dark-Hunters!"

—*Romance Reviews Today*

DANCE WITH THE DEVIL

"Move over, Anne Rice. Kenyon's Dark-Hunter books are changing the face of the vampire novel, making it hip, darker, and all the more appealing."

—*Publishers Weekly*

"*Dance with the Devil* clinches Sherrilyn Kenyon's place as a master of the genre! Zarek is a hero to die for, and his story will pull you in and keep you flipping pages into the wee hours; I couldn't put it down."

—Julie Kenner, author of *Aphrodite's Secret*

"A sensual, fast-paced read with a hero who is definitely worth the risk."

—*Booklist*

"Powerful and unforgettable, *Dance with the Devil* is my pick for Best Paranormal of the Year, and it is my pleasure to give it a perfect 10."

—*Romance Reviews Today*

"Truly exceptional!"   —*Old Book Barn Gazette*

"Using figures from mythology, Sherrilyn Kenyon provides a deep novel that a romantic fantasy lover will cherish. A powerful story that makes believers of skeptics that ancient gods and goddesses, Dark-Hunters, Dayslayers, and other mythological characters walk among us . . . another fine myth from a superb storyteller climbing to the top."

—*Baryon magazine*

"Kenyon pulls out all the stops in this fast-paced, action-filled adventure . . . the passion is fiery-hot and the unique characterizations of shape-shifters will leave readers hanging on the edge of their seats . . . this entire series of outstanding books is a keeper."

—*Rendezvous Reviews*

"Sherrilyn Kenyon's world of Dark-Hunters, Katagaria Slayers, Olympian gods, Oneroi, Apollites, demons and Daimons is a fascinating one. Her Dark-Hunter series sweeps readers away into a dangerous and sensual world . . . *Dance with the Devil* is a tempting delight for both old and new Kenyon readers."

—www.bookloons.com

NIGHT EMBRACE

"With her steamy, action-packed Dark-Hunter novels, Kenyon is ushering in a whole new class of night dwellers . . . an abundance of hot sex and snappy dialogue keep the plot both accessible and appealing. With its courageous, unconventional characters and wry humor, this fast-moving fantasy will fill the void left by the end of the *Buffy the Vampire Slayer* series."

—*Publishers Weekly*

"The second novel in Sherrilyn Kenyon's hot series is just as exciting, sexy, and thrilling as the first. Kenyon has hit on a fabulous premise that promises to be fodder for many more outstanding page-turners."

—*RT BOOKclub Magazine*

"Her heroes are not only the ultimate alpha men, but are also the embodiment of every female fantasy . . . well rounded, with romance as its cornerstone and plenty of action, suspense, humor, and sorrow."

—*The Road to Romance*

"A marathon of discoveries and pleasures—a wonderful addition to the Dark-Hunter series. Ms. Kenyon delivers another exciting, heart-pumping, virile male to titillate us . . . it's full of surprises, but this author's great storytelling talent is no surprise at all."

—*Old Book Barn Gazette*

Also by
Sherrilyn Kenyon

(LISTED IN THE CORRECT READING ORDER)

Limani

Inside all men and beasts is the eternal desire for a haven. Some place free of persecution, free of being hunted or harmed. But long ago there was no such place to be found for those who were both men and beasts. Those who could walk on four legs by day and two legs by night.

They were hunted by all, with no refuge to be found.

Their story, like all stories, had a beginning—a beginning of eternal love gone afoul. Aeons ago there was an ancient Greek king who had a queen who meant more to him than all the world. But his queen harbored a dark secret. She was born of a cursed race.

More than two thousand years before her birth, her people had made a tragic mistake. They had killed the mistress and child of the Greek god Apollo. In retaliation for the murders, the Greek god cursed her people with three things. They would have to drink the blood of their own in order to live. They could never again walk in daylight. But it was the third curse that was the most harsh. They would all die slowly and painfully on their twenty-seventh birthday.

True to the god's curse, the young queen painfully decayed into dust the day she turned twenty-seven. Helpless to stop it, the king watched as his beloved died, calling out his name. Once she was gone, he realized that his two sons were destined to meet the same horrific fate as their mother.

Unable to bear the loss of them, too, the king set out to magically elongate their lives. Using the darkest of magicks, he gathered up his wife's people, who were called Apollites, and he experimented on them. Splicing their cursed humanlike life force with that of the strongest of animals, he created two races. The Arcadians, who possessed human hearts, and the Katagaria, who possessed animal hearts.

The Arcadians were basically humans who were able to take animal form once they reached puberty— an event that for them occurs around the age of twenty-five. The Katagaria were animals who could take human form once they reached puberty at the same time. Two sides of the same coin, both species were born to wield magick and travel through time under the light of the full moon.

At long last, the Greek god's curse was lifted from at least those Apollites who had been transformed into both human and animal. No longer true Apollites, they could not be held to Apollo's curse. Or so the king thought until the ancient Greek god complained to the three Fates.

"Who are you to thwart the god's plan?" the Fates demanded as one voice.

The king answered defiantly. "Like any father worth his salt, I have protected my sons. No one will take their lives needlessly over something they had no part in."

But that wasn't good enough for the Fates. They were angered by the king's hubris. How dare he seek a way to alter the fate of the Apollites he had experimented upon. As punishment, they demanded that he kill the Arcadians and Katagaria, beginning with his own sons.

He refused.

"Then there will never be peace between the two," the Fates decreed. "From this day forward, the Arcadians and the Katagaria will know nothing but strife from each other. They will hunt and kill each other until there are no more of their kind left."

So it has been for thousands of years. Arcadians killing Katagaria who in turn kill Arcadians. Their war has lasted even unto this day . . .

And even beyond it.

But as with all wars, over time, small truces were needed. Savitar, the impartial mediator between the Arcadians and Katagaria, set up limanis or sanctuaries where human and animal could go without fear of being hunted. In these few designated places, both the Katagaria and the Arcadians can rest for a time before they rejoin their ranks and begin warring anew.

It isn't easy to be recognized as such a place, but once that has been achieved, no man or beast can ever breech the limani's sanctity. Not without incurring the wrath of all branches of Arcadians and Katagaria alike.

It is a sacred honor to be a sanctuary and it is a heavy burden. Peace always comes as a result of sacrifice. And few have sacrificed more than the bear clan who controls the Sanctuary bar in New Orleans. . . .

Chapter 1

"Law, much like life, was ever a study of trials. . . ."

The words from her textbook hovered in Marguerite D'Aubert Goudeau's mind and conjured up the familiar phrase of her friend and study partner Nick Gautier: *"Yeah, right. Life is a soul-sucking test that you either survive or you fail. Personally, I think failure blows, so I intend to survive and laugh my ass off at all the losers."*

A sad smile curved her lips as bittersweet pain lacerated her heart. She remembered Nick and his caustic take on life, love, death, and everything in between. That man had been able to turn a phrase like nobody's business.

God, how she missed him. He'd been the closest thing to a brother she'd ever known, and there wasn't a day she didn't feel his absence to the deepest part of her soul.

She still couldn't believe that he was gone. That on this very evening, six months ago, his mother, Cherise Gautier, had been found murdered in their Bourbon Street home while Nick had mysteriously vanished without a trace. The New Orleans authorities were convinced that Nick was responsible for his mother's death.

Marguerite knew better.

No one on earth loved their mother more than Nick had loved his. If Cherise Gautier was dead, then so was Nick. No one would have been able to hurt her without facing his wrath. No one.

Marguerite was certain he'd gone after whoever had killed his mother and ended up dead himself. Most likely, he was lying in the bottom of a bayou somewhere. That was why no one had seen him since. And that knowledge tore her apart. Nick had been a good, caring man. A trusted confidant and generally an all-around fun guy.

In her formal, stodgy world of having to make sure she never said or did the wrong thing, he'd been a breath of fresh air and a wonderful dose of reality. It was why she wanted her friend back so desperately.

As Nick would say, her life basically sucked. Her friends were shallow, her father neurotic, and every time she thought she liked a guy, all her father could do was run a thorough background check on the man and his entire family and then tell her why he was socially unacceptable. Or, worse, *beneath* them.

She really hated that phrase.

"You have a destiny, Marguerite."

Yeah, she was destined to either end up in the mental ward or alone for the rest of her life so that she could in no way ever embarrass her father or her family.

She sighed as she stared at her law book on the library table and felt the familiar tears prick at the backs of her eyes. Nick had never liked studying in the library.

When he'd been in their group, they had all piled into his house four days a week to study together.

Now those days were gone and all she was left with was vapid, insecure blowhards who could only feel better about themselves by belittling everyone else.

"Are you all right, Margeaux?"

Marguerite cleared her throat at Elise Lenora Berwick's question. Elise was a tall, perfectly sculpted blonde. And Marguerite meant "sculpted." At twenty-four, Elise had already had six different plastic surgeries to correct her body's slight imperfections. In high school Elise had been the premier debutante of New Orleans, and now she was the reigning beauty at Tulane University.

The two of them had been friends since grade school. In fact, it had been Elise who had put together the study group three years ago when they'd all been undergraduates. Elise had never been one to really apply herself to schoolwork, and so she'd conceived this as a way to use them to help her pass her classes. Not that Marguerite minded. She actually admired Elise's ingenuity and liked watching the master manipulator get the others to do her bidding.

Only Marguerite and Nick had ever seen through Elise. Like Marguerite, Nick had been immune to the beautiful blonde's machinations. But that was okay. If not for Elise, Marguerite wouldn't have been able to get so close to Nick, and in her mind that would have been a true tragedy.

Now she, Elise, Todd Middleton Chatelaine, Blaine Hunter Landry, and Whitney Logan Trahan were all that was left of the group. And that hurt most of all.

Why aren't you here, Nick? I could really use your sense of humor right now.

Marguerite toyed with the edge of the book as an image of his face hovered in her mind. "I was just thinking of Nick. He always loved this law stuff."

"Didn't he, though?" Todd said as he looked up from his book. His black hair was cut short and worn in a perfect style around his handsome face. He had on an expensive red Tommy Hilfiger sweater and a pair of khaki pants. "Had he not been a criminal of questionable and shady parentage, he might have given your father a run for his office one day, Margeaux."

Marguerite tried not to let them see her grind her teeth as they continued to use a nickname she absolutely loathed. They thought it somehow made them closer to her since they used it while others didn't. But in truth, she much preferred the plain and simple "Maggie" that Nick alone had used. Of course that was too crass a nickname for such a refined family as hers. Her father would have an apoplexy if he'd ever heard Nick use it.

But she preferred it. It certainly matched her looks and personality a lot more than "Marguerite" or "Margeaux" ever would.

Now no one would ever call her Maggie again. . . .

The grief in her heart was overwhelming. How could anything hurt so much?

"I still can't believe he's not here anymore," Marguerite whispered, blinking back her tears. Part of her still expected to see him swagger through the doorway with that devilish grin on his face and a bag of beignets in his hand.

But he wouldn't. Ever.

"Good riddance to bad rubbish," Blaine said bitterly as he leaned back in his chair. At six feet even and extremely well-built, with jet-black hair, Blaine thought himself God's gift to all womankind. His family was rich and well connected, and they had given him an extremely overbloated sense of self-importance.

He'd hated Nick because Nick had never allowed Blaine to get away with his snobbery and had called him on the carpet for it on more than one occasion.

Marguerite pinned an angry glare on Blaine. "You're just ticked that he always outscored you on tests."

Blaine curled his lip. "He cheated."

Right. They all knew better. Nick had been exceptionally brilliant. Earthy and at times downright crude, he'd befriended Marguerite and helped her with schoolwork even outside the confines of this group. If not for him, she would have failed her ancient Greek civ class with Dr. Julian Alexander, who had been her undergraduate advisor.

Todd closed his book, then pushed it aside. "You know, I think we should do something to say good-bye officially to the old man. After all, he was part of this group."

Blaine scoffed. "What do you suggest? Burn incense to banish his stench?"

Whitney lightly slapped at Blaine's leg. "Do stop it, Blaine. You're upsetting poor Margeaux. She actually considered Nick a friend."

"I can't imagine why."

Marguerite stiffened as she narrowed her gaze on

him. "Because he was nice and caring." Unlike them. Nick wasn't pretentious or cold. He'd been real and he cared for people regardless of who they were related to or how much money they had.

Nick had been human.

"I know what we should do," Elise said, shutting her book as well. "Why don't we visit that place that Nick was always talking about? The one where his mother worked."

"Sanctuary?" Blaine looked completely disgusted. Marguerite hadn't even known a man could perfect such a lip curl. Elvis would be envious indeed. "I've heard it's down on the other side of the French Quarter. How positively gauche."

"I like the idea," Todd said as he tucked his book into his designer backpack. "I'm always up for a good slumming."

Blaine gave him a droll stare. "I've heard that about you, Todd. It's the curse of the nouveau riche."

Todd returned Blaine's stare tit for tat. "Fine then, stay here and keep our seats warm while your ass expands to the size of your ego." He stood up and captured Marguerite's attention. "I think we should bid our not quite esteemed member farewell, and what better way than to go and drink cheap alcohol in his favorite place?"

Blaine rolled his eyes. "You'll most likely contract hepatitis there."

"No, we won't," Whitney said. She looked up at Todd with fear in her bright blue eyes. "Will we?"

"No," Marguerite said firmly as she packed up her books. "Blaine's simply a coward."

He arched a brow at her. "Hardly. Being a thorough-bred on both sides, I have no inclination to waste time with riffraff."

Marguerite lifted her chin at his low blow. Every one of them knew that her mother was a Cajun from Slidell who had nowhere near the social status of her father. Even though she had gone to college on a full scholarship and had been Miss Louisiana, her mother's marriage to her father had been scandalous.

In the end, that disaster was what had led to her mother's death.

It was something only a true dog would hurl in Marguerite's face.

"Thoroughbred asshole, you mean," she said between clenched teeth as she rose to her feet. She slammed her book into her Prada backpack. "Nick was right, you are nothing but a prickly wuss who needs to have his butt kicked."

The women around her gaped at her language while Todd laughed.

Blaine turned an interesting shade of red.

"I have to say that I certainly love a little Cajun spice," Todd said as he joined her side. "Come along, Margeaux, and I'll be more than happy to keep you safe." He looked at the other two women. "Care to join us?"

Whitney looked like a child who was about to get away with staying up past her bedtime. "My parents would die if they knew I went into a dive. Count me in."

Elise nodded, too.

They looked at Blaine, who made a disgusted noise. "When all of you contract dysentery, remember who was the voice of reason."

Marguerite pulled her backpack on. "Dr. Blaine, the resident expert on Montezuma's revenge. We have it."

By the look on his face, she could tell he was dying to let fly a vicious retort, but good manners and common sense kept him from speaking. It wasn't wise to twice insult a U.S. senator's daughter when one had ambitions of gaining an internship with said senator in the fall.

And that was most likely what motivated Blaine to join them as they headed for Todd's SUV.

"Oh my goodness!" Whitney exclaimed the instant they entered the famed Sanctuary biker bar.

Marguerite's own eyes widened as she looked around the dark, grungy place that did appear to need a good and thorough cleaning. People were dressed in anything from biker leathers to T-shirts and jeans. The tables and chairs were a hodgepodge of rough design that didn't even match. The stage area was liberally painted black with odd splashes of gray, red, and white, and the billiard tables looked as if they'd survived many a bar fight in their day.

There was even straw spread out across the floor that reminded her of a barn.

The bar area to her right was occupied by rough-looking men drinking beers and yelling at one another. She could see a wooden stairway before them that led to an upstairs area, but she had no idea what was up there. Trouble came to her mind. A person could probably find a lot of trouble up there.

This place was definitely rustic.

But what held her attention most was the high concentration of handsome men working in the bar. They were everywhere. The bartenders, the waiters, the bouncers . . . She'd never seen anything like this. It was a testosterone smorgasbord.

Elise leaned over to whisper in her ear, "I think I might have just died and been sent to heaven. Have you ever seen so many gorgeous men in your life?"

It was all Marguerite could do to shake her head. It really was unbelievable. She was stunned that the news media hadn't caught wind of this and sent in a team to investigate what was in the water to make so many hot men in one place.

Even Whitney was gaping and ogling.

"What kind of music is that?" Blaine said, twisting his lips into a sneer as a new song started over the stereo that was piped through the length and breadth of the bar.

"I think it's called metal!" Todd shouted over the loud guitar solo.

"I call it painful myself," Whitney said. "Did Nick really hang out here?"

Marguerite nodded. Nick had loved this place. He'd spent hours telling her about it and the odd people who called this place home. "He said they had the best andouille sausage in the world."

Blaine scoffed. "Highly doubtful."

Todd indicated a table to the back with a tilt of his head. "I think we should sit and have a drink in memory of old Nick. You only live once, you know?"

"Drink out of the glasses here and you probably won't live through the night," Blaine said. He looked less than enthusiastic as they followed Todd to the table and took a seat.

Marguerite shrugged her backpack off, dug her purse out, then placed it under the table. She hung her purse on her chair, then took a seat. The place was very loud and yet she could easily see Nick in here. There was something about it that reminded her of him. Aside from the rather tacky decor, which he'd always preferred. She often suspected that he dressed tacky just to nettle people.

To her it had been one of his more endearing traits. He was the only person she'd ever known who truly hadn't cared what other people thought of him. Nick was Nick and if you didn't like it, you could leave.

"Can I get you guys something?"

She looked up to see an extremely beautiful blond woman around her own age. She was wearing a pair of skin-tight jeans and a small T-shirt with the Sanctuary logo of a motorcycle parked on a hill that was silhouetted by a full moon. Underneath the picture was the tagline *Sanctuary: Home of the Howlers.*

Blaine gave their waitress a hot once-over that the woman wisely ignored. "Yes, we'll all have the West-vleteren 8."

The waitress frowned at his choice of beer before she cocked her head as if to listen more carefully. "What was that?"

Blaine got that familiar smug look on his face and used his do-I-have-to-talk-to-the-simple? voice. "It's a Belgian beer, sweetie. Please tell me you've at least heard of it."

The waitress gave him a peeved glare. "Boy, I was

born in Brussels and the last time I checked, this was my new homeland, America, not my birthplace. So you can either order an American-made beer or I'll bring you water and you can sit there and act all superior until you puke, okay?"

Blaine looked as if he were ready to choke her. "Does your manager know that you talk to your customers like this?"

The waitress gave him a snide, indulgent smirk. "If you'd like to talk to my mother, who owns this bar, my overindulgent brother, who manages it, or my father, who delights in kicking everyone's ass around, about your treatment by me, just let me know and I'll be more than happy to go get one of them for you. I know they'd just *love* to waste their time dealing with *you*. They're real understanding that way."

Marguerite stifled a laugh. She didn't know the woman, but she was beginning to like her a lot. "I'll have a Bud Light, please."

The waitress winked conspiratorially at her before she wrote it down on her small pad.

"Here, too," Todd said.

Whitney and Elise joined in with their orders.

Then they all looked at Blaine and waited for his next nasty comment. "Bring mine unopened, with a napkin and an opener."

The waitress cocked her head with a devilish gleam in her eyes. "What? Afraid I'm going to spit in it, big boy?"

Todd laughed.

Before Blaine could respond, the blonde left them.

Marguerite's smile faded as she suddenly felt

something odd. . . . The hair on the back of her neck rose. It was like someone was watching her.

Intently.

Menacingly.

Turning her head, she scanned the crowd, looking for the source of her discomfort. But there was nothing there. No one seemed to be paying any attention to them at all.

There were several groups of burly bikers playing pool. Tons of tourists and bikers milling about. There was even a group of seven men playing poker in one corner. Waiters and the waitress walked back and forth to the bar and tables delivering food and drinks while the two bartenders went about their business.

No one was even remotely looking in Marguerite's direction.

I must be imagining it.

At least that's what she thought until she spotted a man in the corner who appeared to be staring straight at her. Dressed in a baggy, untucked white button-down shirt covered by a dirty white apron, and faded, dingy black jeans that had seen much better days, he was a busboy who had paused in cleaning off a table. The sleeves of his shirt were rolled back to the middle of his forearms. His left arm held a bright, colorful tattoo that she couldn't make out at this distance.

She had no idea what he looked like, since his thick dark blond hair obscured most of his face and fell over both of his eyes. The back of it hung just past his shoulders. In fact, given his hairdo she couldn't really tell where he was looking, but every instinct in her body said it was at her.

There was something about him that seemed dark and dangerous. Predatory. Almost sinister.

She rubbed her neck nervously, wishing he would turn his attention back to his job.

"Is something wrong?" Blaine asked.

"No," she said quickly, offering him a smile. If she mentioned it, he would no doubt make a scene and get the poor man fired from a job he probably needed. "I'm fine." But the feeling didn't subside and there was something so animalistic and fierce about it that she was definitely unnerved.

Wren tilted his head as he watched the unknown woman who looked so out of place that he wondered how she'd happened into their bar. Sophistication and money bled from her every pore. She definitely wasn't their usual clientele.

He could also tell that she wasn't comfortable under his close scrutiny. But then, no one was, it was why he seldom made eye contact with anyone. He'd learned a long time ago that no person or beast could stand the intensity of him for very long.

And yet he couldn't take his eyes off her. Her dark chestnut hair that she had tied back into a ponytail held traces of auburn highlights—that and her darker skin tone betrayed a Cajun heritage. She wore a delicate pink sweater set and a long khaki skirt with matching pink espadrilles.

Best of all, she had a lush, curvy body that beckoned a man to hold it close and taste it.

She certainly wasn't the most beautiful woman he'd

ever seen, but there was something about her that held his attention. Something about her that seemed lost and hurt.

Sad.

In the wilds of Asia where he'd been born, such a creature as she would have been killed and eaten by something stronger. Fiercer. Vulnerability of any kind was an invitation for death. And yet he didn't feel that familiar swell of adrenaline that made him want to attack the weak.

He felt an inexplicable desire to protect her.

More than that, he wanted to go over to her and offer comfort, but then, what did he know about comforting a human? He was a feral predator in human form. All he knew was how to stalk and to kill.

How to fight.

He knew nothing of comfort. Nothing of women. He was alone in the world by choice, and he liked it that way.

Marvin, the resident monkey mascot of Sanctuary, came running up to Wren with a new cloth for cleaning the tables. He took it from Marvin's hand as he forced himself to go back to cleaning the table. Still, he felt the unknown woman's presence, and before long he found himself staring at her again while she talked to her group of friends.

Marguerite took a sip of her beer while Elise and Whitney ogled the men in the bar. She reached for a pretzel only to have Blaine slap her hand.

He looked aghast at her. "Are you insane? Do you

know how long that has been out? How many grimy hands have been in it? For that matter, our termagant waitress probably poisoned it just for spite."

Marguerite rolled her eyes at his unreasonable paranoia. She glanced back to the busboy, who had moved closer now. He was working again, but even so she sensed that she was his primary focus.

She frowned as she saw a tiny brown spider monkey run up the busboy's arm to rest on his shoulder.

The busboy pulled a small carrot from his white apron's pocket to hand to the monkey, who ate it while the busboy returned to work. She bit back a smile as she realized who this guy was. He must be Wren. Nick used to talk about him from time to time. He'd told her that at first he'd thought Wren was mute, since he never, ever spoke to anyone. They'd known each other for a full year before Wren had finally mumbled, "Hi," one day when Nick had come in to visit his mother.

According to Nick, Wren was a complete loner who kept to himself and who refused to participate in the world. The only reason Marguerite knew it was him was that Nick would talk about the monkey . . . Wren's only real friend, who was prone to steal their billiard balls while the two of them played in the back corner of the bar.

The monkey was named Marvin. . . .

Blaine caught sight of her watching the busboy. He turned in his chair to see Wren, who had returned to staring at her. At least that's what it seemed like, but again, he kept his hair over his eyes, so there was no way to know for certain.

"Is he bothering you?"

"No," Marguerite said quickly, afraid of what Blaine might do. In a weird way, she felt almost flattered. Men didn't normally notice her unless they knew who her father was. It had been her mother who had turned heads.

Never Marguerite.

"What are you looking at?" Todd snapped at the man.

Wren ignored him as he moved to the table beside theirs that was covered with glasses and a plate of half-eaten nachos.

Marguerite could sense that he wanted to speak to her and she found herself wondering what he looked like underneath all that blond hair. There was an air of danger around him. One of powerful restraint, and yet she sensed that he didn't want to attract anyone's attention.

It was as if he wanted to blend in seamlessly with the background but was completely unable to do so.

A strange image of a sitting tiger in the zoo came to her mind. That's what he reminded her of. A large beast that was carefully watching those around him, detached and yet confident that it could take down anyone who messed with it.

"What a freak," Blaine said as he looked over to see Wren watching them. "Hey, buddy, why don't you do something with those disgusting dreads?" Blaine tossed a few dollars at Wren. "Why don't you use that to get a real haircut?"

Wren completely ignored Blaine and the money.

The monkey started squealing as if protecting Wren. Without a word, Wren patted the monkey's head, then whispered something to him. The monkey jumped off Wren's shoulder and scampered toward the bar.

Wren set his pan of dishes aside.

Her heart pounded as she realized he was coming toward her now. Up close, he was much larger than he'd appeared from a distance. For some reason, he slumped down and appeared to be around six feet, but if he were to straighten to his full height, she was sure he'd be around six two or three.

There was an aura of supreme power that surrounded him. One of speed and agility.

He was simply magnetic.

This close, she could finally see his eyes. They were a vibrant turquoise blue that was so pale they were haunting in their color.

And in their mercilessness.

He indicated her empty glass with a tilt of his chin. "Are you finished, my lady?" His voice was deep and resonant, mesmerizing. It sent a thrilling chill down her spine.

She smiled at his polite title. "Yes," she said, handing her glass toward him.

He wiped his hand off on his apron as if he didn't want to offend or dirty her before he reached for it.

At first she thought their hands might touch, but he moved his away as if he was afraid of making such intimate contact. A strange disappointment filled her.

Dropping his gaze, he took her glass, holding it as if it were precious, and moved away. He set it in the pan, then glanced back at her.

"Excuse me, Rasta-mon?" Todd said rudely. "You

don't need to be looking at her, asshole. She's way out of your league."

Wren cut Todd a bored look that said he didn't find him much of a threat.

"Wren?" the blond waitress said as she came up to him and confirmed his identity for Marguerite. The waitress paused to give them a warning glower before she softened her expression and looked back at Wren. "It's time for you to take a break, okay, sweetie?"

He nodded.

As he started away, Blaine pushed at the pan in his hands. "Yeah, sweetie, hang out with your own kind in the gutter."

Before Marguerite realized what he was doing, Blaine slung his drink in the man's face.

Wren let out a sound that was a strange hissing growl that didn't seem quite human. In a split second, he dropped the pan and lunged for Blaine.

Out of nowhere a group of men appeared to pull Wren back. She staggered to her feet and watched as the four much larger bouncers had to struggle to hold on to Wren. They surrounded him so well that Marguerite couldn't even see him anymore as they formed a barrier as if to protect her group.

The waitress was livid. "Get out!" she snarled at them. "All of you."

"Why?" Blaine asked. "We're paying customers."

Another blond man came up, one who bore a striking resemblance to the waitress. He must be the brother she had mentioned earlier who managed the bar. "You better do what Aimee says, boy. We just saved your life, but even we can't hold him for too long. By the time his vision clears, you better be long gone or we're not responsible for what he does to you."

Blaine sneered at him. "He touches me and I'll sue all of you."

The man laughed menacingly. "Trust me, there won't be enough of you left to feed through a straw, never mind file a lawsuit, dweeb. Now get out of my bar before I throw you out."

"Come on, Blaine," Todd said, pulling him toward the door. "We've been here long enough."

Whitney and Elise balked at having to leave, but like dutiful zombies they got up and followed the men.

Marguerite stayed behind.

"Margeaux?" Todd asked.

"Go on. I'll catch up later."

Blaine shook his head at her. "Don't be stupid, Margeaux. Our kind doesn't belong here."

She was so sick of the "our kind, their kind" mentality. She'd had quite enough of that in her life, and much to her entire family's chagrin, her thought was that there were only two kinds of people in the world. Those who were decent and those who were mean.

Personally, she was sick to death of those who were mean. "Shut up, Blaine. Go home before *I* beat you."

Blaine rolled his eyes before he headed for the door with Elise and Whitney in tow.

"Are you sure you want to stay?" Todd asked.

"Yes. I'll catch a cab home."

He looked less than convinced, but he must have recognized her determination to stay. "Okay. Be careful."

She nodded, then waited for him to leave before she headed off in the direction where she'd seen the bouncers take Wren. This whole fiasco had been her fault. The least she could do was apologize for the fact that she was dumb enough to hang out with assholes.

She found a small hallway that led to the restrooms and to an area marked: *Private. Staff Only.* At first she thought the men might have gone into the private office area, until she heard voices drifting out from the men's room.

"Don't wet his face again, Colt, he'll tear your arm off for it."

Again she heard that fierce, animalistic growl and something that sounded like someone being pushed back.

"I told you," the masculine voice said again. "Stupid humans. That boy's lucky we didn't let Wren have at him. You don't pull a tiger's tail unless you want to get eaten."

"What the hell were you doing talking to that girl anyway?" another voice asked. "Jeez. Since when do you talk to anyone, Wren?"

She heard the growl again, followed by the sound of breaking glass.

"Fine," the first voice said. "Have your tantrum. We'll wait outside."

The bathroom door opened to show her two men who were well over six feet tall. One had short black hair and the other had long black hair pulled into a ponytail. They stopped between her and the door to eye her warily.

"Is he all right?" she asked them.

The one with long hair gave her a strange look. "You ought to go on and get out of here. You've caused enough trouble for one night."

But oddly enough, she didn't want to leave. "I . . ." She forgot her words as the bathroom door opened to show her Wren again as he left the room to enter the hallway, too.

His shirt was wet, making parts of it cling to a very well-muscled chest. He had a towel draped over one shoulder and his head was down. The gesture reminded her more of a predator that was watching the world warily, waiting to pounce, than someone who was bashful or shy.

He approached her slowly, methodically. Something about his movements was reminiscent of a cat right before he brushed up against his owner to nuzzle her or mark her as his.

Wren wiped at his face with the back of his hand before he cut a sinister glare at the men.

"Leave," he growled.

The one with long hair stiffened as if he hated the idea of being ordered about.

"C'mon, Justin," the short-haired man, who must be Colt, said in a conciliatory tone. "Wren still needs time to cool down."

Justin let out a low, sinister growl of his own before he headed back into the bar.

Colt passed a warning look to her, then headed off to the counter.

Marguerite swallowed as she approached Wren slowly. This close she could tell that his baggy shirt covered a lean, hard body. His skin was a deep tawny gold that was so inviting that it should be illegal.

There was something about him that appeared completely uncivilized. He even looked like he'd slept in his clothes. It was obvious this man didn't care what anyone thought of him. He didn't follow fashion or any rule of civility. From what she'd overheard while they'd been in the bathroom, it didn't even appear he was moderately sociable at all.

In theory she should be repulsed by him, and yet she wasn't. All she wanted to do was brush back the mop of blond hair and see if he was as handsome as she suspected.

"I'm so sorry," she said quietly. "I didn't know Blaine was going to do that to you."

He didn't speak. Instead he took a step toward her, so close now that she could feel the heat from his body. He reached out toward her. He paused his hand just before he made contact with her cheek and held it there, hovering while those eerie blue eyes scorched her.

Wren wanted to touch her so badly that he could taste it. He'd never wanted anything more. But then, he knew that he shouldn't.

She was human.

And she was beautiful. Her hair appeared softer than down. Her skin glowed with vital warmth. He would give anything for one tiny taste of that skin to see if she were as delectable as she appeared.

But he couldn't.

An animal like him could never touch something as fragile as her. It was in his nature to destroy, never nurture. He let his hand fall away.

"Are you Nick's friend he used to talk about?" she asked quietly.

Wren cocked his head at her unexpected question. "You knew Nick?"

She nodded. "I went to school with him. We used to study together. He said that he had a friend here named Wren who always kicked his butt at pool. Was that you?"

Wren looked over at the pool tables and nodded as he remembered his friend. Not that Nick had really known anything about Wren. But at least Nick had tried to befriend him. It'd been a nice change of pace.

"It was me," he whispered, not sure why he bothered when he seldom spoke to anyone.

But he wanted to speak to her. He loved the soft, gentle lilt of her voice. She appeared so tender. So feminine. A foreign, alien part of himself actually wanted to cuddle with her.

He leaned forward ever so slightly so that he could discreetly inhale the scent of her. Her skin was warm and sweet and held traces of talcum powder and a spicy wood scent of lotion. It made him hard and aching.

He'd never kissed a woman, but for the first time he wanted to. Her parted lips looked so inviting.

So delicious . . .

"Wren?"

He turned his head as he heard Nicolette Peltier's voice behind him.

The older Frenchwoman approached them from the bar's office. He could sense that Nicolette wanted to reach out and pull him away from the human, but like the others who made Sanctuary their home, Nicolette was afraid of him. His kind was unpredictable. Deadly.

Everyone feared him. Except for the woman before him.

But then, she had no idea that he was a tigard walking in the skin of a human.

"I should go now," he said to her, moving away.

The woman reached out and touched his arm. His groin jerked in response as that touch branded him. It was all he could do to suppress the animal that wanted to take her for his own. Normally, he gave in to those urges.

Tonight he couldn't. To do so could hurt her, and that was the last thing he wanted.

"I'm really sorry about what happened," she said softly. "It was inexcusable and I hope they didn't get you into any trouble or hurt you."

He didn't say anything as she glanced at Nicolette, then turned around and left.

She was gone. It went through him like a knife.

"Come, Wren," Nicolette said. "I think it best if you end your shift now and retire for the night."

Wren didn't argue. He did need some time out of his human form, especially given how volatile he felt right then. It was as if his body were electrified. Elevated. He'd never felt anything like this in his life.

Without another word, he headed for the kitchen, which had a door that led to the building next door where the animal-weres made their home.

Peltier House had long been a refuge for creatures like himself . . . creatures who had been thrown out of their clans for all manner of reasons. As Aimee so often said, they were all refugees and misfits.

Wren was more so than most. He'd never had an animal clan that he belonged to. Neither tiger nor leopard would tolerate his mixed presence. He was a mutant hybrid who should never have been allowed to live.

Here lately he could tell even the bears weren't fond

of him, either. They damned sure didn't trust him. It was subtle. They would gather up their cubs whenever they climbed on him. Or they would do like tonight and isolate him anytime they suspected that he might be getting angry.

That was why he'd valued Nick so much. Nick had treated Wren like he was normal.

"What the hell?" Nick would say. *"We're all screwed up some way. At least you bathe and I don't have to fight you for chicks. In my book, that makes you all right."*

Nick had held a unique view of the world.

Wren pulled his wet shirt off as he headed up the stairs. Marvin came bounding up behind him. He'd only climbed halfway up when a bad feeling went through him.

The woman . . .

She was in trouble.

Wren mentally willed a black T-shirt on his body as he sensed imminent threat for her. Without a word to Marvin, he flashed himself out of the building, onto the street.

Chapter 2

Marguerite slowed as she again felt the sensation of someone watching her from the shadows. She was heading down Chartres, toward Jackson Square, so that she could grab a taxi and get home before it got any later.

Looking around, she half-expected to find Wren there.

She didn't. What she found was four scruffy-looking men who were eyeing her with an unfounded interest. They were keeping to the shadows as if they didn't want her to identify them. Fear assaulted her. Their attention was just a bit too focused. A bit too intense and threatening as they made their way straight for her.

She glanced about, looking for other people, but this time of night, there weren't any around.

Not even a tour group. . . .

It's okay. Stay in the light and keep heading forward. They won't hurt you if you stay in plain sight.

She sped up as she heard the sound of running feet.

Just as she was sure they would run past her, one of the men grabbed her and slung her into a partially opened courtyard.

Marguerite tried to push him away to run.

He slapped her hard. "Give me your purse, bitch."

She was so scared, she couldn't even think to pull it off her arm.

The other men ran into the courtyard and slammed the gate shut. One of them grabbed her bag and tore her shirt in the process of ripping it off her shoulder.

"Hey," he said to the other three. "Y'all want to have some fun with her?"

Before they could answer, the one speaking went sprawling to the ground. Someone came out of the darkness and handed the purse back to her.

Marguerite looked up at the newcomer and wanted to cry as she saw Wren there. No longer slumped, he stood at his full height . . . and it was commanding. Intense. There was a feral gleam in his eyes that wasn't quite sane as he put himself between her and the others. He looked as if he could easily kill everyone there and not even wince.

The men attacked.

She staggered back and watched in awe as Wren fought them off with an incredible skill. One mugger came at him with a knife. He caught the man's wrist and twisted it until it snapped and the knife fell from his hand. Then Wren backhanded the man so hard, the attacker rebounded off the wall.

Another came at Wren's back only to be flung over his head to the ground while another rushed him from behind. He hit Wren full force, but Wren didn't so much as stagger or flinch. He turned on the man and knocked him back.

Marguerite was relieved until one of the muggers pulled out a gun and aimed it at them.

Her breath caught as Wren froze.

A heartbeat later, the man fired the gun. Wren rushed him and knocked it out of his hands. The other three ran off as Wren slugged the one who'd held the gun. The man fell to the ground, then scurried away.

"Are you okay?" Marguerite asked as she ran over to Wren. "Did he shoot you?"

"I'm fine," he said, picking up the gun from the ground. He opened it up and removed the bullets before he smashed it to pieces against the old stone wall. He dropped it, then turned to look at her as he tossed the bullets into the darkness. "Did they hurt you?"

"No. Thanks to you, I'm fine." Relieved beyond belief, she was shaking so badly that she wasn't even sure how her legs could continue to hold her upright. She ached to reach out to touch him in gratitude, but there was something about him that said he didn't want to be touched.

Anger darkened his eyes as he glanced to her torn shirt. She could sense that he wanted to chase the muggers down on her behalf, and it warmed her greatly.

"I don't normally do things this stupid," she said quietly. "I tried to call a taxi on my cell phone, but they said it would be a thirty-to-forty-minute wait. I thought I could make it to the Square to hail one down there or to at least wait at the Café du Monde, where it would be safer. And then the next thing I knew they were after me. . . . Thank God you came when you did."

Her gratitude seemed to make him uncomfortable.

"C'mon," he said, tilting his head toward the street. "I'll walk you home."

She hesitated at his offer. "I live down by the zoo. It's too far to walk."

He looked as if he might argue. "I'll get you home. Don't worry."

Marguerite put her purse on her shoulder as he tucked his hands into his pockets and led her out of the courtyard, back to the street. His white shirt was gone and instead he wore a black T-shirt that hugged a fit and tight body. Even though he wasn't overdeveloped, like a bodybuilder, she could see every muscle clearly defined on him.

He was incredibly hot and sexy. And at that moment, he was her hero. She'd never been more grateful to anyone. Little did he know that he could do anything he wanted to with her right then and she wouldn't mind in the least. In fact, she wanted him to hold her to help calm her ragged nerves, but he didn't appear interested at all.

She felt the familiar pang of being nothing but a friend to guys. Just once in her life, she wished that a man would look at her with passion in his eyes. That a man would find her sexy and attractive. But they never did, not unless they were courting her father and were using her to get to him.

She might as well be invisible. She crossed her arms over her chest and sighed as the familiar grief settled deep in her heart.

As they walked, Wren didn't speak. In fact, he kept his head bent low and his gaze on the ground. Even so, she could tell that he was very much aware of everything around them.

She just wished he was every bit as aware of her.

Wren kept his teeth clenched. He could smell her desire and her uncertain nervousness. But he didn't know how to make her more at ease. He'd never been one to talk very much to anyone. Most people seemed to prefer him silent, or they ignored him entirely. Which was normally fine by him.

Not to mention it was taking a lot of concentration to remain in human form while he was wounded. The gunshot hadn't missed him. It'd hit him in his right shoulder and it hurt like hell. He was burning a lot of extra magic energy to hide the tear in his shirt and the blood.

But he didn't want her to know. It might make her feel bad to realize he'd been hurt defending her. Or, gods forbid, she might want him to seek medical help, which was the last thing he could do.

Or even worse than that, she might feel nothing at all, and that would make him angry. Humans could have strange emotions that he didn't quite fathom.

"Have you worked at Sanctuary long?" she asked.

"A little while."

That didn't seem to quite placate her. "Do you go to school anywhere? Or do you just work full-time at the bar?"

"I go to school." It was a lie and he wasn't even sure why he'd told it. Kyle Peltier—the youngest member of the Peltier bear clan—and a couple of the other waiters went to college, but Wren wasn't the type to mingle enough with humans to bother.

What he needed to know to survive had never been taught in a classroom.

But for some reason he didn't understand, he wanted to appear normal to her. He wanted her to think of him as just an average guy whom she might have met.

Being different had never bothered him before, but tonight it did. It was really stupid. He was odd even in the Were-Hunter world. When it came to the human world . . . they would lock him in a cage if they ever learned of him.

"Which school?" she asked innocently.

"UNO." The University of New Orleans was always a safe bet. Two of the waiters, Tony and Mark, went there, and Wren had overheard them enough to be able to lie about classes, professors, and the campus if he needed to. Not to mention, she looked a little too upper-crust to go to a state school. She most likely attended Tulane or Loyola.

She stopped and offered him a smile that made him instantly hard. "I'm Marguerite Goudeau, by the way."

Recognition hit him at the mention of her name. It was one he'd heard a lot in the past couple of years. "You're Maggie, Nick's study partner."

Marguerite smiled again. "I take it Nick must have mentioned me."

Yeah. Nick'd had a tremendous crush on her. He'd wanted to ask her out but never had. *"She's like Venus, and having met Venus a time or two, I know that no mere mortal man has a right to touch her."*

Wren supposed that went for tigards as well. Nick had been right, there was something about Maggie that was very special.

"He said you were the most intelligent woman he'd ever known, but that you couldn't study for shit."

She laughed. The sound was musical and soft, and it warmed him more than it should. "That sounds like Nick."

Marguerite cleared her throat as Wren pierced her with that intense stare of his. There was something so animalistic about him that it was almost frightening. She felt like someone in the jungle, cornered by a hungry beast.

"Sorry," he said, dropping his stare back to the ground. "I didn't mean to make you nervous again. I know people don't like for me to look at them."

She frowned at his deadpan tone. Even so, she sensed that it hurt him. "I don't mind."

"Yes, you do. You're just being polite." He started back down the street.

How did he know that? Most men were far from intuitive.

Marguerite rushed to catch up to him. "Is the monkey I saw you in the bar with your pet?"

He shook his head. "Marvin owns himself. He just likes to hang out with me."

She laughed at the sweetness of Wren's words. "I've never met anyone who had a monkey for a friend before."

He snorted in disagreement. "I don't know. I think those two guys you were with would qualify as primates, but then, that's an insult to the primates and I don't want Marvin to get pissed at me. He has higher sensibilities, you know?"

Wren's words amused her. "You might have a point

with that. But they're not my friends. I only study with them."

She saw his frown as he glanced at her. "Why do you study with assholes?"

Maybe she should be irritated at him for insulting her group, but then, why? She actually agreed with him. "Habit. I've known Todd and Blaine since we were kids. You have to understand that they haven't had an easy life. They both have severe bonding issues brought on by apathetic and absent parents."

He looked less than impressed by her excuses for their rudeness. "Did their parents ever try to kill them?"

"No," she said, stunned that he would even ask such a thing, "certainly not."

"Did their mothers ever tell them that they were abominations who should have been eaten the minute they were born?"

"Of course not."

"Did their parents ever try to sell them to a zoo?"

He was being ludicrous now and it was all she could do not to roll her eyes at him. "No one's parents would do such a thing."

The look he gave her said she was a fool if she believed that. "Then trust me, their life wasn't so bad."

Marguerite paused as he continued walking. Was he serious? No, he was just toying with her. He must be. No one's parents would try to sell them to a zoo. That was stupid. Wren was throwing out random weirdness just to prove a point.

She rushed to catch up to him. "What about your parents?" she asked, trying to make light of his words. "Did they ever do any of that to you?"

He didn't respond, but something in his manner said that it might not be a far-fetched conclusion. . . .

No, no parent would do that to their child. Her father was a total jerk most of the time and not even he'd ever been *that* bad.

"Wren?" she said, pulling him to a stop. "Be honest. Did your parents ever really try to sell you to a zoo? C'mon. Be real."

He immediately twisted his arm out of her hold. "There's a Dead Milkmen song that the Howlers cover a lot when they play at Sanctuary. It's called 'V.F.W.: Veterans of a Fucked Up World.' You ever heard of it?"

"No."

"You should. There's a lot of truth in it." Something flashed in his eyes like a nightmare he was trying to banish. The deep sadness there tore through her. "Everyone has scars from their life, Maggie. Just forget I said anything and let's get you home so you can get cleaned up." He turned and continued on his way.

She followed after him, wondering just what his scars were. For a young man, he had an ancient wisdom in his eyes. One that said he'd lived far beyond his apparent twenty-something years.

"You know, it helps to talk about it. It really does. It's a lot easier to let go of the past when you share it with someone else."

Wren arched a brow at her. "I notice you're not reminiscing your childhood with me, Maggie. I definitely don't know you well enough to reminisce about mine."

He had a point. There was a lot of pain she kept hidden inside her, and it made her wonder what he had inside of him. He wore the look of a street kid. The kind who'd been thrown out to fend for himself far too young. He had that fierce toughness that often marked them. That jaded look of someone who expected to be used and then cast aside.

It was what made her want to reach out and hold him. But she'd seen enough of his anger to know he wouldn't welcome it. All things considered, she had to give him credit. He hadn't turned completely mean. He did work and he went to school. Those two things said a lot about his moral fiber. Most of the people she'd ever heard of who'd been thrown out had ended up as criminals who preyed on others.

Wren had saved her life, and now he was making sure no one else bothered her. He was a decent human being.

He led her to Decatur Street, in front of the Square, where he quickly hailed a cab to take her to her renovated condo, which was only two blocks from the Audubon Zoo.

As they rode through the Quarter, she could sense Wren watching her even though she couldn't see his eyes in the darkness. The sensation was hot and unsettling.

Without a word, without moving a single inch, he stayed in the shadows like some lounging predator that was eyeing his next lunch. There was something completely eerie about the way he was able to sit like that. If she didn't know better, she'd think he'd stopped breathing. He really was a human statue.

Nervous, she watched the streetlights cut across the angles of his lower face from the corner of her eye. It was extremely unsettling to be with a man who exuded such a primal aura and yet she had no idea what he really looked like.

The silence was only relieved by the low thrum of the cabdriver's Zydeco CD. She wanted to think of something to say, but since Wren wasn't making an effort, she thought it best to follow his lead.

When they finally reached her driveway, Wren had the driver wait for him while he walked her to her door.

There was something strangely sweet about his actions. They were totally incongruous with the air of lethal danger that clung to him.

"Well, this is it," she said as she dug her keys out of her purse. "Home sweet home."

Opening the door, she stepped inside and debated whether or not she should invite him in. Part of her wanted to, but she was afraid of being rebuffed. As a rule, guys thought of her as a friend, never as a girlfriend. It'd always bothered her, and tonight she didn't think she could deal with his rejection after all she'd been through. Not to mention, she wanted to be alone for a while and just calm down.

Wren sensed her uncertainty as he stood on her doorstep. It reached out to the animal in him and set it on edge. It was always in his nature to attack when he sensed weakness, but with her it was different. He wanted to soothe her.

And that scared the shit out of him.

"Good night," he said, stepping away. He needed to put some distance between them.

"Wren?"

He paused to look back at her.

"Thank you so much. I owe you more than I can ever repay."

He inclined his head to her. "It's okay, Maggie. Just stay out of trouble." He headed back for the cab.

"How much do I owe you for the taxi?" she called after him.

Wren just waved at her over his head. He was tempted to laugh at her offer. Why would she think that he'd charge her for seeing her home?

Women . . . he'd never understand them.

He paused at the cab's door and dared a quick look at her to see her framed in her doorway. She looked so fragile and beautiful. He wanted to kiss her so badly that he could already taste those full, tempting lips. But more than that, he wanted to taste the rest of her body. He wanted to know every scent and curve of her flesh. . . .

His hormones were playing havoc with him. His entire body felt as if it were on fire and alive. He wasn't sure how to cope with this. In truth, it frightened him. If he were to lose control, he could easily hurt or even kill her.

In his mind, he could envision her naked. See her underneath him as he claimed her not as an animal, but as a man. . . .

Leave!

He had no choice. He didn't belong here and he didn't belong with her.

There was no place where he did belong. No matter how much he might want otherwise, there never would be. His life had to be spent alone.

. . .

Marguerite forced herself not to react to Wren's hot, devouring stare. She'd never been so interested in any man, especially not one who she really had no idea what he looked like.

It was ludicrous and yet there was no denying the way her body felt. She should have at least asked for his number or e-mail.

He got into the taxi and slammed the door shut with a finality that echoed through her.

Marguerite watched the cab drive away as she felt an inexplicable urge to call Wren back. There was something so lonely about him that it had reached out and touched her deeply.

But it was too late now. He was gone. And she would most likely never see him again.

As Wren paid the driver only a block away from Maggie's condo, he was starting to sweat from the effort of remaining in human form. He had to get out of here and back home ASAP. If he lost consciousness as a human, he would immediately turn into his true state. And the last thing he needed was to be passed out in large-cat form.

That would be a one-way ticket to a government lab somewhere. He'd seen enough episodes of *X-Files* and *Buffy* to know that was the last place he wanted to be.

Ducking into a dark shadow behind a garage, he flashed himself back to Peltier House and into Carson Whitethunder's examination room.

A Were-Hawk, Carson was the resident vet and doctor for all the nonhuman inhabitants of Nicolette Peltier's Sanctuary—of which there were many. Sanctuary had been set up a little over a hundred years ago to be a haven for any and all species. The Peltiers themselves were Were-Bears, while the rest of the inhabitants were leopards, panthers, wolves, and even a dragon. The only species missing from their ranks was the jackal, but then jackals were even more peculiar than the normal oddballs that made up their race. And as such, jackals usually stayed away from the other Were-Hunter branches.

As was typical, Carson was in his office, reading a medical text. Native American in human form, which was due to his human father, Carson had long black hair that was always worn pulled back with a western tie. His black brows slashed above eyes that were a peculiar hazel green. Tonight he was dressed in a dark green turtleneck, blazer, and jeans.

Wren walked over and tapped on the door's glass before he pushed it open.

Carson glanced up. "Hang on a sec, Wren."

Wren tried, but his legs buckled. An instant later, he flashed to his true form of half white tiger, half snow leopard. It was something that disgusted him. Normally, he picked one form or the other, but wounded . . .

This was all he could manage.

Carson got up with a curse and rushed over to Wren. "What happened?"

Wren couldn't respond. He was trying to stay conscious, but the instant Carson touched his wound and pain shot through him, everything went black.

• • •

Carson cursed again as he saw the blood that completely coated the underside of Wren's chest. He grabbed the Nextel phone off his desk and paged his assistant. "Margie, get up here to the lab. It looks like Wren's been shot."

Carson also paged a couple of the bears from downstairs to help pick Wren up and move him to a surgery table. Though Carson as a Were-Animal was stronger than most humans, Wren was an extremely large tigard that weighed in at a good eight hundred pounds whenever he was in animal form. There was no way in hell Carson was going to get the behemoth cat off the floor without help.

Papa Peltier was the first one to appear. At a cool seven feet in height in human form, he posed a fearsome sight. His long, wavy blond hair floated around a face that appeared about forty in human years. In reality, the bear was closer to five hundred. Dressed in a navy T-shirt and jeans, Papa Bear was rugged and tough . . . the kind of man or bear that only a fool would tangle with.

He frowned as he saw the tigard on the floor. "What the hell happened?"

"I don't know," Carson said as he held a pressure bandage to Wren's chest. "It's definitely a bullet wound. I have no idea how he got it. He knocked on the door, then fell down unconscious."

A second later, three of the Peltier quadruplets came in and helped Carson lift Wren to a surgical table. Margie joined them and quickly set about prepping the room for surgery.

Margie Neely was one of the few humans who knew who and what the members of Sanctuary were. She was a petite redhead who had been a waitress in the bar until a mishap had betrayed the Weres to her. She'd been so calm and accepting that they had embraced her as one of their own and then paid to have her trained to be an assistant to Carson.

Dev Peltier, who like his brothers was a younger copy of his father, moved back to let Carson near Wren again. "He was in a fight earlier tonight with some humans," the young bearswain said. "I broke them up and sent them home. You don't think one of them came back and did this to him, do you?"

"Nah," his identical brother Remi said as he stepped away from the table they had placed Wren on. "They were rich pukes. They wouldn't have dared endanger their trust funds for something like this."

Dev sighed. "Since it's Wren, there's no telling who he pissed off. But at least we know it was a human. No Were-Hunter would ever use a gun. It's too crass."

Papa agreed. "C'mon, boys, let Carson work and we'll find out what happened whenever Wren wakes up."

The bears withdrew while Carson scrubbed his hands.

As Margie touched Wren's side to prep him, he came awake with a vicious snarl, then lashed out at her.

She jumped back with a curse and cradled her arm to her chest.

Carson scowled as he realized Wren had torn her arm open. "Dammit, tiger," he snarled an instant before he tranked Wren. Still he tried to fight Carson until the sedative took effect. "Watch that temper of yours."

"I'm okay," Margie said as she wrapped a towel around her savaged arm. "It's my fault. I didn't realize he'd wake back up. I should have known better."

Carson shook his head as he inspected the damage Wren had wrought. She'd definitely need stitches. "I should have warned you. His kind are extremely vicious when wounded. They don't like others anyway, and they've been known to shred anyone who comes near them."

"Yeah, I was down in the bar when the humans threw a drink in his eyes. I'm still not sure how Justin and Colt managed to pull him away from them before he pounced."

Carson let out a tired breath. "Wren's getting more unstable. I don't know how much longer he can stay here."

He saw the concern in her eyes as she looked up at him. "That's what Nicolette said after she sent Wren into Peltier House. If he pounces like that again, she's going to make him leave."

Carson looked back at his unconscious patient. "God have mercy on him then. The best thing we could do is strip him of his powers and dump him back in the past in a rain forest somewhere. It's probably what they should have done to him instead of bringing him here."

"Nicolette is already making those preparations. Since his father went mad, she assumes Wren will follow."

Carson looked back at Wren. His chest tightened. He'd known the tigard since Wren had been brought here almost twenty years ago. Traumatized by the violent and gory deaths of his parents, Wren had just been entering puberty then. His powers had been unstable and shaky. But the powers had been too strong for them to strip, especially since the boy's guard had been up. He'd trusted no one to come near him, and as a result, there had been no way they could control him.

But now . . .

Now Wren's guard was extremely lax around them. At least most of the time. It would be easy to catch him off-guard and strip him of his powers.

Such a thing was a last resort for their kind. It was reserved solely for those who couldn't pass in the human world. Or those who threatened to expose the Were-Hunters to public scrutiny.

Wren had never wanted to blend. He prided himself on being a misfit and outcast. No one had minded since he did his job in the bar and didn't even try to speak to the humans.

Tonight that had changed. He had gone after a human female. Not that contact with females was forbidden. Most of their males took human lovers from time to time. But they had to be careful who they chose.

If Wren's indiscretion threatened them, then there would be no choice.

He would be sacrificed in a heartbeat.

Chapter 3

"Damn, tiger. What the hell did you do? Besides getting shot, that is."

In his tigard form, Wren opened his eyes to see Dev coming into his bedroom. He glanced at the clock on his nightstand to see that it was just after noon—too damned early for him to be up and about, especially when he hurt this much.

He was actually amazed that the bear was awake and in human form, barging into his room. Most of the Katagaria had a difficult time maintaining human form until after nightfall. So as a rule, they were mostly nocturnal.

Not to mention, the occupants of Peltier House knew that tigers didn't like to be disturbed, especially not from a sound sleep.

Without changing his animal form, Wren lifted his head from the pillow to watch Dev walk over to his dresser. Wren growled in warning at the bearswain, who paid no attention to him as he placed an extremely large flower arrangement on top.

Wren started to shift on the bed, but his wound was too tender. Instead, he roared threateningly.

"Calm your tiger-ass down," Dev said, his tone irritated. "If anyone has a right to be pissed, it's us. Notice I'm the one in human form and you're not? You think I want to be awake and looking like this at this unholy hour of the day?"

The bear had a point.

"And do you know why we're up?"

Like he cared. If Wren were in human form he'd be staring drolly at the bear.

Ambivalent to Wren's mood, Dev barely hesitated before he answered his own question. "Because we all thought that these were for Aimee. You've never seen bears move so fast as we did when *Maman* told us there was a truck loaded with flowers that were to be delivered here. We were getting ready to open a can of whup-ass on some local when the delivery guy said they were sent to *you*."

Dev moved to the bed and pulled a small card out of the back pocket of his jeans. "It says 'thanks for last night.'" Dev gave him an amused smirk. "So what? Did you finally get lucky and find someone desperate for a quick lay?"

Wren snapped at Dev, forcing the bear to jump back from the bed.

Dev's eyes narrowed on him. "You better knock that shit off or else we're going to go round. I don't care if you are wounded, I don't play."

"And neither do I, asshole." Wren sent the words to him mentally.

Dev stared at Wren in amazement. "Wow. Multiple syllables and a whole sentence from the tiger. Who'd have ever thought it? Whoever she was, she must have had a lot of talent to make *you* speak. Next thing you know, she'll have the dead walking. Quick, call a Dark-Hunter. I'm sure some of them would like another resurrection."

Wren growled, but before he could lunge, more flowers were brought in by four of Dev's brothers. Lots more. Within a few minutes, the whole room looked like a funeral parlor.

As soon as they had the flowers stacked around the bed and dresser, all the guys left except for Dev and his younger brother Serre.

Serre shook his blond head as he paused by the foot of the bed to stare at Wren. "Man, Wren. I'm impressed. No woman ever sent flowers to thank me."

Dev snorted. "Don't be that impressed. I'm thinking she didn't send flowers to thank him. One flower says thank you. This many says she thought he was dead. Or that she killed him." Dev glanced about speculatively. "Hmm . . . I'm thinking, put a tiger in her tank and that didn't quite rev her up. What she needs is to go hunting for bear."

Wren lunged at Dev, but before he could catch the bear, Serre pulled his brother back out of range.

"Knock it off, Dev. You definitely don't want to come between the tiger and this woman."

"Why not?"

Wren rose into striking position on the bed. This time, he wouldn't miss.

"*That's* why," Serre snapped. He shoved Dev out the door, then turned back to Wren. "Go on and rest, tiger. We've got your back."

Wren settled back on his bed as Serre shut the door. Even so, Wren could still hear them out in the hallway.

"Good God, Dev. Have you completely lost your mind? Don't tease the psychotic tiger. He's getting all angry and frothing at the mouth. Someone's going to think he's rabid."

Dev scoffed, "Yeah, but teasing him is like throwing meat at Kyle. It's highly entertaining."

Serre made a disgusted noise. "Yeah, and I wish you'd stop throwing meat at poor Kyle in the bar. He can't control himself with that. Next thing you know, he's shifted into a bear, *Maman* is having a fit, and all of us are left to control the crowd and keep them from remembering that they just saw a kid become an animal. It's a pain in our collective asses."

"Yeah, but I can't help myself."

Wren heard Serre growl threateningly at his older brother. "You know if you don't learn to, Papa's going to kill you one day."

"But until that day comes, I'm going to have a lot more fun with the whole lot of you."

Serre sighed. "Until then, do us all a favor, and lay off the tiger. I know you've done everything on two legs . . . then again, you've done most everything on four, but this girl is different where Wren is concerned. For once, turn the libido off and go after one of your usual lays."

"What are you? Insane? I'm not interested in Ms. Preppy Uptight Sloan Ranger. Jeez. I'd get khaki between my teeth. Can you imagine? I've never been in khaki and I never want to see a woman out of it. It scares me."

Their voices drifted out of hearing range. Wren collapsed back on the bed, relieved to know Dev was just being his usual asshole self and didn't really have any ambitions toward Maggie. That alone had saved his life.

Then again, Wren shouldn't have any ambitions toward Maggie, either. What was it about her?

Not that it mattered. He wasn't going to see her again. He might be crazy, but he wasn't suicidal. Nothing good could come of him spending time with a human. Nothing.

As soon as she was out of her last law class, Marguerite headed back to the French Quarter. She'd blown off her study group for the afternoon in lieu of going to see Wren. She really wanted to give him a proper thank-you face-to-face for saving her.

It was the least she could do.

By the time she reached Sanctuary, it was just after six in the evening and already dark outside. Glancing around the dim interior of the bar, she saw a tall, dark-haired man who was bussing the tables. Not particularly attractive, he had stringy hair and was marked all over his body with colorful tattoos.

As she continued to look around the thin crowd, she couldn't find a single trace of Wren, but she did spot the waitress from the night before, who was walking over to a table with a tray loaded with drinks.

Marguerite headed over to her as the woman unloaded the drinks to the men who were ogling her.

"Hi," Marguerite said as the woman left the table. "Is Wren working tonight?"

The waitress frowned at her as if she were the worst sort of creature. "You're that woman who was here last night with the dickheads."

Marguerite blushed at her words. "Yes, and I'm sorry about that."

"You should be. You got Wren into all kinds of trouble."

Her stomach shrank at the waitress's words. "I didn't mean to. Please tell me you didn't fire him for it. It wasn't his fault. I had no way of knowing they were going to act like that."

Still the waitress eyed her warily.

"Look, I'm really sorry about it." Marguerite held up the present in her hands. "I just wanted to give this to Wren as a small token, okay?"

"Token for what?"

Marguerite's heart sank as she realized the waitress wasn't going to help her. No wonder she was shy. It was hard to be otherwise when people could be this rude and off-putting. It was so much easier to be alone. "Just, please, see that Wren gets this."

As she turned to leave, the woman stopped her. "Hey, were you there when Wren got shot last night?"

Marguerite went cold at the question. Did she hear that correctly? "Excuse me?"

"Never mind," the blonde said as she turned away with the bag in her hand. "I'll make sure he gets this."

It was Marguerite's turn to stop the waitress as concern welled up inside her. Surely Wren wasn't hurt.

She would have known had he been shot last night.

"What were you talking about?" she asked the waitress. "Wren didn't get shot last night. The bullet missed him . . . didn't it?"

The look on the blonde's face confirmed Marguerite's fear. The bullet hadn't missed.

"What happened to him?" Aimee asked.

Marguerite swallowed as guilt consumed her. "I was being mugged and he came out of nowhere to chase them off. One of the guys had a gun that he fired, but Wren told me that he wasn't hurt. I didn't see a wound on him." Surely she would have seen a gunshot wound, wouldn't she?

If he'd been badly wounded, he would have said something. After all, no man took a bullet without complaint. . . .

"Wren saved you?" The waitress asked the question as if she couldn't believe he would have ever done such a thing.

Marguerite nodded. "The bullet just grazed him, right?"

"No," the waitress said firmly. "Wren almost died last night."

Marguerite felt sick at the news. This couldn't be real. Surely the waitress was just playing with her. "What hospital is he in?"

She could see the debate in the woman's expression about whether or not to answer her, and she couldn't blame her. Good grief, she'd gotten Wren insulted, assaulted, and shot—all in less than an hour. That poor man most likely never wanted to see her face again as long as he lived.

Aimee narrowed her eyes at Marguerite before she took a step back. "You're the one who sent him all those flowers today, aren't you?"

"Yes. Had I known he was hurt, I would have sent even more."

That seemed to amuse her. "Hang on." Aimee handed the bag back to Marguerite before she took her to stand by a door behind the bar. "You wait right here and I'll be back in a few minutes."

Marguerite nodded as she noticed the hostile looks the bartenders were giving her. They were dressed in T-shirts and jeans, and though they were handsome, there was an air of lethalness about them. They appeared to resent her presence there in the bar area, but she couldn't imagine why . . .

Unless they knew about Wren and they blamed her for it.

Nervous and unsure, Marguerite turned to see the man with long black hair from last night. Justin. That had been his name. Like the others, he was staring angrily at her. He didn't say anything while he put away clean glasses.

It seemed to take forever before Aimee came back to beckon her through the doorway. "Follow me."

Marguerite let out a relieved breath as the woman led her into the large commercial kitchen. There were five cooks buzzing around pots and ovens while two men washed dishes in a large sink. None of the workers paid any attention to either of them.

At least not until they reached another door at the end of the long steel tables. A tall blond man was standing in front of it, and he appeared less than pleased that Aimee wanted to take Marguerite through it. He looked just like the man who had thrown them out of the bar last night, except he didn't seem to remember her at all.

"What are you doing, Aimee?" he asked in a growling tone.

"Move, Remi."

"Bullshit."

Aimee put her hands on her hips. "Move, Brother, or you'll limp."

He narrowed his eyes. "You don't scare me, swan. I could tear your head off and not flinch."

"And I could hurt you in a much more permanent way." Her gaze dropped to his groin. "Now move it or lose it."

Curling his lip, he reluctantly complied.

"Ignore the scowl," Aimee said as she opened the door. "It's his natural countenance. Believe it or not, it's far more becoming than his smile. That just looks creepy."

Marguerite didn't know what to think as Aimee led her into a posh old-fashioned parlor. The house was absolutely beautiful. Weirdly enough, it looked as if it were in some kind of time warp or something. There was nothing on this side that looked modern at all. Nothing.

Her eyes fell to the door that held five Stanley dead bolts and an alarm system that would rival NASA's.

Okay, not entirely antique. But other than those telltale items, it was like walking onto an old-fashioned movie set.

Aimee led Marguerite up an intricate hand-carved stairway to the second floor, which was lined with mahogany doors. The waitress didn't pause until they were halfway down the corridor. She knocked on the door, then cracked it open.

"You decent?" she asked, keeping her body so that Marguerite couldn't look into the room.

There was no answer.

"Yeah, well, you have a visitor. So you need to be human for a while, okay?" After a brief hesitation, Aimee stood back and opened the door wider. "I'll wait out here until the two of you are finished. Just call out if you need anything." Then under her breath she added, "Like a priest, cop, or lion tamer."

Marguerite frowned. What an odd thing to say, but then, she was quickly learning that everyone here was a bit strange.

She stepped past Aimee, into the room, and froze as she caught sight of Wren lying on a large sleigh bed under a black comforter that matched the black curtains covering the windows. His skin was ghostly pale. The flowers she'd sent earlier were lined up on his dresser and before it, but other than that, there was absolutely nothing personal in the room to mark it as his. It looked as if he were nothing more than a visitor just staying a night or two.

Her heart hammered as she went to him. His breathing was labored and a large Ace bandage was wrapped around his shoulder and upper chest. With the black comforter draped over his lower half, he was bare from the waist up, showing her a remarkably toned chest and arms. The man was incredibly well built, with a full six-pack of abs. The only hair on his chest was a small trail of dark blond hair that ran from his navel down to disappear under the covers.

But what held her attention most was the amount of obvious pain he was in.

Marguerite knelt beside the bed as guilt tore through her. This was all her fault. All of it. . . .

"Why didn't you tell me about this?"

He didn't answer. Instead he reached out and brushed a strand of hair back from her face. "You shouldn't have come back here, Maggie."

His hand was rough and calloused. Unlike the guys she knew, his hands were used to hard work, not oiled manicures. "I wanted to give you a small token to say thank you for last night."

Wren glanced at the flowers in his room. The bears and other Were-Hunters had been harassing him unmercifully about them. Not that he cared. To him those flowers were unbelievably precious.

No one else had ever given him a present before. No one.

He started to push himself up, only to have Maggie stop him.

"You shouldn't move."

The concern on her face tore at him. "It's okay."

"No." She gestured to the bandage, where a red spot was forming again. "See, you're bleeding. Should I call someone?"

He shook his head. "I'll heal."

Her beautiful brown eyes castigated and doubted him. "I can't believe you didn't tell me you were shot last night. What if you had died?"

He snorted at that. "I've been shot enough to know when it's not fatal."

Marguerite gave him a stunned look. Was he serious? With him she was never quite sure. He tossed things out at her in passing conversations that would be horrifying if they were true, and the bland way he spoke of them led her to believe that they just might be.

"Shot by whom?"

He didn't respond to her question as he propped himself up in the bed. His dreads fell back into his eyes, obscuring his face from her view. She was beginning to suspect that he did that on purpose so that he could watch the world while no one could watch him.

Even so, she saw a small bead of sweat fall down the side of his face from the strain of being awake. "I won't stay long," she said, handing him the bag in her hands.

He stared at it as if it were an alien being. It was actually rather comical. One would think the man had never been given a gift before.

"What's this?" he asked.

"Open it."

She thought he might be frowning as he picked up the tissue paper on top and held it to his face. He seemed to be savoring it. . . .

"What are you doing?" she asked with a frown.

Without responding, he set the paper aside, then reached in and pulled out the gray sweatshirt inside. She smiled at his confusion.

"I know you said you're taking classes at UNO, but I couldn't bring myself to put a pirate on you. I saw the

LSU tiger shirt in a store and had to buy it. I know it's weird, but I've always had a thing for tigers and I thought it'd look good on you."

He cocked his head to the side as if completely perplexed or intrigued by her words. "Thank you, Maggie."

The sound of that nickname on his lips brought a shiver to her. She loved the way he said it—sure, deep, and protective. It was almost like an endearment.

"So is there anything I can do for you?" she asked.

Wren stiffened at her question, in more than one way. The one thing he wanted from her was the one thing he could never ask—to have her naked in his bed. And that added a deep, inexplicable burning to his chest. "I'm fine."

"You sure? I could get—"

"Aimee?" he called, interrupting her.

The door opened instantly to show him the bearswan. She passed a quick look between them as she drew near the bed.

"She needs to leave," Wren told her.

Aimee nodded, then reached for Maggie.

She shrugged off Aimee's touch. "Wren . . ."

"I need to rest, Maggie. Please."

Marguerite hesitated at the strain she heard in his voice. How could she argue with that? He was in extreme pain because he had saved her life when most men would have turned the other way and not bothered.

"Okay." She moved back toward the bed and leaned down to kiss him lightly on the cheek.

Wren couldn't breathe as desire roared through him. It was all he could do to not pull her into his bed. . . .

Before he could think better of it, he caught her

head as she started to pull away and pulled her lips to his. He growled at the sweet taste of her. At the softness of her lips under his. It was the first time in his life he'd ever tasted a woman, but even so he couldn't imagine any woman tasting better than this one. She was incredible.

Maggie's lips were soft and decadent. They awoke a fierce hunger inside him that craved nothing but her. It was a hunger that both scared and thrilled him in a way he would never have thought possible.

He shouldn't feel this. Not for a human. Not for anyone.

God save them both from his ragged emotions.

Marguerite moaned as she tasted the feral wickedness of Wren's mouth. His tongue swept against hers, making her shiver. He smelled of patchouli and antibiotic cream.

More than that, he smelled of raw, earthy male. Of wicked midnight delights that she wanted to spend the entire day sampling.

He pulled away with a deep snarl. "Go, Maggie. Before it's too late."

His words confused her completely. "Too late for what?"

"Aimee," he said between clenched teeth as he refused to look at Marguerite.

Aimee pulled her back. "C'mon, Maggie. He really should rest."

Wren watched as the women left. His heart ached at the loss. Even now Maggie's scent clung to him. It filled his nostrils, making the beast inside him roar with possessiveness. It wanted her in a way that was hard to deny.

He placed the heel of his hand against his groin, which was rock hard and throbbing. He'd never wanted anything more than he did right now to have a night alone with her.

But it was impossible and he knew it.

She was human and he was an animal . . . in more ways than one. There was no way he could trust himself with a woman. No way he could trust himself with anyone. He could turn vicious in a single instant. It was the curse of his people and his breed.

Even his own mother had turned on his father. . . .

Sighing, Wren looked at the gray sweatshirt Maggie had brought to him. He felt a smile curl his lips, and that was the most amazing thing of all. He couldn't remember the last time he'd smiled. Hell, he wasn't even sure if he'd ever smiled before in his life.

A foreign feeling entered his chest. He didn't know what it signified. He held the tissue paper to his face. It held the faintest trace of Maggie's sweet, feminine scent. He crushed it in his fist as a brutal wave of desire consumed him.

Moving the paper aside, he held her gift in his fist as he lay back down.

Someone knocked on his door.

His breath caught as he hoped it was Maggie again, but it wasn't. Aimee entered the room.

"You okay, cub?"

He nodded. Aimee was the only person he allowed to call him *cub*. She didn't use it as an insult but more as a friendly pet name. Of all the people and animals in Sanctuary, Aimee was the only one who had ever made him feel halfway welcome. But she, like the others, feared him. She was afraid even now, though she was trying to hide it.

She crossed the room. As she reached for the bag and paper, he hissed and growled at her. She straightened up instantly. "I thought you'd want it thrown away."

"No."

She held her hands up in surrender. "Just so you know, I sent her home."

It's where Maggie belonged, but the thought lacerated his heart with pain. He didn't want her home. He wanted . . .

He wanted her here with him.

How stupid was that?

"Why didn't you give her her backpack?" Aimee asked in an innocent tone.

He glanced to the corner where Maggie's black Prada backpack was resting. Maggie had left it in the bar, under the table, during the confusion of last night. Aimee had found it not long after Maggie had left and told him about it this morning. He'd immediately ordered Aimee to bring it to him. He hadn't wanted anyone else to touch something so personal to Maggie.

"I forgot."

Aimee nodded. "You want me to take—"

"No!"

The bearswan gave him a sharp stare. "You need to curb that temper, cub. You know what *Maman* has said."

He returned Aimee's stare tit for tat. "I don't want your scent on her property. Understand?"

Aimee rolled her eyes at him. "What is it with you freaky cats? I swear I don't know who's more territorial, you or the wolves. Artemis protect us from the lot of you."

He watched as Aimee left the room and gently shut his door. He cradled the shirt to him as he closed his eyes and conjured up Maggie's face. Nick had been right, she was a beautiful lady. He finally understood what Nick had meant when he'd called her top-quality goods. It bled from every part of her.

And he was nothing but a hunted piece of shit whose life was as worthless as a twig.

It was true. His life was worthless. He was worthless. He'd destroyed everything he'd ever touched.

Aching with the truth, he let his human form dissolve into that of a tiger. He stared at his large white paw on the shirt. What he wouldn't give to be a human male. Then again, he would kill to be anything other than what he really was.

All he'd ever wanted was to belong somewhere. Anywhere. But it wasn't meant to be.

Part of him wanted to rip the shirt apart to rid it from his sight, but the other part refused to let him. Maggie had given it to him. She had gone out of her way to bring it here. It was a gift. A real gift, and he would treasure it as such.

Closing his eyes, he could still taste her kiss. Smell her scent on his skin.

And God help him, he wanted more.

. . .

Marguerite couldn't get the taste of Wren to leave her. She'd never had any man kiss her like that. It'd been sinful and wicked. Decadent. Possessive and hot.

He was so not the right kind of man for her to think about. He was a busboy. Her father would have an apoplexy if he ever learned she'd spoken to, never mind kissed, a man like Wren.

But that didn't matter to her. Wren was wonderful.

"And he saved my life," she said under her breath. There was no way Blaine or Todd would have done such a thing, and even if they had, they wouldn't have walked her home with a bullet wound in them. They would have lain on the ground, screaming for an ambulance and the best surgeon money could buy to be flown in from the Mayo Clinic.

But Wren had never said a word about his injury. Then again, he wasn't exactly chatty. She'd never met anyone who spoke less. And yet she was more attracted to him than she'd ever been attracted to anyone. He said so much more with silence than most others with a thousand words.

She couldn't help wondering if part of his appeal was the fact that he was so socially unacceptable to her father. She could just imagine introducing them.

"Hi, Dad, this is my boyfriend. I know he needs a haircut and that he works in a biker bar, but isn't he great?"

Her father would instantly have a seizure.

Even so, she still tasted Wren's lips. Felt the steel of his hand cupping her head as he tasted her.

How could anyone make her this hot?

"Put it out of your mind."

Yeah, that was easier said than done. All she wanted was to head back to the bar and see him again.

"I can't."

As much as she liked Wren, she loved her father, and her father would never, ever accept her dating someone like Wren. She couldn't do that to him, even if he was an egomaniacal SOB who was more worried about his constituency than his daughter. He was still her father, and since her mother's suicide, he was all the family Marguerite had.

She couldn't see Wren anymore. She couldn't. No matter what these weird feelings inside her thought or argued, their acquaintance was over.

Chapter 4

Marguerite tucked her books into her borrowed backpack. She still hadn't found her Prada. She couldn't imagine what had happened to it. She'd checked the lost and found at the library a dozen times. It wasn't like her to lose something like that.

Sighing, she got up from her desk to head off to the library and meet with her group.

As she left the building and headed across the lawn, she wasn't paying attention until she heard a man calling out, "Maggie." His voice was so deep and rumbling that it sent a shiver down her spine.

There was only one person she knew who held a voice like that. Only one person who called her Maggie nowadays. . . .

Pausing, she turned to see Wren coming toward her from the street. He moved with a graceful, masculine lope that sent a heated wave through her. He had on a pair of faded jeans that had holes in both knees, black biker boots, and a black T-shirt with a ragged red and black flannel shirt worn over it that he'd left unbuttoned.

She'd never known anyone to dress so haphazardly, and there was something about the clothes that made him seem like a young teenager.

But that aside, it was obvious that he was completely ripped. A fact she knew firsthand since she'd seen him without those shirts on. There was also a dangerous confidence about him that said he was a lot older than he appeared at first glance.

He kept one arm behind him as he moved to stand just before her. She shivered at his commanding presence. He was so much taller than her, and those eyes . .

There were times when they didn't seem quite human.

"Should you be upright?" she asked.

He shrugged with a nonchalance that she couldn't fathom. "I told you it wasn't fatal." He brought her backpack around from behind him. "But I thought you might want this back. You left it in the bar the other night."

"Oh, thank goodness!" she said, delighted to have it returned to her.

"You stunned me so much when you came to my room yesterday that I forgot I had it."

She smiled up at him, grateful that he'd gone to such trouble to bring it here. "You didn't have to bring it to me. You could have just called and I would have come for it."

"I didn't have your number."

"Oh," she said as she realized that she hadn't given it to him. Which brought up another question. "How did you find me here?"

He didn't answer. In fact, he looked rather uncomfortable at her question. "I should be going."

"What the hell is this?"

Marguerite looked past Wren's shoulder to see Blaine with a group of his frat brothers. She drew a sharp intake of breath. This wasn't good. Knowing Blaine, he'd see this as a direct violation of his territory by Wren, and with his friends backing him, there was no telling what he might do. Blaine could be a total prick when he wanted to.

"It's none of your business, Blaine," she snapped in warning. "Go on and leave us alone."

He didn't take her obvious hint.

Blaine glared at them. "What are we having here, revenge of the busboy? In case you haven't noticed, pal, there aren't any tables out here in need of cleaning."

She could sense the rage that was swelling inside of Wren. Luckily, he was holding it back.

She glared at Blaine. "Leave him alone, Blaine. Now."

Blaine sneered at Wren as he raked a disgusted stare over Wren's clothes. "What? Can't you afford a real pair of pants? Or are you so hot natured, you need natural ventilation?"

"Blaine," she growled.

"What kind of hair is that?" another of the frat boys asked. "Don't you ever wash it?"

"It's dreads, mon," another answered in a fake Jamaican accent. "All the better for smoking the ganja, don't cha know?"

Blaine tsked, then passed a feigned sympathetic

look at her. "Really, Margeaux, why are you hanging with such lowlifes? I know you can't help who your mother was, but damn, woman, I would think your father's genes would take some dominance."

"I'm sorry, Maggie," Wren said in a quiet voice. "I didn't mean to embarrass you."

"You're not embarrassing me," she said between clenched teeth. "They are."

Still Wren didn't look at her. He started away from her, heading back toward the street.

"Yeah, keep walking, busboy," Blaine said in an acidic tone, "and don't come sniffing around her anymore."

As Wren moved past them, Blaine shoved at him. Wren's reaction was swift and violent. He slammed his fist straight into Blaine's face. Blaine hit the ground hard as his frat cronies jumped Wren.

"Stop!" Marguerite shouted, afraid they would hurt Wren. But to be honest, he was cutting through them with little difficulty. He slung one over his back, onto the ground, then punched him hard while the other two were swinging at him.

All of a sudden, campus security was there, pulling Wren off. He turned on the officer with a growl and slugged him before he realized it wasn't another student.

The other officer pulled out a club and struck Wren's injured shoulder with it. He growled loudly and shoved the officer back. Marguerite realized that Wren was about to attack him as well.

"Wren, stop!" she shouted. "They'll hurt you."

He froze instantly.

"I want that bastard arrested for assault," Blaine

snarled as he wiped at the blood on his face. His nose was a total mess.

"Don't worry," the officer said as he cuffed Wren's wrists together behind his back. "He's going straight downtown."

Wren's face was stone as he said nothing in defense of himself.

Marguerite was livid over this. "He wasn't doing anything wrong. They attacked him first."

"Bullshit," another frat boy said as he wiped the blood from his lips. "He hit Blaine for no reason. We were just protecting our brother from being mauled by this animal."

"He doesn't even belong here," Blaine added. "He's town trash who was trespassing."

The officer Wren had struck tightened the handcuffs to the point where she could see that they were biting into his wrists.

Still Wren said nothing. Nor did he flinch or show any emotion whatsoever.

"Are you a student here?" the officer asked him in an angry tone.

Wren shook his head.

"Then why are you on campus?"

Wren didn't answer.

The officer was getting even angrier as he tugged at Wren's cuffed hands. "Boy, you better answer me if you know what's good for you. Who invited you here?"

Wren kept his gaze on the ground. "No one."

"He was my guest," Marguerite said.

Wren gave her a harsh stare. "She's lying. I don't even know her."

Marguerite's heart clenched that he was trying to protect her so that she wouldn't get into trouble, too. As a student, she was responsible for anyone she invited onto campus.

Meanwhile there was no telling what the police were going to do with him.

She started to speak up and tell the truth, but the look on Wren's face kept her silent. She could tell he didn't want her to contradict him.

A police car pulled up to the curb.

Feeling completely helpless, she watched as they took Wren and placed him roughly into the car.

"Wait until my lawyers get through with him," Blaine said with a laugh. "That bastard will be serving a life sentence for this."

She turned on Blaine with a lethal glare. "You are such an asshole. You can forget *ever* interning with my father. Hell will freeze over before you step one foot into his office."

"Margeaux . . ."

She wrenched her arm away from his grasp and headed in the direction of her car. She needed to find a lawyer for Wren. There was no way she was going to leave him in jail when he hadn't done anything other than protect himself.

Six hours later, Marguerite hesitated in the police station as she felt a wave of fear go through her. She'd never been near such a place. It was cold and sterile. Eerie. More than that, it was frightening. She hoped that she never had to visit such a place again.

As bad as it was for her to be here to get Wren out, she couldn't imagine how much worse it must be for him to be in the scarier part of the building with other men who'd been arrested for God only knew what.

They had to get Wren out of here.

"I told you, you should have stayed home, Ms. Goudeau," her attorney said. He was a short African-American with thinning hair that was dusted with gray. Very distinguished and accomplished, he was one of the most prominent attorneys in New Orleans. Best of all, he was discreet, so no one, not even her father, would ever learn of this.

Both she and Wren would be protected.

She doubted Wren could afford his own counsel, and from what she knew of public defenders, they were often overworked. She wanted to make sure that Wren spent as little time here as possible. Luckily, she had enough money of her own to easily cover Mr. Givry's fees to get Wren out of this.

"I think you should go on back home," Mr. Givry said as he urged her toward the door.

"No," she said hastily. "I wanted to make sure he was okay myself."

Looking less than pleased by her insistence, Mr. Givry led her to the desk where a female clerk sat wearing a police uniform. Even though the woman was heavyset, it was obvious she was well muscled and in great physical condition. Her face was dour and stern as she brushed her short brown hair back from her face. She looked up with a bored stare as they approached.

"We're here to make bail for . . . um . . ." He looked at her expectantly.

"Wren," she said.

"Wren who?" the clerk asked in an agitated tone.

Marguerite hesitated as she realized that she had no idea what his last name was. "Um . . . I'm not sure."

Mr. Givry gave her a stunned look. It probably did seem strange that she was willing to spend several thousand dollars to get a man she barely knew out of jail. But to her it made perfect sense, and she didn't dare explain to the lawyer or clerk that Wren had saved her life.

With her luck, that would make the local news and she would be in deep trouble.

"Well," Marguerite said quickly, "he's around my age, about six three, and has blond dreadlocks. They brought him in about six hours ago for fighting at Tulane."

An African-American male clerk came up and shook his head. "You know who that is, Marie. He's that kid we had to isolate earlier."

The woman screwed her face up in disgust. "The crazy one?"

"Yeah."

"Crazy?" Marguerite asked as she frowned. "How so?"

The man snorted. "When he was first brought in, we put him in with the normal crew of prisoners. He beat the shit out of three of them. It took seven officers to pull him off and stick him in a cell alone. Since then he's been pacing back and forth in his cell like some kind of wild animal. He glares and growls at anyone who comes near him. It's spooky as hell. There's something definitely not right with that kid."

Her lawyer arched a brow at her. "You sure you want to bail him out?"

"Yes. Positive."

Mr. Givry looked extremely skeptical, but he turned dutifully to the female clerk. "How much is his bail?"

"Seventy-five thousand dollars."

Both she and her lawyer gaped.

That couldn't be right, could it? "Are you serious?" she asked them.

"Yes, ma'am," Marie said without hesitation. "He assaulted an officer."

Marguerite was indignant on Wren's behalf. "Not on purpose. He didn't know it was an officer when he struck out."

The male clerk scoffed at that. "Yeah, that's what they all say."

Marguerite felt ill and angry. She didn't have that kind of money. At least not without going to her father, who would stroke if she told him why she wanted it.

"Hi, Daddy, I met this man who is a busboy in a local biker bar and he needs to get out of jail. . . . What did he do? Nothing much. Just assaulted an officer and Blaine. You remember Blaine, don't you? His father is one of your major campaign contributors. But that's okay, isn't it? Wren's a good guy. He even got shot when he kept me from being raped after I was down in the area of the Quarter where you told me not to go.

"Daddy? Are you seizing? Should I get the pills for your heart?"

Oh yeah, that would go over well.

Mr. Givry gave her a sympathetic look. "What would you like for me to do, Ms. Goudeau?"

Loan me the money?

Before she could answer with something more reasonable than that, the outside door opened to admit three men. She knew one of them instantly. He was Dr. Julian Alexander, who had been her undergraduate advisor.

Tall, blond, and absolutely gorgeous, he was with two other good-looking men. One who was two inches taller and blond and another one who had short black hair. The brunette stood even in height to Dr. Alexander.

"Bill," her attorney said to the dark-haired man as he offered his hand to him. "What brings you here? I didn't know you made personal calls anymore."

Bill laughed as he shook Mr. Givry's proffered hand. "I don't."

"Then I must be imagining things."

Bill continued to smile. "I wish, but I have an extremely valuable client to bail out. He always gets my personal attention, if you know what I mean."

The look on Mr. Givry's face said he knew exactly what Bill was talking about. Marguerite had no idea who Bill's client was, but he must be loaded to warrant such personal attention from an attorney who didn't normally give it.

"Marguerite?" Dr. Alexander said as he approached her. "What brings you here? I hope you haven't been in any trouble."

She shook her head. "The lack of news coverage alone shows that I'm innocent. I came in to bail out a friend but found out I don't have enough money to cover it."

She frowned as she suddenly realized who the

dark-haired man was. "You're William Laurens, State Senator Laurens' eldest son, aren't you?"

Bill cocked his head as he searched his mind for clues as to her identity. "Do I know you?"

"She's Senator Goudeau's daughter," Dr. Alexander and her lawyer said at the same time.

"Ah," Bill said as enlightenment came to his features. He extended his hand to her. "We've met at campaign parties."

She nodded. "I love your wife. She's quite a character." Selena Laurens was more than that. Extremely idiosyncratic, Selena was a psychic who owned a new age store down in the Quarter. She was only tolerated by Marguerite's father because Bill's family was one of the wealthiest in the state of Louisiana and Selena's family wasn't too far below his.

Had Selena been poor, she would have been an insane kook. As it was, Marguerite's father referred to the tarot card reader as "eccentric."

Bill laughed. "Yes, she is. It's why I love her." He indicated the blond man with him. "This is my brother-in-law Kyrian Hunter, and you already know Julian."

"It's nice to meet you," she said to Kyrian, who shook her hand and returned her words.

"If you guys will excuse me for a second . . ." Bill went over to the clerk to speak with her.

Marguerite looked back at Kyrian. "You're the man Nick Gautier used to work for, aren't you?"

Kyrian frowned. "You're a friend of Nick's?"

She nodded. "He was a great guy."

"Yes, he was," Kyrian said, his expression extremely sad.

Bill rejoined them. "They're getting him now, but damn, that boy needs to learn to stay out of trouble."

"What happened?" Kyrian asked.

Bill sighed heavily. "Well, he neglected to tell me he'd assaulted a Tulane cop and now they have him in isolation."

"Wren?" she asked hopefully. "You're here for Wren?"

Kyrian looked stunned by her words. "You know Wren, too?"

Marguerite nodded. "We only just met, but yes, I know him." She looked about sheepishly. "I'm ashamed to say that I'm the reason he was arrested."

Bill arched a brow at that. "How so?"

"Wren came to campus to return my backpack to me that I'd left in Sanctuary. When he started to leave, a group of frat boys started harassing him. After insulting him repeatedly, one of the boys shoved him and then Wren slugged him. The rest jumped on him and then the police came and arrested him for the disturbance."

She could see Bill processing the new information with a keen focus on how he could use it to get Wren out of trouble. "Did he really attack a cop?"

"Yes, but it was an accident. The officer came up from behind him and I'm sure he thought it was another student jumping on him. Wren didn't see who it was until after he'd struck the officer."

Bill narrowed his sharp gaze on her. "You willing to testify to that?"

"Absolutely."

"Good," he said with a smile. She could tell that Bill was going to get Wren out of trouble. Thank goodness.

"So who is this kid that he got you out at dinnertime to spring him?" Mr. Givry asked.

"Wren Tigarian."

Her lawyer continued to frown, as did Marguerite.

"Should I know that name?" her lawyer asked.

"Tigarian Technologies," Dr. Alexander explained. "He was the only child to Aristotle Tigarian and the sole heir to their entire international empire."

Marguerite gaped at that. Tigarian Technologies was second only to Microsoft in the corporate world. "Why does he work as a busboy?"

Julian gave her a pointed look. "Why does the daughter of a prominent senator go to Tulane and not Princeton, Harvard, or Yale?"

"I like New Orleans."

"And Wren has no interest in running his father's company," Bill said. "He'd rather leave it to the management in charge."

Still it didn't make any sense to her. Wren didn't live like a wealthy man. He lived like a vagrant.

Bill looked past her shoulder, then scowled. "Hey!" he shouted. "Take the damn cuffs off the man. There's no need in embarrassing him. He's not a criminal."

The police officers with Wren gave Bill a sinister smirk. "Yeah, right, you didn't see the way he tore through those bikers. This 'kid' could give Mike Tyson a run for his money."

Marguerite's heart pounded as she saw Wren. He had a black eye, and his lip was swollen. The police officer gave a vicious turn of the cuff before he opened it. Wren looked up as if he sensed her presence and pinned her with a gimlet stare.

A tremor of heat went through her. There was something so unsettling about him, and at the same time a part of her was drawn to him even against her common sense.

Bill cast a murderous glare at the officers. "Look at him. Has he seen a doctor?"

"He didn't want no doctor."

Bill shook his head. "You okay, Wren?"

Wren nodded as he rubbed his wrists.

Marguerite crossed the distance between them, grateful that he was out of danger.

"Are you sure you're all right?" she asked, brushing the hair away from his face so that she could inspect the damage they'd done to his eye.

He nuzzled her hand ever so slightly before he nodded. "I'm okay. What are you doing here?"

"I was trying to bail you out."

He looked surprised by that. "Really?"

She nodded.

He gave her a hesitant smile.

"You want me to call Carson?" Bill asked.

Wren shook his head.

"You want me to give you a ride home?" she asked Wren.

"Please. Thanks."

By the look on the men's faces, she could tell they were as stunned by his acceptance as she was.

Bill cleared his throat. "You sure you don't want me to take you back?"

Wren shook his head and it was then she realized the only person he'd spoken to so far had been her.

As Marguerite fished her keys from her purse, she saw the outside door open. To her complete shock, Blaine and two of the other frat boys who'd attacked Wren were being led inside the building in handcuffs.

"This is ridiculous!" Blaine was snarling. "My lawyer will have all of your badges for this. Do you hear me!" He froze as he saw Mr. Givry beside her. "Tom! Get me out of this."

His expression concerned, her lawyer went over to Blaine and told him to calm down.

"What are the charges?" Mr. Givry asked the officers.

It was Bill who answered. "Oh, let's see, assault, battery, fighting words, slander, offensive touching, public drunkenness, trespassing, hate crime, and anything else I can think of to toss at him."

Mr. Givry gave Bill an irritated glare. "You're pressing the charges?"

Bill gave him what could only be called a shit-eating grin. "Yep. I swore out that warrant as soon as I got off the phone with Wren. You should counsel your client to be careful who he insults and attacks. Not only did he attack Wren on campus, but also last night at the local bar Sanctuary, where I have plenty of eye-witnesses who will gladly testify to his belligerent and drunken behavior. Ever heard the expression 'never pull a tiger by the tail'? Well, by the time I get through with your client, he and his family will be lucky to have a toothpick left to call their own."

"You've got to be kidding me," Blaine snarled.

Mr. Givry sighed. "No, Blaine, he's not. I'll go call your father and—"

"There's no hurry," Bill said in an emotionless tone. "I can assure you the lot of them will be spending the night in jail."

Mr. Givry gave him a stern frown. "You can't do that, Bill. They're good boys, from good families."

"So is Wren and it's already done. Maybe next time, they'll think twice before they make assumptions about someone." Bill opened his briefcase and pulled out a piece of paper, which he handed to Mr. Givry. "I've also sworn out a restraining order that will be served to your client when he leaves here. If he comes near my client again, he's going to seriously regret it."

Bill looked back at Blaine. "While we're at it, if I were you, I'd warn him that if he insists on pressing charges against my client, he will be implicating Ms. Goudeau in the wrongdoing, since she was the host at Tulane for Wren. We wouldn't want to impugn the good senator's daughter now, would we?"

Blaine rushed at Wren, only to have the police pull him back. "I'll get you for this, you prick."

"Shut up, Blaine!" Mr. Givry snapped. "You're already in enough trouble."

Bill added a speculative look at Blaine, who was being dragged toward a small hallway. "We'll be adding threat to do bodily harm to those charges as well."

The police hauled Blaine and his friends off.

Mr. Givry looked disgusted. "You're not going to make this easy on me, are you, Bill?"

"Not at all. You'll definitely be earning your keep on this case."

Mr. Givry let out a tired sigh. "All right. I'll call you in the morning and see what we can work out."

Bill put his hand on Wren's shoulder, then jerked it back as Wren literally growled at him. "Sorry," he said. "I'll, um . . . I'll call you later."

Kyrian and Julian paused.

"You sure you wouldn't rather we take you home?" Kyrian asked Wren.

Wren shook his head.

"All right, then. Stay out of trouble."

Marguerite indicated the door with a tilt of her head. "You ready to go?"

He nodded. And as they headed out, she noticed that he was rubbing at his injured shoulder. "Do you need to go to the hospital?"

"No, I just need to rest for a while."

"Are you sure?"

"Positive. Just take me home, okay?"

She led him to her Mercedes, which was parked under a streetlight. "I didn't know you were related to Tigerian Technologies."

He stared at her over the top of her car. "Does it matter?"

"Not really."

"Then why should I talk about it?"

He had a point with that. "Why do you live in New Orleans if the company is based out of New York?"

He shrugged. "I don't like New York. Too many people. Too much noise. Too cold in the winter. I don't like being cold."

She supposed that made sense. Offering him a smile, she got into the car and waited for him to join her. He quickly sat down, slammed the door, and buckled himself in.

"Did they feed you while you were in there?" she asked. "Would you like to stop somewhere on the way back and get something to eat?"

He nodded.

"What would you like?"

"I don't care. I'll eat anything not Tylenol or chocolate."

"That's a strange list."

"Not to me."

Okay . . . he was an odd man.

Marguerite headed out of the parking lot while Wren pulled his things out of the manilla envelope that the police had given him. "Was it bad in there?"

He paused to look up at her. "It certainly wasn't the highlight of my life."

She smiled at his sarcasm. "What happened to cause the jail fight?"

He slid his wallet into his pocket. "They thought it would be fun to knock around the 'kid' and show off their manhood. I thought it would be fun to knock a couple of them unconscious."

Well, she could understand that. He did have a unique take on things. "Do you always get into fights like this?"

"No," he said in a low tone as he snapped his Timex onto his arm. "I don't like to fight. I'd rather be left alone. But if someone else starts it . . ."

"You finish it."

He nodded. "My father used to say that it's not enough to just beat an attacker off. You have to hurt them enough that they'll know not to tangle with you anymore. Or preferably, kill them."

"Sounds like our fathers have a lot in common."

Wren didn't comment. Instead, he gestured toward the left. "McDonald's would be good."

She wrinkled her nose at the thought. "You really eat there?"

"It's good stuff."

She cringed at the thought. She'd only seen their food in commercials and had never really considered trying it out for herself. "I don't know about that. I'm not sure I like the idea of fast food." But she pulled in and got in line at the drive-thru.

Wren gave her a suspicious look. "Don't tell me you've never eaten here."

"Never."

"Where do you eat then?"

"Restaurants or at the campus meal hall." She pulled around to the speaker and lowered her window. "This is so weird, to get food like this."

He grinned at her before he leaned over her lap and answered the woman who had asked what they wanted. "I'll have twelve Big Macs, two Filet-O-Fish, three Double Quarter Pounders with Cheese, four apple pies, six large fries, and a large vanilla shake." He looked at her. "You want something?"

She arched both brows as she stared at him and his unbelievably large order. "You're not seriously going to eat all that by yourself, are you?"

He looked stricken by her words. "Am I doing something wrong?"

"No," she said quickly. "Not if you're hungry. I've just never seen anyone eat like that before."

He gave her a confused frown. "I do it all the time."

"And you stay so thin? I'd be bigger than a house."

"Would you like anything else?" the voice asked over the intercom.

She glanced over the menu. "I'll have a cheeseburger meal with a Coke."

Marguerite's eyes actually widened at the total before the server told them to drive around. Who knew fast food could be so expensive?

Wren pulled out his wallet and handed Marguerite the money to pay for it. He sat back in his seat and watched the way the light played in her dark hair. She was so beautiful to him.

While they waited, he reached out to touch her cheek with the back of his fingers. The softness of her skin amazed him. It also made him hard and aching for her.

She turned her head to smile at him. The expression hit him like a sledgehammer and left him oddly dazed. She cocked her head as if studying him in turn. "How do you get your hair to do that?"

"I don't know. You just kind of twist it and it holds."

"How do you wash it?"

He shrugged. "Same as anyone else. You put shampoo on it and run water through it."

Frowning, she reached out to touch a strand. She smiled and wrinkled her nose. "It feels so strange. Kind of like wool." She dropped her hand and pulled up to the window.

Wren sat quietly as he thought about her words. He'd started wearing the dreadlocks to keep other people away from him, and it'd worked. Most people curled their lips in repugnance and immediately cut him a wide berth, which was fine by him. He'd never really liked being touched. But he wouldn't mind Maggie stroking his hair.

His skin . . .

She handed him the change, then his food. Wren opened a Big Mac and took care to eat it like a human, but it was really hard. His kind only ate every three to four days, and he was extremely hungry. In truth, this wasn't enough food. It was only enough to tide him over until he could get back to Sanctuary and eat the rest of what he needed.

He picked up a fry and offered it to her.

Smiling, she took it from his hand and ate it.

Wren watched her closely. She had no idea what a feat that had been for him. His kind didn't share food with anyone or anything when they were hungry. They would fight to the death for a tiny morsel. Yet he wanted to take care of her. It was such a peculiar feeling.

If he didn't know better, he'd think she was his mate. But Katagaria didn't mate to humans. It wasn't possible.

Marguerite drove through the congested streets as she watched Wren from the corner of her eye. He didn't speak as he ate. But then, he didn't speak much anyway.

He was such a fascinating contradiction. She still couldn't get over that he had one of the most exclusive lawyers in New Orleans at his beck and call.

"What do your parents think of you working as a busboy?" she asked. Her father would die if she'd ever done something like that. He'd always carefully screened her jobs so that they would be appropriate to his career and social standing.

Wren swallowed his food. "They don't think much these days."

She waited for him to continue with that thought. Instead, he went back to eating. Frowning, Marguerite prompted him to explain. "Why don't they think?"

"It's kind of hard for them, since my parents are dead."

Her heart clenched at that. "Both of them?"

He nodded.

"How long?"

"About twenty years now."

He'd only been a baby when they'd died. How awful to not know his parents. "I'm so sorry."

"Don't be. I'm not."

She actually gaped.

"They were total assholes," he said quietly. "Neither one could stand me. They couldn't even look at me without their lips curling in disgust. My mom only referred to me as 'it.'"

"Oh God, Wren . . . that's horrible."

He shrugged. "You get used to it. I'm just lucky I was an only child. If they'd had any more children, I'm sure I would have been killed."

The nonchalance of his tone stunned her. "You are joking, right?"

He didn't answer, but the look on his face told her he wasn't. And to think, in fits of anger she'd always thought her father was an uncaring dirtbag. He suddenly looked like Father of the Year.

"So if your parents died while you were so young, who raised you?"

"I raised myself."

"Yeah, but who was your guardian?"

"Bill Laurens. My father and Bill's firm go way back. After my parents died, a guy brought me here to Bill and he hired Nicolette Peltier to let me stay with her and work at Sanctuary for my keep."

"You don't have any other family?"

"Not really. The ones I have who are surviving don't want me anywhere near them."

"Why not?"

"I'm not right."

A chill went down her spine. Was there something about him she needed to know? "What do you mean, you're not right?"

He took a drink of his shake before he answered her. "I'm deformed."

She glanced over at him as she drove. He certainly didn't look deformed to her. He looked completely fine and healthy. "How so?"

He didn't answer as he opened up another Big Mac and started eating it.

"Wren—"

"Don't ask me anything else, Maggie. I'm really tired, I'm hungry, and I'm in pain. If you really knew me, you'd realize that it's a complete miracle that I'm sitting here and not taking your head off, literally. I just want to get home, okay?"

"Okay," she said even though she was dying for an answer.

They remained silent the rest of the way to Sanctuary. By the time she pulled into the small parking lot behind the house, he'd almost finished his food.

Marguerite came around to help him carry the bags.

He led her to a red back door where they were met with the same angry-looking blond man who had wanted Aimee to keep Marguerite in the bar. "She's not allowed in."

"Move away, Remi," Wren said between clenched teeth.

"You know the rules."

"Yeah, I know the rules. In the law of the jungle, the tiger eats the bear."

Marguerite saw Aimee come up behind Remi. "It's okay, Rem, let him pass."

Remi sneered at her. "Have you lost your mind?"

Aimee pulled Remi back. "Come on in, guys."

Marguerite didn't say anything as they headed up the stairs to Wren's room.

"What was that about?" she asked as soon as he closed his bedroom door.

"Lo doesn't like anyone in her house."

"Oh. I guess I should be going—"

"Stay . . . please."

Wren knew he shouldn't ask that of her. He needed rest. Hell, he needed care. But none of that mattered. He just wanted to be with her for a little longer. The danger didn't matter. Nothing did except being able to smell her. To see her.

To touch her.

He dipped his head toward hers until she met his lips. He pinned her to the door as he kissed her.

Without thinking, Marguerite buried her hand in his hair. Wren hissed and pulled back as if in pain. Her hand was still stuck in the twisted blond locks.

"I'm sorry. I'm sorry," she said, trying to extricate her hand without hurting him more.

He frowned at her as he rubbed his head.

She reached out to help, only to have him move away. No sooner had she stepped away from the door than it crashed open. Marguerite turned to see the angry middle-aged woman there who'd been in the bar.

Wren made a strange growling sound low in his throat.

"She has to leave," the woman said in a voice that brooked no argument. "Now."

"I want her here."

"I don't give a damn what you want," she said, her voice laden with a French accent. "This is my house and—"

"I pay you enough."

"No," she said, her tone filled with venom, "you don't. Not for this."

The last thing Marguerite wanted was to get him into trouble. "It's okay, Wren. I'll go."

The anger on his face actually scared her. Wren cast a scathing glare at the woman, then escorted Marguerite downstairs to the back door.

"I'm sorry about this," he said as he led her out of the house and back to her car.

"It's okay. I'll see you later."

He nodded, then opened her car door for her. After enclosing her inside, he placed his hand on her window, and the look of longing on his face tore through her.

She put her hand up on the glass to cover his and offered him a smile.

As she started her car Wren stepped back, and watched until she'd pulled out of the lot before he went back inside.

He met Nicolette in the parlor. Aimee stood just behind her mother, looking completely contrite.

"You ever threaten one of my sons again and I will see you dead, tiger."

He gave a bitter laugh at that. "You can try, bear. You won't succeed."

Nicolette held her temper as Wren left her and headed up the stairs.

"It wasn't his fault, *Maman*," Aimee said. "I told him she could come—"

Nicolette backhanded her. "You ever threaten the safety of this house again, and I will see you cast out. Do you understand me?"

Aimee nodded.

"Papa?" Nicolette shouted for her mate.

He came in from the door that led to the kitchen. *"Oui?"*

"Summon the council. I think it's time we see about putting the tiger out of our misery."

Chapte

Wren was standing in the small bathroom outside of his bedroom, cursing as Marvin threw water at him.

"Stop it, Marvin," he snapped at the playful monkey, who was now making faces at him. "You know I hate it whenever water gets in my eyes."

He couldn't stand to be blinded. None of his species could, which was strange when one considered the fact that they did like to play in water.

They just hated any and all weaknesses. A weak tiger was a dead one.

His father was dead proof of that.

The door, which Wren had left slightly ajar, opened to show him Aimee in the hallway. "What are you two doing?"

Wren pulled the comb from his hair. He looked about for someplace to retreat to, but the only way out was through the bearswan. He hated that she had caught him. He didn't want anyone to know what he was doing.

Aimee entered the room and closed the door behind

...g her head to one side, she studied him with ...t stare that made him extremely uneasy.

...arvin jumped up and down on the sink, chattering.

"You're trying to unmat your hair, aren't you?"

Wren didn't say anything as he set the comb down beside Marvin. It was none of her business.

"It's because of that human female, isn't it?"

He tried to move past Aimee, only to have her block his way.

"It's okay, Wren," Aimee said gently. "I won't tell anyone about her. Believe me, I understand all about impossible relationships."

Yeah, he'd caught her with the wolf Fang a week ago. The two of them had been about to kiss. If anyone other than Wren had discovered her with Fang, Fang would have been killed or at the very least seriously mangled. But luckily for them, Wren couldn't care less who Aimee took to her bed. It was none of his business anyway.

She picked up the comb from the counter. "You want me to help?"

Part of him wanted to growl at her and send her scurrying away, but the other realized that help would be kind of nice. "You can try," he muttered. "But I think it's hopeless."

He'd been trying for over an hour to comb through the mess of his hair, and so far he'd only met with failure and pain.

And all because he wanted . . .

He wanted the impossible. For one moment in time, he wanted to feel a woman's hands in his hair, and it wasn't Aimee he ached to feel there.

He wanted Maggie.

Aimee's face softened as she tried to get the comb through a small matted lock. After a few minutes of trying that only resulted in her breaking the comb in half, she let out a frustrated sigh.

"All right, Wren, what we need is a specialist. Let me call Margie in here to help. She's the best at getting matted hair untangled. If anyone can do this, she can."

As Aimee started out the door, Wren stopped her. "Why are you being so nice to me?" None of the other bears had ever been really nice to him. Most of them barely tolerated him.

But Aimee had always been kind.

She offered him a smile. "I like you, cub. I always have. I know you're not dangerous. . . . I mean, I know that you could kill us, that you are dangerous, but that you don't pose an unfounded danger to anyone other than yourself."

"But you still fear me."

Her eyes softened as she looked at him. "No. I fear *for* you, Wren. There's a big difference."

He frowned in confusion at her words.

She let out a tired breath. "You don't like anyone around you, cub. I know you do inappropriate things just to make people leave you alone, and I fear what you will do one day that could cause the others here to turn on you permanently."

She glanced to Marvin, who was watching her as if he understood and agreed. "I know the ferocity of your people. I know Bill sent you here to keep your father's clan from killing you before you could defend yourself. Believe it or not, I don't want to see you hurt. Everyone deserves some happiness in their life. Even tigards."

Those words touched him deeply. No wonder the wolf was so attracted to her. For a bear, she had a good heart. "Thanks, Aimee."

She nodded, then left. Marvin started chattering at Wren as he tried to detangle his hair again. The monkey didn't understand why Wren was trying to change himself. It didn't make sense to Marvin.

"I know," Wren said to the monkey. "But I want her to be able to touch me without it grossing her out. One day you'll find a Marvina of your own and you'll understand."

"Oh my God, Margeaux! You have got to see what's outside in the hallway!"

Marguerite looked up from where she was packing her books into her backpack to frown at Whitney, whose next class was three doors down. "What?"

"He is the cutest guy on the planet. I swear, I've never seen anyone hotter. He must be gay. No straight man *ever* looks this yummy."

"Oh, doesn't that just piss you off?" Tammy asked from the next seat. "You should try being an art major. All I ever saw as an undergraduate was men looking for other men. It's why I'm in law school now. I need a profession where I might actually run across a dude wanting a female."

Whitney gave Tammy a droll stare for the mere fact that she had spoken without invitation. Marguerite, on the other hand, adored the Goth student, who always had the most interesting stories on Monday morning.

Marguerite smiled at her. "Okay, Tammy, since you're the resident expert on men, go scope him out and tell me what you think. Whose team does he bat for?"

By the time Marguerite had the backpack on her shoulders, Tammy returned with a thoughtful scowl on her face. "I don't know. It's too close to call. Psycho Prep is right, he's stunning. Offhand, I'd say straight, 'cause he has this 'do me' factor all over him that makes you want to take a bite out of his succulent flesh. That being said, he's dressed in a black silk shirt that's open at the neck, sleeves rolled back on his arms, and it's left untucked. Of course he does have a really cool tat on his left arm. But . . ."

Tammy wrinkled her nose. "He has on black slacks and really, really expensive black Italian loafers. Ferragamos, I think. Gotta say that sets off my gaydar big-time. Straight men don't normally dress that good. Not to mention he has one of those expensive haircuts, but at the same time it's kind of shabby. He's not really watching anyone, male or female, who walks by. It's weird. So I'd say our team has a fifty-fifty shot he bats for us. Or maybe he's a switch-hitter."

"Oooh, a mystery," Marguerite said as she headed out of the classroom to see him for herself. "Let me see what I think. . . ."

There was quite a stir in the hallway as women gawked or tried to be inconspicuous in their ogling of him. At first all she could see was the top of his blond hair over the crowd.

It was hard to navigate through the estrogen sea of women who wanted a closer look at him. And as she made her way closer, Marguerite had to admit he was completely stunning. She was far from immune to the " 'do me' factor" that Tammy had mentioned.

His face was perfect, with full, sensual lips that just begged for a hot kiss. He had high cheekbones and a patrician nose. His dark blond hair was shorter in back than in front, with pieces of it falling strategically into his eyes to add an air of mystery to him. He looked extremely uncomfortable as he held a bouquet of roses and a large box of Godiva chocolates. His skin was a deep, tawny gold.

It wasn't until he took a step toward her and she saw the exact color of his turquoise eyes that recognition hit her square in the chest.

It couldn't be. . . .

"Wren?"

He didn't pause until he stood before her and offered her that familiar hesitant smile before he literally nuzzled her cheek, then gave her a light, gentle kiss.

Tammy paused beside them and cleared her throat. "Switch-hitter?" she asked.

Marguerite laughed. "Oh no. This one is definitely on our team, trust me."

Tammy high-fived her. "You go, girl. Make sure you score a few home runs for our side."

Wren frowned as Tammy headed off. "Should I ask about that?"

Marguerite laughed nervously. "No. I would definitely prefer that you didn't."

His scowl only increased as he handed her the flowers and candy. "I got these for you."

It was so strangely corny and clichéd, and yet it made her heart pound that he had done it. No man had ever given her flowers and candy before. "Thank you."

Biting her lip, she reached up and brushed at his new hair, which was incredibly silky between her fingers. The soft texture reminded her more of an animal pelt than human hair.

It looked really good on him, but part of her missed the old Wren. "What did you do?"

Uncertainty darkened his eyes. "Do you like it?"

"Yeah, I think I do." She'd known he was cute, but she'd had no idea he was so incredibly sexy. There was something about this new Wren look that made her even hotter than the old one. Who knew a haircut could make such a difference?

"You didn't do this for me, did you?"

He looked away sheepishly.

Warmth flooded her. "You didn't have to cut your hair, Wren. I liked it the other way, too."

He glanced around at the women who were slowly dispersing. "I didn't want to embarrass you anymore."

She reached up and pulled his face down so that she could press her cheek to his. The masculine scent of his skin and aftershave set fire to her hormones. But it was his sacrifice that set fire to her heart.

"You've never embarrassed me, Wren," she whispered in his ear. "I don't think you ever could."

Wren couldn't breathe as the scent of her washed over him. It was all he could do to control himself. The feeling of her skin on his . . . of her hand on his cheek . . . It was wonderful. Her touch scalded him and it touched the tiny part of him that was human. More than that, it touched his animal heart and tamed it. He never thought he'd feel anything like this.

He was at peace. Calm. Soothed. There was no pain. No past. No taunts echoing in his head.

All there was inside him was Maggie and a foreign, giddy joy the likes of which he'd never known.

It was a feeling he didn't want to end.

To his instant dismay, she pulled back to look up at him. "So how did you know to find me here? Are you like some freaky stalker?"

Wren grinned at that. Honestly, the animal in him could track her with ease anywhere on this planet. She had a unique scent of woman and tea rose laced with the Finesse shampoo that she used. But it would probably scare her to know that she could never hide from him.

"Your schedule was in your backpack. I looked at it before I returned it to you yesterday."

She offered him a shy smile that made him harden before she bent her head down to smell the roses he'd brought for her. He reached out to touch her.

"Who's your friend, Margeaux?"

Wren withdrew his hand instantly as he recognized one of the women who had gone to the bar with Maggie on the night they'd met.

Marguerite turned to see Whitney behind her, eyeing Wren speculatively. "Whitney, meet Wren."

Whitney looked confused by that. "Wren? The grubby busboy who had Blaine arrested?"

Marguerite was quick to defend Wren. "Blaine started the fight."

She doubted Whitney heard her, since she was eyeing Wren like a hungry tigress who had spotted a pork chop on a plate. The only problem was that the pork chop belonged to Marguerite, who had no intention of sharing him with anyone.

She tucked her hand into the crook of his arm and pulled him away. "Wren and I have a date. We'll see you later."

Wren leaned down and did that warm, wonderful action of gently nuzzling her cheek before he covered her hand with his and led her toward the exit.

Wren still didn't really understand why he'd sought out Maggie. Humans had never held any real interest for him in the past. As a Katagari male, he shouldn't be so attracted to her. At least not anything more than physically.

And yet she fascinated him as she drove him to her small cottage by the zoo. All he wanted was to curl up in her lap and purr. Something that didn't make sense, since what he normally wanted was to rip the arm off anyone dumb enough to come near him.

She kept glancing over at him and gifting him with the sweetest little shy smile that he'd ever seen on a woman's face. But even worse on his self-restraint was the desire he felt from her. She was as hungry for him as he was for her, and it was making him feral.

The cat in him wanted to snarl and to stalk.

More than that, it wanted to mate.

By the time she pulled into her driveway, his entire body was throbbing. Alert.

And it wanted her with a ferocity that scared the shit out of him. There was no way he could leave her until he had tasted her.

Marguerite opened her car door and got out. Wren was there on her side of the car before she'd even had a chance to pull her book bag out.

"I'll carry it," he said quietly.

He'd moved so fast that it was practically inhuman. . . .

Nodding, she reached in to get her flowers and chocolate to carry them into her house. Wren followed her to the stoop, then stood back while she unlocked her door and let them in.

She went to set the flowers down on her end table. Before she could even straighten up, he was behind her. He buried his face into her hair and inhaled deeply as if he were savoring her. She'd never felt anything like it. She could feel his entire length against her back. Marguerite actually shivered at the sensualness of that action.

She found herself leaning back against him as his arms came around her to hold her close. In this position, she could feel his erection plainly against her hip. Wren was a large man, powerful.

"You smell good enough to eat," he whispered against her ear.

Marguerite couldn't answer, as her entire body burned from his presence. She laid her hands against his forearms and traced the jungle scene tattoo of a white tiger lurking in tall grass that ran the length of Wren's left one. There was so much strength and power in his arms that it made her feel weak. Trembling. She'd never known any man to make her feel like this.

He turned her in his arms so that she was facing him. His pale turquoise eyes were hot and electrifying. He cupped her face in his hands and kissed her fiercely.

Marguerite held him to her as every hormone in her body sizzled. Never in her life had she been more aroused. More aware of any man. His tongue spiked against hers as he pressed her even closer to his lean, hard body. Her hardened nipples brushed against his chest, making her moan from the contact and from the insatiable desire to touch him without their clothes separating them.

She'd never been the kind of woman to hop into bed with a guy she'd just met. In fact, she'd only known two other lovers in her life. One had been a friend her first year of college and the other had been a guy she'd dated for a little over a year. Those times had been pleasant enough but never stellar.

The men hadn't made her feel like this . . . made her feel like she would die if she didn't touch them. Made her burn in pleasure of the thought of having them inside her.

But Wren did.

Her breasts were heavy and aching. Her breath ragged as it mingled with his while they kissed.

He lifted the hem of her skirt up slowly, so slowly that the expectation was almost painful. She groaned at the feel of his callused hands on her bare skin. At the sensation of the heat of his skin mixed with the cool air as he caressed her with firm, confident hands. It was the most erotic moment of her life. She was already wet and throbbing, needing to feel even more of him. It was all she could do not to beg him to have mercy on her.

Wren explored her mouth, wanting to taste more of her. He'd never felt hunger like this. Needful. Throbbing. Demanding. He closed his eyes and inhaled the scent of her as he lifted her skirt even more so that he could feel the softness of her thighs. She was a warm, perfect heaven.

He'd never touched a woman before, at least not like this, and he was beginning to understand why as the animal inside him roared with ferocity. It was a dangerous beast that wanted to devour her. It roared and clawed, wanting freedom.

Wanting her.

Raw possessiveness swelled up inside him with a stunning ferocity. He finally understood why animals killed those who came near their territory. If anyone else ever touched her . . .

Wren would rip them to shreds.

He left her lips and buried his mouth against her throat where he felt her heartbeat pounding. Licking and teasing her soft skin, he slowly slid his hand down underneath the waistband of her dark blue panties. He half-expected her to stop him, but she didn't. Instead, she parted her legs more, giving him access to the part of her that he craved as she held on to his shoulders.

Oh yeah, this was what he needed. He felt her shiver as he stroked her with a tenderness he'd never known he possessed. If anyone had ever told him that he could hold a woman and not hurt her, he would have laughed at them, and yet he was gently holding Maggie.

No, he was making love to her. It was a human term that he'd never understood until this moment. But even more surprising was the fact that he was enjoying it so much.

Her short, crisp hairs brushed his fingers as he sank his hand down farther, seeking her. He separated the tender folds of her body until he could touch the part of her that he needed most. He closed his eyes and trembled as he sank one long finger deep inside her.

She jumped and moaned against his lips.

Wren growled in triumph as he stroked her. She was so wet. So soft. Her murmurs filled his ears, making him even harder for her.

Marguerite couldn't think as he tormented her with his touch. And when he sank another long, tanned finger deep inside her, she feared her knees would buckle.

"I have to have you, Maggie," he whispered gruffly in her ear.

She answered him by unbuttoning his shirt so that she could feel all that lush, beautiful skin. She hesitated as she saw the bandage still on his shoulder from where he'd protected her. A foreign tenderness went through her an instant before she claimed his lips again.

Marguerite stripped his clothes from him feverishly, wanting to see all of him. Wanting to feel him deep inside her. She'd never wanted anything more desperately.

She had to have him. It was like a madness that she'd never felt before.

They didn't even make it to her bedroom. Instead, they sank to the floor where they were.

Marguerite hissed as Wren unbuttoned her shirt, then nuzzled her small breast with his entire face. Always self-conscious in the past about her cup size, she felt none of that now. How could she when he seemed to savor her body so much? He rubbed himself against her breast from chin to brow several times before he gave her one long, wicked lick to her swollen nipple.

She shivered. "What are you doing?"

He hovered just over her other breast as he blew one teasing, hot breath over the taut peak. His blue eyes bored into hers. "I want your scent all over me. I want to smell your skin until I'm drunk with it."

She moaned as he repeated those actions on her right breast while her body throbbed with needful hunger. How strange to be so at ease with her body . . . with his touch. She wasn't nervous or hesitant in the least. All she wanted was Wren.

His tongue was rough against her skin, and every lick made her stomach flutter in response. He removed her blouse and skirt entirely. And when he pulled her panties off with his teeth, she almost came from the sheer pleasure of it.

He took his time with her. Slowly, methodically, he nibbled every inch of her skin from her foot to her thigh. It was as if he'd never tasted a woman before. As if he wanted to claim every little molecule of her body.

And he was doing a damned good job of it. That man could lick like nobody's business.

Wren paused to look at her. He nudged her thighs farther apart so that he could brush his fingers over her wet cleft and stare in wonderment of her body. It was so very different from his own. Soft and inviting.

So this was what it was like to touch a woman. . . .

He ground his teeth as he brushed his hand over her mons. Not even his dreams could compare to the reality. His hunger overwhelming him, he sank two fingers inside her and watched as she shuddered in response.

She was more than ready for him.

But he didn't want to take her like a human male. He wanted to claim her like the animal that he was. Tigers played with their mates. . . .

Marguerite whimpered as Wren withdrew from her. "What are you doing?" she asked as he picked her up.

"I'm making love to you, Maggie," he breathed in her ear as he pulled her back to his front.

Marguerite wasn't sure what he was doing as he lay back on the floor with her on top of him. It was so strange to be lying fully against his naked body like this. She could feel his chest against her shoulders. His thighs behind her buttocks as he hooked his ankles with hers and spread her legs wide.

"Wren . . ." Her words ended in a small cry as he entered her from behind. She hissed at the width and depth of him finally inside her. He was a large man who filled her completely.

She leaned her head back against his shoulder as he began to slowly thrust himself deeper into her body. She'd never felt more exposed in her life. And yet it was wildly erotic.

He cupped her breasts as he continued to thrust himself into her over and over again with a feverish rhythm that tore her apart with pleasure.

He took her hand into his, then led it down to her spread thighs so that she could feel them joined.

"Touch me, Maggie," he growled. "I want you to feel me take you."

How could she not? He was so hard and thick inside her. So powerful.

He left her hand on him and moved his up so that he could stroke her in time to his thrusts.

Marguerite's head spun as pleasure pounded through her. This was the most incredible moment of her life. It didn't feel like just a physical act, she felt connected somehow with Wren. Like she was giving him something he couldn't get from anyone else. It didn't make sense, but that was what she felt with him.

Wren couldn't breathe as he felt her sleek, hot wetness surrounding him. All he wanted was to be inside his Maggie. To hear her scream out in ultimate pleasure and know that he was the one who gave it to her. He moved faster, grinding himself against her as he carefully buried his teeth against the back of her neck.

She threw her head back and cried out as she shuddered in his arms.

He laughed in triumph as she came for him. But then his own laughter died as he, too, climaxed.

He tightened his arms around her as he felt his body shuddering inside hers. He'd never known anything like this.

His head swimming, he lay back against the floor and reveled in her slight weight above him. He wanted to stay inside her forever. But all too soon his body withdrew from hers.

Marguerite slid off him, then turned to face him. "That was incredible."

He smiled up at her, then lifted her hand to his lips

so that he could gently suckle her fingers. "I love the way you taste, Maggie."

Her heart pounded.

She watched as he laved her palm.

"I've never touched a woman before you," he said, his eyes burning into hers.

"What?"

He sat up to nuzzle her neck. "You heard me, my sweet Maggie. You're the only woman I've ever taken."

Could he be serious? "How could you be a virgin and make love to me like that?"

He smiled at her. "Animal instinct."

She arched a brow, especially as her gaze dropped and she realized he was already hard again. "Wren?"

But he wasn't listening. He laid her back against the floor and placed his body between her thighs. "Show me how a human male loves his woman, Maggie. I want to know what it's like to have you under me."

She frowned at his words until he entered her again with a hard thrust that set her on fire. Marguerite sighed in satisfaction as she cupped his buttocks in her hands. "How can you be hard again?"

He nibbled her jaw. "I have a lot to make up for."

And in the next few hours, he certainly did.

Wren lay snuggled with Maggie, his heart pounding. The scent of her filled his head, making him want to stay here like this forever. He was spooned up behind her while she napped in his arms. He was tired, too, but to sleep would cause him to shift to his natural beastly form.

The last thing he needed was for her to learn what he was. No doubt she would be terrified to find out she was sleeping with a tigard.

Closing his eyes, he savored the feel of her soft buttocks against his loins. Her hair tickled his lips.

For the first time in his adulthood, he almost wished he could mate. But he knew better. He was the last of his line. At least on his mother's side.

On his father's . . .

No self-respecting tiger would ever touch him. He was an abomination to them. It was bad enough to be a hybrid, but to be a white tiger was considered the worst kind of deformity among his people.

He could never belong in the Katagaria world any more than he belonged in the human.

He was alone. There was nothing he could do about it. It was the curse of his breed, and it was one he'd resigned himself to a long time ago.

Sighing, he reluctantly withdrew from the only woman he'd most likely ever know. He paused long enough to kiss her cheek.

It was best to leave her and to never look back. He now knew what he was missing. He'd tasted her once . . . well, okay, it'd been a lot more than once. But that would be enough. It was time to leave her to her world while he went back to his own.

Marguerite felt the dip in the bed as Wren left her. Opening her eyes, she watched as he bent over to pick up the towel she had dropped this morning in her rush to get to class.

Goodness, he had the best backside she'd ever seen on a man.

"Are you leaving?" she asked.

He straightened up to look at her. "I need to get to work."

She laughed at the thought of a man with his kind of money worried about getting to a minimum-wage job on time. "Why don't you call in sick?"

"If I'm not there on time, Tony won't make his class. It wouldn't be fair to him."

She felt a strange fluttering in her stomach that Wren cared about a co-worker. None of the men she'd ever known would have considered someone else above their own interests.

Wren returned to the bed to kiss her. Marguerite melted the instant his lips touched hers. She wanted to beg him to stay but refused to be like that. There would be other moments like this when she could spend more time with him.

He slid his hand beneath the sheet to gently stroke her hip. She sighed at the heat of his skin against hers as she deepened their kiss.

Wren pulled back with a growl. "If we keep this up, I won't leave at all."

"Would that be so bad?"

A veil descended over his face. "Yes, Maggie. It would." He left her so quickly that it brought a chill to her. There was a strange air about him now. One she didn't understand. It was like he'd closed something off.

"What's wrong, Wren?"

"Nothing," he said curtly as he left her to go to the bathroom.

Marguerite got up and pulled her bathrobe on before she followed after him.

"Wren?" she asked as she caught him in the shower. "Tell me what's going on."

His eyes seared hers. "I can't. Even if I did, you would never believe it."

"Try me."

He shook his head. "Look, Maggie. This afternoon was fun . . . you were and are incredible. But we can't keep seeing each other."

"Why not?"

He let out a long, tired breath. "You're the daughter of a senator."

"You're the son of a corporate tycoon. People like us date every day."

He laughed bitterly. "No, Maggie. They don't. I've got a lot of shit in my life that you would never understand."

"Like what?"

His eyes turned dark, tormented. He reached one wet hand out to lay it against her cheek. "I wish I were what you deserve. But I can never be that man. In more ways than one."

His gaze filled with regret, he released her and drew the shower curtain closed.

Marguerite stood there, listening to him bathe. Her mind went over everything that had happened to them since the night they met. There for a time this afternoon, especially after he'd cut his hair, she'd thought that they shared something special.

But wishing for something didn't make it real, and if he wasn't willing to trust her, there was nothing she could do. She wasn't the kind of woman to beg for affection.

Still there was something inside her that shriveled at the thought of not seeing him anymore. She barely knew him and yet she . . .

You know nothing about him. Nothing.

That was true. He really hadn't shared anything with her. So why was she so attracted to him?

Please don't tell me I'm becoming one of those women who are attracted to the bad boys. She'd always prided herself on being levelheaded. And yet she'd spent the whole afternoon in bed with a man she barely knew.

Oh, this sucked!

The water shut off an instant before the shower curtain opened. Marguerite couldn't take her eyes off the sight that he made standing there completely naked with the water glistening on his tawny skin.

His gaze burning her, he reached behind her to pull a towel off the bar. She suddenly felt an inexplicable need to rub herself against him.

"I'll . . . um, I'll take a quick shower and drive you back to Sanctuary."

"Thanks."

Marguerite frowned as she noted his bandage had come loose. But what stunned her about it was the fact that the wound was virtually healed.

"Wha—"

He jerked away before she could get a closer look at it.

"Wren?" she asked, walking after him as he left the bathroom. "Let me see your shoulder."

"There's nothing to see."

"Your wound . . . it looks healed."

Before he could respond, she grabbed the bandage and pulled at it. He hissed, then growled, but she paid no attention as she stared at the scar that looked like several months had gone by, not just a few days.

She gaped at what couldn't be real. "How is that possible?"

"I'm a quick healer."

She shook her head. "What are you, Wren?"

He gave her a flippant look. "What do you think I am? A vampire with extraordinary healing powers? A werewolf?"

She rolled her eyes at his sarcasm. "Don't be ridiculous."

"Exactly. The wound wasn't so severe and I heal fast, okay? That's all there is to it."

"You don't have to be so defensive."

He took a step toward her in a manner so feral that for a second it actually scared her. "It is in my nature to attack when questioned or cornered. *That* along with many other reasons is why I can't have a relationship with you or anyone else. I can't trust myself around you, Maggie. I was born into an extremely violent family, and I honestly don't know how to deal with the emotions you stir inside me." His eyes pierced her with pain. "I don't want to hurt you, but if I stay with you, I will. I know it."

She didn't want to believe that. How could someone so protective ever hurt her? It didn't make sense.

"Have you ever hit a woman before?"

His hand tightened around the towel he had clutched around his waist as he started to move past her.

"Have you?" she demanded.

A muscle worked in his jaw. "No."

"Then why do you think you'll hurt me?"

His turquoise eyes were haunted as he looked away from her. "You have no idea what I'm capable of, Maggie. I don't even know, and honestly, I don't want to find out. My family has a really bad history with relationships."

She shivered at his words. "How did your parents die?"

"You don't want me to answer that. Just believe me when I say that I wish things were different. I wish *I* were different, but I'm not." He leaned down and brushed a light kiss to her cheek. "I just hope I have the strength to stay away from you. For both our sakes."

"And if I don't want you to?"

The anguished look in his eyes burned her. "Please, Maggie, please don't ask me for things that I can't give you."

"Tell me what happened to your parents, Wren."

His eyes burned her with heat. There was so much tormented pain there that when he finally spoke, it surprised her. "They killed each other in a fit of anger. Now do you understand?"

Marguerite was stunned by those words. There for an entire moment, she couldn't even breathe.

"I have both their tempers and now you know why I can't be near other people. I don't want to hurt you, Maggie. I don't, but if I were to stay with you, I know that I would eventually do something wrong."

Still, she didn't believe it. "I don't think you could ever hurt me."

"I don't think it, either, Maggie. I know it. Trust me on this. I have to stay away from you."

Her heart was breaking and yet somewhere inside was a kernel of hope. Maybe he just needed some time to clear his thoughts. They had both said that they weren't going to see each other again and yet here they stood. Naked. Toe-to-toe.

The impossible could happen and he might very well change his mind.

But if it didn't, she wouldn't hold him here. She refused to be one of those clinging women who chased after a man. She was stronger than that.

Suddenly the stupid old adage about "if you love something, set it free. If it comes back, it was, and always will be, yours. If it never returns, it was never yours to begin with" went through her mind. It was true.

Of course the thought was quickly followed by Tammy's favorite addition: "*If it just sits in your living room, eating your food, messing up your stuff, and using your phone while taking all of your money, and never behaves as if you actually set it free in the first place . . . you either married it or gave birth to it.*"

Tammy had an interesting take on life sometimes.

No good would ever come of trying to leash him to her side.

"Okay, Wren, but if you ever need a friend, you know where I live."

He smiled before he nuzzled her cheek. His breath heated her skin, making her hot and weak. It was all she could do not to pull him back to her bed.

"If you ever need someone to protect you, you know where I live."

She laughed at that even though her heart was shriveling at the thought of not seeing him again.

"Go," he said, urging her back. "Get your bath. I'll be waiting in the other room."

Marguerite nodded and watched as he left her there. Missing him already, she bathed and dressed, then took Wren back to Sanctuary.

He opened the car door, then turned toward her. "Thank you, Maggie."

"For what?"

"For being with me."

She scowled at his odd words. Why would he thank her for that? "It was far from a hardship."

"I'll never forget you," he breathed. He took her hand in his, then kissed her palm.

Then he left the car.

Marguerite rolled the passenger side window down. "Wren?"

He turned back toward her. "It's over, Maggie. It has to be."

Before she could say another word, he disappeared into the building without so much as a backward glance. She listened to the radio while the song "I'll Be" by Edwin McCain played quietly to fill the vacancy left by Wren's absence.

But in her heart she knew that nothing would fill the emptiness inside her. Nothing but Wren, and he was determined to stay away.

Maybe that was for the best, though. There was something very dark and very sinister about Wren. Maybe he was right. Maybe there was something wrong with him.

The papers were filled every day with women who'd made the wrong choices in boyfriends or spouses. Many of the women didn't live to regret it.

But Wren wouldn't hurt her. She knew that instinctively.

"Yeah, but unless you're willing to trust me, there's no hope for this."

Wren wanted his freedom and she refused to run after him.

She was Marguerite Goudeau. And if she had nothing else in her life, she had her pride.

"Bye, Wren," she whispered. "I hope we meet again one day after you learn to trust someone."

Chapter 6

Wren felt like warmed-over shit as he walked through the back door of Sanctuary. He forced himself to shut the door gently and not slam it. He didn't want to be here. The only place he wanted to be was with Maggie.

Even now he could smell her scent on his skin, feel her body pressed to his. He craved her with a consuming madness that wanted him to turn into his true form and bound back after her.

But it could never be.

There was no place in his life for her.

"You're late, tiger," Remi growled at Wren as he entered the kitchen. "Where the hell have you been?"

Wren ignored him as he pulled a white apron from the hook by the door, shrugged it on over his head, and tied it around his waist. Marvin came running up to him, chattering in an angry tone as he expressed his upset at being left alone with the bears for so long.

"Sorry, monkey," Wren said quietly. "I had things to do this afternoon."

Marvin pursed his lips before he bounded up Wren's

arm to perch on his neck and muss his hair. Wren smoothed it down but didn't comment.

Remi gave him a hostile glare before he went to get another keg out of the supply room.

Tony came through the kitchen door from the bar area with a load of dishes. He passed a relieved look at Wren as he set them in a large stainless-steel sink. "Man, we have been busy today. I swear it feels like Mardi Gras or something."

Wren glanced to the clock on the wall. He was fifteen minutes late and Tony still had traffic to deal with.

Tony inclined his head to Wren. "Don't worry, I'll make it. But watch out for Remi, he's been in a pissy mood all day."

Wren snorted at that. Remi stayed in a pissy mood. The bearswain had perpetual PMS.

"Don't speed," Wren warned Tony as he shrugged off his apron and pulled his keys out of his back pocket. "There's a cop just down the street."

"Thanks for the tip."

As soon as Tony left, Remi paused with the keg and glared at Wren again. "What? You talking to the help now?"

Wren ignored him as he picked up an empty dishpan.

Remi cocked his head. "You wreak of human, tiger. Where were you this afternoon?"

He could sense the bear wanted to attack—it was as much Remi's nature as it was his own. But luckily the bear had better sense. Without acknowledging him at all, Wren headed out to the bar to bus tables.

It was a typical evening with the tourists and bikers mingling against the backdrop of heavy metal songs that played over the stereo. The Howlers wouldn't take the stage until much later. With the exception of Colt, who was their guitarist, the band tended to sleep all day and only rise at dusk. It was hard for an animal to retain its human form in the daytime.

Only the truly strong could manage it.

Since it was dinnertime, the table areas were packed with people eating. There weren't many Were-Hunters about. Wren was one of the few who came out this early. But then, daylight had never bothered him that much. Even though he was young by Were-Hunter years, he'd never had a lot of trouble remaining in human form before dark. He wasn't sure why.

Maybe it stemmed from the fact that it took just as much effort to hold a pure tiger or leopard form as an animal as it did to look human. He'd honed those skills early in life as a way to at least try to blend in with the other animals.

Unfortunately, it had been moot, since they could smell that he was a hybrid. His scent was the one thing that he couldn't change even with magic. And he hated it.

As soon as he filled his pan, he headed back toward the bar for the kitchen door. Behind the bar, Fang moved to hold the kitchen door open for him.

Wren inclined his head in thanks. Fang was a wolf who had come to Sanctuary almost a year and a half ago. He'd spent the first few months here in a coma brought on by a vicious Daimon attack that had left the wolf completely defenseless. Unlike the vampires of Hollywood legend, Daimons not only drank blood but also sucked living souls into their own bodies to elongate their lives. Since Were-Hunters were able to wield magic, they were particularly sought by the Daimons, who could use the magic themselves after they killed a Were-Hunter.

It was a harsh thing for a Were-Hunter to be attacked by them, and Wren could understand Fang's coma from it. The wolf was damned lucky to be alive.

Since that weird Thanksgiving when Fang had managed to leave his bed for the first time, he'd been slowly coming back around, but the wolf was still seriously scarred by his attack.

"What happened to your hair, tiger?" Fang asked.

"It fell off."

Fang shook his head as Wren walked past him, into the kitchen. He stopped at the sinks. Marvin leapt from his shoulder to the shelf above while he unpacked the pan for the dishwashers.

"How did it go this afternoon?"

He turned his head to see Aimee behind him. As always, she was stunningly beautiful, with a tight red T-shirt and a pair of jeans. A wide smile curved her lips. She looked hopeful.

Wren shrugged. "It was all right."

Her smile faded. "Did the flowers not work?"

"They worked."

"Then why aren't you happy?"

He shrugged again.

Aimee grabbed him by the arm and pulled him out of the hearing range of the others, into a corner. "Wren, talk to me."

She'd been the only person he'd ever really spoken to, which didn't say much, since he seldom said more than a handful of words to her. "I don't belong with a human."

She glanced toward the door that led to the bar where Fang was working. "Yeah, it hurts to want something you know you shouldn't. But—"

"There are no buts in this, Aimee," Wren said between clenched teeth. "Katagaria don't have human mates, you know that. When was the last time one of us was mated with a human?"

"It's happened."

He knew better. "Even if it did, we'd be sterile. An animal can't have children with a human." Which might not be so bad. The gods knew the last thing he needed was to sire more freaks like himself. But that wasn't the point. The point was that Maggie was out of his league. She was everything decent in the world, and he was everything that gave humans nightmares.

It was impossible.

Wren sighed in resignation. "I got her out of my system. Now I need to work."

But the problem was that Maggie wasn't out of his system. If anything, she was more a part of his thoughts than ever before. He didn't understand the hunger he felt. The need.

The beast within him wanted out to hunt for her. It was salivating inside, simmering. It was a good thing he knew how to control the beast, otherwise there was no telling what he might do.

He left Aimee and went to get his pan.

"Wren?" she said, pulling him to a stop.

Wren cast a meaningful look toward the bar where Fang was waiting for the bearswan. "Stop being a dreamer, Aimee. Our reality is too harsh for that."

He saw the doubt in her blue eyes. "But it's the hope of something better that keeps us going."

He scoffed at her blind optimism. "I abandoned the idea of hope the day my own mother lunged at my throat to kill me." He gave Aimee a hard stare. "And if I were you, Aimee, I'd heed that warning well. Neither of us has a human mother. If you think for one moment that Nicolette wouldn't turn on you, too, you're crazy."

"I'm her only daughter."

"And I was an only child—the last of my mother's kind—and yet she didn't hesitate to come after me. Think about it." Wren brushed past Aimee, back into the bar.

Still, Aimee's words rang in his ears.

Hope. He snorted bitterly at the thought of it. Hope was for humans. It wasn't for animals or freaks.

"Hi."

He glanced up to see a young woman in an extremely short skirt and tight midriff shirt approaching him.

She leaned her head back and polished off her drink. "I thought I'd save you some time and bring my glass to you," she said, giving him a hot once-over. She slid her empty glass over her breast before she handed it to him.

Amazed that he felt absolutely nothing for her, Wren inclined his head and took it from her before he moved away to another table.

The woman pouted before she returned to her seat.

"What the hell is wrong with you, tiger?" Justin asked as he joined Wren. "What kind of beast would turn *that* down?"

"Go get her, panther," Wren said quietly. "She's all yours."

"Yeah, I think I will."

Wren watched as Justin made straight for the woman and struck up a conversation. A few minutes later, the two of them were headed off toward the storeroom near the stage that had been soundproofed by one of the bears as a place where they could take willing human females for a quickie or two.

It was weird that Wren felt absolutely nothing for the woman. Not even a slight stirring. If he didn't know better, he'd swear he was mated. But there was no mating mark on his hand, and even if there were, he would never mate with a human. Especially not Maggie. Her father was too prominent a man.

The idea was to keep their world a secret from humans. Mating himself to a member of a politician's family was suicide.

Marvin came running up to drop a glass in his pan before he dashed off again.

Nicolette paused just outside the door to her office as she watched Wren cleaning tables. Every animal sense she possessed told her that it was time he left Sanctuary—not that she had ever really wanted him here.

If she had her way, there wouldn't be anyone staying at Sanctuary except her own family. But that wasn't their laws. It was necessity that dictated she allow other Were-Hunters to come and go and even live in her beloved home.

That didn't mean she liked it.

Her gaze softened as it drifted toward her son Dev,

who was talking to her other son Cherif. She'd lost two sons to the Arcadian Were-Hunters who had once pursued them to the ends of the earth and beyond for no other reason than because her kind were animals. She refused to lose any more children to this bloodthirsty war of Arcadian against Katagaria.

She would do anything to protect her family.

"Lo?"

She turned at the sound of her mate's call. Aubert was staring at her with a concerned gaze. "*Oui*, Aubert?"

He glanced over to where Wren was. "The tiger isn't hurting anyone."

She curled her lips as she watched Wren cleaning. "His very presence offends me. He isn't right and you know it."

"He has nowhere else to go."

"And neither do we." She jerked her chin in the direction of the monkey as he bounded back toward the tigard. "That is unnatural, too. I hate that damned monkey. He is filthy. Animals such as that one are food for us. They should never be kept as pets."

"Marvin isn't a pet," Aubert said quietly. "Wren doesn't own him. They are friends, and the monkey keeps the tiger calm. It is why we allow him to stay."

She made a disgusted sound. "Why must we cater to him? We are bears. We are the more powerful. One strike and we could kill the tiger."

Aubert conceded the point with a nod. "In the wild, beast to beast, yes. But Wren is part human, as are we. He knows not to attack us from the front, but rather to attack us from behind. What he lacks in strength, he makes up for in speed and agility. He could kill us. I have no doubt."

She looked at her mate with rancor. "You fear him?"

"No," he snapped. "But I'm not a fool. Don't let your hatred blind you, *ma petite*. Better to use his strength to fight for us than to make an enemy of him."

She considered that. "Perhaps, but he isn't like the others. He sees through us and our hospitality."

"*Oui*, but he keeps it to himself. Seldom does he speak to anyone."

Still Nicolette didn't trust Wren. She could sense the tigard's unrest. Sense his volatile state. He could turn violent at any moment. "I think we should take our concerns to the Omegrion." The Omegrion was the ruling council for their kind. It made and enforced the laws of all Were-Hunters, and its members could call out a blood hunt for anyone the Weres deemed a threat to their world.

Aubert rolled his eyes. "There is no need for that. Wren is not a Slayer."

"No, but he will be. I can feel it."

Wren let out a deep breath as he finished wiping down the table. With his new haircut he was attracting way too much attention, and he hated it. He'd always liked blending into the background. In the past, people might notice him, but they quickly looked away. Or curled their lips in repugnance.

Either was preferable to the women watching him

now. To the men narrowing their gazes because their girlfriends were ogling him.

Tigers by nature were solitary creatures. They lived their lives alone.

And yet his thoughts kept drifting back to the afternoon. To the sight of Maggie's face.

I have to forget her.

The only problem was that he couldn't.

Marguerite sighed as she straightened her bed. But it was hard to not think of Wren while she made up the bed where they had spent most of the afternoon.

"It's for the best that he's gone," she told herself.

It was true. Law school wasn't easy. Her classes were hard, and they required a lot of concentration. The last thing she needed was the distraction of a troubled bad-boy boyfriend.

The last thing she could afford was to flunk out of school. That would just tickle her father no end.

Marguerite stepped back from the bed and stumbled over something under her foot. Frowning, she saw the small black wallet on the floor.

She grimaced at the sight. "Damn." Of all the stupid luck. It must have fallen out of Wren's pocket while he'd been dressing.

She picked it up and opened it to find his license and money. Yeah, it was his. Not like it could have belonged to anyone else, but she'd still been holding out for a clumsy burglar.

"I should mail it to him."

But he would most likely need it before then. "I can be a grown-up about this."

She'd take it to the bar, leave it with the waitress, and duck out before he even saw her.

Okay, that was a little cowardly and less than adult, but it would be the way to save her feelings. If he didn't want to see her, then she didn't want to be seen.

Wren was in the kitchen unloading dishes when something strange went through him. It was hot and scintillating. Like something had brushed up against his very soul.

Eyes narrowed, he lowered his head and scanned the room.

There was nothing out of the ordinary. But still the beast within him sensed something.

Grinding his teeth, he left the kitchen to head to the bar. He'd only taken one step inside when he found the source of his discomfort . . .

Maggie.

And she was talking to Dev.

Wren's gaze narrowed even more as a jealousy the likes of which he'd never experienced before took hold of him. It was all he could do to stay in human form and not run headlong and attack the bear until he had Dev lying dead in his jaws.

But he did cross the bar in quick, fierce strides.

Marguerite felt the air behind her stir. Even before she turned her head, she knew it was Wren. She could feel his presence like a tangible touch.

She looked up at him over her shoulder. His blue eyes scalded her with heat. The intensity of his stare made her shiver.

"You left your wallet," she said quickly, not wanting him to think that she was tracking him down. She took the wallet from the man she'd given it to and handed it to Wren. "I was just going to leave it for you."

She started for the door.

"Wait," Wren said, pulling her to a stop.

"Wait for what?" she said more harshly than she meant to. "I'm not a yo-yo, Wren. You made it clear that there's nothing more between us. I was—"

He cut her words off with a scorching kiss. Marguerite actually moaned at the feral taste of him.

Even so, she pulled back. "This is cruel." She saw the bitter longing in his eyes as he stared at her.

"Have you ever wanted something that you knew was bad for you? Something that you ached for so much that you could think of nothing else?"

"Yes, which is why I always end up eating the whole chocolate bar anyway."

His grip loosened on her arm as he laughed. She saw the shock on the man's face over his shoulder.

Wren pulled her against him, nuzzled her, and took a deep breath in her hair. "And I want to inhale my chocolate, kitten. Even if it kills me."

She frowned at his words. "I would never hurt you, Wren."

He tensed as if he heard or felt something. "You need to go now. It's not safe here for you."

"How so?"

Wren didn't answer. The two of them were getting

way too much attention from the other Were-Hunters in the bar. He couldn't afford to let them know just how much this woman was coming to mean to him.

"I'm taking my break," he said to Dev before he took her arm and led her for the door.

"What's going on here?" she asked him as they walked outside.

"I can't explain it. I really can't." There was no way to tell her that the feelings inside him were completely wrong. He wasn't supposed to feel for a human. Not like this.

He felt . . .

Like a human being. And that was something he most definitely wasn't.

Wren took her to her Mercedes, which was parked on the side street. He clenched his fists as his body roared to life, demanding he take her again.

Why was he feeling like this? Dammit, it was wrong.

Lifting one hand, he laid his fingers against the blush of her cheek.

He wasn't what she needed in her life. He wasn't what anyone needed, and he knew it. But for the first time ever, he wanted to be with someone.

And a human woman no less.

What was wrong with him? Was this the *trelosa* that could come upon Were-Hunters when they hit puberty? He'd never really felt it as a young man and hadn't understood the rabies-like madness that appeared with hormonal surges.

But he felt it now. It gnawed and it demanded.

Maybe the *trelosa* had been delayed because he was

a hybrid. He didn't know. But humans weren't supposed to attract him. Not as anything more than a possible bedmate or prey.

She stared up at him with those accusing brown eyes that were shining in anger. "I don't understand what's going on here, Wren. You push me away and yet you look at me as if you're a starving beggar and I'm the only steak in town."

"That sums it up about right," he said softly. "You are so out of my league."

"How do you figure?"

"I'm not right, Maggie. Physically, emotionally, socially . . . I shouldn't be with you."

"That's just stupid. You keep saying that and I don't see anything abnormal with you. What is so wrong with you that we can't date?"

How he wished he could tell her, but that was stupid and he knew it. To tell her he was an animal would scare the life out of her. Instead, he settled on human arguments. "I'm antisocial."

"So am I. I'm socially awkward and I hate parties and mixers."

"I hate people."

"Then why is your hand still on my face?"

He swallowed at the truth he couldn't deny. "Because I don't hate *you*."

"Well that's a relief to know, especially after this afternoon."

A tic started in his jaw as he dropped his hand away. "I need to get back to work."

"Will I see you later?"

He wanted to say no, but there was a part of him that

was so calm around her. It was the only time in his life that he had felt such.

Dear gods, she had actually tamed some part of him. *Shove her away.*

He couldn't. He needed to feel her against him. Against his will, he felt himself nodding.

Marguerite breathed a sigh of relief. She hadn't realized that she'd been holding her breath in expectation.

He hadn't rejected her this time. It was a good sign. "Wren?"

She looked past him to see the mean older woman on the street, glaring at them. Apparently the woman hadn't warmed up to either one of them since the last time she'd thrown Marguerite out of her house.

Wren glanced at the woman, then growled a sound that didn't seem quite human as he returned to stare into Marguerite's eyes. "I have to go now."

"Okay." Marguerite leaned forward and placed a chaste kiss on his cheek. As she pulled back, she saw the way he savored it.

He picked her hand up and brought it to his lips, where he placed a hungry kiss on her knuckles. "Be careful."

"You, too."

He stepped back as she got in her car and he didn't move until she'd driven away.

Turning, Wren walked to where Nicolette was still standing. The bear didn't say a word as he walked past her, but he felt the heat of her stare.

Ignoring it, he returned to the bar and went back to work.

Nicolette followed the tigard inside and paused by

her son Dev's side. "It is unnatural for our kind to be attracted to a human."

"He's becoming unstable."

She nodded. "I spoke with a cousin of his a few hours ago."

"And?"

She narrowed her eyes on the tigard. "He said that Wren had killed both of his parents."

Dev looked stunned by the news, but she hadn't been. It was what she'd expected to hear. There was something evil about that tigard.

"How?" Dev asked. "He was barely more than a cub when he was brought here."

"It is the curse of his breed. Why do you think the snow leopards are nearly extinct? They go mad and turn on the ones they depend on. The ones who care for them."

"You think Wren is going mad?"

"What do you think?"

Dev glanced to where Wren was cleaning a table with Marvin on his shoulder. "I think he's in love with that woman. I actually heard him laugh."

Nicolette sneered at the very thought. "It is unnatural for a Katagari to love a human. Not to mention, that *woman*," she spat the word, "is death to all of us. Can you imagine what would happen if her father ever learned of us? We would be hunted and killed."

Dev nodded. "The humans would panic, no doubt."

Nicolette ground her teeth as raw, bitter anger consumed her. "I will not allow that hybrid beast to jeopardize all of us."

"What do you plan to do, *Maman*?"

She didn't speak as she watched the tigard curl his lip at her before he took his dishes to the kitchen.

She couldn't tell Dev what she had planned. For some reason, her son was rather fond of the tigard. Something that truly appalled her. But then most males were weak. It was why bearswans were the stronger of the species and why she was the one who led this household.

"Don't worry, Devereaux. *Maman* will handle everything. You go back and monitor our door."

And soon her house would again be safe from the threat that Wren posed to them all.

Chapter 7

Marguerite sighed heavily as she walked alone in the zoo, watching the animals play together or rest. Three days had gone by without a single word from Wren. Worse, her father had called two hours ago to yell at her about Blaine's arrest and pending trial. Apparently neither Blaine nor his father had bothered to inform him just who Wren really was—Blaine most likely refused to believe it. After all, whose family could ever be more important than his own? And how could anyone with Wren's kind of money ever do anything other than bask in his own greatness?

It was enough to make her sick, and even now she could hear her father's angry voice in her head.

"He will have a permanent mark on his record and for what? A worthless vagrant you decided to befriend? Really, Marguerite, what is wrong with you? Blaine's father has helped to raise tens of thousands of dollars at a time for my campaign, and my daughter had his only son arrested? Are you trying to kill me? Do you want me to drop dead from cardiac arrest so

that you can have your inheritance early? Just take a gun out and shoot me then. Get it over with. . . ."

And then he'd pulled out the one zinger that never failed to tear straight through her.

"This is what I get for marrying a Cajun against my family's wishes. I should never have had children. They're a liability no politician can afford."

She hadn't even been able to get a word in edgewise during his entire forty-five-minute rant. After a while, she hadn't even tried. She'd set the phone down on the counter, munched chips, and flipped through a magazine while he railed. Once he'd finished, she'd simply apologized and hung up.

Her father had never been the kind of man to listen to reason. Of course, she could have ended the whole thing by telling him who Wren was and why Blaine hadn't been able to bribe his way out of trouble, but she took sadistic pleasure out of not telling him. Let her father go on with his delusions.

Knowing her dad, he'd do a full turnaround as soon as he learned about Wren's wealth.

But she didn't want her father to like Wren because Wren was wealthy. She wanted him to see the man, not the money.

Shaking her head, she walked down the wooden pathway between the cages in the zoo as she tried to put the whole thing out of her mind. But it was impossible. She didn't want to fight with her father.

All she wanted was to have her father be proud of her. To accept her. And yet he was so unreasonable. She'd never known anyone who could make up their mind so fast with so little information and then argue into infinity that they were right while everyone else was wrong.

"One day I'm going to stand up to you, Dad," she whispered. At least she hoped she could, but it was hard. No matter what, she loved him. He was her father and he had profound moments of tenderness . . .

At least sometimes.

He just had higher expectations for her. He wanted her to be like Whitney or Elise, a perfect debutante. A stunning beauty who could be some rich man's consort. One who threw strategic parties to help her husband climb the ladder of success in whatever venue he chose.

But that wasn't her. She was plain and far from skinny or petite. As for parties . . . she'd rather be alone in a corner somewhere reading. She hated being nice to people she didn't like because her father wanted their contributions. She hated being fake. All she wanted was to be herself.

She wanted to make her own mark on the world like her mother had done before her marriage, not be the helpmate for someone else. That kind of life had destroyed her mother, and she knew intrinsically that it would kill her, too.

"I just want to breathe." She didn't care what she did so long as it was a job or career *she* chose. She wouldn't be locked in a cage like the animals here. No matter how much she loved her father, she refused to let him treat her the way he'd done her mother. Sooner or later, she was going to force him to see her for herself.

Marguerite stopped her walk in front of the white tiger exhibit. Since she was a little girl, she'd always

loved to come to the zoo. It had been her mother's favorite place on earth.

Her mother had grown up here. It'd been Marguerite's maternal grandfather who'd led the crusade
to save the zoo in the seventies and early eighties.
He had been a visionary who had taken the zoo out of
the dark ages and turned it into one of the leading zoos
in the country.

Everywhere she looked, she saw her mother's side
of the family here.

For that matter, she saw her mother.

When her mother had been a college student at Tulane, she'd worked here as a docent. She had planned
on being a veterinarian or zookeeper after college, but
her marriage had stopped all of her dreams.

The only time Marguerite could remember her
mother smiling and laughing was when she'd brought
her here and told her stories about the different animals
and how they lived and hunted. It was here that Marguerite found peace.

Here that she could again feel her mother's presence.

Marguerite's father hated this place. To him was
gauche, common, and filthy. But to Marguerite it was
beautiful.

"I miss you, Mom," she whispered as she watched
the two tigers play in a small facsimile of their wilderness home.

She'd only been twelve when her mother, sick of being a politician's wife, had overdosed on antidepres-
sants. Of course Marguerite's father had covered it up
so that everyone thought it'd been an accident, but she
knew the truth. Her father had refused to divorce her

mother or even live apart. It would have been bad for his career.

Unable to stand the prospect of being castigated for her friends, her wardrobe, and her taste in everything for the rest of her life, her mother had taken matters into her own hands. She'd left a final note telling Marguerite to be stronger than she had been.

> *Follow your heart, Marguerite. Don't let anyone tell you how to live your life. It's the only one you have,* mon ange. *Live it for both of us.*

Marguerite's lips quivered as grief swept through her. Her mother had been a truly beautiful and gentle soul.

For the longest time, Marguerite had hated her father after her mother's death. And in truth, she'd hated God for leaving her alone with him. But as she grew older, she'd begun to understand him a bit.

Like Blaine and Todd, he was at the mercy of his own family's ambitions for his future. Her grandfather had run her father's entire life from birth. Her grandfather still did in many ways. Even as a powerful senator, her father always deferred to his father for advice. If Grandpa was upset, Dad was upset and contrite.

The only time her father had ever stood up to her grandfather had been by marrying her mother.

Marguerite wasn't even sure that her father ever really loved her mother. Her mother had been one of those absolutely stunning women. The kind of beauty who turned everyone's head. Any man would have wanted her.

No doubt her father had been attracted to her for her exceptional looks. Not to mention, as a former Miss Louisiana and a Cajun whose father had saved their beloved Audubon Zoo, she was a major benefit to a man with political ambitions. With her mother by his side, her father had been able to claim that he understood the needs of all members of Louisiana—both rich and poor.

Well, he might understand their needs, but he'd never understood his daughter's and he never would.

"Hi, Maggie."

Marguerite froze as she recognized that deep, hypnotic voice. She looked over her shoulder to see Wren standing back from her. Wearing a loose denim shirt and jeans, he was the best thing she'd seen in days. His blond hair was a bit shaggy, and the blue of his shirt made his eyes practically glow. He completely took her breath away.

Before she could think better of it, she literally threw herself into his arms and held him close, needing to feel warmth from someone.

His timing couldn't have been better.

Wren was shocked by her reaction. He wrapped his arms around her as she clutched him to her. No one had ever been so happy to see him before. He swallowed as unfamiliar emotions tore through him.

"I'm so glad you're here," she whispered.

"I noticed."

She pulled back with a grimace and he sensed her instant dismay. Wren offered her a smile as his heart pounded with a foreign ache. "It was a joke, Maggie."

Her expression softened back into one of joy. "How did you know I was here?"

He hesitated as he tried to think of a plausible lie. "You weren't home."

"Yeah, but I could have been anywhere in New Orleans."

Wren rubbed his neck nervously. He had to distract her away from this line of questioning before he let something slip.

"I like coming here." That was a complete lie. He actually hated zoos. He couldn't stand to see the animals who were caged. As one of them, he could hear their thoughts and sense their discomfort. Not that all of them were unhappy with their situation. There were a number of animals who liked the attention and who were grateful to have a safe environment.

But others . . .

They were like him. Predators. And they despised cages of any sort.

When he was a child, his mother had always threatened to sell him to the zoo.

"It's a freak. They'd pay good money to have something like it on display. Just imagine how much money we could make." His father had been the only thing that had kept Wren out of such a place as this.

Wren ground his teeth as he looked away from the white tigers. They were the number one attraction at the zoo here. His mother hadn't been wrong.

He hated her for that.

Pushing those thoughts away, he turned back toward Maggie. "Why are you here?"

She gave him a winsome smile. "I told you I have a thing for tigers." She looked past him, into the pit where the white tigers were playing. "I think Rex and Zulu are the most beautiful creatures I've ever seen and I love to come over and watch them."

Her words amused him. "You like white tigers, huh?"

She nodded. "I would give anything to pet one."

He smiled at the irony of that. Little did she know, she'd already done it. "They're not so hard to tame."

She laughed. "Yeah, right. They'd probably eat anyone dumb enough to go near them."

Maybe, but not when the hand stroking them was one as gentle and delicate as hers. Any tiger would lie down at her feet. . . .

At least he would.

Wren took those beautiful hands into his. Her skin was like warm velvet against his, and it reminded him of just how soft the rest of her body was. He could sense a deep sadness inside her, and it made his own heart ache for her. "Why aren't you studying?"

She sighed as if the weight of the entire universe was on her shoulders. "I couldn't concentrate. I had a crappy call with my father a little while ago and I was trying to zen myself into some semblance of a happy place."

His stomach shrank at her words. He hadn't meant to disturb her. "You want me to leave you alone?"

She shook her head. "No. I found my happy place the minute I saw you."

His heart stopped beating as he heard words he'd never thought to hear from anyone. This was such an impossible relationship. Were-Hunters didn't choose their mates; the Fates did that without any input from them.

Whenever a Were-Hunter was to be mated, a mating

mark would appear on their hands. It almost always appeared after sex, which was one of the reasons why unmated Were-Hunters were promiscuous. The more they slept around, the more likely they were to find their mate. But there was no visible mark to show him that Maggie was his.

The only mark was the one in his heart that craved her.

He didn't speak as she bicycled their hands with her fingers laced with his. The smile on her face warmed every part of him.

Her hair was pulled back, with a single strand of it loose to fall down the side of her face to her neck. He longed to brush his lips against that spot so that he could inhale her precious scent.

Her eyes were full of passion and caring. She was without a doubt the most beautiful creature he had ever seen in his life.

A group of schoolkids ran past them, laughing and shouting as they saw the two male tigers.

Wren barely noticed the kids. "What are your plans today?"

She shrugged. "I'm open. What about you?"

"It's my day off."

"Really?"

He nodded, then gave her a devilish grin. "Want to go get naked?"

Marguerite squeaked at his offer as she felt heat scald her face. But the truth was, she wanted nothing more. "Is that all I am to you?" she asked in a teasing tone.

"No," he said with sincerity burning deep in his eyes. "You're much more to me than that."

SHERRILYN KENYON

She swallowed at the deepness of his voice. At the needful look on his face. She was completely captivated by him. He let go of her hands to cup her face and tilt it up toward his. Marguerite closed her eyes in expectation of his kiss.

His lips brushed hers.

Until a scream rent the air.

"Help! Oh God, someone call the zookeepers! Hurry!"

Wren pulled away from Marguerite as the children started screaming and people began running all around them.

"What happened?" she asked.

A lady was shrieking a few feet away. "Oh my God, that kid is in the cage with the tigers!"

"They're going to eat him!"

Marguerite couldn't breathe as she turned to see a boy around the age of eight in the cage. His face bloody and clothes torn from his fall, he was crying and screaming as he tried to climb back up to the fence, but the concrete wall kept him from it. He splashed around in the water, drawing even more attention from the tigers.

Worse, the tigers were growling and hissing as they stalked down their landing toward the water that separated them from him.

She was sure the kid was dead, as was everyone else in the crowd.

Suddenly, Wren bolted past her, toward the wooden railing that kept the visitors from the fence. She watched in horror as he vaulted over the fence and barbed wire into the cage, to land in a crouch not far from the boy on one of the concrete pads that formed small islands in the water. With his head bent down in that familiar feral pose, Wren rose slowly to his feet and turned toward the child, who was screaming and crying.

She covered her mouth with her hand as she expected the tigers to kill them both.

Wren moved carefully toward the child, who obviously had been hurt from his fall.

"It's okay, kid," Wren said in a calm, even tone as he waded through the water to reach the boy. "What's your name?"

"Johnny."

Wren reached up to pull him from the concrete pad, but the boy wouldn't let go.

"Trust me, Johnny. They're not going to hurt you. I won't let them."

Johnny was crying as he reluctantly let go of the concrete. Wren cradled him to his chest as he looked around for a way to get the boy to safety. With Wren's animal strength, he could easily jump back up to the spectator area above their heads, but that would most likely clue in the people watching them that he wasn't quite human.

Not that they wouldn't have some suspicions anyway, since he was going to get out of this cage without either him or Johnny being bitten or mauled. Wren ground his teeth as he realized a number of people were taking pictures.

Damn.

Turning his face away, he glanced around. The best way to get them out of this would be through a gate in the back that the zookeepers probably used to feed the tigers. Wren moved toward it.

Rex and Zulu came closer, roaring and prancing in warning to him. Wren turned around and glared at them. They wanted to attack him, he could sense it, and yet they were confused by his human state and tigard smell.

He hissed at them.

They backed up.

Johnny screamed.

"Sh," Wren said calmly. "Don't be afraid. They can smell it, and it's that scent that makes them want to attack you. Pretend they're nothing more than pet kittens."

"But they're tigers."

"I know. Pretend you're a tiger, too. Pretend that they can't see us at all."

The boy's tears slowed. "Here, kitty, kitty."

Wren nodded. "That's it, Johnny. Be brave."

The tigers came closer but stayed back long enough for Wren to reach the gate. A group of zookeepers were already there to unlock it. As soon as Wren handed Johnny to the female keeper, one of the tigers ran for him.

"Run!" the keeper screamed.

Wren didn't move as the tiger leapt at him. He caught the tiger and rolled to the ground with him. Rex only wanted to play with Wren. He lay on the ground with the tiger on his chest as Rex nipped teasingly at Wren's skin. He patted Rex's head playfully.

"You better let me up, Rex," he said quietly. "Otherwise they might trank you."

The tiger licked his face before he bounded away. Wren got up and went back to the fence.

"What the hell was that?" the keeper asked.

"I grew up around tigers," Wren said. "They're just big cats."

"Yeah," the keeper said in a disbelieving tone. "Right. You're lucky you weren't lunch."

Wren stepped out of the cage.

As the keeper locked the gate behind him while another keeper tended to the boy, Maggie came running up to Wren. "Are you okay?"

He nodded.

She held him at arm's length to examine him as if she couldn't believe he was completely intact. "I thought you were dead when that one tiger ran at you."

"He just wanted a playmate."

"Yeah, and hell is just a sauna. You could have been eaten alive."

He smiled at her concerned tone. "Eaten alive's not so bad, depending on who it is doing the biting."

A rich blush covered her face. "How can you make light of this? What you did was incredible."

People were starting to come up to them, asking questions that Wren had no intention of answering.

"C'mon," he said to Maggie. "Let's get out of here."

She nodded before she took his hand and led him toward the exit. They had to dodge a lot of people wanting answers before they could safely make it to her car.

As soon as they were in it, Marguerite drove him back toward her house. "Were you really raised around big cats?" she asked.

"Yes."

"In New York?"

By her tone he could tell she didn't quite buy it. "You don't believe me?"

"Well, New York isn't exactly known for its wilderness areas."

Wren gave her a wry grin. "Okay. The truth is I'm like Doctor Dolittle. I can speak to all animals. I know what they're thinking at all times. I jumped into the cage and told the tigers to back off. They obeyed me because I'm one of them."

Marguerite rolled her eyes. "Now you're being ridiculous."

Wren let out an exasperated sigh. He couldn't win for losing. Even when he told her the truth, she refused to believe it. "Then you tell me, Maggie. Why didn't the tigers kill me?"

"Were you ever around lion tamers?"

He laughed at that. "I'm around you. I could easily classify you as a tiger tamer."

"Oh, forget it. I can't get a straight answer out of you, can I?"

Ironically, she'd been getting them, she just didn't want to hear them. Not that he could blame her. In her world, people were people, they weren't animals in disguise. Her kind didn't belong in his world. Very few humans could even begin to understand, let alone survive in it.

"I've missed you, Maggie," he said in a hushed tone. "You're all I've been thinking about for days. I lie in bed and all I can think about is being with you, touching you."

She pulled into her driveway and turned the engine off. He sensed irritation and unrest from her.

"I don't get you, Wren," she said as she faced him. "You're one of the richest men in the country and yet you live like you're penniless and work as a busboy in a biker bar of all places. You tell me you don't want to see me anymore at the same time you tell me all you want to do is get naked with me. That you've missed me even though I haven't had one word from you in days. What is the truth of you? Are you just playing with me? Because if you are . . ."

"I don't understand me, either. Okay? I never have. Until the night you came into Sanctuary, everything was basic. I got up, I ate, I worked, and I went to bed. Now . . . I don't know what I want."

That wasn't the truth. He knew exactly what he wanted. He just couldn't have it.

"I know I'm bad for you, Maggie. If I had a brain in my head, I would walk away and leave you alone, but God help me, I can't. I just want to be with you even though I know it's wrong."

"Wrong how?"

He ground his teeth in anger, wishing he could tell her the truth and have her believe it. But he couldn't. Telling her would most likely get her killed. "I don't belong in your world."

"*I* don't belong in my world."

He scowled at her. Now she was the one being ridiculous. "Of course you do."

"No, Wren, I don't. I might wear the clothes and drive the car, but my heart isn't in my life. I hate that I let my father make me feel like I'm somehow unworthy of what I have. I hate that I'm living here in the house Daddy picked out because he was afraid that if I lived in a dorm—which is what I wanted to do—I'd be hanging out with the wrong kind of people. There have been so many times in my life when I prayed that I'd have the courage to run away from all this. And yet here I am, still in Daddy's house, still taking classes I hate, and all because I don't know what else I should be doing with my life."

Her sadness reached out to Wren in a way nothing ever had before.

"If you could be free of your father, what would you do?"

She let out a slow breath. "I don't know. Travel maybe. I've always wanted to see all the different cultures of the world, but my father won't allow it. He says it's too dangerous and he's afraid I might get caught in some scandal that could backlash onto him or his career. I can't imagine being you and having no one to answer to. What's it like to have that kind of freedom?"

Wren laughed bitterly. "It's lonely. No one cares what happens to me. Had I been shot dead the night we met, they would have buried me without a tear and that would have been the end of it. And I'm not as free as you think I am. There are a lot of people who would have rejoiced had the bullet hit me a little further to the left and pierced my heart. People who would love to see me dead."

"Why?"

Bitterness swelled inside him. "Money motivates, and there are several people who would be a lot richer if I were no longer here."

"Well, there's one person I know of who would be a lot poorer if you vanished."

Wren's heart clenched at her words. He leaned

forward to capture her lips with his. She tasted of woman and sweetness. Of pure decadence. But most of all, she tasted of heaven.

She wrapped her arms around him as they embraced in the tight confines of her car.

His cock hardened with a primal need that only she could fulfill. It wasn't just sexual. She touched something else inside him. Something both human and animal.

Breathless, Wren pulled back to stare at her. He could use his powers to take them from the car to the bed, but that would be really stupid.

The last thing she wanted to know was that she was sleeping with an animal.

Wanting her more than he'd ever wanted anything, he reached across her and opened her car door.

Marguerite practically fell out of her car. Wren crawled over to come out of the car behind her on her side. Before she could even catch her breath, he scooped her up in his arms and virtually ran with her toward her house.

"Impatient much?"

He laughed at her question. "Get that key ready or I might kick the door in."

The tone of his voice told her he wasn't joking. Marguerite was laughing as she tried to get the key into the lock. Wren growled before he tossed her onto one shoulder and took the key away from her. He had the door opened a heartbeat later.

He entered the house, slammed the door shut, then set her down in front of it.

Marguerite was still laughing as she faced him. His

eyes scorched her with heat as he pulled his shirt over his head. Her humor died at the sight of his bared tawny chest. The scar on his shoulder was a harsh reminder of what he'd sacrificed for her. He seized her for a scorching kiss that stole her breath.

She wrapped her arms around him and groaned at the wicked taste of him, at the sensation of his hot skin under her hands. She could feel his heart pounding against her breasts as he deepened his kiss.

He moved from her mouth to her neck, where his breath scorched her. Chills spread all over her as he gently suckled the tender skin there. She had missed him so. . . . Much more than she would have thought possible. It didn't make sense, but then, feelings almost never did.

"I love the way you smell," he said in a ragged breath beside her ear.

"I love the way you feel."

Most of all, she loved the way his whiskered cheeks prickled her skin. His body was so hard compared to hers. So incredibly masculine.

Wren couldn't think with her in his arms. All he wanted was to be inside her again. It was a desire so potent that it overrode all reason. She trailed her lips along his jaw as he lifted her skirt so that he could cup her and press her closer to his swollen cock.

Part of him wanted to take his time savoring her, but the other was beyond that. He would play with her later. Right now the beast in him needed her.

His breathing ragged, he slid her panties down her legs.

Marguerite shivered at the sight of Wren kneeling

between her feet. She lifted her feet up one by one so that he could strip her underwear from her. He looked up at her, and the heated intensity of those pale blue eyes scorched her.

He rose slowly, lifting her skirt again as he did so, his gaze never wavering from hers. Marguerite moaned deep in her throat as he brushed his hand through the small triangle of hair. His touch was incredibly tender as he slowly separated the folds of her body to touch her. It was all she could do to remain standing as he pleasured her, and when he slid his finger inside her she moaned in ecstasy.

Wren watched her closely as she slowly rode his fingers. There was nothing more beautiful than this woman taking her pleasure from him. Unable to stand it, he pulled away long enough to unfasten his pants and free himself. The beast within growled as it came to the forefront and possessed him. He could feel his teeth growing inside his mouth as he fought to remain in human form with her.

But it was hard.

Burying his head against her neck, he lifted her leg enough so that he could enter her. She cried out in pleasure as he buried himself all the way to his hilt.

Marguerite couldn't think straight as he filled her completely and they made love furiously. She wasn't sure how he could hold her up and still thrust, but he managed and it was incredible. She'd never had a man so desperate to be with her.

He licked and nuzzled her neck as she leaned her head back against the door while he plunged himself in and out of her.

"Oh, Wren," she breathed as she buried her hand in his soft golden hair.

She could hear his own ragged breathing as he held her against the door. "Come for me, Maggie," he whispered. "I want to see the pleasure on your face."

She arched her back against the wood as he continued to slam himself into her. She wrapped both of her legs around his waist so that she could draw him even deeper into her body.

The rhythm of his thrusts . . . it was more than she could stand. Two seconds later, her orgasm claimed her as she cried out his name.

Wren smiled as he watched the ecstasy on her face. He could feel her body clutching his. He moved faster until he joined her in that one perfect moment of complete physical bliss.

Throwing his head back, he roared with the pleasure that coursed through him as he finally felt the beast inside him cry out in triumph.

Marguerite smiled at the sight of Wren coming in her arms. It wasn't until he started to pull out that a horrible thought occurred to her.

"We didn't use protection."

He frowned at her. "What?"

"I just realized that I could be pregnant! I could—"

"Maggie," he said firmly. "Don't worry."

"That's easy for you to say," she said, angry at the typical male response. "You're not the one—"

"Maggie, listen to me," he said in a calm, rational tone. "I can't make you pregnant. I can't."

She frowned. "What do you mean?"

His face was sad as he brushed the hair back from her forehead and kissed it. "I'm sterile, okay? I know this for a fact. There's no way I could ever make you, or any other woman, pregnant."

She let out a relieved breath. "You're sure?"

"Absolutely."

She felt better until a new thought struck her. "But what about diseases?"

He scoffed at her. "I've only been with *you.* I told you that."

Was he telling her the truth? Honestly, she had a hard time believing it. "Are you sure about that? You don't make love like a novice."

He made a small X on his bare chest, over his heart. "Cross my heart. You are the only woman I've ever wanted to be this intimate with. I swear it."

Those words touched her deeply. She smiled up at him. "I'm so sorry you're sterile."

He gave a short, bitter laugh. "Don't be. Believe me, it's for the best."

But how could that be? A man like him should have a house full of kids. He was protective and gentle. Patient.

She reached out to touch his cheek. Closing his eyes, he kissed her palm as he unbuttoned her blouse.

Marguerite shivered as he ran his hands over her right breast and caressed her through her bra. She could see he was already growing hard again. "How do you do that?"

"I don't know. I only do it around you."

She shook her head. "You keep saying all the right things, and I just might have to keep you."

He peeled her blouse off of her before he reached around and unhooked her bra, then he slowly removed her skirt. Marguerite swallowed as she found herself naked in her living room. Wren kicked his shoes off, then removed his pants completely.

The look on his face scorched her as he reached for her and kissed her. She ran her hand down the colorful tattoo on his forearm. It was such a beautiful work of art that featured a hiding tiger that was peeking out through jungle grass.

Wren pulled back with a devilish grin. "You know what I want to do with you?"

"I think you already did that."

He laughed, then pulled her toward the sliding glass door that led to the small courtyard in the back.

Marguerite balked the instant he moved her curtain aside. "What are you doing?"

"I want to make love in your pool."

She made a noise of complete disagreement. "Are you insane? It's broad daylight. Someone could see us."

"No one will see us."

"Bull! You don't know that."

He dipped his head to lightly lave her breast. Marguerite groaned at the sensation of his hot tongue on her skin.

"No one will see us, Maggie. I promise." He straightened up. "Trust me?"

This was so not something she should do. "For all we know there could be reporters out there with cameras."

"If there are, I'll kill them before they can turn the film in."

"Yeah, right."

"I swear, there's no one out there, Maggie. C'mon, be adventurous with me."

Marguerite bit her lip as she considered it. Her father would die . . .

But this wasn't her father's life. It was hers. She'd never done anything like this before. It was strangely exciting . . . invigorating.

Erotic. . . .

"Okay, but if we get caught . . ."

"I'll let you geld me."

She gave him a faux angry stare. "I will."

"I know."

She bit her lip in trepidation as he opened the door and pulled her out onto the patio. This was absolutely horrifying and yet it was strangely titillating to be outside in the sunlight, completely naked.

She looked about nervously, half-expecting to find someone spying on them, but to her relief it was just the two of them. Always paranoid about privacy, her father had hired gardeners to plant high shrubs all around her yard. There really wasn't any way for anyone to spy on them.

Wren released her to dive into her pool. He broke the surface of the water to find her still standing on the cement, covering herself as best she could with her hands. She was absolutely beautiful with the sunlight kissing her skin.

"Join me, Maggie."

Her smile was shy an instant before she waded into the pool with him. Like all tigers, Wren loved to play in water. He could hold his breath under the surface for a lot longer than a human.

He dove under and propelled himself toward his prey. He nipped her thigh under the water before he broke the surface.

Marguerite shivered as she felt Wren's naked body up against hers in the water. He nudged her thighs apart to place his hips between her legs. She moaned at the sensation of the water lapping against the tenderest part of her body as the tip of his swollen cock pressed against her core.

She stared up at Wren. He was gorgeous with his hair slicked back from his face. His features really were perfect. But it wasn't until then that she realized he no longer hid his eyes from her. In public, he still kept his gaze down and his hair over his eyes.

But around her he didn't. If she brushed the hair out of his eyes, he left it that way.

"Why are you looking at me like that?" he asked.

"I was just thinking of how different you are from the night we met."

She closed her eyes as he slid himself inside her again.

How could any man be ready to have sex again so soon?

"I'm not different, Maggie. I'm still the same."

But not around her he wasn't. He was much more open and trusting. He spoke to her, while he didn't normally speak to others. It made her extremely tender toward him.

Hissing, she lowered herself onto his shaft, taking him all the way into her body, before she pushed him away. She swam away from him.

"Maggie?" he called. "Did I do something wrong?"

She treaded water. "No. But if you want me, you have to catch me."

He smiled before he dove under the water and headed for her. Marguerite squeaked before she raced him toward the cement steps that led out of the pool.

Wren caught up to her just as she reached the steps. To his shock, she actually flipped him over in the water and pinned him against the steps. Of course he wasn't really pinned, he could easily overpower her. But he was curious as to what she had planned for him.

She kissed his lips before she cupped him in her hand. Pleasure blinded him as she gently stroked his cock from tip to hilt.

She moved herself so that she was between his legs. Wren sank down to the steps, then moved up them so that she could get on top of him if she wanted to.

Instead, she cupped his butt in her hands and lifted his hips until he was out of the water. He started to ask her what she was doing, but before he could speak she took him into her mouth. Stunned by the unexpected pleasure, he let his hand slip and ended up with his head under the water.

Wren came out of the water, sputtering to see Maggie's brown eyes teasing him. "I didn't mean to drown you."

He couldn't speak as he continued to cough.

She nudged him closer to the edge so that he could lean his head on the dry concrete while she returned to teasing him with her mouth.

Wren's head reeled in ecstasy as he watched her pleasure him. He cupped her face in his hand as her tongue swirled around his cock. The sight of her there . . . it was more than he could stand. He'd never known anything more blissful or sweet.

He came in a fierce, blinding wave of pleasure. But still she didn't pull away. She continued to tease him until she had wrung the last bit of pleasure from his body.

Wren was completely stunned by her actions, by the strange tenderness inside him.

He looked at his hand, expecting the mating mark. Surely no woman could make him feel like this without being his mate. But still there was no burning on his flesh, no magic sign that they were destined mates.

Grinding his teeth in frustration, he wanted to curse in disappointment. He pulled her body flush to his and held her in his arms.

"Thank you, Maggie," he said before kissing her cheek.

Marguerite sighed in complete bliss as she held him close. If she could, she would stay lost in this perfect moment for the rest of her life.

She never wanted to leave the pool.

"Wren?" she asked, lifting her head up from his chest to stare at him. "I don't want to be a downer or anything, but I need to know that you're not going to walk out on me again. I've never felt like this before and I don't want you to think that I just jump all over any guy who comes into my house."

He teased her cheek with his fingers as he offered her a timid smile. "I would like to keep seeing you, Maggie. Let's just take it one day at a time and see what happens. Okay?"

She nodded, then leaned her head back on his chest.

Wren closed his eyes and held her while his thoughts churned inside him. Katagaria and humans didn't mix. Not to mention there were a lot of Katagaria and humans who wanted him dead. He didn't even know if he had a future at all.

All he knew was that if he did have one, he wanted her in it.

But that wasn't up to him, either. He better than anyone else knew the cruelty of the Fates. One moment they blessed you and the next they cursed you.

And he'd been cursed enough to know better than to expect something better. No, something was going to happen. He could feel it deep inside. His time with Maggie was limited. He only hoped that when the trouble he sensed came, it fell solely to his shoulders. The last thing he wanted was for Maggie to be hurt because of him.

But one thing was sure. He would gladly lay down his life to protect the woman in his arms, and he would kill anyone who ever threatened her.

Chapter 8

Neratiti
A mysterious island off the shores of Australia
At least for the moment . . .

Dante Pontis paused to get his bearings as he material-
ized into the large circular chamber that was decorated
in burgundy and gold. Through the open windows that
spanned from the black marble floor to the gilded ceiling, he could see and hear the ocean on all sides of the
room.

Savitar, their dubious and mysterious mediator,
liked the water . . .

A lot.

The room was reminiscent of an ancient sultan's
tent. It was lushly decorated, with an enormous round
table in the center that had always made Dante wonder
what the rest of the palace looked like. But no Were-
Hunter had ever received an invitation to venture into
the rest of the palace.

Their mediator seriously guarded his privacy. To the
point of extreme paranoia.

The human saying that "curiosity killed the cat" actually came from the Arcadian panther who had once

tried to sneak past the council's door to take a look around the palace.

Savitar had fried him on the spot.

As a point of interest, satisfaction didn't bring the cat back. There wasn't enough magic in the world to reanimate the big black, smoldering spot that had once been a living creature. That one incident had gotten Savitar's point across with panache. Don't screw with the big man.

He didn't really have a sense of humor.

For all his laid-back persona, Savitar could break medieval on your ass at a moment's notice. And since Dante had once lived in the Middle Ages, he understood that concept better than most.

Dante let out an aggravated breath as he heard the seagulls cawing outside. The summons to appear at the Omegrion couldn't have come at a better time . . . insert all intended sarcasm.

His brother Romeo had been down with a bad case of the flu for the last three days while the panther's cubs ran amok through Dante's house without their daddy there to corral them.

Dante's wife, Pandora, was about to drop an entire litter of panthers any second, and his other two brothers, Mike and Leo, had decided they could run his bar without him.

Yeah, he needed to get back home before they burned the place down or, worse, Pandora went into labor without him. In which case his pantherswan had promised to see him thoroughly gelded. He cupped himself at the mere thought. Knowing his spunky little pantherswan, it would be most painful indeed. And given the discomfort of her pregnancy with his cubs, she would thoroughly enjoy it.

He scanned the small crowd that was already gathered there for the meeting. Eight members, all of whom appeared as thrilled to be there as he was. The only ones here so far were all Katagaria. Not that that surprised him. The Arcadians tended to appear at the Omegrion together, as if they were afraid to face their animal cousins alone.

And well they should be. There wasn't a Katagaria family who didn't owe a blood debt to the Arcadians who loved to hunt and kill the animals.

It'd always amazed him that the Arcadian and Katagaria leaders or Regises of each clan could come and sit together without fighting. Not to say that there hadn't been outbursts in the past. But those transgressions were dealt with swiftly and painfully by the Omegrion's mediator.

Savitar didn't play. If anyone breached his rules, he quickly toasted them.

Literally.

And with great relish.

Some of Dante's ire faded as he saw Fury and Vane Kattalakis in one corner, talking to each other. Dante had met the wolves years ago, but what he found odd was that they were here together. The Omegrion was a meeting where only the Regis, or head, of each animal-were branch was sent to represent all of their species.

Only one Katagaria wolf should be present.

A fierce creature like Dante, Vane had long, dark brown hair that he wore loose around his shoulders.

Fury had his blond hair pulled back into a ponytail. Like Dante, Fury was dressed all in black, while Vane wore a pair of jeans with a white T-shirt and brown leather jacket.

"Wolves," Dante said in greeting as he neared them.

Vane shook his hand first, then Fury. Dante grinned as he noted Vane had a mating mark on his palm.

"Looks like we've both been tagged since last we met," Vane said.

"Yeah," Dante said with a laugh. "Hell hath frozen over, eh?"

Fury laughed. "You've no idea."

Dante eyed the two brothers. "So how is it that the Katagaria Lykos have two reps?"

Vane gave him a sinister smile. "They don't."

Dante frowned.

Fury's blue eyes danced with humor. "I'm the Katagaria Regis. Vane's the Arcadian Regis."

That news stunned Dante. It wasn't possible. Vane was Katagaria. "No way in hell."

Vane nodded. "As you said, hell hath frozen."

Dante shook his head. "Yeah, but how is that possible?"

"Birth defect," Vane explained. "I switched from being Katagaria to Arcadian at puberty, but I never told anyone until recently."

Dante went cold as one-half of Vane's face showed the stylized markings of an Arcadian Sentinel. They were the human soldiers sent out to murder their Katagaria cousins. As such, Dante despised them with every piece of his being.

"Easy, Dante," Fury said. "Vane grew up as one of

us. As Katagaria. He's not like the other Sentinels, who kill without reason."

"You better not be," Dante said as his humor fled. "I might run a limani, but I have no love for a Sentinel."

"That makes two of us," Vane said as the markings faded. "Believe me, I've lost a lot in my life to insane Sentinels and I have not taken up their crusade. Peace?" He extended his hand to Dante.

Dante hesitated before he shook it. All things considered, he did respect the wolf. "Human, huh? I'm really sorry for you."

Vane gave him a wry grin. "Yeah, me, too."

His humor restored, Dante smiled at the wolf. "Man, I have to respect you, though. Two votes in the Omegrion. That's impressive. Maybe I'll luck out and one of my cubs might switch to Arcadian at puberty, too, and give me another vote."

Fury arched a brow at that. "Your mate's Arcadian? Does she know how you feel about her people?"

Dante sobered. "She knows. But the only thing that matters is how I feel about her, and *that* she never doubts for a minute."

Fury and Vane nodded in agreement.

Dante looked around as a couple more Katagaria flashed into the room. "Do either of you have any idea why we're here?"

Vane sighed. "I heard it's about a Katagari with *trelosa.*"

Dante sucked his breath in between his teeth. *Trelosa* was a disease that was somewhat similar to rabies. It was a madness that infected their kind during puberty. No one was sure what caused it. But once in the blood, it consumed the host, making them an indiscriminate killer. There was no known cure. Once a Katagari or Arcadian was determined to have it, then they were hunted down and killed.

"Who's bringing the charge?" Dante asked.

Vane indicated a tall blond man in the corner. "One of the tigers."

Dante studied the man, who was dressed in an expensive tan silk Versace suit. The tiger dripped money and sophistication from every pore.

Dante's gaze narrowed on him. "That's not Lysander." Lysander Stephanos was a dark-haired tiger who was about as surly as anyone Dante had ever met and wouldn't be caught dead in tan anything, unless it was tanned black leather. "Was he replaced as the Tigarian Regis?"

"Oh, hell no," Fury said in a disbelieving tone. "I'd like to meet the tiger with the balls and skill to take down Lysander. That boy eats bear for breakfast."

"Better bear than panther," Dante said with a sinister laugh.

Vane rolled his eyes. "That one is named Zack. He's waiting for Lysander to show, but apparently Sander isn't as convinced of the charge as Zack is."

"Why do you say that?"

"If Sander thought his claim had merit, I doubt Zack would be here."

That made sense to Dante. As was typical among the tiger species, Lysander was very solitary and didn't like anyone or anything treading on his space. "Then who's backing him?"

"I'm not sure," Vane said, "but it should be interesting."

Dante hoped so. There was nothing worse than a boring meeting.

A bright light flashed, making Dante flinch as Lysander appeared on the far side of the room. Dressed in loose black Indian silk pants and a long sleeveless black vest that was heavily embroidered in gold, the tiger was bare from the waist up. His entire right shoulder and bicep were covered with a colorful tattoo of a heart pierced by a sword. His black wavy hair fell haphazardly around his face.

The blond tiger sneered as he saw Lysander's unorthodox appearance. "Fresh from the jungle?"

Lysander narrowed his gaze threateningly on the shorter tiger. "Don't fuck with me, *hijda*. I only like human form, for one thing, and since I'm not attracted to men, I'm not happy about being here."

Dante exchanged an amused look with Vane, who had been right about Lysander not backing the other tiger. He particularly liked the Hindi insult to the tiger's manhood that had gone over his head.

Lysander pushed past the tiger to take a seat at the large round table, but it was obvious he was as anxious to leave as the rest of them.

No sooner had Dante turned away than something flashed just to his right. Dante watched as Damos Kattalakis appeared a few feet away from them. Damos was an Arcadian Drakos. The dragon was dressed in medieval armor, which made sense, since most of the dragons lived in the past where open fields and unchartered regions made it easy for them to hide from the humans.

Like Fury and Vane, Damos was a direct descendant of the royal brothers whose father had magically created their races.

Damos inclined his head to them. "Wolves. Panther."

"Dragon," Dante said, but he didn't offer his hand to Damos. With the exception of his wife and Vane a few seconds ago, Dante never touched an Arcadian by choice.

Damos seemed amused as he held his hand out to Vane. "Good to see you again, Cousin."

"You as well," Vane said, shaking his hand.

While Damos shook Fury's hand, the other nine Arcadians flashed into the room and took their seats at the large round table without acknowledging any of the Katagaria.

Dante tsked at their actions. "Look at the scared little children. I'm surprised they had the balls to show before Savitar was here to protect them."

"Who says I'm not here?"

Dante jerked his head at the deep, lightly accented voice behind him. Standing at six feet eight, Savitar was an imposing sight. Not that Dante was afraid of him, but he did have a hefty amount of respect for the ancient being.

There was a mutual gleam of respect in Savitar's black eyes. His long dark brown hair brushed his shoulders, and his skin tone was as dark as Dante's Italian complexion. Savitar wore a small, well-trimmed goatee. No one was sure of Savitar's heritage, but he could easily pass for either Spanish, Italian, or even Arabian.

As always, he was dressed in a long, dark blue flowing

robe that reminded Dante of an ancient Egyptian design. But what stood out was the pair of dark brown Birkenstocks on his feet.

"Let me guess," Dante said with a laugh. "The big one is due in on the north shore?"

"Yes." Savitar's tone was deadly earnest. "So let's make this quick. I have a board, a wave, and a babe with my name on them and I would like to take advantage of all three."

Savitar left their side.

"Animals. People," he said as he strode through the room with a gait that announced him as the very top of this food chain. "Cop a squat."

Dante grimaced at Savitar's choice of words. He really hated that expression.

Constantine, an Arcadian jackal, sneered at Savitar, which was a very bad move. "We don't listen to—"

His words were cut off instantly as Savitar waved his hand in the jackal's direction. The jackal began gasping for breath as if an invisible hand was choking him.

"You're a new little punk," Savitar said in a sinister tone as he neared the Were-Jackal. Savitar narrowed his eyes on him. "You'll learn."

The jackal sat immediately . . . as did the others. The poor animal continued to wheeze as he rubbed his bruised throat.

Dante was a little more leisurely, but even he knew better than to test Savitar's extremely limited patience. Savitar's powers made a mockery of every creature here.

Savitar took his throne, which wasn't at the table. It was off to the side, much like the seat of a lifeguard . . . or referee. Rather fitting, since that was why Savitar was here. To guard all their lives as well as those of the people and animals they represented.

Leaning back on his cushioned throne, Savitar passed a bored look to each of them. "Okay, folks and animals, we have exactly forty-two minutes and thirteen seconds until the next great wave comes my way, and I expect this to be finished in time for me to be on my board, waiting for it."

Savitar let out a long-suffering sigh. "But since we have several new faces among us, let me dispense with the ridiculously boring pedagogy. . . . Hear ye, hear ye, welcome to the Omegrion Chamber. Here we gather, one representative from each branch of the Arcadian and Katagaria patrias. We come in peace to make peace." Savitar snorted as if the very thought of that made him want to laugh. "I am your mediator, Savitar. I am the summation of all that was and what will one day be again. I make order from chaos and chaos from order—"

One of the women sneered, interrupting him. "Who is this guy and why do we have to listen to him? Since when do any of us take orders from a human?"

Dante looked across the table to where a petite brunette sat in the Arcadian Litarian seat. The poor lioness had no idea what she was saying.

He half-expected Savitar to zap her into dust.

Instead, Paris Sebastienne, the Katagaria Litarian rep, leaned over and spoke to her. "Hon, he ain't human. You see Leo over there?" He pointed to the old, gray-haired Arcadian bear who was three seats down from Dante. "He's sat here on the council for what, Leo? Nine hundred years?"

"Nine hundred and eighty-two, to be precise."

"Yeah," Paris continued. "And Savitar predates him. He has presided over this council since the very beginning, and notice, Savitar looks about thirty. We don't know what he is, but he ain't one of us and he ain't human. And trust me, you don't want to mess with him."

"Thank you for that highly unamusing summation," Savitar said drily. "Next time I have insomnia, I know who to call. In the meantime, little lioness who would probably like to live another year, don't interrupt me again. I don't like it and I tend to kill the things I don't like."

Savitar indicated the seat to her left that was empty. "That's where the Arcadian jaguar Regis used to sit. Notice no one's there now."

The woman frowned as she saw it. "What happened to him?"

"He pissed me off."

She looked confused by that. "Why hasn't one of the other jaguars taken his place?"

"He pissed me off . . . big-time."

Paris leaned over to whisper loudly, "There aren't any Arcadian jaguars left. Savitar destroyed their entire bloodline."

Her eyes widened as she made a large O with her mouth. She cleared her throat and made a placating gesture. "Please, Savitar, continue."

"Yeah-h-h," Savitar said, stretching the word out and inflecting it to show his agitation. He checked his watch. "We're running out of time, kids."

He pinned his stare on Nicolette Peltier. "So why was I called?"

Nicolette stood up slowly to address them all. "Forgive me for wasting your time, my lord. But I have distressing news. It appears we have a Slayer in our midst, and I need help dealing with him, since he is housed in one of our protected sanctuaries. As our laws dictate, I cannot kill him without sanction."

"We'll be happy to care for your problem," Anelise Romano volunteered. An Arcadian Niphetos Pardalia, or snow leopard, the woman had a glint in her eye that reminded everyone there that women were far more bloodthirsty than the men.

Savitar shook his head. "And who is your Slayer, Lo?"

"Wren Tigarian."

Savitar arched a brow at that. "Where is Wren? As the last Katagaria Niphetos Pardalia, he has a seat here in the Omegrion. Why hasn't he taken it?"

"He can't if he's a Slayer."

Savitar turned to look at the blond tiger who'd spoken out of turn. The tiger moved forward.

By Savitar's face Dante could tell the man wasn't amused. "And who are you?"

"I am Zack Tigarian, cousin to Wren."

Anelise frowned as she sniffed the air. "But you're not a snow leopard. You're a tiger."

"I'm related to him on his father's side. His father was a tiger."

Savitar stroked his chin as he narrowed his black gaze on the tiger. "And what do you know of this matter?"

"I know that Wren murdered both of his parents in cold blood. *Both.*"

Savitar gave him an arch stare. "If you knew this, why did you wait to bring it before the Omegrion?"

"Because I was afraid to come forward. I was young

then and afraid of my cousin. Not to mention that the human Bill Laurens snatched him away and hid him in Nicolette's Sanctuary before I could tell anyone. Once Wren was ensconced there, I was powerless to pursue him for justice."

Savitar looked less than convinced. "And now you're all better?"

"I no longer fear him. No. The time has come for him to pay for his crimes. Not to mention that he is showing signs of the *trelosa* which runs rampant through his species. He must be stopped before he kills anyone else."

Dante shook his head as anger went through him.

"What is it?" Fury asked in a whisper.

"He's lying."

"I don't smell a lie from him."

"Yeah, but when this much money is involved . . ." He shook his head glumly. "I don't trust Mr. Versace."

Savitar let out a long, tired breath. "Well, it appears that this is a Katagaria problem. Arcadians, go home."

As they started to object, Savitar zapped them out of the room, back to their respective time periods.

All but one anyway.

Vane Kattalakis.

Nicolette came to her feet as Vane moved to sit beside his brother Fury. "Why is he still here? He is an Arcadian."

Savitar arched a brow at her. "Truly you are one hell of an observant bear, Lo. But Vane technically straddles the fence. He is by all rights the head of the Katagaria Lykos."

Fury passed an evil grin toward the bear. "I'm just a

figurehead and I have no desire to challenge Vane and get my ass kicked by my own brother."

Her gaze narrowed angrily at the two wolves. "He's partial to the tiger."

Vane shrugged. "I'm partial to the truth, Lo. Good, bad, or indifferent."

Zack moved forward to stand behind Nicolette's chair. "The truth is the *trelosa* is borne through Wren's mother's family. Almost every member of her family succumbed to it. It is why Wren is the last of their kind. Even she was going mad there at the end of her life. Some say that Wren killed her only after she attacked him first."

Dante watched Savitar's face as he considered the tiger's words.

"Maybe," Savitar said after a brief pause, "but Wren isn't pubescent now. He's long into his maturity."

Zack contradicted him. "He is only forty-five. Puberty for his kind can last until the age of sixty."

"Not necessarily," Savitar said. "It depends on the genes."

"He came into puberty late," Nicolette said. "I know this for a fact. And he's only become sexually active in the last few days. Since then he has become more and more violent. Unstable. He was even arrested for it and for attacking human police officers."

She shook her head. "This very afternoon, he had his picture taken and was on the local news because the humans saw him running in the zoo as a human in a cage with other white tigers. Tell me that wasn't madness."

She looked at each of the remaining Katagaria members to implore them to her side. "His actions pose a threat to all of us. If the humans were to ever learn . . ."

"Bullshit," Dante said out loud. "This reeks of greed to me."

"That's ridiculous," Paris said. "We are the animals, not humans. Since when do any of us care about money?"

Dante held his hands up. "Hello? Ever been to my club, The Inferno? I give a major damn about the bottom line. In fact, I'm the second-richest Katagari in the world. And who am I second to? Wren Tigarian. This whole thing smells of a setup." He glared at the tiger, whose stare was completely blank.

Lysander stroked his jaw. "I don't know. If he's exposed us . . ."

"Wren is not a danger," Vane said. "I know this kid. He is quiet and withdrawn. He would never do anything to draw attention to himself."

Nicolette scoffed at Vane. "And what do you really know of Wren? Has he ever once spoken to you?"

Vane growled low in his throat, but in the end he admitted the truth. "Well . . . not much."

"Has he even acknowledged you in any way?"

A tic started in Vane's jaw. "No. Not really. As I said, he's withdrawn from the world."

"That's right," she said, curling her lip. She looked at Savitar. "He is completely antisocial. He refuses always to listen to anyone or anything. He has threatened the lives of my sons and me. Now he is dating the daughter of a senator. Tell me what Katagari in his right mind would do such?"

Even Dante had to admit that was living dangerously.

"Are we to wait until he kills an innocent?" Nicolette asked. "Wait until he shows himself as a changeling to the senator? I have already lost enough children. I will not lose another. I want him out of my house. If I try to force him out, he will kill me or one of my cubs. I know it. He has never been right mentally."

"He killed both of his parents when he was only twenty," Zack added. "They were both highly trained and powerful predators. Imagine what he can do now that he has trained, too."

Savitar passed a disgusted look to Dante. "I'm just an observer in this. At the end of the day, the final vote falls to you guys." He looked back at Nicolette and Zack. "But remember this, if you're wrong, it will be my wrath you face. Greed is for humans; it's not for the Katagaria." He gave Zack a gimlet stare. "Force a wrongful hunt and it will come back on you."

"Wren is a killer," Zack reiterated. "I say we call out the Strati and put him down."

"I second that," Nicolette said.

Savitar let out a heavy sigh. "We have two motions to hunt and kill Wren Tigarian. All those in favor, say aye."

Wren sighed as he shrugged his shirt off and ran water to wash his face. He was tired, yet all he could think of was going to see Maggie again. The compulsion inside him was like a madness.

"Why do I feel like this?" he said between clenched teeth. It was suicide to pursue anything else with a woman like her and he knew it. It wasn't as if they were mates.

He checked his hand again. Even now, there was no mark. Why did he feel like this? He'd spent all evening with her and still he wanted more.

It didn't make sense.

He washed his face, then turned off the water and ran his damp hands through his hair. As he reached for a towel, he felt a strange fissure in the air around him. . . .

Wren cocked his head in a very tigerlike pose as he listened and sensed the air around him.

Two seconds later, he smelled the scent of a predator.

Wren turned, but before he could even focus his gaze, something sharp pierced his chest. He cursed as he staggered back.

"Get the collar ready."

The voices seemed to come from far away. His vision dimmed. Wren cursed as he realized he'd been tranked, but he refused to succumb to it.

"Fuck this," he snarled, shifting from human to tiger.

He lunged out to find four humans in the hallway.

"Shoot him!" one snapped.

He jumped at the one with the gun. As he made contact, the human turned into a tiger. Wren felt another sting to his back as two of the humans tried to get a holding noose around his neck. If they succeeded, they would have him.

Shifting to the form of a leopard, he knew his only hope was to outrun them. He ran at the closed window and jumped out to the street below. Glass shattered and shards of it embedded his flesh.

His entire body throbbed as he hit the ground hard.

He lay on the asphalt for only an instant to catch his breath before he forced himself to get up and sprint up the back alley, toward the convent down the street. He could hear the others giving chase.

Blood was pouring from his cuts as he raced. He had to get away from them. They would kill him if he slowed down. But at the rate he was going, he couldn't last much longer. Between the trank and his cuts, he was fading fast.

His heart pounding, he knew he'd have to find a new haven or he was dead.

Marguerite was finishing up her dishes when she heard the sound of someone knocking on her back door.

She frowned, half-afraid of going to it. No one should be in her backyard at this late hour, and she'd watched enough episodes of *America's Most Wanted* to know not to even peek outside.

Instead, she reached for her phone to call the police.

"Maggie?"

Her frown deepened as she recognized Wren's voice from outside. Why would he be in her backyard?

Maybe she was imagining it.

"Maggie, please let me in."

Still clutching the phone just in case, she pushed the curtains aside to see him on the patio completely naked. But more than that, he was covered in blood. His breathing ragged, his face was scratched and bruised. It looked like he'd been in some sort of accident.

"Oh my God, Wren," she breathed as she opened the door to let him inside. "What happened?"

He didn't speak as he stumbled into her kitchen.

"Wren?"

He fell to his knees and looked up at her as he continued to pant. "I'm sorry, Maggie. I didn't know where else to go."

Her heart hammering in panic, she knelt beside him. "I'll call—"

"No police," he said with a groan. "No doctors."

"But you're—"

"No!" he snapped, grabbing the phone out of her hands. "They'll kill me."

"Who'll kill you?"

She watched helplessly as his eyes rolled back in his head and he passed out at her feet. An instant later, instead of a man on her floor, there was . . .

Something.

She staggered back, away from the creature. It looked as if it was a strange mixture of snow leopard and white tiger, and it was huge.

Marguerite had never seen anything like it. Part of her wanted to scream and another part of her was held transfixed by what she saw.

"This isn't happening. . . ."

She had to be dreaming.

Yet there was no arguing with what was on her floor. She looked to the bloody footprints that led inside her house. They were human.

They were Wren's.

And they stopped at the tigard. . . .

"I'm having a nervous breakdown. I'm delusional."
That was it. She was having a flashback.

You don't take drugs.

"Well then, mind, please explain this shit to me,
huh?"

But there was no explanation. At least not a logical
one. Wren had come into her house, looking like someone had beaten him up, and now there was a bleeding
animal on her floor.

A *big* bleeding animal on her floor.

"Okay, Marguerite, you live in New Orleans. You
read Anne Rice and Jim Butcher. You've seen *Silver
Bullet.* . . . But he ain't no werewolf."

No, he was something else.

And now she understood what he'd been trying to
tell her without saying it explicitly. Then again, he'd
told her exactly what he was and she'd stupidly
brushed it aside.

Now she understood why he'd been able to jump
into the tiger cage and not get hurt. How he had healed
from that bullet wound so fast.

He wasn't human.

At least not entirely.

"I didn't know where else to go."

His words went through her. Most likely, he'd
known what would happen the minute he passed out—
it was probably why he'd refused to spend the night
with her before. Yet he had trusted her enough in his
hour of need to seek her out.

His life was now in her hands. If she called the police, an ambulance, or even animal rescue, they would
lock him in a cage and never let him out.

Or worse, as he'd pointed out, they would kill him.

Her heart pounding, she moved closer to the large cat on her floor. With a shaking hand, she reached out to touch his soft pelt. It was like stroking a thick, silky cat. She'd never felt anything softer. Impulsively, she buried her face in the fur and let it caress her skin.

"Is it really you, Wren?"

He didn't respond in any way.

And he was still bleeding.

Terrified of him dying there on her floor, she tried to move him, only to learn that he seemed to weigh about as much as her car. With no other idea of what to do, she went to her bathroom to get alcohol, antibiotic cream, and bandages.

"What the hell," she said as she gathered them. "He healed fast enough after the gunshot. All freaky Were-People heal quickly, right?" If she bandaged him up, he should be up and around in no time.

At least that's what she hoped.

But as she returned to his side and started cleaning his wounds, she couldn't help but wonder who or what had hurt him and why. Most important, she couldn't help wondering if whoever had done this would be able to find him.

And her.

Chapter 9

Wren came awake slowly to find a severe, pounding ache in his skull that seemed to be echocd in every single part of his body. His ears were buzzing as he slowly blinked open his eyes and tried to focus them.

The first thing he saw was a dark green sofa.

Where the hell am I?

Suddenly it all came rushing back. The tigers who were chasing him. The people who'd tried to trank him. The mad dash through the back alleys of New Orleans. The car that had slammed into him as he darted across the street to avoid another predator.

The impact had sent him flying into a store on Decatur Street and the ensuing pandemonium of tourists running from a snow leopard, and men with guns, had allowed him to escape his pursuers.

With no other choice, he'd gone to Maggie's. . . .

His tail twitched.

"Oh God."

He looked up at the startled sound of Maggie's voice to see her standing in her kitchen, her eyes wide as she watched him. She was terrified. The pungent smell of it called out to the predator inside him.

A predator that had been tamed by her. . . . For once, the beast within was at peace. There was no desire to attack. No desire to harm.

Instead, it wanted only to feel her warm hand in its fur. . . .

"It's okay, kitty," she said in that odd high-pitched voice that humans reserved for small children and pets. "Don't eat the nice lady, okay? She's not going to hurt you, boy. She's only going to step over here so that you don't pounce. Please don't pounce."

She moved a little closer, eyeing him carefully. Her voice dropped two octaves as she spoke to him again. "Are you really in there, Wren? Do you know it's me?"

Wren took a deep breath to brace himself for what he was about to do and flashed himself back to human form. His pain increased tenfold, but he stamped it down before it dragged him back into unconscious cat form. He focused on her. "I know it's you, Maggie."

Marguerite swallowed in relief as she finally saw the confirmation of what she'd feared and hoped. Wren really was the cat.

Scared and nervous, she crossed the small distance where he lay facedown on the floor with one of her blankets covering his bare backside and legs. There were scratches and bites all over his back as if another kind of cat had attacked him. His blond hair fell into his eyes, obscuring them as he rose up ever so slightly in a way that reminded her of a cat stretching.

She knelt down beside him and placed a comforting hand to his bare back. He rolled over slowly, groaning softly as he moved, so that he was lying on his back, looking up at her.

Cuts and bruises marred his chest as well. There was one particularly nasty black bruise that practically covered the whole of his left rib cage. The mark rose up, high onto his chest, all the way to his heart. It had to be killing him to just breathe, and yet he bore his agony with a stoicism that astounded her.

His head resting on her pillow, he looked up at her with those searingly blue eyes. They alone betrayed the pain he was in. More than that, she saw his own fear of her rejecting him now that she knew the truth of him.

As if she would ever do such a thing.

"Don't be afraid of me, Maggie."

She nodded as she reached to brush his soft hair back from his face. In human form, he had a bad fever. His skin was so hot and clammy that it scared her even more. There were still some cuts and bruises on his face, including one cut on his bottom lip, but they were nowhere near as bad as they'd been the night he'd showed up at her back door.

Days of lying on her floor unconscious had left him with a thick dark blond beard growing on his face. Though to be honest, it looked surprisingly good on him.

"How do you feel?" she asked.

"Like I got hit by a bus that decided to back up a few times and make sure it finished the job." He wrinkled his nose at her. "I think it must have ground its tires on my ribs during the last run. You know, just in case I might actually want to breathe again in my lifetime."

She smiled at his misplaced humor as she rested her hand on his chest. His heartbeat was strong under her hand. Grateful for that small favor, she gave a small, silent prayer of thanks. "What happened?"

Wren hesitated. She could see the debate on his handsome face as he wrestled with what to say.

"Be honest with me, Wren. I already know you're a shape-shifter and I haven't freaked out . . . much. You might as well tell me the whole thing."

He winced as if something hurt before he spoke. "Yeah, I wish I could have stayed awake long enough to see your face when I changed over."

"No, you don't. I assure you, it wasn't pretty."

He cocked his head and took her hand into his so that he could toy with her fingers as they rested on his chest, just over his bare nipple. He rubbed her palm against his hardened nub before he lifted her hand to his chafed lips to place a tender kiss on her fingertips.

"There's never anything about you that isn't pretty, Maggie. You're the most beautiful woman I've ever seen."

Her heart pounded at his words as heat went through her. No one had ever said anything so sweet to her before. "I knew you had a concussion."

He started to shake his head at her, but it ended up as a wince, as the gesture must have hurt him.

"So what happened?" she asked again.

"Nothing major. It's just a group of assholes out to kill me."

She wasn't sure what dismayed her most, his stoic tone or the fact that his confession didn't really come as a surprise. She'd figured as much. "Who are they?"

"Other Were-Animals."

There were more of him? She forced herself not to

react to that. But to be honest, she'd assumed the ones who hurt him had been human. Given his solitary nature, it would have made sense that he was completely alone in the world.

Stupid her to not be more imaginative.

"Why are they trying to kill you?"

"Because I shouldn't be seeing a human. We're not supposed to have anything more than casual relationships with your kind. They're afraid that by being with you, I'm becoming dangerous to them."

As much as she hated hearing him say "your kind," she realized for once that there really was a difference between her and him. She was human and he wasn't.

At least not entirely.

"Are you dangerous?"

"I don't know. You're all I can think about. When I'm away from you, it hurts in a way I wouldn't have thought possible and I don't know why. I shouldn't feel like this for a human woman. I know that. I crave being with you so much that it's like some kind of madness inside me. Maybe they're right. Maybe I should be put down."

"Or maybe they're wrong. I don't think you're dangerous, Wren. At least not physically. But what you do to my body might be considered criminal in some states."

He offered her a smile. "Thanks for taking me in and not calling the cops."

"No problem. Believe me, letting a gorgeous naked man into the house isn't a hardship for most women."

He gave a short laugh at that. "I can't believe how well you're taking all this."

"That's only because you were unconscious for the worst of it. I've had enough time to adjust to the fact that there was a half-dead tigard on my floor that had come into my house in the guise of my boyfriend."

Wren still found it hard to believe how calm she was. He'd expected her to flee and leave him alone at the very best. At the worst, he'd expected her to turn him over to the authorities.

Normally, he would have never trusted anyone with his well-being. But with the trank taking effect, he'd had no choice except to hope that Maggie wouldn't betray him.

And she hadn't. She'd kept him safe, and from the looks of the makeshift pallet he was on, she'd tended to him while he was out.

As Wren started to sit up, she helped him. Her hands felt good on his naked skin, soothing as he leaned back against her couch. He would give anything to keep those precious hands on his body, but unfortunately, she pulled back.

"How long have I been out?"

"Four days."

He froze at her words. That couldn't be right. Could it? "What?"

She nodded. "I told you, I had ample time to get used to you being a big cat. I've been terrified every day that you wouldn't wake back up."

Terror consumed him. If she'd left her house . . .

It was a thousand wonders that the ones after him hadn't already found them both and killed them. "What have you been doing while I was out of it?"

She indicated a small pallet on the floor beside him.

"I stayed close by in case you needed something. All I did was clean the blood off the back porch, then I locked the house down. I didn't know who was after you, but I was afraid that whoever they were, they might find you, so I kept the phone ready to call for help if they did."

Tenderness flooded him over her actions. It was unthinkable that someone would do all that for him. Not once in his life had anyone ever sought to protect him. He'd never had any delusions about Nicolette. Had he ever done anything to endanger her life or those of her family members, she'd have tossed him out in a heartbeat.

But Maggie hadn't. She owed him nothing and yet she had kept him safe even though it endangered her own life. It was inconceivable.

He let out a relieved breath that she'd had the good sense to stay put. "Has anyone else come by?"

"No. I kept the windows and doors shut tight, just in case."

He was amazed they hadn't found him, but then again, unconscious, he hadn't been putting off his scent or a trail. He had to be careful now. His kind would be sending out psychic feelers. If he used his magic, such as he was doing right now to remain human, they could find him.

Closing his eyes, he masked his powers. But he wouldn't be able to do that long before it weakened him even more.

Sooner or later, he'd have to leave a trail that they could very easily trace.

"We have to get out of here ASAP."

She looked confused by that. "Why? I have plenty of groceries."

"I can't let them find me in your house, Maggie. There's no telling what they might do to you."

"I'm a big girl, Wren. And I have a mighty big gun, fully loaded."

He scoffed at her bravado. "If you think back to the night we met when I got shot, you'll remember that guns aren't real effective on us. At least not unless you shoot us in the head at very close range."

She twisted up her face in disgust.

"Yeah," he breathed. "Like I said, we need to go."

Marguerite didn't know what to say. She didn't want him to leave. "How many more are there like you?"

"Enough to make the cast of a Cecil B. DeMille film look like a two-man opera." He reached up and cupped her cheek in his palm. "They'll be coming for me, Maggie, and they won't stop until I'm dead. You've been to Sanctuary and they know it. Sooner or later, they will find you if I leave you behind. They'll use you to get to me."

Her head swam at what he was saying. "I can't leave. I've got school. Responsibilities. . . ."

"You can't go to school if you're dead."

She began to panic as the true horror of her situation dawned on her.

This couldn't be happening.

"I'll go to my father. He can protect us."

Wren vanished from in front of her. Two seconds later, he was behind her. "He can't protect you from my people," he whispered against her ear.

"How did you do that?" she asked, unable to believe the extent of his abilities.

"It's easy. My people can travel through time and they can use magic at will. There's no human on this earth who can keep you safe from them. Trust me."

Anger welled up inside her at what he was saying. She felt powerless, and that was the one thing she hated most of all. She was a grown woman in charge of her own life, and she didn't like the thought of having no way to protect herself. There had to be something they could do.

"If I can't use a gun to protect me and we can't hide, then what are we supposed to do? Am I supposed to give up my entire life because I slept with you?"

Wren pulled back at her words, which struck him like a physical blow. She was right. He was asking too much of her. It wasn't fair. Why should he expect her to sacrifice the rest of her life for him?

It was too much to ask of anyone. Not to mention she'd had a life that had been perfect until he'd entered it. No, she didn't need something like him screwing up her future. He'd never brought happiness or joy to anyone. She'd been one of only a very small handful of people who'd ever really been nice to him. He wouldn't pay her back by hurting her.

There was only one way to settle this. . . .

Marguerite frowned as Wren kissed her lips tenderly.

"I'm sorry I fucked up your life, Maggie," he said in a low tone as he pulled back to stare down at her. His eyes burned her with their sad resignation.

With regret.

He stroked her cheek with his fingers as he stared at her as if trying to commit her features to memory.

Then two seconds later, he vanished from in front of her.

The heat from his hand still lingered on her cheek while the rest of her felt cold from his sudden absence.

"Wren?" she called, looking around the room for him. Surely he would pop right back like he'd done a minute ago . . . wouldn't he?

"Wren? Where are you?"

Someone knocked on her door.

What is he doing now?

Sure it was him, she went and swung open the door to find Dr. Alexander standing on her front porch.

"Hi, Marguerite," he said. "I've been—"

"Not now, please, Dr. Alexander. I've got a serious problem."

"Is there anything I can do to help you?"

Disgusted, scared, and frustrated by what was happening to her, she spoke without thinking. "No. Not unless you know some way to track a vanishing tiger."

She saw the color drain from his face. "Then Wren really is here."

It was then she knew. . . .

That was why Dr. Alexander and the others had shown up to bail Wren out of jail. "You know what he is?"

"Do you?"

His defensive vagueness was starting to piss her off. "Why are you here, Dr. Alexander?" she asked in a cold tone.

"You haven't been in class for four days and you haven't answered your phone."

Her stomach tightened in reservation. "How do you know that? You're not my advisor anymore."

His handsome face was grim. "No, I'm not. But I knew you were most likely the last one to see Wren and I have to find him."

"Why?"

"Because he's dead if we don't."

Marguerite shrieked at the deep voice behind her. She turned to see a tall, blond man dressed in black. "How did you get into my house?"

He didn't answer as he went to where Wren had been sleeping. "He was here," he said to Julian. "His scent is all over the place." The man pierced her with an angry stare. "Where did he go?"

"Who the hell are you?" she demanded.

"Fury," he snarled, "and it's not just a name, it's my temperament. So stop being defensive, human. I don't got time or patience for it. We're here to save your boyfriend before he gets himself killed."

Dr. Alexander cleared his throat in a warning gesture. "You know me, Marguerite. Believe me when I say that we're on Wren's side. Do you know where he is?"

She hesitated as she considered her options. Wren had called for Dr. Alexander and Bill when he'd been locked in jail. But then, he hadn't sought them out while wounded.

Did that mean they couldn't be trusted?

Or did it just mean that he had trusted her more?

Unsure of the answer, she decided that the only way to help him now was to take a chance and pray it was the right decision.

"No. He vanished a second ago."

"What did he say before he left?" Fury asked.

"I don't know. He told me I needed to run with him and I told him I can't just leave. He got this weird look on his face and then he apologized for screwing up my life. Two seconds later, he was gone."

"Shit," Fury snarled as he met Dr. Alexander's gaze. "He's headed you know where."

Dr. Alexander looked disgusted.

"Grab Vane and have him meet me there." Fury had barely finished those words before he, too, vanished.

Dr. Alexander cursed as he pulled his cell phone out of his pocket and pressed a button.

"Vane," he said after a few seconds, "we found where he's been. But we just missed him. Literally. I think he's headed back to Sanctuary to confront them."

Dr. Alexander frowned at her as he paused to listen. "No. I have the woman he's been with. I'll keep her with me for the time being. Can you and Fury handle the others?"

Marguerite chewed her nail as she waited.

"I'm taking her to Jean-Luc's. Let me know what happens." He hung up the phone. "Pack an overnight bag."

"Why?"

His gaze was severe and cutting with its intensity. "They know who you are, Marguerite. It's why I'm here. I checked with your professors, who told me you'd been missing classes. I was terrified that they'd already found you and were holding you to bait Wren. You're both damn lucky that they haven't tracked you down yet, but believe me, it's only a matter of time until they do. It's imperative that we get you to safety. Now."

Still, she wanted some answers. "Who are 'we'?"

"Look, I'll explain all this later. Right now, I need you to get the hell out of here before I have to kill people who I generally consider my friends."

He was right. She was being stupid when she'd already seen what they were capable of.

Nodding, Marguerite turned and ran to her room, where she grabbed a small bag that she quickly filled with a change of clothes, underwear, some makeup, and a nightgown.

By the time she returned, Bill Laurens had joined Dr. Alexander in her living room.

She arched a brow at the lawyer.

"Yeah, I know," Bill said. "I look like a mild-mannered corporate attorney. But I can wrestle a bear or tiger any day. C'mon, we need to get you out of here."

"How long will I be gone?"

Bill exchanged a nervous look with Dr. Alexander. "We don't know."

Agitated at how fast her entire life was changing and how powerless she was to stop it, she grabbed her cell phone and charger from the counter. She led the men out of her house, then locked the door.

"You don't really think Wren went to get himself killed, do you?" she asked Dr. Alexander as he led her to his black Land Rover.

Both men answered at once. "To save you? Yes."

Marguerite had never felt more selfish in her life as she climbed into Dr. Alexander's car. "I can't believe this is happening. . . ." She wasn't even aware she'd spoken aloud until Bill spoke.

"Welcome to our world. It's not a pretty place. But then, it's never boring, either."

She sighed as pain swept through her. "I keep thinking this is all a dream and tomorrow I'm going to wake up in my bed and wonder what the hell I had for dinner."

Bill laughed at that as Dr. Alexander pulled out of her driveway. "You want a real rude awakening, ask your classics professor how old he really is."

By the tone of Bill's voice, she could tell it was going to send her over the edge. "I don't want to know, do I?"

"Not really," Dr. Alexander said. "Let's just say that I have firsthand knowledge of my subject matter."

That made her head swim. No wonder Dr. Alexander was so impressive in his knowledge. It would be a lot easier to teach a subject you'd actually experienced, which meant the man was probably several thousand years old. It was enough to boggle the human mind.

Marguerite watched the traffic pass by as they headed off toward the Warehouse District. The world outside the car looked normal, and yet nothing was the same as it had been five days ago. She wondered how much of what was out there wasn't what it seemed. Heck, for all she knew, the bar they were passing right now could very well be owned by demons or some other freaky Were-Animal. For that matter, gargoyles.

But that wasn't really what concerned her most. Right now her thoughts were on one particular Were-Beast. "Tell me Wren's going to be okay."

Bill turned to look at her over his shoulder. "At this point, you should be more worried about yourself, Marguerite. If the ones after Wren ever learn that you know they exist, they'll come for you."

She scowled at him. "I don't understand that. You know they exist. Why don't they go after you?"

"I have a vested interest in keeping their existence quiet. You don't."

"Don't I?" she asked, her voice heavy with her fear and anger. "The last thing I want is for Wren to be locked in a government lab someplace."

Bill smiled approvingly. "Good answer."

Marguerite sighed as she fought off the tears that were stinging her eyes. "I can't believe they're trying to kill him because of me. Can't he just tell them that he won't see me anymore?"

Bill frowned at her. "What are you talking about?"

"Wren said that they're after him because they don't want him involved with a human. If we don't see each other—"

"I'm afraid it's too late for that," Bill said in a sympathetic voice. "This isn't about you anymore, Marguerite. This is about big business. Wren's family has been aching for a chance to kill him for years now. As long as he had the protection of Sanctuary behind him, they couldn't touch him or his money. Now that he's been thrown out, there's nothing to stop them."

But that didn't make sense. "I'm completely confused. Sanctuary is just a bar, right?"

"No," Bill said, his voice laden with gravity. "It's more like an animal shelter where people like Wren can go and not be hunted by those who want to kill them."

"Can't he find another sanctuary?"

Bill shook his head. "They don't exactly grow on trees for his people. Not that it matters. Right now the Omegrion has him marked for death. Until they lift that sentence, no one can take him in and protect him. If they do, they die, too."

She frowned. "What's the Omegrion?"

"It's the governing council for his people," Dr. Alexander said as he turned right. "Kind of like their version of Congress."

She hoped their Congress was a little more effective and had more cooperation, especially since their decision determined whether Wren lived or died.

"How do we get them to lift the sentence against him?" she asked.

Bill sighed. "You have to prove he's not a danger to his people."

"And how do we do that?"

Bill gave her a hard stare. "*We* don't. Basically Wren is going to be hunted down eventually and killed. All we can do at this point is delay it and keep you alive until they determine that you're not as much a threat as he is."

That was so unfair. How could this be?

A single tear fled down her cheek as Bill's words went through her like daggers.

"Wren doesn't deserve this. Man or animal, he's the gentlest soul I've ever known."

Bill's eyes widened as Dr. Alexander made a sound of disagreement.

"You're the only one I've ever met who said that about him, Marguerite," Dr. Alexander said. "Wren is about as wild and dangerous as they come."

Maybe to them, but he wasn't like that with her.

Marguerite closed her eyes as she imagined Wren the way he'd been the night they met. He'd been so shy and bashful. He'd kept himself to the shadows, only coming out to speak to her.

Then her thoughts turned to the way he'd held her while they made love. The way he'd been when he fought off her muggers. They were right, Wren could be dangerous. But he wasn't out of control. He had never attacked anyone without provocation. That didn't make him a threat. It just made him not a wimp.

"We have to save him," she said to the men. "Tell me how to kill the things after him."

In tiger form, Wren crept through the upstairs of Sanctuary, seeking out Nicolette. He had no doubt who had turned on him, and it was time to end this. It was one thing to come after him, but to put Maggie in harm's way . . . that was another story.

The time had come for them all to realize that solitary didn't mean pushover. This tiger had teeth and he was more than ready to use them.

"Shit!"

He turned to find Fang in human form standing in an open doorway behind him. The wolf wore nothing except for a pair of jeans. Even his feet were bare.

Crouching low, Wren prepared himself to attack.

"Get your ass in here," Fang snapped. "Now!"

Wren started away from him.

"Listen to him, Wren. Please."

He froze at Aimee's voice. In human form as well, the bearswan was standing behind the wolf. One side of her face was red and her lips were swollen, as if she'd been necking with Fang in his room.

Damn, the two of them had even bigger problems than he did.

Before he could move, another door opened. Aimee dashed out of sight as her younger brother Etienne froze in his doorway. Tall and blond like the rest of his brothers, the bear was only a few decades older than Wren but didn't appear any older in human form.

Etienne instantly flashed to his bear form.

"There's no fighting in Sanctuary," Fang said, closing his door to protect Aimee as he moved to stand between them. "You both know the Eirini Laws that govern us."

"He is marked, wolf. Stand down."

Wren turned at the sound of Aubert's voice and flashed himself to human form to confront the famed Papa Bear, who only took orders from Nicolette. "I did nothing wrong. This is bullshit and all of you know it."

"You've gone mad," Aubert said. "You've threatened my cubs and my mate."

Wren narrowed his gaze at the bear. "No, I haven't. But you can tell your bitch that I'm here for her now."

Aubert ran at him.

Fang put himself between them and caught the bear as he lunged. Wren tensed, expecting Aubert to break past the wolf, but to his amazement, Fang held his own.

Roaring, Aubert knocked Fang aside and came at Wren.

Wren flashed to tiger form and launched himself at Aubert, who transformed instantly to a bear. Wren caught the larger animal about the throat as Etienne attacked him from the back. He hissed as Etienne threw him against the wall and laid one leg open with his huge claw.

Dazed, Wren sprang back to his feet only to have his wounded leg buckle as pain lacerated him. His wounds were still too fresh, and these new ones were taking their toll on his stamina. Not that he cared. He'd come into this knowing they would most likely kill him.

But he was planning on getting some satisfaction out of this before he died.

The bears reared before they started toward him.

They'd only taken two steps when a bright light flashed in the hallway.

Wren backed up, ready to fight, only to pause as he saw Vane and Fury in the hallway now.

In human form, Vane took one look at Fang's bleeding shoulder and growled low in his throat. "Aubert? Have you lost your mind?"

Aubert flashed back to human, while Etienne remained a bear. "He is marked for death," Aubert snarled. "We took you in, wolf, when you had nothing. Is this how you repay us?"

Vane's green eyes were blazing. "No, Aubert. I haven't forgotten my debt to you or Nicolette. But I will not stand by and see this happen to an innocent. Wren has no clan to back him. Therefore I offer him mine."

Wren was completely stunned by the offer. It was suicide to stand by him now, and he couldn't believe that Vane would even consider such an action.

Aubert was every bit as incredulous. "You would back him against the Omegrion's decree?"

Vane didn't hesitate with his answer. His face was grim and deadly. "You damn straight."

Wren saw the flash of panic on Fang's human face as he looked past Wren's shoulder.

"No!"

They all turned to see Aimee in the middle of the hallway behind them. Only Wren and Fang knew whose room she'd been inside.

She swallowed as she looked from her father to Fang. "Papa, please. Don't do this. This is wrong and you know it. Wren poses no threat to us."

"Are you insane, Daughter? He's here to kill your mother."

More doors were opening now. More animals were coming out to investigate the disturbance. Dammit, Wren would have to run through them all to reach the one animal he wanted a piece of. . . .

Even after Vane's bold words, Wren didn't really expect anyone to side with him, so when the three wolves formed a barrier between him and the others, he was shocked.

"You'll never make it out of here alive," Aubert said in warning. "None of you."

Wren cocked his head as he saw something strange pass between Fang and Aimee. He knew they were speaking telepathically.

A heartbeat later, Fang grabbed her into his arms, manifested a knife in his hand, then held it threateningly to her throat. "Don't you dare follow us. I'll kill her if you do."

Fang turned to look at the three of them. "Fury, Vane, get Wren out of here."

Wren started to protest, but before he could, Vane grabbed him by the neck and flashed him from the hallway into a room he'd never seen before.

It was dark, with no windows anywhere. The only light came from two dim lamps on two tables at opposite ends of the room. He looked around, wondering where Vane had brought him. The modern furnishings were chic and high-tech, not to mention the walls were made of dark gray steel.

By those walls and the rolling motion of the floor, he could tell they were on a ship somewhere.

Hissing in anger, Wren flashed to human form to confront the wolf. "What the hell are you doing?"

"Saving your life."

He curled his lip at Vane. "I didn't want you to save my life, asshole."

Fury, Fang, and Aimee flashed into the room beside Vane. Aimee threw herself into Fang's arms.

"Have you two lost your friggin' minds?" Vane asked them. "Between you and the tiger, we're so screwed."

"No, you're not." Wren tried to flash himself back to Sanctuary to finish this, only to learn that he couldn't. "What the hell?"

"I've got you locked down," Vane said.

Wren knew better than to go after Vane—the wolf was too powerful to take down—but it was taking every bit of his self-restraint not to at least try to kill him. "Lift it."

"No," Vane said firmly. "I didn't just jeopardize my entire clan to see you commit suicide."

"This isn't your fight."

"Yes, it is. I'm not going to sit by and watch an innocent die because some asshole got greedy."

Wren scoffed at Vane's heroism. "Well, thank you, Mr. Altruist, but the tiger doesn't want your help. So sod off."

Someone started clapping. Wren turned his head to see the Dark-Hunter Jean-Luc entering the room from a door on his left. A pirate in his human life, the immortal vampire slayer still retained much of his old look. With a small gold hoop flashing in his left earlobe, he was dressed all in black in a pair of leather pants, a silk button-down shirt, and biker boots. His long, straight black hair was pulled back into a queue that emphasized the sharp angles of his face. His eyes were so dark that not even the pupils were discernible, and those eyes were dancing with amusement. "Nicely put, tiger."

"Shut up, lapdog, this isn't your fight, either."

Jean-Luc sucked his breath in sharply at the insult. "Boy, you better counsel that tongue before you find yourself without it."

Wren took a step toward him, then froze as Maggie came through the door behind the pirate. The relief on her face held Wren immobile.

She rushed to his side and threw her arms around him. "I'm so glad they got to you before it was too late. You weren't really going to do something stupid, were you?"

"Oh no, hon, we were too late," Fury said snidely. "Tiger-boy done pissed down the wrong honey tree and got all the bees, or in this case, bears, going wild."

Fury glanced to Fang. "Then again, knowing the bears, they'll be gunning for wolf before tiger. Good move, Fang. Making time with their only daughter.

Real swift. You know chocolate is lethal to our kind. I'm thinking if you want to commit suicide, that's the much less painful way to go about it."

"Knock it off, Fury," Vane said, moving over to where Fang and Aimee were standing. "We have to send her back. Now."

"I know," Fang said.

Tears glistened in Aimee's eyes. "I don't want to leave."

The two of them stared pleadingly at Vane, who looked sick to his stomach. "And I thought my relationship with Bride was doomed. Dammit, people and animals, this shit sucks."

Fury snorted. "You're the leader, Vane. Lead."

Vane looked up at the ceiling and sighed. "If I had any brains at all, which obviously I don't, I would never have gotten involved in this. I would hand my brother and Wren over to the bears and just take my wife and go find a nice, quiet place to raise our children."

He swept them all with an irritated glare. "But obviously, I am truly the dumbest man on the planet."

Jean-Luc pulled a long, thin stiletto out of his boot. "Here, *mon ami*. Either for you or for them. One cut and all your problems are solved, eh?"

"Don't tempt me." Vane growled low in his throat as he surveyed the lot of them. "Wren, listen close, 'cause, buddy, your chances are running slim. You kill Nicolette and you're dead. There's no way back from that."

Wren scoffed at him. "There's no way back from an execution order. Period."

Shaking his head in denial, Fury stepped forward. "You weren't there when the vote came down. The council was divided on the order."

Wren frowned. "What are you saying?"

"That you have a shot at redemption," Vane said, "but not if you kill Nicolette for vengeance."

Wren hesitated as he felt a small twinge of hope. Did he dare believe them? It seemed a little too implausible even to a man who was really a tigard.

Vane sighed. "You give the council proof that you're innocent of killing your parents and Savitar will rescind the Omegrion's order."

Wren froze as those ludicrous words went through him. Was the wolf on crack? "What the fuck are you talking about? They're trying to kill me because I'm dating Maggie."

"What are you, stupid?" Fury asked. "Your dating the human is only the catalyst for why Mama Lo tossed your ass out. The death warrant is because you murdered your parents."

"Says who?"

"Your cousin Zack."

Wren clenched his jaw shut to keep from gaping as rage took root deep inside him.

This, this just got ugly. He couldn't believe that bastard had gone to the council with his lies. . . .

"We can help you, Wren," Vane said calmly. "But you have to trust us."

Wren sneered at the wolf. "I'm not putting my faith or life in anyone's hands. All that ever got me was screwed, and my ass is currently sore from it."

Fury curled his lip in repugnance. "Nice imagery

there, tiger. Graphic. Ever think of writing children's books?"

Fang popped his brother lightly in the back of his head.

"Ow!" Fury snapped, rubbing the spot where he'd been hit. He glared at Fang.

"Was I this annoying before my attack?" Fang asked Vane.

Vane didn't hesitate. "Yes, and you still are most of the time. And we have now gotten off-topic."

"There's nothing to discuss," Wren said. "You can't keep me here forever, wolf. Putting me on a boat was a nice trick to keep them off my scent, but it won't take them long to figure out where I am. All you've done is drag the Dark-Hunters into our fight, and knowing Acheron, I'm sure he won't be amused by this."

Wren let out a tired sigh as he shook his head at them. "They'll be coming for me and we all know they won't stop. I would rather face them on my own terms than have them attack me on theirs."

Too tired and hurt to argue anymore, Wren headed for the door.

As he passed by Jean-Luc, the Dark-Hunter grabbed him. Before Wren could react, he felt the sting of a needle in his arm.

Infuriated, he growled and changed, but before he could do anything more, everything went black.

Marguerite went cold at the sight of Wren falling to the floor at the Dark-Hunter's feet. "What did you do?"

"Tranked him."

Fury let out a slow breath. "He's going to be seriously pissed off when he wakes up."

"No doubt," Jean-Luc concurred. "Therefore I suggest we keep him under at least for a day or two, until he can heal and you can plan out what it is he needs to do."

"Yeah, but if he doesn't listen—"

"Come up with your plan," Marguerite said, "and I'll make sure he listens to it."

Fury, who she had quickly learned was the doubting Thomas of the group, laughed at her. "Don't be so cocky, human. Wren isn't the kind of beast you manipulate."

Aimee shook her head at him. "No, Fury, you're wrong. With her, Wren is different."

Fury moved over and took Marguerite's hand into his. He turned it over to see her palm. "They're not mates."

Aimee passed an adoring look at Fang before she looked back at Fury. "You don't have to be mated to care deeply for someone. I think Wren will listen to her."

Marguerite stood back with Aimee as the men picked Wren's tigard form up and carried him down the narrow hallway to a lush bedroom that was adjacent to the one they had given her. She'd learned from Bill that this ship was a converted tanker. On the outside, it looked like a rusted heap, but inside it held every luxury known to mankind, including a satellite room that would give NASA a run for its money.

Dr. Alexander and Bill had determined that a ship was the safest place for them to hide. While they were over water, the Were-Hunters after Wren wouldn't be able to track him by scent, and so long as he kept his use of magic to a minimum, they wouldn't be able to find him that way, either.

She only hoped this worked. "Do you really think there's any way Wren can prove his innocence?" she asked Vane as he covered Wren in tigard form with a blanket.

"I don't know. Hell, I'm not even sure he didn't kill his parents. His cousin made one hell of an argument."

"He didn't kill them," Aimee said firmly. "I was there when they brought him in. He was too traumatized by it. He sat in a corner for three weeks solid with his arms around himself, just rocking back and forth whenever he was in human form. As a tigard, leopard, or tiger, he stayed coiled up."

Vane frowned. "Was he wounded when he was brought to you?"

Marguerite saw the reluctance on Aimee's face. "He was a little scuffed up."

Vane looked skeptical. "A little or a lot?"

"Okay, a lot," Aimee admitted reluctantly. "But had he been in a fight with two full-grown Katagaria, he would have been a lot more injured than what he was."

"Unless he poisoned them," Fury said. "Zack didn't really say how he'd killed them."

"I still don't believe it," Marguerite said. "It's not in him."

"Yeah, and you are delusional," Fury said. "Babe, news flash, With the exception of you and the pirate, we're all animals here. And we all have a killer's instinct."

Aimee sighed as she looked wistfully at Wren's unconscious form. "He did have a really hard time in puberty. He couldn't maintain his forms and he did have extremely violent outbursts over minor things."

"Such as?" Vane asked.

"Well, the first night he was working in the kitchen, Dev startled him, and Wren cut Dev's throat with the knife he had in his hands. Luckily, Dev pulled back fast enough that it was only a small wound, but had his reflexes been slower or if Dev had been human, it could have been fatal."

"That doesn't mean he killed his parents," Fang said as he moved to stand beside Aimee.

Jean-Luc made a noise of disagreement. "It's rather damning. Normal people don't do that."

Fang looked doubtful. "No, but someone who's been severely attacked and who was powerless to stop it would do it."

Fury didn't seem to buy Fang's argument, but Marguerite did.

"I don't know, Brother," Fury said. "I think you're projecting what happened to you onto Wren."

Marguerite looked at Aimee. "When was the last time Wren ever attacked anyone without them attacking him first?"

Aimee didn't hesitate with her answer. "Just that one time with Dev, but Wren was scared and shaking when it happened."

Marguerite nodded. "That's what I thought. Wren is innocent in this. He told me that his parents killed each other, and I believe him. Now we just need to put our heads together and think of some way to prove it."

Chapter 10

Marguerite lay on the bed beside Wren, who was still sleeping in cat form. She'd learned from Vane that the Were-Hunters as animals had full human cognition.

"If Wren won't hurt you in human form, then he won't hurt you as an animal."

That knowledge had eased her mind a great deal. It was so strange, though, to be touching a huge, wild cat and have no fear of it.

How could this animal be the man she knew?

Marguerite touched his velvety soft ears. His fur was incredibly white, and when he was in his "true" form, there were no stripes or spots on it. He looked like a big, fluffy cat. As a tiger, he had the typical black tiger markings that bisected the white fur.

She moved her hand to sink it deep in the pelt of his neck. It was like clutching the softest silk imaginable. She could feel the strength of him. It was scary and oddly comforting.

Without a second thought, she sank her face there

and held him close. Poor Wren had been through so much. If she could, she would ease the pain.

But how?

All she could do was offer him comfort and hope that their plan would work. The last thing she wanted was to see him hurt anymore. Vane had told her much about Wren's childhood, about how alone he had always been. It was something she understood very well. All her life she, too, had been an outsider. Never good enough. Never what others wanted her to be.

It was a lonely place to live.

Her heart aching, she nuzzled the soft fur as she gently petted his uninjured side.

Wren came awake to the most incredible feeling of his life. Someone was stroking him. . . .

No one had ever laid a gentle hand on him in animal form before. The hand on his side was warm, soothing. It stroked and smoothed his fur in a sensuous rhythm that wasn't sexual in any way. It was comforting. And that meant more to him than anything else ever had.

Other Were-Hunters knew better than to touch him when he was like this. Humans feared him as an animal.

And his parents . . . they had never been affectionate.

At least not to him.

He knew instinctively that it was Maggie who was petting him now. Her scent was heavy in his fur and he loved it.

He also remembered what he'd been about to do when the damned Dark-Hunter had drugged him.

But at the moment, suicide was the furthest thing from his mind. He just wanted to stay here and feel the delicate strength of Maggie's hand on his body. There was nothing else like the peace he felt inside. The happiness.

How he wished there was nothing else in the world except the two of them. . . .

Marguerite gasped as Wren rolled over, changing as he moved from the tigard into a man. Those pale blue eyes seared her with heat.

She touched the healing cut on his bottom lip. "Are you okay? How do you feel?"

"Dizzy. Hazy. Nauseated."

She wrinkled her nose at his honesty. "Do you need to go to the bathroom?"

He shook his head. "I just need a few minutes to let the last of the drug burn through my system. I hate friggin' tranks."

"I can imagine." She brushed the hair back from his beautiful face. "You still planning on being stupid?"

"I don't have any choice."

"Vane says that you do. If you can prove—"

"How?" he asked. His voice sounded so very tired. So reserved and resigned to his bum fate. "There was never any evidence to show who killed my father or my mother."

She refused to believe that. There had to be something left behind to help Wren. Something that could prove his innocence. "Tell me what happened."

Wren grew quiet as he remembered the last few hours of his father's life. He'd never spoken about it to anyone before. But the nightmares still haunted him at times.

"I'd just been learning to shift forms and I couldn't hold on to anything for long. One minute I'd be human and helpless, and then in the next I was a leopard or tiger or tigard. My mother was completely disgusted by me and my appearance. It was why they never had any more children. I overheard from others that they'd gotten along well together until my birth. After that, my mother refused to let my father touch her for fear of having another thing like me."

Marguerite's heart ached for him. She couldn't imagine having her parents flat out reject her. Her father could be judgmental, preoccupied or missing at times, but he'd never been deliberately cruel.

Wren toyed with a lock of her hair as he continued talking. "My father seldom looked at me as a cub. They kept me locked away in a small cage in their house until I started going through puberty. My father knew I needed someone to train me on how to use my powers, so he hired a cousin to come in and teach me . . . Zack."

The one Vane said had accused Wren of the murders. But Marguerite didn't bring that up at the moment. First she wanted to understand the chain of events. "So your cousin showed you how to use your powers?"

"No. He was too disgusted that I couldn't hold a solid form, so he quit a week after my father had hired him." Wren drew a ragged breath. "So my father decided he'd have to do it himself. It was the only time in my life that he'd ever spent any time with me. At first, he was so angry at me, so cold, that I kept trying to leave any way I could. I'd run out of the room, or use my burgeoning powers to flash myself into other parts of the house or outside. Angry and disgusted, he'd drag me back and try to teach me again."

"Drag you back how?"

Pain haunted his eyes. "It's not important."

She knew better. The tightness of his body told her differently. His father's actions had cut Wren straight to his soul.

"Once I began having some degree of control, my father calmed down. He was even starting to like me, I think. It's what hurt most when he died. I'd spent my whole childhood alone, only seeing my keeper who came in once a day to change my food and my box. Every now and again, my father would come in, stare at me with a look of disappointment or hatred, and then leave without saying anything. So when he started paying attention to me, it was the most incredible thing."

He paused and looked away. She could see the memories that ached. She only wished she knew some way to soothe them.

"He'd moved me from my cage into a bedroom," Wren said quietly. "I was asleep when I heard something crash down the hall. I changed into human form to see what it was and I found him in his bedroom with his throat open. There was so much blood and bruising that you couldn't even see his face."

"What did you do?"

"I sat there crouched in human form, with my hand on his. I couldn't move, couldn't think. I'd never seen a fresh kill before. All I could do was stare at him."

"But you don't know who killed him?"

"I knew," he said in an angry tone. "I heard my mother and her lover. They were off laughing about it in another room."

Marguerite swallowed as panic consumed her at the bitter hatred in his voice. Maybe he'd killed his mother after all.

"I was so angry that I wasn't thinking. I went into the room where the two of them were toasting each other with champagne. I ran at my mother, but her lover caught me and threw me to the ground. He was going to kill me, too, but she stopped him. I found out then that that had been their initial plan. She was supposed to kill me and my father so that my uncle could take control of Tigarian Tech. But she said that she didn't trust my uncle. If I died, she was sure he'd leave them with nothing. Their only hope to keep any of my father's money was to keep me drugged and control it as my guardian."

Anger coiled through Marguerite that anyone could do such a thing, never mind to their own son. What had been wrong with his mother?

"So what did they do?" she asked.

"I'm not sure. I was trying to use my magic to get away from her lover, the next thing I knew, I woke up in a locked room as the whole house was burning down around me."

She frowned. "How did you get out?"

"The floor burned out from under me. I went crashing downstairs and a firefighter saw me and thought I was a pet. They threw a blanket over me and pulled me out right before the whole house went down. As they took me out, I saw the bodies of my mother and her lover and my father, who were lying on the lawn where they had placed them."

A tic beat rapidly in Wren's jaw. "Before they could hand me over to animal control, I bit the firefighter and escaped. I headed straight for the trees and shrubs that surrounded the house. And I just kept running until I came across another man who told me to jump into his car."

"Wasn't that unbelievably dangerous?"

He snorted. "Probably, but he knew who and what I was and he said that my father had sent him to take care of me. I wasn't really thinking clearly at the time. I was wounded and scared, and had nowhere else to turn. All I knew was that if he had a chance, my uncle would kill me, too, and the man who came to me smelled human. My uncle hated humans, so I figured he was my safest bet."

Marguerite was amazed by Wren's tale. She couldn't imagine just how terrifying that night must have been for him. "Why didn't you ever tell anyone what had happened to your parents?"

He gave her a droll look. "Who would believe me? Animals don't kill for money. That's a human crime."

"You're not an animal."

"Yes, Maggie," he said, his eyes burning her with their intensity. "I am. Never delude yourself on that count. Until I was twenty-five years old, I was nothing but a tigard cub. The ability to become human is a by-product of the magic that some insane king forced onto my people centuries ago. But at the end of the day, I have the heart and instincts of an animal. And I will always act like an animal."

Still she didn't buy it. "And yet your so-called animal uncle killed for a very human reason and he's now setting you up. I think there's more human in you than you admit."

He looked away from her. "I've been living my whole life in Sanctuary. I knew if I ever left it that my father's family would come for me. Now they have." He locked gazes with her. "They'll kill you to get to me. Do you understand that?"

His words sent a wave of fear over her, even so, she refused to cower. She didn't know what would or even could happen, but she wasn't going to run from this. She wouldn't let them intimidate her.

"Yes."

Wren let out a ragged yet determined breath. "I have to face them."

"And that is the animal in you talking. Face them and fight to the death." She brushed his hair back, hoping she could dissuade him from killing himself so needlessly. "Stop for a minute, Wren, and think like a human. What's the best way to get back at someone who's greedy?"

"You kill them."

She rolled her eyes as she dropped her hand to his bare chest. "No, you make them poor. You take away the money that means so much and you lock them in a cage."

He scoffed. "I'd rather kill them."

She narrowed her eyes at him.

To her surprise, he smiled at her. "Okay, let's say for a minute that I'm listening to you. What do you suggest I do?"

"Vane said that we could go back in time to—"

"Us?"

"Us," she said firmly. "It's the one place where they won't be looking for me. If I stay here, you won't have any way of knowing that I'm okay and I won't have any way of knowing that you're all right. If we go back together, we can find something that ties your uncle to the murders."

Wren clenched his teeth and gave her a skeptical grimace. "It's going to be dangerous."

"They're already trying to kill us. What could be more dangerous than that?"

By his face she could tell he conceded that point to her. "I've never tried to carry someone across time before. What if I screw it up?"

"Vane swears you won't."

"Vane ain't got nothing to lose by this. I do."

She took his hand into hers and met his gaze without wavering. "I trust you."

Wren let out a deep breath at that. No one had given him trust before. And he couldn't believe she would give it to him now, when she had so much to lose.

Gods, if he had any brains at all, he'd leave her here for Jean-Luc to guard, and yet Wren knew she was right. He'd have no way of knowing if she was safe or not. He'd be so concerned for her safety that he wouldn't be able to focus and do what he must to prove his innocence.

He dropped his gaze down to her hand on his chest. She was human. Fragile. And yet she had a strength inside her that stunned him. He'd been alone all his life. . . .

Wouldn't it be nice to have someone by his side, just this once?

He let out a tired breath as a profound desire burned through him. Honestly, he didn't want to live without her. Not even for a minute.

"All right, Maggie. We'll try this your way, but if it doesn't work—"

"You can kill them your way."

Wren pulled her face toward his, intent on kissing her. But as soon as their lips touched, her cell phone rang.

Marguerite growled in irritation as she pulled back. Normally she would ignore it, but this was one call she had to take. "It's my dad's ring," she explained. "Hang on a sec."

She answered the phone.

"Where have you been, young lady?"

She cringed at the anger in her father's voice. "Hi, Dad, nice to hear from you, too."

"Don't get smart with me, Marguerite. I just got a call from your school saying that you haven't been to classes in days. They're going to flunk you. What are you thinking? Have you any idea how embarrassing that will be?"

Marguerite hated the fact that tears were wanting to pool in her eyes. Most of all, she hated the fact that his words really hurt her. "Sorry to be such a disappointment, Dad. But I have—"

"I don't care what you have, little girl. You need to get yourself back into your classrooms and your study group. Blaine said that instead of studying, you've been spending all your time with the local riffraff. I paid too much money for you to just blow off your responsibility because some cheap piece of trash looks good in a pair of jeans. I wish I could just decide not to show up for work for a week."

And that set her anger off. For all he knew, she'd

been in a car wreck or was ill. Did he bother to find out why she'd missed school? No.

"Sorry, Dad, but I have something more important to do."

"And that is?"

She gripped the phone tight as she glanced back at Wren, who was watching her with anger in his own eyes. "I'm running away with a tiger. I'll call you when I can."

And with that, she hung up the phone and turned it off.

Wren's jaw went slack. "I can't believe you just told him that."

"Oh, please," she said irritably. "He'll just think you're some LSU student."

She took a deep breath as she considered the repercussions of what she'd just done. "But he will start calling out government agencies to find me. So if you don't take me with you, my 'recovery' by him will be quite public and your friends will know right where to find me."

He tsked at her even though his turquoise eyes were shining in humor. "You're sneaky."

She bit her lip playfully. "Yes and no. You do need someone at your back, and I don't think you trust many people there."

His gaze hardened to lethal blue ice. "I don't trust anyone there . . ." Then those harsh eyes softened. "Except you." He cupped her face in his palm.

Marguerite sighed as he kissed her. God, this was the most hopeless relationship on the planet. A senator's runaway daughter and a tigard wanted for murder.

In spite of herself, she started laughing.

Wren pulled back with a frown.

"I'm sorry," she said, kissing him lightly. "I was just thinking that this would be one heck of a headline for *Weekly World News*: 'Prominent Senator's Daughter Goes Back in Time to Save Tiger Boyfriend.'"

She fingered his cheek as the complete reality of this sank in. "I can't believe the world you live in is real. I keep thinking that this is a dream and I'll wake up any minute."

"I wish for your sake that it was a dream. I wish I were human. But you do know that if I survive this, I can't stay with you."

As much as she hated it, she knew he was being honest. "I know."

Wren froze as he heard something outside their room.

Cocking his head, he listened closely.

"What's wrong?" Marguerite asked.

To her shock, clothes appeared on his body as he moved slowly from the bed. He motioned for her to be silent.

He took a step nearer the door.

Out of nowhere, a man appeared in the center of the room.

Marguerite gasped as Wren spun around to confront the intruder.

As he lunged, the man vanished.

"Damn it!" Wren snarled. "They've found us."

The door opened an instant before Vane rushed into the room. "Did I just sense a breach?"

Wren looked at him drolly. "If you're talking about the asshole tiger that was here right before you, yes."

Vane cursed. "You guys are out of time."

"I can't jump until a full moon," Wren said.

Vane gave him a wicked grin. "Yeah, you can."

One minute they were on the ship, the next they were in an ornate room that had open windows where she could hear traffic rumbling from outside.

Wren's face was ashen as he looked around as if he couldn't believe what it was he was seeing.

"Where are we?" she asked.

His eyes were wide as he looked back at her. "My father's bedroom."

Chapter 11

Wren felt as if he were caught in a vicious nightmare as he looked around a room that he hadn't seen in over twenty years. Hell, he hadn't even really remembered what it looked like. He'd only seen the room a time or two in his youth, and even then only briefly.

He flinched as he remembered the sight of his father lying dead on the floor between the bed and door.

Shaking the image off, Wren glanced around. The room was the height of high-tech, 1980s fashion, done in dark blues and greens, with a king-sized water bed. Abstract art hung on the walls along with the skin of a tiger his father must have killed. It was a common Katagaria trait to mount their first kill as a reminder of their prowess and a warning to any other animal who might want to tangle with them.

By the size of the skin and the wound marks on it, Wren could tell his father must have had one hell of a fight on his hands at the time. But the important thing was that his father had survived while the other beast had perished.

His heart hammering, Wren walked slowly to the open windows to see the bustling traffic that ran behind his father's carefully guarded estate.

"Is this the house that was burned down?" Maggie asked.

Wren nodded slowly, wondering again who had set the fire and when. "We have to get out of here before someone sees us. My father tended to eat trespassers, and I don't want to prove my uncle right by being the one who kills my father when he attacks us by mistake."

She shook her head at him. "We have to find evidence."

"There won't be anything in here," he said simply. "My mother wasn't that stupid."

Suddenly, there were voices outside in the hallway that seemed to be coming nearer to their room. It was definitely a man and a woman . . .

And they were fighting.

Wren grabbed Maggie and pulled her into an extremely large closet that appeared to only have his father's clothes in it. He briefly considered flashing them out of the house with his powers, but since he didn't really remember the layout of the place or the schedule of the staff or his parents, he could end up reappearing right in front of himself as a cub or his father.

Both of those could be disastrous.

For the time being, the best thing would be to stay here and wait until he got a better grasp on the situation.

He heard the bedroom door open and then slam shut.

He went cold as he recognized his mother's angry tone. There was a harsh brittleness to her voice that was unmistakable even after all these years of not being subjected to it.

"Why have you called me back from Asia, Aristotle? I need to run wild for a while."

His father gave a dark laugh. "You've been running wild for too long now, Karina. It was long past time for you to come home."

"Why?" She slammed something down.

"I've learned some interesting things about Wren. As his mother—"

Something shattered. "Don't you dare start that. I gave you your heir that you stupidly accepted. You have no further need of me."

He heard his father's voice deepen. "You need to see what Wren can do."

"So it can change into a human now," she said in a bored, sarcastic tone. "Well, la-di-da. It's long past time for it to start changing. I told you it was retarded."

Marguerite drew her breath in sharply at those harsh words. She saw the pain on Wren's face that he tried to hide and felt rage consume her. Honestly, she wanted to kick open the door and beat his mother for her cruelty.

How could anyone say such a thing about a child she'd birthed?

"Don't you dare walk out of here, Karina," his father growled.

Marguerite heard cold laughter from Wren's mother. "I'm not one of your people you command, Ari. Nor am I your bitch. I don't have to listen to you."

"Fine. But just so you know, I changed my will while you were gone."

Dead silence came from the bedroom for several heartbeats.

"You did what?" Karina finally screeched in a tone that should have shattered glass. As it was, Marguerite was rather certain her eardrums would never be the same again.

"You heard me." Wren's father's voice was cold and emotionless. "I'm sick of you catting around and flaunting it in my face while I pay your bills. I know about your leopard lover and I know he came back here with you. Fine. I set up a separate residence for you in New Jersey."

"New Jersey?" she snarled. "Are you insane?"

"No, I'm pissed. If you think I like the fact that the Fates damned me to mating with you, you're wrong. You are my mate by their decree and yet you won't let me touch you. I am damned to celibacy while you whore around with any leopard male who comes near you. Yet you expect me to keep you up. Dream on, my love. Your days of freeloading are over."

"You owe me," Karina said from between clenched teeth. "I didn't ask to be your mate any more than I asked to give birth to a mutant abomination. If you were really a tiger, you would have killed that thing when it was born instead of stopping me from doing what was necessary to preserve our species."

"Wren is my son."

"You human," Karina sneered in a way that said "human" was the worst insult she could imagine.

"Yes," his father said angrily, "and like a human, I've made Wren my sole heir. If something happens to me, your entire future rests in his hands. So if I were you, I'd be praying that he's more human than animal. Maybe he'll take some mercy on you. But I wouldn't count on it."

"You bastard!"

"Yeah, and before you tear the house apart looking for the will to destroy it, it's already on file with the Laurens firm in New Orleans."

"I hate you!"

His father's response was immediate and filled with the same scathing hatred. "The feeling is entirely mutual. Now if you'll excuse me, I'd like to go spend some time with *my* son. When I come back to this room, I expect you to be gone. Permanently. Taylor will drive you over to your new home, where you'll find your new checkbooks and credit cards waiting there for you. You're off all my accounts entirely and eternally."

A door closed an instant before something shattered. Marguerite could hear Karina screaming and breaking things in the room. It sounded like she was about to tear down the walls. Then Marguerite heard the sound of a feral cat roaring and hissing.

Finally, it stopped.

The sudden silence was unnerving.

Marguerite froze, half-afraid the woman would come into the closet to shred Aristotle's clothes or something.

She didn't.

Instead, Karina made a phone call. "Grayson?" she said in an almost reserved tone. "It's Karina. I believe you now. Aristotle has completely lost his mind. I'm back in town. Is there someplace where we can meet and discuss what needs to be done?"

Marguerite was stunned by how rational Wren's mother sounded while speaking on the phone. It was hard to believe this was the woman tearing the house down only a few heartbeats before.

His poor father for having to tolerate such a volatile beast. Marguerite was just grateful that Wren hadn't inherited his mother's personality.

There was a brief pause. "Yes, I know where that is. Three o'clock. I'll see you then."

Then Marguerite heard Karina hang up the phone and leave the room.

Marguerite turned to Wren, unable to believe what had happened over the last few minutes. "I think your mother and my father should have married each other."

There was no trace of amusement on Wren's face.

"I'm sorry, Wren," Marguerite said, feeling instantly contrite. How could he find humor in the fact that his mother was a vicious cur who was about to murder his father? A cur who had practically ruined his life. "But at least you know your father did love you."

"That's what hurts," Wren said in a low whisper. "I keep thinking that if only he'd lived . . . My life would have been so different."

She hugged him as she felt for his pain. "I know. I spent a long time hating my mother because she left me. At least your dad didn't go by choice."

Wren's eyes flared at that. "No, he didn't." He gave her a harsh stare. "Thank you."

She was completely baffled by his words. "For what?"

"For making me come back here." There was a grim determination that burned brightly in his eyes. "I was happy to let them get away with what they did to me and my parents. You were right. There is more human in me than I thought. 'Cause right now I want revenge, and I'm not leaving here until I get it."

"So what do we do?"

He glanced away as an angry tic beat furiously in his jaw. "First thing, we have to make sure that we don't alter anything here in this time period. We need to try and stay away from anyone who might remember us in the future. Second, we have to make sure I don't run into myself."

She nodded in understanding. "It'll cause a paradox."

"Yes, and it would cause me to drop completely out of existence—really not a good thing for either me now or me then. But luckily, at this time and place, I'm pretty much confined to a bedroom down the hall."

He opened the closet door and peeked outside, into the bedroom. "It's clear."

She followed him back into the bedroom. "Any game plan?"

"Follow my mother. Grayson is my uncle, and since they're meeting, my money says that this is when they planned my father's murder."

That made complete sense to Marguerite. "Okay, but how do we do that?"

Marguerite gasped as her clothing changed into a bright red, ruffled shirt and a beige prairie skirt. It was an outfit very similar to some of the ones she'd seen her mother wearing in old pictures taken around the time she'd been born.

Wren grinned at her confusion as his own clothes changed to a black Izod and dark jeans. "We need to look like we belong in this time period."

"How do you do that?"

His grin widened. "It's magic."

Yeah, but his magic was starting to creep her out. It was one thing to travel through time, quite another to find herself wearing outdated clothing that was actually the height of fashion right now.

A woman could really lose her mind thinking about these things. . . . Then again, maybe she had. Maybe all of this was nothing more than a grand hallucination . . .

It was certainly a possibility.

As Wren took a step toward the door, it swung open.

Time seemed to hang still as they both faced a man who was an exact, only older, copy of Wren. Dressed in an elegant black suit, the man had blond hair cropped short. His blue eyes were electrifying as he narrowed his gaze threateningly on them.

Wren wasn't sure what he should do. He could flash him and Maggie out of the room, into another part of the house, or even outside, but his father would be able to trace them and follow.

Damn, they were caught and they were screwed.

His father sniffed the air, then frowned in obvious disbelief. "Wren?"

Wren swallowed as he met Maggie's wide brown eyes. Repressed emotions tore through him. Grief, rage, but at the bottom was the part of him that had wanted to love his father.

The part of him that had wanted his father to love him.

His father moved closer to Wren with a deep scowl marking his brow. "It is you, isn't it . . . from the future?"

There was no need to lie. His father was far from a

stupid man, and there was no other explanation for the two of them being in his house.

Double damn. This was against every rule Wren knew of time traveling . . . not that he knew many. Since he didn't practice jumping, he wasn't all that familiar with the laws of it.

He took a deep breath before he answered his father's question. "Yes."

"Why are you here now?" His father frowned as he looked back and forth between them. "You're not supposed to be, are you?"

As every second ticked by and nothing odd happened—like he didn't cease to exist—Wren began to wonder about that. "No . . . Yes . . . Maybe? Since I'm not dead now, I'm not sure anymore. If I wasn't supposed to be here, wouldn't I have died when you came through the door?"

His father let out an exasperated sigh. "You still haven't mastered your powers?"

Anger flashed deep inside him. How dare his father judge him lacking? He wasn't a callow cub anymore. He was an adult who was more than able to take care of himself, and he resented his father thinking otherwise. "I could take you down, old man, and not blink or flinch."

His father looked at him with pride in his eyes. A slow smile curved his lips. "But you don't time jump?"

"No," he answered honestly. "I was told a long time ago that it wasn't in my best interest to learn it."

"Why?"

"He was raised in Sanctuary," Maggie said. "There are a lot of people who want Wren dead."

Wren narrowed his eyes on his father in case he misunderstood Maggie's words. "Not that I've ever feared a fight or backed down from one—"

"That's the truth," Maggie inserted. "I swear he's half beta fish. He'd fight his own reflection to prove a point."

Wren ignored her interruption. "But likewise, I'm not stupid and I've never wanted to make it easy on anyone. Especially not my enemies."

There was no mistaking the pride on his father's face. "Good, boy. I'm glad to know they haven't killed you yet."

"And they're not going to."

His father looked at Maggie. "Is she your mate?"

Wren took her hand into his and squeezed it as Maggie watched him expectantly for that answer. "Not exactly . . . but we're working on it."

His father laughed until he sniffed the air again. He cocked his head curiously. "She's human."

Wren wrapped his arms around her as if to protect her. "You have a problem with that?"

"Not at all," his father said firmly. Sincerely. "My mother was human, too."

Wren gaped, letting Maggie know that his father had just imparted a secret to him. "Pardon?"

His father moved to lock the bedroom door as if he was afraid of someone overhearing them. "You heard correctly. It wasn't something that we ever spoke about outside of the immediate family, but yes. My mother was an Arcadian tiger." His face softened. "Hell of a woman she was, full of fire and spirit. I wish to the gods that I had been mated to a human, as opposed to the bitch I fathered you with."

Marguerite felt Wren tense around her, but she wasn't sure why. She rubbed his arm to offer him her support. Poor guy was having one hell of a day.

But then, they had come back here for answers. Even hard ones.

"I want you to know that I don't regret you," his father said, reaching out to touch Wren's shoulder. "I never did." And then his handsome face turned sad and wistful. "I take it by your presence here that I'm not around in your future."

Wren leaned his head against hers. His tenseness increased before he answered. "No."

His father winced as he dropped his hand and sighed. "Do I . . . Did I do right by you in the end?"

Wren didn't answer the question. Instead he asked, "What day is today?"

"August 5, 1981."

Marguerite gasped at the date as a chill went down her spine.

"What?" both of them asked.

"I'll be born at noon tomorrow," she said incredulously. "It's just kind of eerie, isn't it?"

Wren's father snorted. "Not in our world. You get used to such weirdness."

Wren took a deep breath while he continued to hold her close. "Three days from now, I'll be in the back of a car headed for New Orleans."

His father opened his mouth as if to say something, then snapped it shut. Emotions played across his face while the reality of his imminent death hit him.

Marguerite couldn't imagine anything worse than to

know just how limited your future was. All the regrets. All the concerns. His poor father.

He sighed heavily. "I'm going to assume that I'm not the one who sends you there."

"No."

His father sat down on the edge of the bed with a sad, faraway look in his eyes. She could tell he was struggling with the news.

"I only have three more days left alive," he breathed.

"You shouldn't know that," Wren said.

"No." His father looked up at them. "If you're here, then it was meant to be."

A weird feeling went through Marguerite as she considered that. "I think he's right, Wren. Remember what you said about running into the man in the woods who took you to Sanctuary? He knew who and what you were. He knew to be there. How?"

Wren looked as perplexed as she felt.

His father frowned. "Why didn't you go to Grayson for protection? He's your guardian."

Wren shook his head. "Bill Laurens was my guardian until I came into my own."

His father scoffed at that. "Bill is a child."

"No, he's twenty-one right now, and for reasons I never understood, you made him my guardian. Bill's the one who saw to it that I was tutored in my powers and kept safe until I could protect myself."

"Grayson is the one who kills you," Marguerite told Aristotle. "He would have killed Wren, too, had Bill not been his guardian."

Wren's father snarled as he came off the bed. "That sorry sack of shit. I always knew he was a scabbing bastard." Hatred and anger burned deep in his blue eyes as he paced back and forth in the room. "I should have killed him. I should have . . ." His voice trailed off.

Aristotle paused as he looked back at the two of them. "Your mate is right. You were here before. You had to be. Because if you weren't, Grayson would have had full rights to you. I would never have left my only son in the hands of a human child."

Aristotle growled and cursed . . . and returned to pacing even faster. He definitely reminded her of a caged tiger that was ready to tear the arm off anyone who came near it. "Who runs my company after I die?"

"Aloysius Grant."

He screwed his face up in disgust. "He's an incompetent nerd."

"Yes, but he's a visionary," Wren said quietly. "In the next twenty years, he makes this company second only to Microsoft."

Disgust gave way to incredulity as his father stopped pacing again. He gaped at them. "Microsoft? Don't tell me that kid from the West Coast really got that stuff to fly?"

"Oh yeah," Marguerite said with a laugh, "Bill Gates pretty much takes over the world as we know it."

Wren's father growled again. "Damn, see what happens when you get killed before your time? Someone else dominates the market you've spent your entire life grooming. It's just not right."

"It's okay, Dad. Your company makes it on the hardware side anyway. That and the World Wide Web. Not to mention plasma TVs and cell phones."

His father's eyes burned with intensity as he locked gazes with Wren. "Not my company, cub. *Your* company." He wrinkled his brow as if another thought occurred to him. "What's this World Wide Web thing?"

Marguerite laughed again. "In short, money. Lots and lots of money. Especially for Tigerian Tech."

Wren's father smiled. "Good. I like money. Always have. It doesn't ever betray you, and unless someone steals it, it stays where you put it. But mostly, money keeps us safe from the outside world." The humor fled from his face as he let out a long sigh. "I guess my problem was that I wasn't looking within. I should have kept a better eye on my family."

He returned to pacing with his hands behind his back and his gaze on the floor. "So I only have three days to get everything in order." He glanced back at them. "But that doesn't explain why the two of you are here, does it?"

Marguerite stepped away from Wren. "We're both being hunted."

"Why? By whom?"

"Grayson wants to finish what he started," Wren answered. "He wants me dead so that he and his son Zack can take over the company."

"That'll be over my . . ." Aristotle ground his teeth. "I guess it *is* over my dead body."

Marguerite moved to pace beside him. She wasn't sure why, but it seemed a natural thing to do. "They framed Wren for the deaths of you and your wife."

Both of his eyebrows shot upward. "Karina dies as well?"

Wren nodded. "But not until after she kills *you*."

He wrinkled his nose as if that was the most disgusting thing he'd ever heard. "How the hell does that bitch kill me? There's no way she could do it."

"She had help," Marguerite said. "Her lover is here with her."

Aristotle shook his head in denial. "That worthless leopard cub? He can barely tie his own shoelaces. Never mind take me on. That's just stupid."

"I never understood it, either. But as a cub, I will hear something break in this room and I will come in here and find you dead. Mom and her lover will be in the study across the hall, laughing about it."

Still Aristotle shook his head in disbelief. "And who kills her?"

Wren shrugged. "My money says Grayson. But I don't know. When I woke up after her lover attacked me, she and her lover were dead, too. I never saw hide nor hair of who did it."

His father ran his hand over his face before he sighed wearily. His eyes were sincere as he looked at Wren. "I'm so sorry that I wasn't around for you, Son. Here I've been thinking that I would have time to make it up to you that I left you alone so much as a cub. I should never have ignored you."

She could tell exactly how much those words meant to Wren. And she was grateful that she and Wren had come back so that he could hear them.

"It's okay."

"No," his father said sternly, "it's not. I spent all my time building a company that I won't even be around to see prosper. You must hate me."

"I never hated you, Dad. Not really."

He reached out and pulled Wren into a tight hug.

Marguerite watched the look on Wren's face as he tensed, then returned the hug. Tears welled in her eyes as she reached out and patted Wren's back.

"I love you, Wren. I'm sorry if I ever said or did anything that hurt you."

"I love you, too, Dad."

Wren pulled back and cleared his throat, but even so she could see the tears that were glistening in his eyes.

His father turned toward her. "I hope you've been taking good care of my boy."

She smiled at Wren. "I've been trying to. But he can be very difficult. He doesn't listen."

Wren rolled his eyes at her before he spoke to his father. "Karina's going to meet Grayson this afternoon. Would you keep Maggie safe while I track her?"

Marguerite growled at that. "Wren . . ."

"No, Maggie," he said, his voice thick and commanding. "It's better this way. It'll be easier for me to search her out alone."

"Bull!"

Both of them ignored her.

"I'll guard her with my life," Aristotle promised.

"Wren!" she snapped.

He cupped her cheek in his warm, callused palm. "It's okay, Maggie. Really. I have to do this."

Marguerite didn't want to listen to him, but she saw the turmoil inside him. The fear he had for her. That reached down and touched her deeply.

She wouldn't be stupid. Her luck, she'd just get them caught anyway. Spying wasn't something she was good at.

For that matter, she'd been busted anytime she tried to get away with anything.

She let out a long, exasperated breath. "Don't you dare strand me here without you."

"I won't." He kissed her cheek, then vanished from in front of her.

Marguerite seethed at his actions. "I hate it when he does that."

His father laughed. "I'm glad to know he's at least mastered that trick."

"He's mastered many. I think you'd be very proud of him. He's managed to stay alive against incredible odds just since I've known him." Then she held her hand out to his father. "I'm Maggie Goudeau, by the way."

He shook her hand gently. "Pleased to meet you, Maggie. I have to say you are a beautiful companion for my boy."

Aristotle's words warmed her. At least until a weird thought went through her. "You wouldn't happen to have any old photographs of Wren, would you? I would love to know what he looked like as a young boy."

His father smiled devilishly. "I've got something even better than that for you."

She didn't understand what he meant until he led her down the long, elegant hallway to another room at the very end of it.

He opened the door, then stood back so that she could enter the darkened room first. Marguerite entered, then froze as she saw a young Wren on the other side of a two-way mirror.

"Isn't this dangerous?" she whispered.

"No." Aristotle closed the door and moved to stand right behind her. "Wren can't see, hear, or smell either of us. I had this room built a long time ago so that I could watch him without his knowing it."

She scowled. "Why?"

There was much regret and hurt deep in those turquoise eyes that reminded her so much of Wren's. "Because I have always loved my son even when he repulsed me, and I want you to make sure that he knows that. That he really understands it."

She looked at Wren, who appeared to be around the human age of thirteen or fourteen as he lay on the floor of the other room. His blond hair was long and shaggy, his body frighteningly skinny. He looked so vulnerable. So scared and unsure. Things she had never known the man Wren to be.

"How could he have ever repulsed you?" she asked Aristotle.

He indicated the window that showed Wren on his back in human form. He was completely naked and writhing as if he was in pain.

"It is the nature of animals to kill those who are weak. Those who are different. For the last twenty-five years, I let Karina's coldness color my own views of my child. Wren was born neither tiger nor leopard, but a mixture of us." His gaze burned her. "You've no idea how much of a handicap that is in our world."

He moved over to the glass, so close that she was surprised Wren couldn't see him there, staring at him. "All his life, I thought it was a deformity. I didn't know that when he hit puberty, it would be a gift. You see, as a rule, our kind can only be two things. Human and whatever animal we're born to. There's no choice in it. But Wren . . . he's special. He can be the tigard that he was born—"

"Or a tiger. I've seen him as a tiger."

His father nodded. "And he can be a leopard. Snow or normal. Day or night. He's not bound by the same laws that the rest of us must heed. It's an incredible gift he has. I had heard myths of such creatures. But like the fabled unicorn, I thought it was bullshit. Until I saw him."

He looked back at Wren, who was starting to tremble. "At his age now, he shouldn't be able to take human form until after dark. It's very hard for Katagaria to be humans in the daylight. I have an advantage because my mother was human. I'm able to maintain this form longer than most of my kind. For Wren to be able to take human form in the daylight at the age of twenty-five is unbelievable."

Marguerite's heart pounded as she watched Wren struggle with some unseen discomfort. "We should help him. He looks like he's in pain."

His father shook his head. "There's nothing we can do."

"But—"

"Watch and see."

He left her alone in the viewing room, then entered the room with Wren.

As soon as Wren heard the doorknob turn, he shifted into the form of a tigard. He growled low in his throat as he saw his father joining him.

"Easy, Wren," his father said, crouching down. "Come here."

Wren backed up as he eyed Aristotle warily.

He moved toward Wren as he continued to back up into the corner. When his father reached out, Wren swatted him with his claws.

His father pulled back.

She could see the disappointment on his face. The more he tried to reach out to his son, the more Wren rejected him.

After a few minutes, he left.

She watched as Wren shifted back into human form. He tried to stand, but for some reason his legs buckled.

His father rejoined her.

"What's wrong with him?"

"He doesn't know how to walk or talk as a human. He's like a baby now. Everything that you learned as an infant he has to learn as an adult. If he would accept me, it would be easier to teach him. But I'm afraid we left him alone too long. He's feral. If anyone enters the room, he lashes out at them."

Marguerite wanted to go to him so badly that she ached. But she knew she couldn't—it might alter their future, and that was the last thing she wanted.

"Would you do me a favor, Maggie?"

She had no idea what Aristotle might ask, so she answered hesitantly. "I guess so."

"Tell Wren that if I could change the past, I would have kept him by my side and not locked him away."

Her heart clenched at Aristotle's words and the tragedy that would become their relationship. "It seems cruel that you can travel through time and not fix it."

He agreed. "It is cruel and it's why many of us don't jump. It's way too tempting to right the past, but every time you try—"

"You screw it up more."

He nodded.

Marguerite watched as Wren pulled himself by his arms across the floor into a corner. His entire body was trembling while he tried to make what seemed to be words. He reminded her so much of the Wren she had met in Sanctuary.

Withdrawn and solitary. Hurting.

Wanting something he didn't think he was allowed to have.

But the man she knew now . . . he was a whole other being. Wren was slowly starting to come into his own, and she hoped that maybe part of it was because of her.

His father let out a sad sigh as he watched Wren struggling. "I hope you never know what it's like to look at your child and know that you hurt him. I think back to when I was a cub how my mother would roll on the ground with me and play. She didn't care that I was an animal while she was human. She loved me regardless. Just as she loved my father. You would have thought that I'd be the same way with my own son. And now . . . now there's no time to apologize."

"I think you're wrong. I know Wren, and what you did while he was here . . . it helped more than I think either one of you realize."

Aristotle gave her an appreciative look. "I need to

make sure that everything is set so that when I die, he gets to the future he's supposed to have. But first, there's one other thing I want to give him."

"And that is?"

"The future he deserves."

Chapter 12

Aimee took a deep breath as she entered the back door of Peltier House. This was the last place she wanted to be, but she better than anyone else understood why she had to return.

Her family would kill Fang and his entire clan if she didn't.

Steeling herself for what was to come, she closed the door and headed for the stairs.

She'd only gotten as far as the hall table when her brother Dev came out the door that led to the kitchen to see her. She saw relief in his eyes a second before it was replaced with anger.

"So you're back."

"It's my home."

He scoffed at her. "I would find another one, if I were you."

She stiffened at the coldness of his tone. "I'm being thrown out?"

"You're being warned. You picked your side and it was the wrong one."

"Leave us."

Aimee looked up at her mother's commanding tone. *Maman* was at the top of the stairs, glaring down at them. Dev shook his head at Aimee before he headed back toward the kitchen.

She flashed herself up to her mother's side. "Don't even think about striking me, *Maman*. I'm not in the mood for it. And I will hit back this time."

Her mother narrowed her eyes on Aimee. "You would sacrifice all of us for a hybrid orphan without clan?"

"Never. But I will not stand by and see an innocent condemned for nothing. Can you not see the lie that is being told, *Maman*? I know Wren. I talk to him. He's no threat to anyone but himself."

Still her mother's face was angry and cold. Her family, and in particular her mother, wasn't stupid. Aimee had no doubt that her mother and father knew she'd left voluntarily with Fang.

"You betrayed us all."

Aimee sighed. "If doing the right thing is betrayal, then yes, I suppose I did. So what are you going to do now, *Maman*? Kill me?"

Her mother growled ferociously at her, but Aimee stood her ground.

The air around them sizzled an instant before something shattered in Wren's room.

She followed her mother, who rushed to the door and slung it open. Aimee half-expected to find Wren there.

She could tell by the scent that it was a tiger all right, but the blond man wasn't Wren.

"What are you doing here, Zack?" her mother asked.

The tiger curled his lips as he opened a drawer. "The bastard escaped us. I need something with his scent on it to disseminate to the Strati."

Aimee arched a brow at that. The Strati were elite Katagaria soldiers who were carefully trained to hunt and to kill. Her brothers Zar and Dev, along with her father, were Strati warriors.

"You need nothing of his," her mother said, to Aimee's surprise. "Get out of my house."

Zack didn't listen. He moved to open another drawer.

Her mother used her powers to slam it shut. "I said for you to leave."

The tiger moved to confront her. "Don't screw with me, bear. You have as much to lose by this as I do."

"What do you mean?"

But Aimee already knew. "You're the one who spoke out against Wren at the Omegrion. You lied."

Her mother jerked her head to look at Aimee. "Do not be foolish, cub. I would have smelled a lie."

Aimee shook her head. "Not if the animal makes a habit of lying. He could easily mask his scent."

Zack took a step toward her only to find his path blocked by her mother.

"Is Aimee telling the truth?"

Zack answered with a question of his own. "Were you?" He arched a brow at her. "Do you really think Wren's gone mad? Honestly? You just wanted him out of here and you seized on any excuse to expel him. Admit it, Lo. You don't want anyone here but your family and it galls you to have to play nice with the rest of us."

She growled low in her throat.

Zack narrowed his gaze. "If Savitar ever learns the truth, he'll come for you and all your cubs. There won't be a brick left of your precious Sanctuary."

Her mother seized him and threw him against the wall. He landed with his back against it, but it didn't appear to faze him at all.

Zack actually laughed at her. "What happened to the rules of Sanctuary, Nicolette?"

Aimee caught her mother before she could attack the tiger again.

"Get out, tiger," Aimee snarled. "If I let go of my mother, there won't be enough left of you to worry about Savitar or anything else."

Zack pushed himself away from the wall. He glared at them both. "You have even more to lose than I do. Give me what I need to cover both our asses."

Now it was her mother who laughed. "Are you completely stupid? Wren has never left his scent on anything. Look around you, idiot. There is no personal item here. As soon as an article of clothing comes off his body, he has always washed it or destroyed it. He even keeps a monkey here so that its scent camouflages his own. You will never be able to track him. Face it, Zack, the cub has more intelligence than you and your father combined."

Aimee was suddenly impressed by her mother. She'd never really thought about why Wren had arrived at Sanctuary with Marvin, but obviously her mother had known all along.

Zack's nostrils flared in anger. "This isn't over."

"*Oui*, but it is. You come here again and code or no code, I will see you dead."

Growling, Zack vanished.

The tension in the air eased considerably.

Her mother let out a slow breath as she turned toward her. "Aimee, call your wolf and warn him what has happened. I am sure he knows where Wren is and he can warn him that the tiger is cornered and desperate. In his position, Zack is capable of anything."

She frowned at her mother's sudden reversal. "I don't understand. Why are you being unbelievably understanding all of a sudden? No offense, *Maman,* it scares me."

Her mother gave Aimee a harsh stare. "I have no love of Wren, this you know. But I respect the predator within him and I do not appreciate being manipulated by another. Nor do I relish being made a fool." She shook her head. "I should have questioned why Zack and his father continually called to check on Wren after he was sent here. I allowed them to plant seeds of doubts in my mind and I saw in him what they wanted me to see. I can't believe I was so foolish."

Her gaze softened. "I give you credit, cub. You weren't blinded. Now we must repair this before the weight of Savitar's wrath comes crashing down on all of us." She urged Aimee toward the door. "Go warn them. You, they will listen to."

"What are you going to do?"

"I am going to speak with your father and brothers. I fear we are on the edge of a very dangerous situation and I want them all prepared."

Aimee took a step toward the door, then paused. "I love you, *Maman.*"

"*Je t'aime aussi, ma petite.* Now go and let us make this as right as we can."

In tiger form, Wren located his mother on a bench in Central Park. Luckily the place was crowded, which would help conceal his scent and allow him to blend into the background.

Hiding in a copse of bushes, he flashed into a human with black hair, jeans, sunglasses, and a Ramones T-shirt. The kind of human his mother would never pay attention to. He probably could have kept blond hair, but he looked enough like his father that he didn't want to chance it.

Watching her as she rummaged in her purse for something, he had to give her credit, she was beautiful in human form. Elegant. Her white business suit and red silk blouse set off her impeccable figure to advantage. Many human males paused to try to speak to her, but she quickly chased them off with caustic barbs.

For an animal, she had a great command of the human language. Her tongue was as deadly a weapon as her claws.

Shaking his head as she emasculated another would-be admirer, Wren stayed back until he saw his uncle approaching. With blond hair and dressed in a navy pin-striped suit, he was the masculine equivalent to Wren's mother. The two of them looked like a Fortune 500 power couple.

Grayson inclined his head to her as he sat down on

the opposite edge of the bench. Wren noticed that his uncle kept a safe distance so that he could bolt if Karina suddenly lunged at him . . . smart man.

"So what's up?" Grayson asked.

Wren drifted a little closer so that he could hear them plainly.

"The tiger has lost its mind," she said evasively. "You were right. It's been spending time with its offspring while I was away."

"I told you to poison the cub before you left."

She gave him a peeved glare. "Aristotle would have been suspicious, and since we haven't been on the best of terms in the last twenty-five years, I thought it in my best interest to leave it alive."

Wren clenched his teeth at her words. Even now it was hard to hear her callous condemnation of his life.

She curled her lips in anger. "He's now cut me out entirely. I've been given a tiny hovel in New Jersey of all places. My credit cards have the limits of a human peasant. He's left me with nothing."

Grayson's eyes lighted as if her rage amused him. "I told you not to flaunt your lover in his face. My brother is a proud beast. You're lucky he hasn't killed you both."

She scoffed at that. "I defy him to try it. I assure you, I can hold my own against any tiger."

Grayson passed a doubting look to her. "Perhaps you shouldn't be so arrogant. You know tigers are known to tear the throats out of leopards."

"Only in your dreams." She leveled a sinister glare at Grayson. "I want out of this relationship. So long as that tiger lives, I can't mate within my own species."

"I thought you loved him."

"Love?" she spat. "Are you stupid? Love is for humans."

She jerked the white glove off her right hand and held it up for Grayson to see. "I mated with him because of this. Mating is what our species does when the mark appears. It never equates to love for the Katagaria, you know that. Do you *love* your mate?"

"She satisfies me."

Karina got a faraway look on her face as if she was remembering something in the past. Sadness marked her perfect features. "I, too, was satisfied once," she said softly. Her face hardened again into the bitch countenance Wren knew so well. "Until I saw what our mating produced. I am the very last of my kind. If I can't prolong the snow leopard breed, then at least let me reproduce a pure leopard and not some freakish hybrid."

Thanks, Mom. Love you, too. He would love to show her exactly what her freak was capable of.

Even she would be impressed with his ability to rip her throat out before she could even defend herself.

Grayson folded his arms over his chest and spoke in a calm, level tone as if they were discussing the weather and not the life and death of Wren and his father.

The very nonchalance made Wren want to kill them both.

"Then you know what you need to do, Karina."

"It's not that simple now," she said with a sigh. "He's left everything to the mutant. I'm quite sure it will see me out in the cold before it allows me near it."

Grayson snorted. "What does a leopard care about a tiger's will?"

She hissed at him. "Don't be stupid. Our habitats

are dwindling every day. At least in the facade of a wealthy human I can make sure that I always have a refuge to be in my true form. I also know how badly you want Tigarian Technologies, but Aristotle is too suspicious of you to ever trust you at his back again. So here's what I propose. I kill him and the mutant, and you give me a share of the estate."

"If I say no?"

"Then I take my chances with the mutant."

Yeah, Wren thought angrily. That would be an even worse mistake. Even as a cub he'd hated his mother. Too bad she hadn't taken her chances with him.

Grayson fell silent as he considered her words. "Very well, I accept."

Duh, like he'd expected his uncle to say anything else. But then, Wren was watching a history that he already knew the outcome to.

"Good, but I know you, Grayson. I don't trust you, either. I want some assurances."

Wow, Karina actually had had a brain. At least for a moment. Too bad her assurances had failed her in the end, but maybe they would give Wren some way to prove Grayson guilty of this deed.

"And what would that be?" Grayson asked.

"I want you to set me up as a major stockholder in your own company and I want a million dollars up front, transferred from your account to mine before I make any moves against the tiger."

Even Wren could tell that went over like a weighted cannonball with his uncle. Grayson's features actually looked pinched and drawn. Wren half-expected the tiger to tell her to shove it.

He didn't. "How long do I have?"

"Not long. I know Aristotle. By now, he'll have me banned entirely from the house. But he did say that he wanted me to look at the mutant. I feign interest. Tell him I've calmed down and would like to see it. When he opens the door, I can kill them both."

Now that pleased his uncle. His eyes were actually alight and happy. "I need time to liquidate a few things to have the cash for you."

"You have forty-eight hours." She pulled a business card out of her purse. "That's my account. Once the money is in there, you'll be a far richer man."

Wren watched as she stood up and walked off. It was the hardest moment of his life to stand there and let history make itself when all he had to do was lunge at them both and kill them.

I could save my father's life . . .

But his father was supposed to die. If he didn't, then Wren wouldn't go to New Orleans and he would never meet Maggie.

She's not your mate.

It was true. As his mother had pointed out to Grayson, it wasn't in his people to love. Not like humans did, and yet Wren felt something for Maggie that defied any other explanation.

He only wanted to be with her and yet he knew he had nothing to offer her.

But right now, he could save his father's life . . .

And lose Maggie forever.

His father or Maggie. But then, there was no real choice. If Wren saved his father, he would alter many more fates than just his own.

His mind turned back to when Vane had been living at Sanctuary. One of Vane's packmates had come to kill him. Only Wren had kept him from pursuing Vane.

If Wren hadn't been there . . .

Vane might be dead now. And that was just one instance that Wren knew about. One life touched hundreds of others, either directly or indirectly.

"The slightest stirring in the air can set a hurricane in motion a thousand miles off."

Chaos theory. The Dark-Hunter Acheron had been the one to teach Wren that years ago. To change even the smallest thing could have extremely damaging repercussions.

No, he had to let history play itself out.

Grinding his teeth, he turned away and drifted into a secluded area so that he could shift back to his father's house.

"You two can stay in here once Wren returns," Wren's father said as he closed the door to seal the two of them into a guest bedroom alone.

Marguerite frowned at his actions as something inside her became frightened. She didn't want to be alone with Wren's father. But it didn't make any sense. Aristotle had only been kind to her so far.

Still, she felt extremely uncomfortable.

Aristotle took a deep breath as he fidgeted with a small porcelain box on the cherrywood dresser. "Do you think Wren will be able to find the evidence he needs?"

"I hope so."

Aristotle shook his head. "My mother always told me to watch out for Grayson. She said that he had too much human in him for his own good."

Marguerite frowned at his words. "How so?"

Aristotle put the lid on the box, then turned and leaned back against the dresser. "Animals as a rule aren't particularly jealous, but Grayson always was. He was the eldest of my parents' offspring. I was the youngest . . . born very late in their lives. I had two littermates who didn't survive. Because of that, my mother doted on me. I can remember being just a cub and catching Grayson eyeing me with malice. My mother was always afraid to leave us alone together. It was why I banned him from my company a long time ago."

Marguerite could understand Aristotle's concern, but his actions struck her as extremely paranoid. "Yes, but jealousy doesn't always make people homicidal."

He laughed at that. "We're not talking about people, Maggie. We're talking animals. In our world, it's survival of the fittest. Winner take all."

He crossed the room to stand before her. "You love my son, don't you?"

"I . . ." Marguerite hesitated. But in the end, she knew the answer. There was no denying it. "Yes."

Aristotle smiled. "A human's love. I couldn't wish anything better for him. Animals protect what they know. They protect what they are bound to, but humans . . . humans have a greater capacity for sacrifice for those who live in their hearts."

Before Maggie could move, Aristotle grabbed her by the throat and threw her to the ground. She tried to scream, only to find that she couldn't even get air into her lungs.

She couldn't move, couldn't fight. It was as if some unseen force held her paralyzed.

His eyes blazed at her. "Forgive me for doing this to you. I hope you'll understand in time."

Her desired scream came out as a whimper as he changed into a tiger and bit her shoulder.

Marguerite was completely paralyzed as pain ripped through her. She saw colors swirling around as a foreign buzzing started in her ears.

Her breathing became labored, painful. It was as if she were suffocating.

She was dying. She knew it.

Why?

Why was he doing this to her? Her thoughts turned to Wren. He would be devastated.

Fight, damn it, fight!

But she couldn't. She had no control over her body. No control over what his father was doing to her. It was terrifying.

I'm so sorry, Wren.

It was her final thought before everything went black.

Wren found himself alone in his father's bedroom. He cocked his head as he heard faint music playing from another room. It was the song "The Lion Sleeps Tonight."

Wren snorted. No doubt it was his father's way of letting Wren know where they were.

He cracked open the door to the hallway and looked

down it to make sure his younger self wasn't about. Not that there was much chance of that. If he remembered correctly, he only ventured out after dark and then only a time or two. He'd been too afraid to let his father see him. Afraid of how much more his father would hate him if he knew what he could do.

God, he'd been such a fool. The very thing that had caused his father to change his feelings toward him had been the thing that had scared him most.

If only he'd known.

Wren headed down the hall, in the opposite direction of his childhood room. He found the door where the music was playing.

Just in case he was wrong, he knocked lightly on the door.

No one answered.

Hesitant, he opened it slowly to find a large white tiger on the bed. He froze not so much at the sight but at what he smelled. The air was thick with the scent of tiger mixed with that of Maggie.

But there was no sight of her.

Wren's heart hammered at the significance. "What did you do?" he snarled at the beast that lay facing the opposite wall. "How could you eat my girlfriend, Dad? She was all I've ever had. Damn you!"

His rage boiling over, Wren charged the bed, intending to kill his father as he changed into a tiger's form. He caught the tiger, then skidded to a halt.

Wren's gaze locked with the tiger's, whose eyes weren't blue. . . .

They were brown.

They were *Maggie* brown.

And they were large in panic.

Wren let go of her and changed back to human form. Scared of what he was seeing, he reached out to touch her, half-expecting this to be a trick of some kind. How could Maggie be a tiger?

She was human. Completely human.

"Baby?" he whispered, stroking the tiger's face. "Is it really you?"

The tiger crawled closer to him. She nuzzled his bare chest and raised a paw to rest on his hip. He could sense her fear that was mingled with relief.

Wren wrapped his arms around her to hold her close in comfort. "It's all right," he said, stroking her soft fur. "I've got you."

Two seconds later, she was lying as a naked human in his arms.

Wren pulled back to see those familiar brown eyes.

"I'm scared, Wren," she said, her voice trembling. "What's happening to me?"

He cupped her face in his hands. "I don't know. What happened while I was gone?"

"Your father brought me into this room and I thought he killed me."

Wren frowned at her words. "What?"

"He attacked me as a tiger, then everything went black. When I woke up, I was . . ." She changed back into a tiger before she could finish speaking.

Her panic doubled.

"It's okay, Maggie," Wren assured her. "Take a deep breath and imagine yourself as a human."

She came back to him.

"That's it," he said with a smile he didn't really feel.

But he didn't want to scare her any more than she already was. "Stay focused as a human and you'll remain one."

"I have to tell you, being a tiger really sucks."

He laughed darkly at her words. "Sometimes. Sometimes it's not so bad."

"This isn't one of those times."

He smiled as he gently stroked her hair. "No, I guess for you it isn't." He tilted his head as he tried to sense his father, but all Wren could feel was Maggie. "Do you know where my father went?"

"No, but the next time I see him, I intend to return the bite."

"Don't worry. I'll bite him for you." Wren pulled back from her. "How do you feel right now?"

"Woozy. Do you ever feel like you're going to vomit when you change shapes?"

"It usually goes away quickly. Stare at something for a minute and your senses will settle down."

She stared at his lips.

Wren didn't know what it was about that that turned him on, but his body reacted instantly to it.

"You're right," she said. "It helps."

Wren kissed her lightly. She moaned deep in her throat as he parted her lips to taste the sweetness of her mouth. His body hardening even more, he gently cupped her breast in his hand.

He rolled her to her back just as someone knocked on the door.

He quickly dressed them both as the door opened to show his father. Hesitating in the doorway, he appeared sheepish. "I didn't know you were back. I was coming in to check on Maggie. How's she doing?"

Wren left the bed as rage took hold of him. "What did you do to her?"

He looked past Wren to the bed where Maggie was still lying in human form. "I'm so sorry, Maggie. But it's for the best. You're stronger now. You'll live longer than you would have as a human. Believe me, you're much better off this way."

Wren grabbed him and slammed him back against the wall. "What did you do to her?"

"I gave her my mother's powers."

Wren couldn't have been more stunned had his father racked him. He loosened his hold on his throat. "You did what?"

"I gave her animal powers. I figured that by the weekend I wouldn't need them anymore anyway, right?"

Wren shook his head in denial. "It's impossible. No one can give up their powers."

His father snorted at that. "Yes, they can. It's not something done often. Very few of our kind are willing to let go of their magic. But it can be done."

Wren still didn't believe it. "No. I know a Were-Hunter who's mated to a human. She has no powers."

"Because he didn't share them with her."

"Believe me, if Vane could share his powers with his wife, he would."

Wren's father arched a brow at that. "Even if it meant weakening his own?"

Wren hesitated. No, maybe not. "How is it I've never heard of this?"

"It's not exactly something that's talked about in open circles. I learned about it from my mother, who gave up her powers to me when she knew she was dying of cancer. I was young and she was terrified Grayson would kill me. So she made me strong enough to hold my own against him. Now I've passed her gift along to your girlfriend."

Maggie sat up slowly on the bed. "Why not give it to Wren?"

His father gave an odd half laugh. "His powers are enough that he can hold his own against virtually anyone. But you . . . you would always be a weakness for him. Now you're not. In a few days, you will grow accustomed to your new life and you will master those powers."

"But we're not mates," Wren said, still unable to believe this was happening.

"You will be. I know it."

Wren shook his head. "Maggie is the daughter of a U.S. senator, Dad. How is she supposed to go back to her life now?" He watched as the horror of that sank in.

"Why didn't you tell me?" his father asked.

"Had I known you were going to foist our world on her, I would have. But I never dreamed in my wildest imagination that you could do this."

Maggie touched Wren's arm as she joined them. "It's okay, Wren. Although to be honest, a choice in this would have been nice. Your father's heart was in the right place. You can't be angry at someone who did something because they loved you."

Wren ground his teeth. "Sure I can."

His father looked stricken.

"But I won't."

His father pulled Wren into his arms and hugged him.

She smiled at them. "So before I shift into a tiger

again, did you learn anything about your father's murder?"

Wren nodded as he pulled away and moved to Marguerite's side. "My mother's brilliant plan is that she kills Dad and me, and then she and Grayson split the estate. He's to wire a million dollars into her account in advance of the murders."

"But she doesn't kill you," Marguerite reminded him. "After your father dies—"

"You know," his father said between clenched teeth, "it really disturbs me to be talking about my death like this."

"I'm sorry," Maggie said. She looked at Wren. "Are you sure we can't save him?"

"No," Wren said. "It would alter things and the Fates would punish us for it."

His father concurred. "And I'd most likely end up dead in some other fashion within a few hours of his saving me. The Fates have an eerie way of keeping things in balance."

Marguerite felt for Aristotle. "So how do we prove their involvement?"

"I don't know," Wren said. "The deposit doesn't mean anything. I suppose I could get a copy of it, but Grayson could lie and say that he put the money there for another reason. His argument will be based on the fact that both of my parents are dead. He'll say I killed them both."

"So you'll need to find out who killed your mother and provide proof of it."

Wren nodded. "Could Grayson have been in the house when she died?"

Aristotle shook his head. "It's not possible."

"Are you sure?" Wren asked.

"Positive. I banned Grayson from here a long time ago." Aristotle turned thoughtful. "What all do you remember about the night of my death? I need every detail."

Wren passed an uncomfortable look to Marguerite. "It happened around ten. I remember because I heard the clock chime just as something crashed. I sensed that something was wrong, so I left my room to go to yours. I found you there and I held you."

She saw the pain on Wren's father's face.

"Then I heard them laughing and I went to kill them. Mom's lover attacked me and knocked me out. When I woke up, the house was on fire and I escaped when the floor burned out from underneath me. A fireman took me outside and I escaped into the woods. There was a man there who called out to me. He said he would take me to Sanctuary."

His father frowned. "What man?"

"I don't know. He never told me his name and I don't even know why I trusted him, in retrospect. He just seemed to be honest."

Marguerite considered that. "What did he look like?"

Wren shrugged. "He looked and smelled human. He was really tall, with black eyes and long, dark brown hair."

Aristotle shook his head. "I don't know a human who looks like that."

"Are you sure?" Wren asked.

"Positive."

"How weird," Marguerite said as she considered that. "Who could he have been then?"

Wren shook his head. "I don't know."

Aristotle let out a long, tired breath. "Very well then. It doesn't sound like there's much we can do until the night they kill me. I'll have the bank keep me posted about your mother's account. You stay here and teach your girlfriend how to use her powers."

Wren's frown increased. "Where are you going?"

His father gave Wren a meaningful stare. "I want to go spend a little time with my son so that he won't hate me entirely when he finds me dead."

"I didn't hate you, Dad."

He smiled sadly. "Thanks, Wren. I'm glad to know it before I die."

Marguerite was amazed by the man's strength, at the fact that he could face his death so bravely. It was unbelievable. "You're being incredibly understanding about all this."

He scoffed at that. "Only on the outside. I assure you, inside I'm screaming right now. There's nothing worse than knowing you're going to die and not being able to stop it."

She cringed at the very thought. "No, I guess not."

Aristotle opened the door. "I'll be back in a few hours. In the meantime if either of you need anything, have Maggie buzz me on the intercom."

"Okay."

As his father started to leave, Wren stopped him. "Thanks, Dad."

He patted Wren on the arm before he left them alone.

Wren sighed heavily. "This has been one seriously fucked-up day, huh?"

"You might say that. This morning it was 2005 in New Orleans, I was staring at you wondering what it would be like to have the ability to change into a tiger. Now it's the day before I enter the world in 1981 and I *can* turn into a tiger. Yeah, just your average day . . . if you're in a Ted Raimi production."

Wren snorted at her sarcasm.

Marguerite rubbed her arms as the real horror of all this settled deep inside her heart. "What's going to become of us, Wren?"

"I don't know. But whatever it is, it should be interesting."

"And that is what really, really scares me."

Chapter 13

Marguerite quickly learned that life as a Were-Tiger wasn't easy. For one thing, her appetite quadrupled almost instantaneously. And as she was searching the deserted kitchen for chocolate to consume, since her new metabolism would burn through gross amounts of calories, Wren warned her that it was eternally off her menu. Apparently too much of it could kill her.

So could Tylenol.

The Tylenol she could take or leave, but the chocolate . . . that was a cruel blow. No more Easter bunnies for her.

But the good news was that her body quickly acclimated to the changes and within hours she was able to maintain a human form again with ease.

Wren explained that during the daytime being human wouldn't be a problem for her since that was her "base" form. His was technically that of the tigard, which was why whenever he slept or passed out he reverted to tigard form.

She also learned that it would be easier for her to

change into a tiger at night. Being a tiger in the day-time would be a little tricky for her until she grew more accustomed to her powers.

Until she mastered them, during a full moon her human form would most likely change even against her will. The magnetic pull of the full moon would play havoc with her powers—this was where the human myth of the werewolf came from.

Under the light of a full moon, all young Were-Hunters were at the mercy of their powers. They were also much more likely to attack an unwary human, since the animal in them tended to take over their human rationale.

"All human myth is rooted somewhere in reality," Wren said as he showed her how to control her ability to change.

The change from one form to the other wasn't painful. It was the struggle to hold on to the form that caused mental and physical stress.

But as her body settled down, Marguerite began to feel ferocious. Intense. Everything was more vivid now.

Her sight. Her hearing. Smells—another thing she could have done with less of.

At least for certain things. For others, such as the way Wren smelled when he was near, it wasn't so bad.

She leaned her head against Wren's neck so that she could inhale the unique scent of him. It was more intoxicating than a fine wine.

And it made her salivate.

Always timid in life, she was now possessed of something else. Something feral and wild. She was still the same Marguerite, only now she was much more confident about her place in the world.

Wren smiled as she gently nuzzled his neck. "You're feeling the tiger's pull, aren't you?"

"The what?"

"The beast that shares your body. It's different from being human. It sizzles inside you like another person. Calling to you."

She nodded as she crawled into his lap, then pushed him down on the bed. She rubbed her face against his, delighting in the sensation of his roughened cheeks scraping the smoothness of hers. Her body was on fire.

And the animal inside her craved him with a need born of madness.

She stared at his shirt, then wished it away.

It vanished instantly.

It was good to be a magical tiger. Marguerite smiled in satisfaction.

At least until her own top and bra vanished. "Hey!"

"Turnabout is fair play," Wren said an instant before all of her clothes disappeared.

For the first time in her life, she wasn't self-conscious. The beast inside her knew nothing of modesty. It only knew desire. Hunger.

Wren.

And it wanted a taste of him.

Wren leaned back and watched the fire that burned bright in her dark brown eyes. He was already hard and aching for her as she lashed his chest with her hair. Grinding his teeth, he had to force himself not to take control of this.

But it was part of her coming into her own. She needed to experience the new aspect of herself. Needed to come to terms with the hunger of a tiger's soul.

Lying there while she explored him was the hardest thing he'd ever had to do. Her soft body brushed torturously against his. As she nibbled his ear, the crisp hairs at the juncture of her thighs brushed against his hip, reminding him of his own hunger for her.

Her desire set fire to his own.

Wren hissed as she teased his ear with her tongue. Her breath on his neck blistered him and caused chills to run the whole length of his body. There was something inside him that calmed to her touch, and yet she excited him more than anything else ever had.

He ran his hands over her smooth back to cup her bottom in his hands. She moaned in his ear before she moved so that she was straddling his body. Wren reached up to cup her face as he deepened their kiss.

All he'd ever wanted in his life was to belong, and with her he found that special place. It was why she meant so much to him. Why he never wanted to lose her. She was everything to him.

And he couldn't keep her.

It was so unfair and yet he refused to let himself think of that. For the moment, they were together and that was all that was important to him. Sighing in satisfaction, he gently nuzzled her cheek.

Marguerite growled at the sight of Wren's defined muscles straining as he held himself in check and allowed her to have her way with him. What was it about this beast that made her entire being burn?

Really, no one should be so irresistible. Her heart

pounding, she pulled back from his lips and growled ferociously. His scent and taste ran through her, making her drunk with need. She had to have him. . . .

Unable to stand it anymore, she impaled herself on him.

They growled in unison.

Wren lifted his hips, driving himself even deeper into her. Marguerite bit her lip in satisfaction as she reveled in the hard thickness of him inside her body. There was nothing better than the feeling of him buried there as they made love furiously.

Her body shook and burned, demanding more and more of him. Biting her lip, she watched as her pleasure was mirrored in his eyes. Oh yeah, this was what she'd craved from him and she had no doubt that no man would ever be able to make her feel this way again.

He was everything to her.

And both she and the tiger within intended to keep him. Unable to stand it anymore, she quickened her strokes until she found the release she needed.

Wren watched as Maggie came calling out his name. Smiling, he rolled over with her so that he could finally take control of their play. He moved faster against her supple hips, heightening her pleasure as her nails bit into his back.

And when he found his own orgasm, he could swear he saw stars from it.

He collapsed on top of her, his heart pounding as he felt the most incredible bliss of his life. There was nothing on earth that could match the warmth of her lying beneath him. Of the sensation of her hot hand against his cool skin.

The beast inside him could devour her. It was already growling and straining for another taste of her body.

Marguerite played in his hair as Wren's breath tickled across her skin. She loved the feel of his weight on her. Of his body still joined to hers. It was warm and wicked.

And she never wanted to move again.

She ran her feet over the backs of his legs, delighting in the feel of all his lean muscle. She could feel her hunger for him starting to build again deep down inside. Now she finally understood how Wren could make love to her for hours.

It was intrinsic.

She laughed deep in her throat as she felt him growing hard again inside her. Biting her lip, she moved against him, slow and easy, savoring the whole length and breadth of him.

Wren lifted himself up by his arms to stare down at her as she continued to control their play. "I think my little tigress is still hungry."

She moaned as he thrust himself into her deep and hard.

And she still wanted more. Cupping his bottom, she urged him faster and lifted her hips to draw him in even deeper. It still wasn't enough.

As if he could sense it, Wren pulled away. Marguerite whimpered until he rolled her over onto her knees. He took her hands and braced them on the headboard as he separated her thighs with his.

"Trust me, Maggie," he breathed in her ear a moment before he was inside her again.

She gasped at the deepness of his penetration. Her breasts tingled as he thrust against her. Using leverage from the headboard, she met him stroke for stroke. He cupped her breasts an instant before he buried his lips against the nape of her neck.

Marguerite groaned at the hotness of his lips, at the feeling of his hand cupping her breast while he trailed the other down her stomach, to her wet cleft. Her breath caught as he toyed with her in time to his thrusts. She'd never felt anything more incredible than him in and around her. It was as if she were consumed by him.

And when she came again it was so intense and ragged that she literally screamed.

Wren laughed in satisfaction until his own blinding orgasm took him. He buried himself deep inside her as his entire body shook. Never had he felt anything like it. His heart hammering, his powers sizzling, he wrapped himself around her and pulled her back on the bed so that she was lying on top of him, completely exposed.

Marguerite gave a ragged but contented sigh as Wren gently stroked her breasts while she lay atop him. She was so sated that she felt like a well-fed kitten ready for a long nap.

Wren hooked his ankles to hers and spread her legs wide. "I don't think I could ever get enough of you, Maggie," he whispered as he slowly began to toy with her again.

She shivered at the sensation of his long, lean fingers stroking her cleft. Of them delving deep inside her body, stoking yet another fire inside her. She reached down to cover his hand with hers as he pleased her even more.

"What is it like to be mated?" she asked, wondering if it could get any better than this.

"For the female, heaven. For a male, it sucks."

She frowned at his deep, almost angry tone. "How so?"

"Once our kind mates, it really is until death we do part. There is no freedom from each other so long as both mates live."

She started to correct him about the "our" until she realized that she was his kind now.

She was no longer fully human.

"Is that so bad?"

"Not if both are loyal to each other. The male's job is to protect the female. To keep her and their children safe. So long as she lives, he can never again touch another woman sexually. Essentially we become impotent around anyone but our mates."

Now she understood his father's anger. "Your father can't even take a mistress?"

"No. No male can. But the females are free to share their bodies with anyone they choose to. They just can't reproduce with anyone other than their mate."

"That doesn't seem fair."

"It isn't. It was one of the curses that the three Fates handed out to my people when we were created."

She hissed as he continued to stroke her and moved her hips against his hand.

All in all, what he described didn't sound too bad. 'But if one of the mates dies, the other is free?"

"Yes, unless we have bonded our life forces together. Then if one dies, both die."

She closed her eyes and smiled. "That sounds romantic."

He nuzzled her hair with his face as he continued to stroke her. "In a way it is. It's the ultimate sacrifice between two beings who never want to live apart. They say that not even the Fates can break such a bond. If one of the lovers is reincarnated, then the Fates must reincarnate the other so that they can be together again in their new lives."

She opened her eyes as Wren pulled away from her. He slid her off of him, onto the bed. She frowned at him until he moved on the bed until he was lying between her open thighs.

"You are so beautiful," he said raggedly, his eyes burning into hers.

Marguerite wanted to tell him then how much she loved him, but she was afraid to. She wasn't even sure why. But something inside was scared that if she said it, she would ruin this moment, and she didn't want it to end.

Wren took her hands into his and led them to the center of her body. "Hold yourself open for me, Maggie," he said, his voice thick. "I want to see you touching yourself while I taste you."

She shivered at his words as she reached to comply. The instant she did, he dipped his head and took her into his mouth. Marguerite choked on a cry of pleasure as he tongue-tormented her with the sweetest ecstasy she'd ever known.

How could any man feel this good?

And in that moment, she realized something.

She wanted to be mated to him. Forever.

Are you insane?

But her heart didn't listen to her head. Then again, hearts were seldom rational. All she knew was what she felt. She loved this man with a depth of emotion she had never known before.

How could she not?

He had given her more than anyone else she'd ever known. He listened to her. He cared for her.

She had actually tamed him. At least partially. When they had met, he had never known a woman's touch. He'd been wild and feral.

Now he was tender with her. He took care of her.

And she wanted to take care of him.

Marguerite threw her head back as she came again. She shook all over from the intensity of her pleasure mixed with her volatile emotions.

He can never be yours. . . .

No, Wren Tigarian could never belong to Marguerite D'Aubert Goudeau. In her blue-blood, plastic world of conformity, he would always stand out.

But she was no longer Marguerite D'Aubert Goudeau, at least not entirely.

She was Maggie Goudeau.

Human.

Tigress.

And she wanted Wren Tigarian as her own. She just had to convince three very stubborn Fates that she was a beast to be reckoned with. One who was more than willing to fight for this man.

Chapter 14

Wren lay naked, spooned up against Maggie while she slept in his arms. He had his cheek pressed against hers as he listened to her breathe. She had the faintest little snore that warmed him through and through. He was tired, too, but he wanted to hold her as a man at least for a little while longer while the scent of her hung heavy in his senses.

It was heaven to be in her arms, and he cursed the Fates for not allowing them to mate. It wasn't fair or right. Surely they were meant to be together. . . .

Suddenly he heard something out in the hallway.

Wren moved slowly from the bed as he felt an odd fissure ripple down his spine. It wasn't like the one he got when his father was nearby.

It was . . .

Eerie, powerful, disturbing.

He crossed the room, his attention focused on what he'd heard outside.

Closing his eyes, he dressed himself and Maggie an instant before he felt a presence behind him.

Wren spun around to find one of the tigers in human form who had assaulted him in Sanctuary.

The tiger moved forward to try to put a collar over Wren's neck.

Wren shoved the Katagari back, into the wall. The collar fell to the floor with a thud as the tiger growled at him.

Maggie came awake with a gasp.

"Run, Maggie," Wren said as he put himself between her and the tiger.

Two more tigers popped in.

Marguerite's eyes narrowed at the sight of the tigers and man after Wren. An unbridled fury started deep inside her. She'd never felt anything like it as it rose up.

It was the beast inside her. She knew it. She actually felt it straining and hissing.

Aching.

And it wanted blood. *Their* blood.

Acting on pure animal instinct, she launched herself from the bed at the tiger closest to her. It turned on her to fight. For a fleeting instant, fear gripped her, and then it was gone, washed away by her fury.

And in its place was a confidence the likes of which she'd never experienced before. Trusting herself completely, she stood her ground and caught the tiger by the neck.

Wren was stunned as he watched Maggie take the tiger. He smiled an instant before something shocked him. He couldn't breathe as the electrical energy went through his entire body, flashing him from tiger to human and back again.

He hit the ground hard, terrified of what would happen to Maggie while he was completely incapacitated.

Marguerite froze at the sight of Wren. He was on the floor writhing as if in excruciating pain as he changed forms back and forth at an alarming rate.

The tiger she'd been fighting manifested itself as a human male. "Collar the bastard."

She didn't know what that was, but she was sure it was bad. She changed back to human form. "No!" she shouted, rushing at them. She threw herself down on top of Wren and wished herself out of the room.

Please let this work!

Two seconds later, she was in his father's bedroom.

Aristotle looked up from his desk with a frown. "Maggie?"

Before she could answer, the tigers poofed into the room with them.

"They're trying to kill Wren," she warned his father.

He came out of his chair ready to battle them.

As the human moved for Wren, Marguerite sprang at him. She shoved him back so hard that he actually cracked the wall.

"Stay out of this, woman, or die," he warned her.

She glared her hatred at him. "The only one who's going to die tonight is you, asshole."

Aristotle caught the man as he lunged toward her. He twisted the man's head around until a gruesome crack sounded. The man turned into a tiger before he slid to the ground, where he lay motionless.

The other two tigers vanished.

Only partially relieved, Marguerite knelt beside

Wren, who was still flashing back and forth between his forms.

"Baby?" she said, wanting to help him.

"They must have hit him with a Taser," Aristotle said. "You should probably be told that if you get shocked at all, this is what will happen to you, too. You can't hold on to a form after such a thing."

Well that was nice to know, but it didn't help Wren. "What can we do to help him?"

"Nothing," Aristotle said sadly. "The electricity has to stop bouncing around his cells. Once it does he'll be back to normal, but in the meantime he's helpless."

Aristotle locked gazes with her. The heat and fear in his blue eyes scorched her. "And you two are out of time. Now that they know you're here, they'll be back for both of you. In force."

"What are we to do?" she asked, willing to fight or do whatever was necessary to protect Wren.

His father placed a hand on Wren's arm. "The full moon is cresting. It's time to send you both back to where you came from."

Marguerite shook her head as a new fear gripped her. "It's too soon. We have no proof of his innocence."

Still those eyes burned her with an intensity that was frightening. "Trust me. Go to the Laurens law office and ask them for a package. I will send it from here and they will have it in their safe, waiting for the two of you. It will prove Wren's innocence."

It sounded way too easy. "Are you sure?"

"You have no choice, Maggie," he insisted. "If you stay here, you're both dead. I only hope I have enough of my powers left after turning you to accomplish this."

"And if you don't?"

He looked away. "It's all in the hands of the Fates. Let us hope they're not entirely lacking in compassion."

Marguerite opened her mouth to argue, but before she could, everything around her went hazy.

A minute later, she found herself on a grassy lawn not too far from her small house in New Orleans.

Shocked and a bit confused, she looked around. It was the middle of the day, and everything looked as if it were normal. The sun was bright and shining over her head. The day appeared calm and tranquil.

Only there was nothing tranquil about what was happening to them right now. There was nothing tranquil about the fear and anxiety she felt.

In human form, Wren hissed, then slammed his head against the grass. She held her breath, expecting him to transform into a tigard again.

He didn't.

He lay still against the grass, his eyes open with a distant gaze that was filled with remorse and guilt.

"Wren?" she asked hesitantly.

"Damn it, Dad," he breathed angrily. "How could you?"

She saw the anguish in Wren's eyes and it set fire to her own. "I'm sorry, Wren. I should have stopped him."

He looked as if he wanted to scream out at the injustice. It only lasted an instant before he was up on his feet with a grim determination on his face.

Wren held his hand out to her. "C'mon. Let's go settle this. I'm not about to let him have died in vain."

She understood exactly what he felt and she was every bit as ready to set this right. "You got it."

As soon as she touched his hand, he flashed them from the street to a small alcove in the alley behind the Laurens Law Firm. Much to her relief, their clothes changed back into their usual 2005 attire.

"Thank you," she said, looking down at her pink sweater and khaki pants. "I feel much more normal now, which is really freaky when you consider just how abnormal I've become."

Smiling, Wren gave her an encouraging look before he led her inside.

The dark-haired receptionist frowned at them as they entered. A middle-aged woman who had obviously been chosen for her job because she could intimidate Evander Holyfield, she eyed them suspiciously. It was obvious she didn't recognize Wren. "Can I help you?" she said coolly.

Wren brushed a hand through his hair. Maggie could sense his unease as he addressed the woman, who had a snobby attitude that would make Marguerite's father proud.

"Yeah. I'm Wren Tigarian and I was told that my father sent something here for the firm to hold for me."

The name immediately registered on the woman's face as she stood up. She looked at him with much more respect. "Oh, you're one of Mr. Laurens' personal clients. If you and your friend will wait right here, Mr. Tigarian, I'll go get him for you." She paused as she reached the door to the office area. "Would either of you like anything to drink?"

Wren looked at Marguerite.

"I'm fine," she said quickly.

The woman looked at Wren, who shook his head in declination. "Very good, sir. I'll be right back with Mr. Laurens. Y'all just make yourselves at home."

Wow, the change in her tone was remarkable.

Marguerite could feel Wren's agitation as they waited for Bill.

Not that they had to wait very long. He entered the reception area one step behind his receptionist, who returned to her seat.

Bill frowned nervously as soon as he saw them. Not that Marguerite blamed him. They were still being hunted.

"What are you doing here, Wren?"

"My father sent something to you. He told me you'd have it in your safe."

Bill shook his head. "No, we didn't."

Wren lowered his voice so that only she and Bill could hear him. "I just left him, Bill, and he said he was going to send something here for you to hold on to. He said it would prove my innocence."

Bill's eyes showed his own upset for Wren. "No letter ever came from him. Believe me. There's nothing here. I would have told you a long time ago if I'd had something for you."

She saw the disappointment she felt mirrored on Wren's face. "Are you sure?"

"I would never joke about this."

Damn. Marguerite shivered. How could his father have not sent it? Or, God forbid, it fell victim to the mail service. This was awful.

"What are we going to do?" she asked Wren.

Wren rubbed his head to relieve the ache that was starting just behind his eyes. He was angry and disappointed.

But most of all he was sad. His heart ached for the father he'd barely known. A father who hadn't hated him after all.

That knowledge alone had been worth the trip into the past. So what if he couldn't prove his innocence? At least he finally knew that his father had loved him.

He looked at Maggie, who was dependent on him to keep her safe. And in his heart he knew what he had to do.

"I'm going to the Omegrion." His tone was low so that the receptionist couldn't overhear him.

"Are you insane?" Bill hissed. "They'll kill you."

"They'll kill me if I don't. You know that." Wren looked at her, hoping to make her understand why this had to be done. "Savitar is my only hope. I'll ask for a *diki* and then we'll see what happens."

"What's a *diki*?" Marguerite asked, her tone barely more than a whisper.

"Trial by combat," Bill explained. "Wren confronts his accuser and they fight it out."

She was aghast at the idea. "No!" she said firmly.

"We have no choice, Maggie. They'll run us into the ground. Neither you nor I will ever have rest from them. There's nowhere we can go they won't find us. Tell her, Bill."

Bill sighed heavily. "He's right. As much as I hate to admit it. They won't stop until he's dead."

Marguerite straightened up and eyed Wren with raw determination. "Fine. Then I go with you."

"Maggie—"

"No, Wren," she said sternly. "You are not going to do this alone. You need someone in your corner."

Wren stared at her. And it was then he knew the truth.

He loved this woman. He loved her strength and her courage. She was absolutely everything to him. Mated or not, he would never feel like this toward another female.

In truth, he didn't want to go alone. If he had to die, he wanted to die in Maggie's arms, with the touch of her hand on his skin to ease him on his way.

"Okay." Wren looked at the receptionist.

Bill followed his line of sight. "Terry? Could you go grab the file I have on my desk and bring it to me?"

"Sure, Mr. Laurens. I'll be right back."

Wren waited until she was out of their sight. Wrapping his arms around Maggie, he closed his eyes and teleported them to Savitar's home.

Wren didn't move for several seconds as he glanced around the large circular room. Even though he had a seat on the council, he'd never been here before. The room was large, almost overwhelming.

"Where are we?" Maggie asked as she gaped at the opulence of the place.

"A traveling island."

She arched both brows. "A what?"

"It's an island kind of like Brigadoon. It vanishes and reappears at Savitar's whims."

She looked even more confused "And who is Savitar?"

"That would be me."

They both turned to see an incredibly tall man standing behind them. Dressed all in white like a typical surfer, Savitar had shoulder-length dark brown hair and deeply tanned skin.

Wren's jaw went slack as he recognized Savitar. "You?"

"You know him?" Maggie asked.

Wren nodded. "He's the man I met in the woods after my father died."

"The one who took you to New Orleans?"

"That was me," Savitar said again as he walked past them, toward a throne that was set against one wall.

Marguerite was gaping at the man's nonchalance.

As he sat down, the room filled with people who appeared to have been in the middle of doing other things. One man was even holding a fried drumstick against his lips as if he'd been in the middle of eating dinner.

"What the hell is this?" a dark-haired man asked as he quickly flashed clothing onto his naked body. "Savitar? I was in the middle of my shower."

Savitar looked completely unrepentant.

Marguerite was about to laugh until her gaze fell to one of the tigers who had been pursuing them. The man curled his lip an instant before he changed to a tiger and rushed at them.

He leapt at Wren.

Just as he would have reached them, he slammed into what appeared to be an invisible wall. He fell to the ground yelping.

"Don't piss me off any more, you stupid punk," Savitar growled. "Now get up, Zack."

The tiger became human. His mouth was bleeding as he turned to face Savitar's throne. "I demand justice!"

Savitar laughed evilly. "Be careful what you wish for, you just might get it."

Marguerite exchanged a completely confounded look with Wren, who seemed to understand about as much of this as she did. What was going on here?

"Animals," Savitar said. "Sorry to disturb all of you. But it seems there is new evidence for you to consider."

"He knows something," she whispered to Wren.

Wren took her hand into his and held it tight.

"Nicolette?" Savitar addressed the bear who had been so nasty to them. "Care to share with the council what you told me earlier?"

"Oui."

Zack growled a warning to Nicolette. "Think of what you have to lose, bear."

"Worry about your own ass, tiger," Savitar said snidely. His gaze softened as he looked back to the bear. "Speak, Nicolette. To be rather clichéd, the truth shall set you free."

Nicolette glanced at Wren and Marguerite before she spoke again. "Zack Tigarian admitted to both me and my daughter that he knew Wren hadn't gone mad. That he and his father were accusing him only to get his money."

Another dark-haired man frowned at Nicolette. "What about your earlier testimony? You said you had witnessed his madness yourself."

Nicolette nodded. "He has been more hostile lately, I did not lie. And he has exposed us to unnecessary human scrutiny."

Zack sneered. "He's standing here right now with the daughter of a senator. Tell me what kind of animal would do such a thing? It's obvious he is insane. He even launched himself into a tiger cage at the zoo, where he was filmed by the humans."

Savitar looked at Maggie and Wren with a stoic expression. "Do you have anything to say, Maggie?"

"How do you know my name?"

One corner of his mouth twisted up wryly. "I know everything, kid. And the vast majority of it, I wish I didn't . . . especially those girly thoughts you're having about Wren right now. They're really grossing me out, and I seriously wish Dante would stop thinking about Pandora's . . ." Savitar made a face, then appeared to shake it off. "Now speak if you have something to say that refutes these allegations."

Marguerite let go of Wren's hand to step forward as she addressed the Were-Animals who were gathered at the round table. "In every event that you accuse Wren of, I was there as a witness. He never once attacked unless it was in defense of himself or me. He only jumped into the tigers' cage because a small boy's life was in danger and he knew he could save him. That wasn't madness, it was kindness."

A blond woman sneered at her. "What does a human know?"

Savitar snorted. "Oh, I think our little human knows quite a bit about animals . . . especially now."

Marguerite frowned. By the tone of his voice she could tell that somehow Savitar knew she was part tiger.

Good grief, the man did appear to know everything. It was really scary to think about that.

Wren moved to stand in front of her. "I'm not mad

or insane. There is no *trelosa* inside me. I'm here to be judged as the Omegrion sees fit, but only so long as you promise me that nothing will happen to Maggie."

Zack scoffed at him. "I would fear more for my own life than the human's."

Wren tilted his head as he felt something odd. He turned just as something flashed right behind him.

Before he could react, a man grabbed Maggie, then vanished with her.

Zack laughed an instant before he vanished, too.

"What the hell?" Fury demanded from the round table.

Savitar didn't react at all physically. He sat on his throne completely emotionless. "Well, that was certainly special," he said, his voice laden with sarcasm.

"Are you going to allow someone to threaten the sanctity here?" the jackal representative asked.

"Oh no," Savitar said. He checked his watch. "Let's give them a few minutes before I send the tiger in to finish this."

"Where the hell did he take her?" Wren demanded.

Savitar gave him a droll look. "Hold your horses or, since you're part tiger, your tail."

"She can't stand alone!" Wren roared as his anger boiled inside him. Savitar might not care about Maggie's well-being, but he most certainly did. "You have to send me to her now."

"Fehrista nara gaum."

Wren scowled at words he didn't comprehend. "What does that mean?"

"To make an omelette you must first break some eggs."

. . .

Marguerite was slightly disoriented as she found herself in a posh, overly decorated room. It looked like something one might find in a home-and-gardens magazine. Everything was highly polished and meticulously clean.

She tried to move, but the tiger still held her in a grip from behind that kept her from escaping. For that matter, she could barely breathe.

Closing her eyes, she summoned her powers and tried to make herself a tiger.

It wasn't easy.

But as Zack flashed into the room, she succeeded. The man holding her cursed before he turned into a tiger to attack her. Marguerite caught him a gash to his throat before she bit him hard in the neck.

They weren't going to take her without a fight.

He limped away from her as Zack lunged, then grabbed her from behind. She roared as she tried to bite him, too, but he held her in such a way that she couldn't.

A middle-aged man gasped as he entered the room. Dressed in an expensive black suit, he was the poster boy for the Fortune 500 set.

Marguerite cocked her head. It was Grayson. She knew him instantly due to the fact that he bore an amazing resemblance to Aristotle.

"You got him?" Grayson asked.

"No. It's his human companion."

Grayson shook his head in denial. "How is that possible?"

"Don't ask me," Zack said in an aggravated tone. "You're the elder, Dad." He indicated where the other tiger was lying on the floor, dead and bloody. "She's already killed Theo, and I'm sure Wren will track her to us any minute now."

Grayson approached them cautiously.

Marguerite snapped at Grayson, wanting to tear him apart for what he'd done to not only Wren but Aristotle as well. How could any man kill his own brother?

And over what?

Money?

It was ridiculous and both the woman and animal in her wanted vengeance for the undue pain Grayson had caused Wren.

She did her best to return to human form so that she could tell Grayson exactly what she thought of him, but her body wasn't listening to her at the moment.

Grayson moved toward her, with a deliberate intent. He manifested a butterfly knife in his fist. Twirling it open, he gave her an evil smirk. "Then I say we put her out of her misery and let Wren find her with her throat slit."

"Don't you dare touch her."

Marguerite, as well as Grayson and Zack, froze at the sound of a voice she was sure she'd never hear again.

It couldn't be . . .

She wasn't sure who was the most stunned as Aristotle appeared in the room before them. With his arms crossed over his chest he seemed strangely calm, and yet at the same time his anger was tangible. It was an eerie combination.

"You're dead!" Grayson snapped.

Aristotle laughed. "Do I look dead, Brother?"

"Karina killed you."

Aristotle arched a brow at that. "I thought Wren killed me. Is that not what you claimed?"

Grayson moved away from her slowly, toward the door. "You're a ghost. You have to be. Your mate killed you more than twenty years ago."

"Did she?" Aristotle unfolded his arms and threw a small Japanese throwing star into Zack's arm.

Cursing in pain, Zack let go of Marguerite.

His face a mask of malice, Aristotle turned toward his brother. "I told you a long time ago, Gray, never come between a tiger and his mate."

Grayson changed into a tiger and lunged at Aristotle. Aristotle caught him in his arms and held him close to his heart.

He gave her a grim look. "Do what you have to do to protect Wren, Maggie. He needs you," he said, then vanished.

Marguerite turned on Zack with a snarl.

Wren was livid by the time Savitar allowed him to locate Maggie.

He flashed into an unfamiliar house, ready to do battle with the devil himself if he had to.

But what he found absolutely floored him. Maggie was huddled naked in a corner, shaking and crying, while Zack's tiger body lay a few feet away from her.

Stunned and terrified of what had been done to her, Wren moved slowly toward Maggie until he could pull her into his arms. She looked up at him with tears in her eyes. His gut knotted as he mentally prepared himself for the worst.

"I killed him, Wren," she breathed, "just as I killed the other one. It was so awful." She wiped at her mouth so hard that he was amazed she didn't rub the skin off. "I can't get the taste of blood out of my mouth."

"Did they . . . are you okay?"

She nodded, then sobbed even harder.

Relieved that they hadn't raped her, he held her close and sent up a silent prayer of thanks. "Shh," he said, pulling her into his lap and putting clothes on her. "You did what you had to do to protect yourself. There's nothing wrong with that."

"But I killed someone."

"You're a tiger now, Maggie. The animal inside you is stronger . . ." He paused as he thought that through. It wasn't true and he knew it. "No. The woman inside you is strong enough to know it had to be done. If you hadn't killed them, they would have killed you."

Marguerite drew a ragged breath as she remembered Wren telling her about how harsh his life was. How brutal. At the time she'd thought he was just being melodramatic.

Now she understood.

He was right, the animal part of herself was satisfied even as the woman in her was horrified. The two parts of her were at war and at peace.

It was so strange.

How could she feel like this? Those had been people, kind of. And she had killed them.

For Wren and for herself. No, he was right. It was self-defense. Had she not killed them, they would have taken a lot more from her.

Wren got up and pulled her to her feet. His eyes were

dark with worry, and it warmed her even through the pain and the horror. "Did you get hurt in the fighting?"

"A few scratches, but I'll live." She looked up at him as the whole event replayed through her thoughts and she shivered. "Your father was here."

Wren stared at her in disbelief. "What?"

She nodded. "Right after Zack brought me here, your father came in and grabbed his brother. I think he took him to the past."

"That doesn't make sense. Why?"

"I don't know. Maybe to confront him?" But even that didn't make sense. It was completely bizarre.

Wren let out an elongated breath. "There's no way to prove my innocence now. We can't even force Zack or Grayson to a confession."

"But they're dead. There's no one to accuse you."

His gaze burned her. "Our justice doesn't work that way." He lifted her hand to his lips and placed the tenderest of kisses on her palm. "C'mon, let's return to the Omegrion."

"No," she said, stopping him. "Let's run. We can—"

"No, Maggie. I've never been a coward and I will not run in this. Besides, Savitar can find me."

Hope flared inside her. "He knows the truth. He said he knows everything. If we can get him—"

"Savitar won't interfere with what the others decide. It's not in his nature."

"Then what good is he?"

Before Wren could answer, they found themselves back in the Omegrion's council room.

Chapter 15

Marguerite swallowed at the extremely unamused look on Savitar's face as he stared straight at her. Surely he hadn't heard what she'd just said to Wren . . .

Had he?

"Yes," he said darkly. "I did, and I ask myself every friggin' day exactly what you did. What good am I? The answer is simple. There's nothing good about me and I like it that way. Pride myself on it, in fact."

Savitar was a really strange man.

And still, he looked ticked off.

She glanced around the room at the council members, who were all staring, not at them, but at the doors. She followed their gazes and then gasped.

Wren frowned until he looked to where everyone else's gaze was. His jaw went slack.

He blinked, trying to clear his vision. But still he saw what couldn't be.

"Dad?"

Wren's father smiled and nodded.

Wren took a hesitant step forward, then caught him-self. This wasn't real. It couldn't be.

His father crossed the distance to pull Wren into a hug. He just stood there in shock, unable to return the embrace. Wren looked at Maggie, who appeared every bit as confused, then at Savitar, who just looked stoic.

Afraid it was a trick, Wren pushed the man who looked like his father away.

"What the hell is this?" Wren demanded.

"Your father didn't die," Savitar said blandly. He pushed himself up from his throne to approach them. "It was one hell of a night. Too bad you passed out and missed the fireworks."

Wren shook his head. "*I* touched him. I saw his body. He was dead. Killed."

"You saw Grayson's body," Wren's father explained.

Savitar waved his hand and on the far wall images appeared. Wren couldn't breathe as he saw his father and uncle fighting as tigers. With one harsh move, Wren's father laid open his brother's throat.

Grayson limped away and died on the floor where Wren remembered finding his father. Two seconds later, the tiger became a man.

"Didn't you ever think it was weird that the dead body appeared human?" Savitar asked him. "By rights, should your father not have been a tiger as a dead man?"

Wren's eyes widened. It was true. He should have thought of that himself, but in the ensuing trauma it had never occurred to him. Not even when he thought back on it. Not that he made a habit of dwelling on that night.

"I don't understand."

His father placed a hand on Wren's shoulder. "My brother was actually Arcadian, like our mother. And he hated it about himself. Like you, he hid what he was from the world. He never learned to come to terms with it. It was why I didn't trust him. He had all the power of a tiger and all the jealousy and hatred of a human."

"I told you bastards it was all about the money."

Wren frowned at Dante Pontis, who was giving the council an I-told-you-so smirk from his seat at the table.

Wren's father cleared his throat, drawing his attention back to him. "While you and Maggie were off, I started thinking about what the two of you had said about the night you found me. And I remembered you saying I was human. I realized it wasn't me you had seen. It couldn't have been. I am a tiger and I would have been a tiger in death."

"But you gave me your powers," Maggie said, confused.

Aristotle shook his head. "I gave you the powers my mother conferred on me. I kept my own." His eyes turned haunted as he faced Wren. "I knew that Karina must have seen Grayson, and his face must have been so badly damaged by whatever killed him that she assumed it was me, since I would never have allowed my brother to enter my home—unless I brought him there myself to fight. I kept trying to think of why I would have done it and when."

His gaze sharpened as he tightened his grip on Wren's shoulder. "Then it occurred to me. If Grayson was alive to accuse you before you came back, then I must have brought him back in time to kill him after you left."

Wren looked at Marguerite. "Are you following this?"

"Not really, but in a weird way, I think I get it." She looked at his father. "If you killed Grayson, then who killed Karina?"

Wren's father took a deep breath. "I did. I assumed that I was still supposed to die that night, so after they penned you, I confronted her and her lover. We fought, and during it, her lover fell into the fireplace. He dragged the coals out into the room and it set fire to the house before he died. Karina and I went down fighting hard. By the time I killed her, there were flames everywhere and I assumed I was meant to die in the fire. I passed out, and when I awoke, I was in an animal shelter."

Wren was completely stunned by the revelation. His father had been alive all these years? "Why didn't you ever tell me?"

"Because he knew you had to grow up without him," Marguerite said quietly. "Otherwise everything would change."

Aristotle nodded. "You wouldn't have come back to warn me about my death, and had you not done that, I would have died, as would *you*. I wouldn't have changed my will and you would have gone into Grayson's custody."

Savitar moved to stand beside them. "It's true. Everything played out just as it was supposed to."

Wren still couldn't believe it. How was all this meant to be? "Where have you been hiding all these years?" he asked his father.

He gave a sheepish grin. "Running the company be-hind the scenes in the guise of a human. It's why no

one ever bothered you while you were at Sanctuary."
He winked at Wren. "You didn't really think I'd let a
human handle things, did you? But I really appreciate
the tips you two gave me. World Wide Web. You were
right, it's one hell of a thing."

Marguerite was completely stunned by all this.

Aristotle tsked. "I have to say it was hard not getting
the jump on Microsoft after what you said, but I was
too damned grateful to be alive to screw with the Fates
over that. Second-best is better than dead."

Dante whistled from the table to get their attention.
"You know this is all real charming and interesting . . .
well, not really. I'm bored and I have things to do at
home. So are the rest of us free to go now?"

Savitar shrugged. "Depends. Is the death order on
Wren lifted?"

"The man is alive," Vane said to the others. "And he
admits he killed his mate in self-defense. I don't see how
Wren could possibly be responsible. I move to rescind."

Savitar nodded his agreement. "Anyone second it?"

"I do," Dante said.

Savitar scanned the group. "All in favor say aye."

It was unanimous.

"Then you're all free to go," Savitar said drily.

They poofed out. All except Dante, who sauntered
over to them.

"Congrats, tiger," he said, extending his hand to
Wren. "I knew you were innocent. And if you ever
need a sanctuary, Dante's Inferno is there for you. . . . I
just hope you don't mind freezing your ass off in the
wintertime. Bring a parka. It's cold in the Twin Cities."

Wren was warmed by his offer. "Thanks, Dante."

"No prob." He smiled at Maggie, then winked at her. "Good luck. I have a feeling the two of you are going to need it." He vanished.

Wren turned to face Savitar. He did something he'd never done to another living soul. He offered the immortal his hand. "Thank you. For everything."

Savitar shook it. "I don't take credit for this. All I did was pick your rank ass up and cart it off to New Orleans. The rest was you and your father." He let go of Wren's hand and stepped back. "Now if you'll excuse me . . . surf's up."

Savitar placed a pair of sunglasses on his face as his clothes faded into a black wetsuit. Then he, too, vanished.

Wren stared at his father as he tried to come to terms with all this. "I can't believe this is real. I can't believe you're really alive."

"You can't?" Aristotle asked in disbelief. "I'm the one who's been living with an alias all these years." He shivered. "Josiah Crane. Is that crap or what?"

Maggie smiled at him. "I think it's a wonderful name."

Aristotle sobered as he looked at her. "I'm sorry I left you alone with Zack when I grabbed Grayson. He didn't hurt you, did he?"

She shook her head.

"Good." Aristotle pulled his wallet out and opened it. "Look, I know the two of you have a lot to do when you get back to New Orleans." He pulled a business card out and handed it to Wren. "Give me a call sometime. If you ever get up to New York, drop by."

Wren took the card and nodded. "I'll be by, Dad."

Wren's father looked at her hopefully. "And Maggie?"

"I'll be right by his side."

Aristotle beamed at them. "Excellent. Now if I could only take those powers back so that I'd be fully charged . . . Ah, what the hell? They look better on you anyway."

Wren hugged his father, who then pulled away to hug Maggie. "You two take care."

Maggie stepped back from him. "You, too."

He nodded, then left them alone.

Marguerite watched as Wren put his father's card into his pocket.

"So what now?" she asked, wondering how they could just simply go home after all that had happened to them.

To her complete shock, Wren dropped to his knee in front of her. He took her hand into his and stared up at her. "Marguerite, lady tiger, will you marry me?"

She couldn't breathe as she heard those words. He couldn't be proposing to her? Not as a human. It wasn't possible. "We're not mated."

He shrugged nonchalantly. "Fuck the Fates and what they want. Mark or no mark, I love you and I want to spend the rest of my life with you."

Marguerite's vision dimmed as tears filled her eyes. Obscenities aside, she'd never heard anything more lovely.

His grip tightened on her hand as if he were afraid she'd deny him. "Will you marry me, baby?"

"Of course I will." She gave him a devilish smile. "Besides, it's not like I could marry a regular guy now anyway. I might accidentally eat him during a full moon or something."

Wren returned her devilish smile with one of his own as he rose slowly to his feet and pulled her into his arms. He cupped her face in his warm hands. "You don't have to wait for the light of a full moon, Maggie. I'll be your dinner anytime you're hungry."

Marguerite laughed as she held him close. This was without a doubt the happiest moment of her life.

Until she remembered something. "We can't have children, can we?"

Wren pulled back and shook his head. "We can always adopt. That is, if you don't mind."

"I don't mind, but are you sure that you don't?"

"No. As long as I have you, I'll always be happy."

Marguerite pulled his head down toward hers to give him a hot, sizzling kiss.

Now, she just had to find some way to explain all of this to her father.

Chapter 16

Two days later

With Maggie by his side, Wren walked through the doors of Sanctuary like he owned it. It was so strange to be back after all that had happened. There was an eerie sense of déjà vu that he couldn't quite shake.

He'd spent the last twenty years cleaning tables here, never once thinking about a time when he wouldn't call this place home. Never thinking about the world that existed outside these walls. He'd lived here as a recluse and a hollowed-out shell.

Now he was facing a whole new life with a whole new family. Maggie, Marvin, and his father. It was scary in a way and yet he looked forward to it. It was almost as if he'd been reborn. The old Wren was gone and in his place was a man who knew exactly what he wanted.

And that was the woman at his side.

His heart pounding, he held Maggie to him as he walked up to Dev, who was sitting in front of the door.

"Welcome back," the bear said to him as if nothing had happened.

"Yeah," Wren scoffed. "Don't worry. I'm not staying. I'm only here to get Marvin, unless one of you bastards ate him."

Dev's eyes danced with humor. "Remi tried to, but that little bugger is fast. He's been hiding out in Aimee's room ever since."

Wren wasn't amused. Without another word, he led Maggie through the bar, to the kitchen, and to the door that led to Peltier House. As was typical, Remi was there with a scowl on his face.

"Blow me, bear," Wren snarled at Remi's intimidation. "Move your lumbering ass or get it kicked."

Remi crossed his arms over his chest as he glared defiantly at Wren.

"Let him pass, *mon ange.*"

Wren glanced over his shoulder to see Nicolette behind them. Her face was stoic, but for once he sensed no animosity from her.

Remi's face registered shock at his mother's words. "The woman—"

"She is cleared to go with him," Nicolette said, interrupting Remi. "She's one of us now."

Wren inclined his head to her before he smirked at Remi. Remi wanted to fight, he could smell it. But fortunately for the bear, he moved aside.

Wren opened the door and let Maggie enter first. He still didn't trust the bears, and he wanted to keep his eye on her while they were here to make sure no one hurt her in any way.

Lo followed him into the parlor. "I'm sorry for what happened, tiger."

He laughed bitterly at that. "No, you're not."

Nicolette pulled him to a stop as he reached the stairs. "It was your own fault, you know? You were never really one of us here."

"Never one of your dupes, you mean." Wren shook his head. "No, Lo, I wasn't. Unlike the other fools here who would lay down their lives for you, I do know the truth. You do what you have to, but in the end, you don't want any of us here. We're nothing to you but a means to an end, and in a weird way, I almost respect that. It's Darwin's law. Either you eat the bear or the bear eats you. My goal is to be the diner, never the dinner."

Wren looked to where Maggie waited on the first step, watching him with pride gleaming in her brown eyes. "I only owe my loyalty to one person."

Nicolette nodded. "I understand. And our laws still apply. Now that you've been pardoned—"

"Save it, Lo. I've got enough human in me that I don't intend to let bygones be bygones. You turned on me and I can't forget that. I have too much to lose now."

Nicolette inclined her head to him. "Then you will understand if I ask you to leave?"

"I'm just here for the monkey."

"Then get it and get out."

"Believe me, I intend to." Wren headed up the stairs with Maggie in front of him. He led her down the hallway to Aimee's room before he knocked and waited.

"Come in."

He pushed open the door to find the bearswan on her bed in human form, watching TV. Marvin dropped the banana in his hands, then ran screaming at Wren. He launched himself into Wren's arms.

Wren caught him against his chest with a laugh. "Hey, buddy," he said as the monkey latched his arms around his neck and hugged him tight. "I missed you, too."

By Aimee's face, Wren could tell she was stunned to see him here.

"Thanks for watching out for him."

"My pleasure."

As Wren turned to leave, Aimee stopped him. "I have a few things for you."

He frowned as she knelt by her bed and pulled out a plastic box. "It's the handful of things that you left behind."

Wren was stunned to see the sweatshirt Maggie had given him along with the rest of his clothes.

"I know how weird you are about your scent, so I put it in an airtight container."

A wave of tenderness for the bearswan swept through him. Unlike her mother, Aimee was human, and for once he didn't mean that in a derogatory way. "Thanks, Aimee."

She smiled at them. "No problem."

"How's Fang doing?" Maggie asked.

Sadness darkened Aimee's features as she looked away. "I don't know. I'm not allowed to see him anymore. They're watching me now. All the time."

Wren felt for her. He couldn't imagine what it must be like to be banned from the person he loved. He would kill anyone or anything who came between him and Maggie. "I'm really sorry."

A bittersweet smile curved Aimee's lips as she looked back at them. "Don't be. You two give me hope."

"For what?" Wren asked.

"For my own future." Aimee kissed him lightly on the cheek. "You two take care."

He inclined his head to her. "You, too, Aimee."

Marvin leapt from Wren's shoulder to Maggie's. He ruffled her hair, then placed a kiss on her forehead.

Maggie laughed. "I think he likes me."

"He better," Wren said in a light tone. He looked back at Aimee. "Good luck, bearswan."

"Thanks, cub."

Wren wrapped his arm around Maggie and flashed them back to her house.

No, it was *their* house now.

He finally had a home. After all this time, he had somewhere he really belonged. The feeling washed over him with a joy the likes of which he'd only known in one place . . .

Maggie's arms.

"Poor Aimee," Maggie said as she took Marvin to see where his food and water were kept on the kitchen counter. "Do you think she'll ever find a way to be with Fang?"

"I don't know. To have him, she'd have to give up her family. I doubt that'll ever happen."

Marguerite sighed dreamily as Wren came up behind her while Marvin splashed in his water cup. She leaned her forehead against Wren's cheek as he held her close. The scent of him enveloped her and made her hungry for him.

Everything was perfect. Or at least very close to it. Because of the time travel, she'd only missed one week of school. With the help of Dr. Alexander, she'd be able to make it up without an incident and without failing.

She and Wren had decided that she would finish up her last semester of law school and then they would travel for a while before she even thought about taking the bar exam.

That sounded like heaven to her.

As Wren held her, she watched Marvin explore her kitchen cabinet. "Where did Marvin come from?"

She could feel Wren smiling. "I don't know. He was in Savitar's car when he saved me. He's been with me ever since."

"He's a cute little monkey." She sighed as she felt Wren's bulge against her hip while he gently nuzzled her neck.

"Marvin," Wren said in a husky voice. "Go check out your bedroom and shut the door."

The monkey squealed at Wren before he complied.

"Smart monkey," Marguerite said with a laugh.

"Mmm," Wren breathed against her throat before he gently laved her skin.

Fire coursed through her veins as he lifted the hem of her short leather skirt and ran his hands over her.

"You are a hungry little tiger, aren't you?" she said as he pushed her panties down her legs.

"Insatiable." He loosened his pants before he lifted the hem of her skirt to bare her from the waist down. He raised her up to sit on the countertop.

Marguerite hissed as he slid himself deep inside her.

She wrapped her body around his as he thrust against her hips.

She loved feeling the power of him inside her. Loved the fact that he was all hers. There was nothing else like her Wren.

She clasped him to her as she came fiercely.

Wren growled as he felt her body convulsing around his. There was nothing in life he treasured more than this woman. He quickened his strokes and in a few more thrusts he joined her in her paradise.

He held her to him and let her breath scorch his skin. Their bodies still joined, he reveled in the feel of her. For her, he was willing to do anything.

"Do you mind if I stay right here inside you for the rest of the day?"

She actually purred. "Not at all."

Biting her lip, she stroked him with her body, making him hard all over again.

Wren growled at how good she felt as he reached down to unbutton her silk blouse. He smiled at the fact that she wasn't wearing a bra.

"I know how much you hate them," she said as if she could read his thoughts.

He smiled at her before he dipped his head down to taste the taut peak.

Marguerite moaned at the sensation of his tongue flicking back and forth so very torturously. With every stroke, her body contracted, moving her dangerously close to another orgasm.

Just as she was sure she'd come again, she heard Marvin screaming from the other room.

Wren pulled out of her with a curse.

"What is it?" she asked, half-afraid someone else was coming for them.

"He says there's someone pulling into your driveway."

Marguerite frowned. No one should be visiting. She'd already told Todd, Blaine, and the others that she wasn't interested in their study group anymore.

Who could it be?

She buttoned her blouse while Wren refastened his pants. As she straightened her skirt, someone started pounding on her door.

She exchanged a scowl with Wren as she went to open it. The minute she swung it open, she felt the instant need to slam it shut.

It was her father, and he was flanked by two Secret Servicemen. All three of them were dressed in black power suits. They made quite a spectacle on her stoop.

"Oh goody," she said under her breath. "It's the X-Files."

Her father glared at her. "Don't be smart with me, young lady. Have you any idea what you interrupted? I don't have time to be flying down here to see what's going on with you while you flunk out of school and hang up on me."

Marguerite let out a tired breath as she gave him a bored stare. Without speaking to him, she left the door open and walked nonchalantly over to her small desk. She looked over at Wren and sent a silent warning to him: *"I'll handle this."*

Wren looked less than pleased. *"Are you sure?"*

She nodded even though she could feel his irritation at her father rising.

Her father curled his lip as he entered the house with his men flanking him. "And what is that get-up you have on, Marguerite? You look like a streetwalker."

She glanced down at her black miniskirt and high heels. She'd bought the outfit just yesterday after Wren had told her how much he loved seeing her legs. Her burgundy silk blouse was a little slinky, but it was sedate enough. She hardly looked like a prostitute.

And deep inside, her own anger rose. She wasn't thirteen anymore and this man didn't run her life.

"Yes, but the question is, Daddy, do I look like a cheap ho or an expensive one?"

"You don't look like either one," Wren growled.

She smiled at him.

Her father curled his lip at the sight of Wren. "Is this the busboy you've been gallivanting around with?"

Marguerite walked over to Wren, who pulled her into his arms. "Yes, Daddy. He's my busboy and I'm in love with him. We're going to get married at the end of the month."

Her father took a threatening step toward her.

She felt Wren tense as if to fight. *"I have him, love, let me do my thing."*

Wren relaxed only a tiny degree.

"What in the hell are you thinking?" her father snarled.

Marguerite refused to make any apologies to him. "This is my life, Dad, and from now on, I'm going to live it. I would really like for you to be a part of it, but if you can't, then fine. I'm through trying to please you."

His handsome face hardened. "You better listen to

me, young lady. I happen to *own* your life. That car, this house, the school you attend . . . You can't afford even the bill for your cell phone on your own. You marry this bum and you're out of this house. I'll cut you off so fast, your head will spin."

"Fine," she said in a bored tone. "We'll move, then."

Her father looked sick to his stomach. "And where will you go? Oh wait, I forgot. You can go anywhere they need a busboy to clean tables. Think about it, Marguerite, don't be a fool. Don't throw your life away for a cheap piece of trash you picked up in a bar. People don't live on love. It won't feed you and it won't protect you."

"There you're wrong, Dad. Wren can, and will, keep me safe."

He screwed his face up in anger. "Damn you! After all I've done for you . . . given you. How dare you spit in my face? And for what? So that you can get back at me by doing this?"

"This isn't about *you*, Daddy. This is about me and Wren. You have nothing to do with why I'm in love with Wren. Nothing."

He narrowed his eyes on them. "I want you both out of this house by tomorrow."

"Fine."

His face turned to stone. "This isn't a game, Marguerite, and I'm not joking. I'll see you on the street before I let you toss away your life. I'm canceling your credit cards as soon as I leave here and I'm cleaning out your student bank account. In the next few hours you will have absolutely nothing."

She leaned back against Wren and looked up at him.

"So where do you think we should live, hon? Which pathetic little hovel appeals to you?"

Wren shrugged. "Well, we have the estate in northern Scotland, but it's kind of cold there and you know how I feel about the cold. There's the estate on a game preserve we have in South Africa. An island in the Pacific that's supposed to be really nice. I've never been there, but my mother used to love it and my dad said it's ours anytime we want it. It's not a really big place, only about ten square miles or so. But we own it. And then there's the boat that's docked in the Bahamas." He paused at that. "Well, it is a boat, but it has ten bedrooms, so it's kind of like a house. Then we own the upper two floors of the Tigarian building, but that's like living above the shop, in my opinion. Not to mention the city is loud."

He made a thinking noise with his teeth. "But you know, since you want to finish school, we could buy that house over in the Garden District that you liked so much."

"You mean the three-story mansion with the pool?"

He nodded. "Yeah. It's only what? Four and a half million? I'll get my accountant on it and we should be able to move in by tomorrow."

Her father's eyes were getting bigger by the second. "What bullshit is this?"

"It's not bullshit, Daddy. It's truth."

Still her father refused to believe it. "He's lying to you, Marguerite. Wake up and don't be stupid."

She arched a brow at her father. "I have a question, Daddy. I know how much you've been wanting to cozy up to State Senator Laurens and shmooze him for contributions because he, as you so often say, has more money than God. Do you know where his family got their money?"

"Of course. They're stockholders in the Tigarian corporation."

She nodded. "Want to meet the man who holds fifty-two percent of those stocks?"

His jaw actually went slack. "It's not possible."

Marguerite smiled at him. "Yes, Daddy, it is. Meet Wren Tigarian. The man who owns the enchilada."

It was the first time in her life that she'd ever seen her father speechless.

Marguerite turned and did something completely crass and gauche. She whistled for Marvin. As soon as the monkey was in her arms, she stepped away from Wren and picked up her keys from the counter.

With a confidence she'd never known before, she walked over to her father and handed the keys to him. "No offense, Dad, I don't want the life you gave me. I want the one I'm going to make for myself . . . with Wren. You're welcome to everything here. I'm through letting you control me."

She closed his hands over her keys. "I do love you, Daddy, and I would like for you to be a part of my future. But if you can't, that's your decision. I'm not your scared little girl anymore who's terrified that she's going to embarrass you. I'm Maggie Goudeau now and I know what I want. When you decide that you can love and accept me without conditions, give me a call."

She let go of him and turned to take Wren's hand. For the first time in her life, she felt free. Happy. The future stretched out before her with a vastness that would have scared her a few weeks earlier.

Now she looked forward to the challenge of it.

As they left the house, she half-expected her father to call her back, but he didn't.

And that was okay. Her father would need time and she had . . . literally centuries ahead of her.

Without looking back, she got into Wren's vintage red Mustang and held Marvin in her lap.

"Are you sure about this?" Wren asked as he joined her in the car.

"Absolutely."

Wren picked her hand up and kissed her palm lightly. "So where are we off to?"

She gave him a hot once-over. "I vote for a quiet hotel where we can finish what my father interrupted."

Wren gave her a wicked grin at that. "Here, here, lady tiger. Sounds like a plan to me."

Maggie's smile faded as she looked back to see her father on her front porch, watching them leave. The little girl in her wanted to run back to him and hug him.

But she wasn't a child anymore, and until he could accept that, there was nothing more to be said between them.

Good-bye, Daddy.

She only hoped that one day he would come to his senses. But until he did, that wasn't her problem. She refused to let him hold her back anymore.

Her heart lighter, she looked down at her unmarked palm. "Wren? Do you think we'll ever be mates?"

Wren glanced over at her. "We already are, Maggie. I don't need some external mark to tell me what I know."

She smiled at him. "I love you, Wren."

He reached over and took her hand into his. "I love you, too, baby."

And that was the greatest miracle of all. "So you're sure you still want to marry me? Bad in-laws and all?"

He snorted. "In-laws don't frighten me. If he doesn't come around, I can always eat him."

She laughed. "Okay, so I at least know what to put on the caterer's menu. One senator's head. Cool."

Wren joined her laughter, but even as he did, he felt the sadness inside her, and for that he really could kill her father. He couldn't understand how the man could be such a jerk to his only child. If Wren ever had one of his own, he would make sure that they never doubted his love.

But that didn't help Maggie. "It'll be okay, Maggie, trust me."

"I do."

Wren squeezed her hand before he let go and headed toward the French Quarter. As he stopped at a light, he looked over at her and made himself a promise. Her father might not love her, but Wren would give her so much of his own that she would never miss it.

And that was something she could definitely take to the bank.

Epilogue

One month later

Marguerite smiled up at Wren as they stood in the small yard behind their new house in the Garden District. The air was a bit warm and muggy, which was why she'd chosen to get married in a very sedate strapless, tea-length wedding dress. She had her hair up with tiny white flowers in it, but no veil.

Wren looked gorgeous, if not a little warm, in his black tie and tails. For the first time, his hair wasn't worn in his eyes. He'd actually brushed it back from his face.

"I'm going into this with my eyes wide open and I want nothing to blur my vision . . ."

Those words that he'd spoken earlier still warmed her.

Their wedding party was small with only Elise, Whitney, Tammy, Vane, Bride who held her infant son, Fury, Fang, Aristotle . . . and of course Marvin who was dressed in a small monkey tuxedo since he was the best man.

Marguerite's father had been invited, but apparently he'd been too busy to come and that was fine with her.

She didn't want anything to mar this day anyway. Better he be absent than here and scowling.

Wren kissed her ring finger where her sedate gold band was before he kissed her lips as the priest announced them as husband and wife. A part of her was more than amused at that since they were more tiger and tigerswan these days, but that was another story.

As soon as Wren released her, her friends came forward to hug and congratulate her. Marguerite embraced them while she listened to the wolves harass Wren.

"Now you're like Vane, tied down for eternity," Fury said with a shudder. "Man, you're stupid. Unlike Vane, you don't even have a reason for it."

"You better be quiet, Fury," Vane said, laughing. "Or I'll turn Bride loose on you."

"Yeah," Bride agreed as she handed her son off to his father. "I know a little demon who likes the taste of wolf meat . . ."

They all laughed, except for Elise, Tammy, and Whitney, who just looked confused.

When they adjourned inside the house for the reception, Marguerite pulled up short as they met Savitar in the hallway. Arching his brow, Vane paused to stare at the man who was dressed in a pair of white slouchy pants and a blue-and-white beach shirt that was left hanging open to show off his eight-pack of abs. "Do you ever wear anything except beach clothes?"

Savitar shrugged. "Everything else chafes. Besides, easy on . . . easy off."

Marguerite wrinkled her nose at his words. "Ew. TMI . . . way too much information."

"Agreed," Wren said as Vane shook his head and followed the others into their dining room.

Once they were alone, Wren frowned at Savitar. "So, to what do we owe the honor?"

Savitar gave them a cocky half-grin. "I'm sorry to crash your wedding, but I won't be long."

"You don't have to rush off on our account," Maggie said quickly.

Wren agreed. "We have plenty of food if you'd like to stay. We would have invited you, but I didn't think weddings were your scene."

"They're not," he said drily. "But I wanted to give the two of you a gift from a friend."

Wren's frown increased. "You don't have to do that."

"I know, but I want to do it." Without anything more, Savitar joined Wren's left hand with her right one and held them in his.

Gasping, Marguerite felt a sudden burning. She withdrew her hand to find a small, intricate tattoo-like mark on her palm. "What the—"

"It's a mating mark," Wren said in a low tone as he looked from his hand to Savitar. "I don't understand. Is this real?"

Savitar nodded. "I don't trust the Fates. Those three bitches have a nasty sense of humor, and the last thing I want is to see them mate you to someone else just for spite. Besides, I'm sure the two of you would like to have kids some day." A deep sadness entered his eyes, but it quickly passed. "Everyone should have a chance to see their kids grow up."

Wren looked aghast. "But you can't screw with fate."

Savitar gave him a wicked grin. "*You* can't, little tiger, but I do what I please. Fates be damned. If they want a piece of me, then bring it on. I couldn't care less what they think and at the end of the day, they know who not to tangle with." He winked at them. "You two kids have a great life. I'm gonna go catch a wave and zen."

Marguerite's jaw was slack as Savitar faded into nothing. She rubbed the mark on her right hand with her left one. "Is this legit?"

Wren took her hand into his. "I think it is."

"Then we can have children . . ."

Wagging his eyebrows at her, he gave her a smile that was completely lecherous. Seductive. "There's only one way to know. I vote we ditch the wedding party and find out."

She laughed at the eager look on his face. "You are so bad."

He growled low in his throat as he gave her a hot once-over. "I can't help it. You look way too edible in that dress."

Wren pulled back at the sound of someone clearing his throat.

Marguerite blushed to see his father standing in the doorway.

Aristotle shook his head at them. "Some of us *in here* are also hungry, so do you mind if we eat the food without you?"

Wren visibly cringed. "Sorry, Dad. We're coming."

His father gave him an arched stare as if he didn't believe it.

As they started into the dining room, they were interrupted yet again by the doorbell.

Wren and Marguerite exchanged a frown.

"It's not anyone on my side," Wren said, "we don't knock."

She rolled her eyes at him. "It's probably UPS. I vote we add the delivery man who dared to interrupt us to the menu."

Wren laughed. "I don't know. I think your friends would be grossed out." He headed for the door.

She watched as he opened it, then went ramrod stiff.

Scowling at his actions and curious what caused them, she walked forward at the same time as he opened the door wider. Marguerite faltered as she saw her father on the doorstep, looking a bit sheepish.

Wren moved back to let him into the house. A flash of relief went over her father's face as he saw her, until it was replaced by disappointment and grief.

"I'm sorry I'm late, buttercup," he said gruffly. "I really did try to make it, but there was an all-night session in Congress and the weather was so bad that the flight was delayed. I got here as soon as I could."

Marguerite didn't know what stunned her most. His apology or the use of a nickname she hadn't heard from his lips since she was a little girl.

"It's okay, Daddy."

"No, it isn't." He cleared his throat before he pulled a small box out of his coat pocket. "I started to send this to you, but I thought I'd come here to give it to you in person." He handed her the box.

Marguerite frowned at it. It was an old 1950s-style, light-blue necklace box. "What is it?"

"Your grandmother's pearls. Your mother wore

them at our wedding and she wanted you to have them for yours."

Tears welled up in her eyes. It had been years since her father had spoken of her mother in such a way.

Wren came up behind her to place a comforting hand on her back as she opened the box and saw the perfect strand of white pearls and matching earrings.

"They're beautiful."

Her father inclined his head. "Like your mother . . . and like you."

Her lips trembled as her tears started falling. And then Marguerite did something she hadn't done since her mother's death. She hugged her father.

For the first time in her memory, he didn't tense and move away. He wrapped his arms around her and held her close.

"I love you, Daddy," she whispered against his cheek.

"I love you, too, Marguerite." He tightened his arms around her an instant before he straightened up and wiped at the tears on her face. His smile was tinged by sadness. "I'm sorry I wasn't here to give you away. I should have at least called."

"It's okay."

Wren took the pearls from the box. As he moved to put them on her, her father stopped him.

"You have the rest of your life to help her with these. If you don't mind, I'd like to do it just this once."

"Sure," Wren said as he handed them over.

Marguerite gave a less than ladylike sniff as she met Wren's turquoise eyes. The love in his gaze warmed her.

Her father fastened the pearls, then moved to stand

in front of Wren. "I know I've been a prick to you both, but I'm a big enough man to admit when I've been wrong." He glanced at her. "You are my daughter, Marguerite, and if he makes you happy, then that's the best I can ask for. I've given a lot of thought about what you said over the last few weeks and I do want to be part of your life . . . if you'll let me."

"Of course, Daddy. No matter what, you'll always be my father."

His eyes softened until he looked back at Wren. "Shall we bury the hatchet? No more hard feelings?"

Marguerite held her breath as she waited expectantly for Wren's response.

He hesitated a moment before he took her father's hand and shook it. "None whatsoever so long as you only make her cry in happiness."

Her father placed his other hand over Wren's. "Don't worry. I have no intention of ever hurting her."

Yet again they heard someone clear his throat. Marguerite turned to see Aristotle standing once more in the doorway.

"Are we *ever* going to eat?" he asked.

Marguerite laughed. "We are definitely going to eat," she said before she introduced her father to Wren's.

And as the four of them rejoined the rest of the dinner party, she felt a warm rush go through her.

"You okay?" Wren asked as he took her hand to lead her to the table.

"I was just thinking that I wish my mother was here."

"I'm sure that she's looking down on you and smiling."

Marguerite kissed his cheek. In a weird way, she felt that he was right, and in that moment she realized that this day really was perfect.

And she had one person to thank for it, and it was the one person she intended to spend the rest of her life thanking. She squeezed that person's hand before she took a seat with his help, and he sat down by her side.

As they started their meal, Marguerite smiled at Wren. There might not be another perfect day in their future, but they had this one and as long as she had Wren beside her, she knew that no matter what the future held, they would always face it like this. Together.

Savitar forced a blank expression on his face as he neared the lone figure who was sitting on his beach, watching the surf roll in. Dressed in a tacky Hawaiian shirt and a pair of surfer shorts, the dark-haired man was leaning back on his arms with his attention off somewhere else entirely.

He knew that faraway look. It was one he wore a lot himself. And it was why the beach was the only thing that offered him any kind of comfort.

The ocean, like time, was endless and ever changing. Vast. Empty. Overwhelming.

Folding his arms over his chest, he neared the man on the beach. "I delivered your present to them."

Nick Gautier looked up at him then. From Nick's face, Savitar could tell it took a few seconds for those words to register.

"Thanks for the favor, Savitar."

"No problem. They're good kids."

Nick nodded as a sad smile hovered at the edges of his lips. "I would never have thought Maggie had it in her to fight for her future. Wren either for that matter. It's good to see your friends happy, isn't it?"

Savitar snorted. "How would I know? I have no friends. People basically suck and all friends will screw you over in the end. Take my word for it."

"Then why am I here?"

"Hell if I know." But that wasn't the truth. Nick was here because Acheron had asked it of him and Acheron was one of the very few beings Savitar would never deny.

"Tell me something, Sav. Will they—"

"They'll live happily ever after. Don't worry. Raise lots of little tigers and think of you from time to time. Hell, they'll even name their firstborn after you . . . of course it'll be a girl, but little Nikki won't mind her name. She'll think it's cool."

Nick nodded, but even so, Savitar could feel his pain. Nick hadn't wanted to die, and his death had screwed him over in more ways than one.

But life and death went on. He knew that better than anyone.

"C'mon, kid," he said, inclining his head toward the waves. "Surf 's up."

Nick rolled his eyes at him. "Are you ever going to train me as a Dark-Hunter?"

"Yeah, but right now, I've got bigger things on my mind. A twenty-footer is heading to shore and I want a piece of it."

Nick sighed as he pushed himself up. Savitar was already dressed in his wetsuit as he waded his way into the water. A surfboard appeared alongside him.

He was grateful Savitar had taken him in since right now he couldn't face Acheron without wanting to kill the bastard for what had happened the night Nick died. But honestly, he was getting tired of sitting on his ass, waiting for his training to begin.

His old life was over. He knew that. There was no way to go back to what he'd known. No way back to New Orleans.

Now, like Wren and Maggie, it was time for a new chapter to begin in his life.

And he could feel it coming, just like the wave that was cresting . . .

Here's a taste of the next
Dark-Hunter book from
Sherrilyn Kenyon

DARK SIDE
of the
Moon

Available from St. Martin's Paperbacks

Seattle, 2006

"BOY EATEN BY KILLER MOTHS"

Susan Michaels groaned as she saw the headline for her latest story. she knew better than to read the rest of the article, but something inside her just wanted to feel kicked this afternoon. God forbid that she ever take pride in her work again . . .

Bred in a lab in South America, these top-secret moths are the next generation of military assassins. They are genetically engineered to think their way into an enemy's lair where they bite the neck of the target and infect them with a concentrated poison that will render their victim dead within an hour.

Now they have escaped the lab and were last seen heading north, straight for the U.S. . . .

Dear Lord, it was worse than she had thought.

Her hands shaking in anger, she got up from her desk and headed straight into Leo's office. As usual, he was online, reading someone's blog and making copious notes.

Leo was a short, lean man with long black hair that he always wore in a ponytail. He also had a goatee and cold, gray eyes. He was dressed in a baggy black t-shirt and jeans with a giant Starbucks travel mug at his elbow while he worked. In his late thirties, he'd be cute if he wasn't so damned annoying.

"Killer moths?" she asked.

He looked up from his notepad and shrugged. "You said we were going to have a moth invasion, I just had Joanie rewrite the story to make it more marketable."

She gaped in total astonishment. "Joanie? You had *Joanie* rewrite the story? The woman who wears tinfoil in her bra so that the people with X-ray vision can't see her breasts? *That* Joanie?"

He didn't flinch or miss a beat. "Yeah, she's my best writer."

Talk about insult to injury . . . "I thought *I* was your best writer."

Sighing heavily, he swiveled his chair to face her. "You would be *if* you had any imagination whatsoever." He held his hands up dramatically as if to illustrate his point. "C'mon, Sue, embrace your inner child. Embrace the absurd that lives amongst us. Think Ibsen." He put his hands down and gave another weary sigh. "But no, you never do. I send you out to investigate the bat boy who lives in the old church belfry and you come back with a story about moths infesting the rafters. What the hell is that?"

She gave him a droll stare as she crossed her arms over her chest. "It's called reality, Leo. Reality. You should stop 'shrooming sometime and try it."

He snorted at that before he flipped to a blank sheet of paper on his notepad. He set it beside his coffee. "Screw reality. It don't feed my dog. It don't make my Porsche payments. It don't get me laid. . . . Bullshit does that, and I like it."

She rolled her eyes at his beaming face. "You are such a toad."

He paused as if an idea had struck him. He reached for his pad where he quickly scribbled something. "Employee Kisses Toady Boss to Discover an Ancient Prince . . . I like it. Can you imagine? Women all over the country will be kissing their bosses to test the theory." Then he looked back at her with a wicked grin. "Shall we try the experiment and see if it works?"

"Hell, no. And that wasn't a come-on. Trust me, even with a thousand kisses you'd still be a toad."

He was totally undaunted. "I still think we should give it a try." He wagged his eyebrows at her.

Susan let out a long, exasperated breath. "You know, I would bring you up on sexual harassment charges, but that would imply that you actually have had sex and I intend to maintain that you are a prime example of what happens to people when they're sexually frustrated."

That brought another glassy look to his eyes before he scribbled again. "Sexually Frustrated Boss Turns into Screaming Lunatic. Disembowels Woman Who Excites Him."

Susan groaned deep in her throat. If she didn't know better, she'd think he was threatening her, but that would involve actual action on his part, and Leo was nothing if not a complete delegater. His maxim had always been, Why do it yourself when you can hire or bully someone else to do it for you?—which meant he'd probably delegate her to kill herself.

"Leo! Stop turning everything into a cheesy headline." And before he could respond, she quickly added, "I know, I know. Cheesy headlines pay for your Porsche."

"Exactly!"

Disgusted, she rubbed at the sudden pain she felt behind her right eye.

"Look, Sue," he said, as if he felt an uncharacteristic wave of sympathy for her. "I know how hard these last two years have been for you, okay? But you're not an investigative reporter anymore."

Her chest tightened at his words. Words she didn't really need to hear since they haunted her every minute of every day. Two years ago, she'd been one of the foremost investigative reporters in the country. Her former boss had nicknamed her Hound Dog Sue because she could sniff a story from a mile away.

And in one moment, her whole world had come crumbling down. She'd been so hungry that she'd run headlong into a setup that had completely destroyed her reputation.

It had almost cost her her life.

She rubbed at the scar on her wrist as she forced herself not to remember that awful night in November.

But for Leo, she'd never have worked in journalism again. Not that working for the *Daily Inquisitor* could ever be construed as true journalism, but at least it allowed her to pay off some of her gargantuan debt and court costs. And though she hated her job, it kept her fed and off the street. For that she owed the little toad.

Leo tore off a sheet of paper and slid it toward her.

"What's this?" she asked as she took it from his desk.

"It's a Web address. There's this college kid named Dark Angel who claims she's working for the undead."

She stared at him. "A vampire?"

"Not exactly. She says he's an immortal shapeshifting warrior who annoys the hell out of her. She's local so I want you to check it out and see what else she has to say."

Oh, this couldn't be happening to her and yet that old internal voice in her head was already laughing at her. "Shapeshifter. Is that before or after she drops acid?"

Leo made an irritated noise. "Why don't you at least try to get into the spirit of the job? Enjoy it, Sue."

Enjoy it . . . enjoy being a laughingstock after she'd been working for the *Washington Post* . . . yeah. It was hard to Carpe Crap when what she really wanted to do was get her reputation back.

But those days were over. She'd never be a real reporter again. This was it. Her life. Joy, oh joy—the bad luck fairy had really screwed her over.

No, that wasn't true. She'd screwed herself over and she knew it. Heartsick, she turned around and headed back to her desk as she looked at the blog address in her hand.

It's stupid. Don't do it . . .

But she did and there it was . . . a black page with

some hand-drawn gothic artwork on a Web site called *deadjournal.com*. But her absolute favorite part had to be the header that read "Musings from the Dark and Twisted Mind of a Damned College Student."

The girl, Dark Angel, was certainly that.

June 3, 2006, 06:45 a.m.

Someone please shoot me. Please. I really can't stress the please enough. So here I was trying to study for my test tomorrow. Note the word trying. So here I am engrossed in the complexities of Babylonian Math when all of a sudden my cell phone rings and scares the total shit out of me. At first I thought it was my brother harassing me, until I look at it and no. Not him. Those who've been reading my journal know that it's my boss. 5:30 in the morning, there he is. Calling to tell me that he's been attacked by more undead people and that I need to pick him up since it's about to be dawn and he can't make it home before the sun turns him into grilled toast.

Oh, and I have to bring him clothes since he'll most likely be in cat form at Pike's Market and when he switches back into human form he'll be naked. All right, it pisses me off, but I go since he pays me and what do I find? Nothing but a couple of homeless people who think I've lost my mind as I search for my "cat" while holding male clothing.

I'm sure he found some bimbo to shack up with for the day, but dang it all. Couldn't he have called and told me that? No. So here I am, chugging coffee and hoping I stay awake for my test. Thanks, boss. Appreciate it.

Mood: Pissed
Song: "Everything About You": Ugly Kid Joe

Oh yeah. The girl needed some serious psychiatric help. But what the hell? It wasn't like Susan had anything better to do.

Glossary

Abadonna: Atlantean term of honor. Means "the heart of the destroyer."

Act of Vengeance: In exchange for their souls, Artemis allows all new Dark-Hunters to have twenty-four hours to exact revenge on those who wronged them in their human life. After the twenty-four-hour period, they belong to her and are trained by Acheron.

Adelfos: Greek for "brother."

Agrotera, Katra (Kat): She is handmaiden to both Apollymi and Artemis and serves as a bodyguard to Cassandra Peters. She has a mysterious affinity for Acheron, and is known as the Abadonna. In *Seize the Night*, Artemis releases her from her service in order for Apollymi to help Acheron.

Agrotera is also one of the Greek names for Artemis, meaning "strength" or "wild hunter."

Akelos Daimons: A branch of Daimons who have taken an oath to kill only the humans who deserve it—murderers and criminals.

Akra: The Atlantean term for "lady and master."

Akri: The Atlantean term for "lord and master."

Akribos: Greek endearment meaning "dear" or "precious."

Alastor: A demon who sometimes works with the Were-Hunters to cause mischief. Conjured in *Night Play* by Vane's mother, Bryani, to bring Bride back in time to Dark Age Britain.

Alexander, Grace: A down-to-earth psychologist, Grace has the fortune (or misfortune) to count psychic Selena Laurens as a best friend. She is the wife of Julian Alexander and heroine of *Fantasy Lover*. And yes, both she and her husband are immortal.

Alexander, Julian: An ancient Greek general who trained and fought alongside Kyrian of Thrace (and was originally his commanding officer). He is a demigod who was cursed by his half-brother Priapus to become a sex slave. Julian is now the husband of Grace Alexander and a professor of classics at Loyola and Tulane. He is an Oracle, and the hero of *Fantasy Lover*.

Alexion: Atlantean word meaning "defender."

Ambrosia and Nectar: Food and drink of the gods. Consuming them will make a mortal into an immortal demigod.

Anaimikos Daimon: A Daimon who feeds only from another Daimon in order to drain him.

Apollites: Apollites are a race created by the Greek god Apollo. More beautiful and stronger than mankind, they were blessed with psychic abilities. Apollo loved his people and wanted them to replace mankind. They were sent to Atlantis where they intermarried with the

Atlantean natives. Until the day that the Apollite/Atlantean queen, in a rage of jealousy, sent her people to kill Apollo's Greek human mistress and his son. In retaliation, Apollo cursed his people threefold:

1. Because they made it appear that an animal had killed his beloved, they would have to feed off each other's blood in order to live. They were given fangs and the eyes of a predator.
2. They could never again walk in his daylight realm.
3. On their twenty-seventh birthday (the age his mistress was murdered), they would all disintegrate slowly and painfully over a twenty-four-hour period until they were dust. (See also **Daimons**.)

Today many of them blend seamlessly into the human world while others live in segregated communes.

Apollymi: An Atlantean goddess known as "the Great Destroyer." Protects and uses the Spathi Daimons and keeps an elite group of around thirty Illuminati as her guards, in addition to Charonte demons and ceredons. She is Archon's wife and Apostolos's mother. For centuries, she has been trapped in Kalosis where she can see the human world and other gods, but not affect them. However, she can still control the Charontes.

Apostolos: The son of Apollymi. He is the Harbinger who will bring about the end of the world.

Arcadians: See **Were-Hunters**.

Archon: Atlantean counterpart to Zeus. He is the son of Chaos, who first established order throughout the universe his father had created. Mate of Apollymi.

Also called Kosmetas, which means "orderer." He is the one who ordered the death of Apostolos and who trapped Apollymi in Kalosis.

Aristo/Aristi: A rare breed of Arcadian with the ability to wield magic effortlessly. They are the most powerful of their kind. Aristi are considered gods in the Arcadian realm and are guarded zealously by patria who would gladly die for them.

Artemis: The redheaded, passionate Greek goddess of the hunt, and creator of the Dark-Hunters. She has twin obsessions with Acheron Parthenopaeus and her own comfort.

Astrid: Astrid is the daughter of Themis, and the sister of the Three Fates. She is a Justice Nymph, an immortal impartial judge who is sent down to earth to rule on possible rogue Dark-Hunters. Olympian justice states that once accused, the defendant must prove himself worthy of mercy. Since the gods only accuse with good cause, Astrid has only been called in to judge guilty Dark-Hunters, and she is beginning to give up hope that there are any innocents. She is the heroine of *Dance with the Devil* and married to Zarek of Moesia.

Atlantis: An ancient island nation with an advanced culture and its own pantheon of gods. It sank into the Aegean Sea eleven thousand years ago.

Atropos: Oldest of the Three Fates, responsible for cutting the threads of lives. Daughter of Themis and sister to Astrid. Also known as Atty.

Blood Rite Squires: The Squires called out to hunt rogue Dark-Hunters or to execute humans/Squires who betray their world. They are all marked with a spiderweb tattoo on their hands.

Blue Blood Squires: Squires who come from a family with many generations of Squires.

Bolt-holes: Portals between Kalosis and the human world, often used by Spathi Daimons to escape Dark-Hunters. Also known as laminas.

Brady, William Jessup: See **Sundown**.

Callabrax: Spartan or actually Dorean (the ancient precursors of the Spartans) Dark-Hunter. One of the first three Dark-Hunters created by Artemis, along with Kyros and Ias.

Callyx: An Apollite who seeks vengeance against Zarek for his wife's death in *Dance with the Devil*. The most recent incarnation of Thanatos.

Camulus: A Gaulish god of war, forced into retirement. Wants to reclaim his godhood.

Carvaletti, Otto: Half Italian mafia, half Blue Blood Squire, with a Ph.D. in film from Princeton. He has a black spiderweb tattoo over the back of his knuckles. Now assigned to Valerius in New Orleans, where he often pretends to be a stupid, loudly dressed lout to annoy his boss.

Ceredon: A creature with the head of a dog, the body of a dragon, and the tail of a scorpion. Several of them protect Apollymi.

Charonte demon: An ancient type of demon that the Atlantean gods managed to tame. Fearsome, powerful, all but unstoppable, they can bond to gods, Hunters, or humans as companions. Once bonded, they can rest in the form of a tattoo on their bonded's body. Charontes are all appetite—they love to shop, kill, and eat everything. They are very easy to annoy and very dangerous when angry. Simi is Acheron's bonded Charonte, and like a daughter to him.

Clotho: One of the Three Fates who is in charge of spinning the threads of lives. Daughter of Themis and sister of Atropos, Lachesis, and Astrid. Also known as Cloie.

Corbin: Born an ancient Greek queen, Corbin was married and widowed young. She fought to keep her husband's throne as her own, and was a beloved queen. Her reign was uncontested until her brother-in-law made a pact with a barbarian tribe to sack the city and burn it to the ground. She died trying to save her servants and their children.

Cronus: Greek god of time.

Cult of Pollux: Apollites who take an oath to die exactly as Apollo cursed them to die—to neither commit suicide nor turn Daimon.

Daimons: Daimons are Apollites who refuse to die at age twenty-seven. They have to steal human souls to artificially elongate their life span. However, once a human soul is taken it begins to die, leaving Daimons always looking for their next victims. So long as they have a living human soul within them, they can continue to live indefinitely. Any Apollite who takes a human soul into his or her body is classified a Daimon.

D'Alerian: Oneroi Dream-Hunter, son of Morpheus, he is a healer and helper to the Dark-Hunters. D'Alerian is a straight man who never met a rule he didn't love. He keeps a constant vigil over the Dark-Hunters and is quick to step in with aid whenever one of them needs it. He and Acheron are close friends.

Danger: A Dark-Huntress who died during the French Revolution. She is the heroine in *Sins of the Night*.

Dark-Hunters: Dark-Hunters are immortal warriors created from those who died wrongfully. Whenever such a person dies, the soul screams out for vengeance. The strongest and angriest of the screams echo through the halls of Olympus. Whenever one reaches Artemis, she considers offering a deal to the one who screamed:

Give her your soul, agree to fight the Daimons who are trying to kill and enslave mankind, and she will make you immortal.

Once the bargain is struck, the new Dark-Hunter is branded with Artemis's double bow-and-arrow logo and allowed an Act of Vengeance. He or she trains with Acheron Parthenopaeus, the enigmatic leader of the Dark-Hunters, and is assigned a location on earth. The Dark-Hunter then spends the rest of eternity fighting Daimons and other evil. Like the Daimons they kill, they have fangs, light-sensitive eyes, and a prohibition against going out in the daylight. The only things that can kill a Dark-Hunter are sunlight, beheading, or total dismemberment. Those who have read *Dance with the Devil* also know that piercing the bow-and-arrow mark can kill them as well. It's something Acheron keeps from them since he doesn't want them to panic and concentrate on it while they're fighting. To do so would give that knowledge to the Daimons who would have a very easy way to kill them.

Artemis pays them well for their services, and provides them with human helpers. (See **Squires**.)

The only way for a Dark-Hunter to become free of Artemis is to find the one true soul who loves him or her enough to pass Artemis's test. That person must take the medallion that contains the Dark-Hunter's soul and hold it to the bow-and-arrow mark on the Dark-Hunter's body until the soul returns. The medallion is lava-hot and will scar the hand. If the person can't maintain his or her grip and the medallion is dropped, the soul is released into nothing. This traps the Dark-Hunter into a painful existence as a Shade. If, on the other hand, the lover succeeds, the Dark-Hunter is once again a mortal with a soul, restarting life at the age they were when they first died.

Dark-Hunter Code: Honor Artemis. Drink no blood. Harm no human or Apollite. Never touch your Squire. Speak with no family, no friends who knew you before you died. Let no Daimon escape alive. Never speak of what you are. You walk alone. Keep your bow mark hidden.

Dark-Hunter.com: An online community of Dark-Hunters and Squires disguised as a fiction and role-play Web site.

Dayslayer: Apollite myth of a Daimon/Apollite who can walk in daylight. (See **Thanatos**.)

Desiderius: Dangerous demigod Spathi Daimon with a grudge against the Devereaux family. Appears in *Seize the Night* and *Night Pleasures*. Can control minds and throw bolts of lightning.

Devereaux: A close-knit family of sisters with a lot of magical talent. Daughters include Esmerelda (Essie); Yasmina (Mina); Petra; Ekaterina (Trina); Karma; Tiyana (Tia)—a voodoo princess; Selena (Lane)—a psychic; Tabitha (Tabby)—a human Vampire-Hunter; and Amanda—an accountant. (See also **Devereaux, Tabitha**; **Hunter, Amanda**; and **Laurens, Bill and Selena**.)

Devereaux, Tabitha: A member of the Devereaux family who hunts Daimons. Owns Pandora's Box, an adult shop on Bourbon Street. Has the ability to sense others' emotions, a quick temper, and an unmatched vibrancy. Twin sister to Amanda Hunter and wife of Valerius Magnus.

Dionysus: Greek god of wine and excess—now amuses himself as a corporate raider. Usually appears as a tall man with short brown hair and a neat goatee. Appears in *Night Embrace*. Not a very good driver . . .

Divine, Marla: Drag queen friend of Tabitha Devereaux. Loves to steal men's coats. Was once escorted in a drag pageant by a very uptight Dark-Hunter.

Dorean Squires: Dorean Squires don't serve a particular Dark-Hunter, but rather serve the whole group. These Squires set up businesses that fulfill the more bizarre needs of the Dark-Hunters such as making specialized weapons or cars. They are also bankers and lawyers who know all about the Dark-Hunter world and who help keep up the appearance of normality.

Doulos: A human servant of Apollites and Daimons.

Dream-Hunters: Dream-Hunters are the children of the Greek gods of sleep. Some of them are born of human mothers, but most are born of the Greek goddess Mist.

Dream-Hunters are also known as Oneroi. Long ago, one of the Oneroi played a trick on the Greek god Zeus. In anger, the god cursed all of their kind to have no emotion whatsoever. Now the only time they can feel anything is when they are in a human's dreams.

Because this is seductive, Oneroi may only visit dreams; they may never participate and never revisit the same human.

There are also a few Dream-Hunters who prefer to stay out of dreams, except to police their own brethren. All Dream-Hunters take a prefix to their name so that everyone will know their role:

M' are the enforcers, they work like a police force and are the leaders.

V' are the ones who help humans who are having trouble sleeping or who have nightmares.

D' are the ones who help the gods and immortals. One of these is almost always sent in to aid newly created Dark-Hunters. Since the Dark-Hunters usually come from horrible pasts, they tend to be plagued with nightmares. Their designated Dream-Hunter will usually watch over them throughout their entire DH existence.

The Dream-Hunter world is complex, but not hard to understand. The main thing to remember is that they are born gods or half-gods. They can be either male or female, and for the most part, they leave the human realm alone and are found only in your wildest dreams as lovers or demons.

Sometimes a Dream-Hunter will become enamored of a dreamer. Sometimes they even instigate the dreams and alter them to enhance their borrowed emotions. When this happens, they are termed Skoti. Oneroi are charged with seeking them out to punish them for their actions.

However, many of the Skoti go unchecked and uncaught. They inhabit our dreams as incubi and succubi.

Eda: Archon's sister, Atlantean Earth goddess.

Elekti: Atlantean word meaning "chosen."

Elysia: A secret underground Apollite city, where Apollites live hidden from humans and Daimons alike. One of the oldest Apollite cities in North America. Home to Phoebe Peters. Featured in *Kiss of the Night*.

Eriksson, Christopher (Chris) Lars: Wulf Tryggvason's Squire and a direct descendant of Wulf's brother. Since Chris is the sole surviving member of Wulf's family, he is the only human who can remember Wulf and who he is.

Eros and Psyche: Married Greek gods of sexual desire and the soul. Often seen playing pool and poker at Sanctuary.

Eycharistisi: Atlantean word for "pleasure." Also a potent Atlantean aphrodisiac that floods the body with endorphins and destroys all inhibitions.

Gallagher, Jamie: Gangster Dark-Hunter from the American Prohibition era. Killed when he fell in love and tried to go straight. Featured in "A Dark-Hunter Christmas."

Gataki: Term of endearment, meaning "kitten."

Gautier, Cherise: Nick Gautier's mother, who had him when she was only fifteen. A beautiful, kindhearted woman in her early forties who works at Sanctuary.

Gautier, Nicholas (Nick) Ambrosius: Kyrian's Squire. A young man with a rough past, a loving mother, and an irreverent attitude. Nick is fiercely loyal and as close to being a friend of Acheron's as any mortal can be.

Gilbert: Valerius Magnus's trusted servant and butler, who would like to be a Squire.

Godeau, Marguerite D'Aubert: The daughter of a Louisiana senator and a Cajun beauty queen, Maggie wants to escape her straight-laced social world. As a student at Tulane University, she joined a study group with Nick Gautier. Heroine of *Unleash the Night*.

Hold the human hair: A phrase used at Sanctuary to indicate that a Were-Hunter wants an especially strong drink, one that would inebriate a human with one shot. Weres have a higher metabolism and can handle a lot more alcohol.

Hunter, Amanda: One of the Devereaux sisters, Amanda always wanted to be more normal than the empaths, voodoo priestesses, and psychics she was raised with. Tabitha Devereaux is her twin sister. Amanda became an accountant, but the supernatural found her anyway. Heroine of *Night Pleasures*, she is a human sorceress, married to Kyrian Hunter, and the mother of Marissa Hunter.

Hunter, Kyrian: Ancient Greek Dark-Hunter. Born prince and heir to Thrace, Kyrian was disinherited when he married an ex-prostitute against his father's wishes. As a legendary Macedonian general, he cut a trail of slaughter through the Mediterranean during the Fourth Macedonian War. Chroniclers wrote that he would break the Roman stranglehold on the known world and claim Rome for his own. He would have succeeded had he not been betrayed by his wife and delivered into the hands of his enemies. He was tortured for weeks and then executed by Valerius's grandfather. Hero of *Night Pleasures*. He is the husband of Amanda Hunter and father of Marissa Hunter.

Hunter, Marissa: Amanda and Kyrian Hunter's daughter, Marissa is a baby with astounding powers and a favorite with Acheron and Simi.

Hypnos: Greek God who holds dominion over all the gods of sleep.

I am the Light of the Lyre: Phrase used by Daimons and Apollites to seek shelter from another Daimon or Apollite. Refers to their kinship to Apollo, god of the sun.

Ias of Groesia: An ancient Greek Dark-Hunter. One of the first three created, along with Callabrax and Kyros. Cruelly betrayed by his wife.

Icelus: Greek god who creates human shapes in dreams, and father of some Dream-Hunters. His children tend to be the more erotic Dream-Hunters. They live for sex and drift from dream to dream seeking new partners.

Idios: A rare serum made by the Oneroi that allows the user to become one with the dreamer for a short time. Used in dreams to guide and direct, allowing one sleeper to experience another's life so he can better understand it.

Illuminati: The Spathi Daimon bodyguards of Apollymi, led by Stryker and comprising between thirty to forty members. They include the oldest and most powerful of the Spathi.

Inferno: Also known as Dante's Inferno. The nightclub run by Dante Pontis, located in Minnesota.

Inkblot: A derogatory term for Daimons stemming from the strange black mark that all Daimons develop on their chests when they cross over from being Apollites to human slayers. This is what a dagger or sharp object must pierce to kill a Daimon.

Kallinos, Jasyn: A Katagaria Were-Hunter, Jaysn changes into a hawk. He is one of Sanctuary's deadlier inhabitants.

Kallitechnis: A Greek term meaning "dream master."

Kalosis: Atlantean word for "hell." The place where Apollymi is imprisoned so that she can see the human world but not participate in it. It is also where the Spathi Daimons live in perpetual darkness. No Dark-Hunter can enter and few Were-Hunters are allowed to live after visiting this realm, but it is accessible to Daimons through bolt-holes or laminas.

Katagaria: See **Were-Hunters**.

Katoteros: The Atlantean term for "heaven," and where Acheron makes his home. All Apollites and Daimons dream of being able to reclaim their right to rest here.

Kattalakis: A family name that indicates direct descent from one of King Lycaon's sons. The name belongs to the Drakos and Lykos branches on both the Arcadian and Katagaria side. Family members include Vane, Fang, Fury, Sebastian, Damos, Makis, Illarion, Bracis, Acmenis, Antiphone, Percy, Markos, Dare, Bryani, and Star, among many others.

Kattalakis, Bryani: An Arcadian Lykos Were-Huntress; mother to Vane, Fang, Anya, Fury, Dare, and Star. She has three vicious-looking scars on her face and neck and is a Sentinel. Bryani dresses like something out of a *Xena* episode. She hates Vane and his Katagaria father who tried to force her to accept him as mate. Lives in Dark Age Britain.

Kattalakis, Fang: A Katagari Were-Hunter who changes into a brown timber wolf. Fang loves to crack bad jokes and is currently recuperating from wounds under the care of Aimee Peltier at Sanctuary. Brother of Vane and Fury.

Kattalakis, Fury: Vane's littermate. Like Vane, he is a large white timber wolf in animal form, with a distinguishing brown spot. Fury was born in human form and was Arcadian until puberty when his Katagari half took over.

Kattalakis, Markus: Katagari Were-Hunter. Changes into a brown timber wolf. Tried to force Bryani to accept him as mate and failed. Father of Vane, Fang, and Fury, among others.

Kattalakis, Sebastian: Arcadian Drakos Were-Hunter, grandson of King Lycaon. Was excommunicated from his patria after the death of his sister. Now he walks as a solitary Sentinel, and has done so for four hundred years. Hero of "Dragonswan (*Tapestry*)."

Kattalakis, Vane: Arcadian Were-Hunter. He is a large, solid white timber wolf in animal form. Vane was born Katagaria but changed to Arcadian when puberty gave him his magic and his human form. He was protected from his pack by his brother Fang and his sister Anya. Vane is an Aristo and a Sentinel. Brother of Anya, Fang, and Fury. Hero of *Night Play*.

Kell: A former Roman gladiator from Dacia, now a Dark-Hunter stationed in Dallas. Makes weapons for the Dark-Hunters.

Kori: Handmaiden to Artemis, the most noted of which is Kat Agrotera.

Kouti, Pandora: Heroine of "Winter Born (*Stroke of Midnight*)," Arcadian were-pantheress. Pandora is of a patria whose women are subject to a bargain with a Katagaria panther patria, but she is not willing to honor it—she will fight back. Pandora is mated to Katagaria panther Dante Pontis.

Kyklonas: A ceredon guarding Apollymi's temple in Kalosis. Its name means "tornado."

Kyrios: A respectful Atlantean term for "lord."

Kyros of Seklos: An ancient Greek Dark-Hunter. One of the first three created, along with Callabrax and Ias. Stationed in Aberdeen, Mississippi.

Lachesis: The middle of the Three Fates, responsible for weaving the pattern of fate. Sister to Astrid and daughter of Themis. Also known as Lacy.

Laminas: Atlantean term for "haven." It can refer to a

portal between Kalosis and the human world, often used by Spathi Daimons, that is also known as a bolt-hole. This term can also applied to any Were-Hunter sanctuary. These are established safe houses where the Were-Hunters can go without fear of being hunted by their own kind. Apollites and Daimons in those havens are safe from Dark-Hunters.

Laurens, Bill and Selena: Bill is a politically connected lawyer, who sometimes does work for the Dark-Hunters, but his real ties are to the Were-Hunters. His wife, Selena, is a psychic who tells fortunes in Jackson Square in New Orleans. Selena is a Devereaux sister, and the best friend of Grace Alexander. In fact, Selena is the one who gave Grace the enchanted book at the beginning of *Fantasy Lover*. She is impulsive and emotional—the perfect foil for Bill.

Limani: A Were-Hunter sanctuary where Arcadians and Katagaria alike can go without fear of being hunted. No violence is permitted in a limani. Limani status is difficult to achieve.

Liza: A Dorean Squire who owns a doll shop on Royal Street in New Orleans. She makes custom dolls and special weapons for the Dark-Hunters.

Loki: The Norse trickster god.

Lycaon: The king who used his magic to make the Were-Hunter races.

MacRae, Channon: A history professor at the University of Virginia specializing in pre-Norman Britain. Heroine of "Dragonswan (*Tapestry*)."

M'Adoc: An Oneroi Dream-Hunter, he is the son of

Phantasos. He is an Enforcer who watches over both the Oneroi and the Skoti. He is quick to issue orders, but seldom takes them. M'Adoc is the Oneroi of last resort. When he comes after you, you know you're going to pay. He often takes the jobs no one else wants to do.

Magnus, Valerius: A Dark-Hunter from ancient Rome, Valerius was once the son of a Roman senator. As a Roman general, he led conquests throughout Greece, Gaul, and Britannia. He doesn't play well with most Dark-Hunters, since so many come from Greece or other countries he conquered. Val is truly ostracized from the rest of his brethren. He is very formal and currently posted in New Orleans. He is the half-brother of Zarek and hero of *Seize the Night*.

Marvin the Monkey: Sanctuary's mascot, Marvin is the only *real* animal in Sanctuary. Good friends with Wren Tigarian.

McDaniels, Erin: Corporate drone who has repressed her more creative impulses and thus is a prime target for Skoti. Heroine of "Phantom Lover (*Midnight Pleasures*)."

McTierney: A human family with connections to the Were-Hunter world. Members include mother Joyce, father Paul, and children Bride, Dierdre, and Patrick. Paul is a veterinarian famous around the New Orleans area for his ads promoting neutering. The family have several pets: Titus, a black rottweiler; the Professor and Marianne, two cats; Bart, a gator; and a rotating cast of recuperating animals.

McTierney, Bride: A human who owns the Lilac and Lace Boutique on Iberville in the French Quarter.

She lives in an apartment behind her shop and is the heroine of *Night Play*.

Metriazo collar: A thin silver collar that sends tiny ionic pulses into the body of a Were-Hunter to prevent him or her from using their magic powers.

M'gios: The Atlantean word for "my son."

M'Ordant: Oneroi Dream-Hunter, son of Phantasos, he is an Enforcer who watches over both the Oneroi and the Skoti. He is hard-nosed and down-to-business. Still, he has a degree of compassion that is forbidden to his kind. It doesn't stop him from doing whatever is necessary to do his job. He makes his appearance in "Phantom Lover (*Midnight Pleasures*)."

Morginne: A Dark-Huntress who tricked Wulf Tryggvason into trading souls and cursed him so that no human except one of his bloodline can remember him.

Morpheus: Greek god of dreams; father of many Oneroi.

Morrigan: The Celtic Raven goddess. Talon swore loyalty to her during his human lifetime, but she seemed to have abandoned him long before his death. She is the grandmother of Sunshine Runningwolf.

Mount Olympus: Home of the Greek gods.

Nynia: Talon's first love, during his human lifetime. She was an ancient Celt, and a fisherman's daughter whom Talon insisted upon marrying despite the clan's disapproval. She died giving birth to his still-born child.

Nyx: Greek goddess of night.

Omegrion: The ruling council of the Were-Hunters. Similar to a senate, one representative from each branch of the Arcadian and Katagaria is sent to represent them all. They make laws that govern all the Were-Hunters and are responsible for setting up sanctuaries. A = Arcadian representative, K = Katagaria representative.

 Its members are: Litarian (lions) Patrice Leonides (A), Paris Sebastienne (K); Drakos (dragons) Damos Kattalakis (A), Darion Kattalakis (K); Gerakian (hawks, falcons, and eagles) Arion Petrakis (A), Draven Hawke (K); Tigarian (tigers) Adrian Gavril (A), Lysander Stephanos (K); Lykos (wolves) Vane Kattalakis (A), Fury Kattalakis (K); Ursulan (bears) Leo Apollonian (A), Nicolette Peltier (K); Panthiras (panthers) Alexander James (A), Dante Pontis (K); Tsakalis (jackals) Constantine (A), Vincenzo Moretti (K); Niphetos Pardalia (snow leopards) Anelise Romano (A), Wren Tigarian (K); Pardalia (leopards) Dorian Kontis (A), Stefan Kouris (K); Balios (jaguars) extinct (A), Myles Stephanopoulos (K); Helikias (cheetahs) Jace Wilder (A), Michael Giovanni (K).

Oneroi: Dream-Hunters responsible for watching over human dreams and protecting them from Skoti. Often assigned to newly created Dark-Hunters to heal them mentally.

Oracle: Anyone who communes with the gods.

Orasia: The Atlantean goddess of sleep.

Ouisa: Distinct from the body and the soul, the Ouisa is the personality—the part of a person that is left when a Dark-Hunter becomes a Shade.

Parthenopaeus, Acheron (Ash): Ancient immortal Atlantean, leader of the Dark-Hunters. Born in 9548 B.C. on the Greek isle of Didymos to King Acarion and Queen Aara. His promises and curses are binding and can have unintended consequences. Tall and naturally blond, he dyes his hair different colors and dresses like a Goth most of the time. He looks about twenty-one and makes his home in Katoteros.

No one knows anything about him and he likes it that way. In reality, he is a god-killer and an Atlantean god with powers that no one knows the full extent of. He refuses to answer any personal questions and he must keep his word no matter what. The correct Atlantean/Greek pronunciation of his name is *Ack-uh-rahn Pahr-thin-oh-pay-us*. These days, only the older Dark-Hunters and Artemis pronounce it that way. The rest either call him Ash or *Ash-uh-rahn*. The exceptions to this are his demon, Simi, who calls him akri, and Talon, who calls him T-Rex.

Patria: A family grouping of Were-Hunters of the same race and animal genus.

Peltier: The family of bear Katagaria Were-Hunters who run the Sanctuary bar in New Orleans. Family members include Nicolette, Aubert, Dev, Kyle, Aimee, Remi, Quinn, Zar, Serre, Etienne, Alain, Cody, Griffe, and Cherif. Mama (Nicolette) and Papa (Aubert) Bear decided to found Sanctuary as a safe zone after their cubs Bastien and Gilbert were brutally killed by Arcadian Sentinels.

Peltier House: Adjacent to the bar, Peltier House is the living quarters for Sanctuary's hidden animal population. There they can assume their animal forms without fear of discovery and their young cubs are protected. It has more alarms than Fort Knox and is always guarded by at least two Peltier family members.

Peters, Cassandra Elaine: Half human and half Apollite, she is one of the last Apollites in the direct bloodline of Apollo. Daughter of Jefferson and sister to Phoebe and Nia. The Peters family is subject to a prophecy that if they all die, the Apollites will be free of their curse, so they are hunted by Spathi Daimons who want their freedom. The truth, however, is that if their bloodline dies out, so does the earth and all who live here. Heroine of *Kiss of the Night*.

Peters, Jefferson T.: Cassandra and Phoebe Peters's human father. Wealthy owner and founder of one of the world's largest pharmaceutical research and development companies.

Peters, Nia: Cassandra's sister and Jefferson's half-Apollite daughter. One of the last direct descendants of Apollo. Died with her mother when Spathi Daimons blew up their car.

Peters, Phoebe: Cassandra's sister and Jefferson's half-Apollite daughter. One of the last direct descendants of Apollo. She was rescued from the Spathi attack that killed her mother and sister Nia. After their deaths, Urian turned her Daimon. Lives in Elysia as Urian's wife.

Phantasos: Greek god who creates nonsentient dream objects, father of some Dream-Hunters. His children tend to be more cerebral and they are most often the Oneroi who police the Dream-Hunters.

Phaser: An Arcadian Sentinel weapon developed for

use against the Katagaria. Stronger than a Taser, it sends a vicious jolt of electricity through the victims, causing their magic to go berserk. They are unable to hold either of their forms and a strong enough jolt will cause them to literally fall out of their bodies and become noncorporeal beings such as ghosts.

Phobetor: God of animal shapes, father of some of the Dream-Hunters. Phobetor's children tend to make nightmares. They often take the shapes of demons, dragons, and other terrifying images.

Pontis: A patria of Katagaria Were-Panthers. Includes Dante, Romeo, Michelangelo (Mike), Leonardo (Leo), Gabriel, Angel, Donatello, Bonita, Sal, and Tyla, among others.

Pontis, Dante: A Katagari Panther who owns Dante's Inferno in the Twin Cities, Minnesota. Though he technically owns one of the known Were-Hunter sanctuaries, he's not nearly as tolerant as other sanctuary owners. He is the head of his family and tends to take no crap from anyone. He first appears in *Kiss of the Night*, is the hero of "Winter Born (*Stroke of Midnight*)," and is mated to the Arcadian panther Pandora Kouti.

Priapus: Greek and Roman sex god, half brother of Julian Alexander.

Regis: Leader of a Were-Hunter pack who is essentially their king and representative.

Rogue Dark-Hunter: One who has breached the Dark-Hunter Code and must die. Hunted by Blood Rite Squires or Thanatos.

Runningwolf, Sunshine: Daughter of Starla and Daniel. A free spirit and an artist of tremendous talent who is easily distracted from the practical. Sells her art in Jackson Square and likes the color pink. Heroine of *Night Embrace* and now married to Talon Runningwolf.

Runningwolf, Talon: An ancient Celtic Dark-Hunter known as Speirr (which meant "Talon" in his language) in his human life. He was the son of a Druid high priest and a Celtic queen, and was high chieftain of his clan. After the deaths of his aunt, uncle, wife, and son over a short period of time, he was told that his ancient gods had cursed him. To appease the gods, he allowed himself to be sacrificed. Once his clan had Talon secured to the altar, they killed his sister before his eyes and then turned on him. As a Dark-Hunter, Talon has the power of telekinesis. He walks between this realm and the next with the help of Spirit Guides, and loses power when he feels negative emotions. The hero of *Night Embrace* and married to Sunshine Runningwolf.

Runningwolf's: A club on Canal Street in New Orleans run by Starla and Daniel Runningwolf.

Ryssa: A Greek princess who was one of Apollo's favorite mistresses. She bore him a son, which led the Apollite queen to such jealousy that she sent a team of Apollites to kill them. They were ordered to make it look like an animal had done it. That act caused Apollo to curse all the Apollites.

Rytis: An invisible stream of waves that move through everything. The waves echo, flow, and occasionally buckle. The Rytis is what Were- and Dream-Hunters use to move through space and time.

Saga: The Norse goddess of poetry.

Sanctuary: The premier New Orleans biker bar, owned by the Peltiers, a clan of Katagaria bears. It is a limani: a safe zone for all types of Hunters where natural rivalries are put aside and no fighting or killing is allowed.

Santana, Wayne: Convicted and imprisoned for involuntary manslaughter while still young, Wayne lucked out when the Runningwolf family decided to hire him despite his record. They lucked out, too, in gaining a faithful friend and a good lookout for absentminded Sunshine.

Sasha: Astrid's Katagari Were-Hunter companion in *Dance with the Devil*. He's a large white timber wolf in animal form and a lot of attitude in any form.

Savitar: Even more mysterious than Acheron, he is rumored to have been the one to train Ash in his powers. He oversees the Omegrion even though none of the Were-Hunters are sure how this came about. He has a strong fascination for the beach and surfing, and is usually found dressed as a surfer or beach bum. No one, not even Acheron, knows anything at all about him. He is extremely powerful and deadly. Most of his body is covered with tattoos.

Sentinels: Out of the Arcadian patrias are born the Sentinels—the Guardians of man- and were-kind. Only a select few are born to each patria. They are the strongest Were-Hunters and they pursue and execute Slayers. A colorful geometric design covers one side of an Arcadian Sentinel's face once they reach maturity, but the Sentinel can hide the design if he or she chooses.

Sfora: A scrying globe that people in Katoteros can use to watch events in other realms, including the human realm. Sometimes those being viewed can sense that someone is watching.

Shade: What a Dark-Hunter becomes when he is killed and does not immediately get invested with a soul. Shadedom is an existence of unrelenting hunger and thirst, but its worst aspect is that the Shade is invisible to all mortals and denied contact with everyone—so it quickly goes insane screaming for attention in its solitary confinement. There are rumors of an out clause for Shades.

Simi: Acheron's Charonte demon, who can manifest as a human or a demon, and who rests as an ever-changing tattoo on Ash's body. Though she is thousands of years old, she is equivalent to a human eighteen-year-old. She is like a daughter to Acheron. Loves barbecue, movies, and QVC. Hates to be told no.

Also, the Charonte term for "baby."

Skoti: Usually the children of Phobetor, but can be any Dream-Hunter who goes bad. Nightmare demons who infiltrate the dreams of humans to suck emotions and creativity from them, they are also incubi and succubi who derive sexual pleasure from their dream-hosts.

Slayer: Katagaria Were-Hunters driven to madness at puberty when they come into their powers, but fail to find a way to control them. They become ruthless slayers who kill anything or anyone who cross them. Similar to rabies, it is an infection for which there is no cure. Hunted by Sentinels.

Smith, Janice: An African-American Dark-Huntress with a Carribbean accent. Currently posted in New Orleans.

Spathi: Warrior Daimons. Apollymi's guards and pets, who can be reincarnated after they die if someone cares enough; their essence remains intact. See also **Illuminati**.

Squires: To help the Dark-Hunters appear "normal," Acheron set up a Squire's Council of humans who serve them. A Squire works with a Dark-Hunter, usually living in the same house, and—to the outside world—appearing to be the owner. It is a Squire's job to attend to all the day-to-day monotony of running the household so the Dark-Hunter can focus on killing Daimons. Squires are often at risk since the Daimons know a Squire is an emotional attachment for the Dark-Hunter.

If a Dark-Hunter is in danger, it is the Squire's responsibility to pull him or her out, although the Squire doesn't have immortality or psychic abilities. Like the Dark-Hunters they serve, they are extremely well paid for their services. (See also **Dorian Squires, Blue Blood Squires**.)

Strati: Term used for Katagaria soldiers who seek out Arcadians to fight. They are the Katagaria equivalent to Sentinels except they have no facial markings.

Strykerius (Stryker): The leader and trainer of Apollymi's Spathi Daimons and leader of the elite Illuminati force. He is the son of Apollo and turned on his father after Apollo cursed him and his race. He is the adopted son of Apollymi and father to Urian. Holds a grudge against Acheron and plots the deaths of all whom Ash holds dear.

Styxx: Acheron's human brother, and an identical twin. Styxx was born in 9548 B.C. on the Greek isle of Didymos to King Acarion and Queen Aara. His and Acheron's life forces are connected, so he can't die until Acheron does. Styxx has spent centuries hating Ash.

Summoning, the: A Daimon homing beacon the Dayslayer can use to summon Daimons and Apollites to conference or for war.

Sundown: Sundown is a Dark-Hunter from the nineteenth-century American West. His real name is William Jessup "Jess" Brady. Jess was orphaned at age five and grew up under the harsh hand of a preacher man who owned the local orphanage. At eleven, he ran away and headed out West where he quickly learned life wasn't fair and it wasn't easy for a boy with no family. At sixteen, he was making his living as a gunslinger, train robber, and cardsharp. He lived his life hard and was ruthlessly shot in the back on his way to his wedding by his best man—the only man he'd ever trusted—who wanted to collect the bounty on his head. He is currently stationed in Reno, Nevada.

Swain: Suffix for a male Were-Hunter, e.g., dragon-swain, pantherswain, bearswain, etc.

Swan: Suffix for a female Were-Hunter, e.g., dragon-swan, pantherswan, bearswan, etc.

"Sweet Home Alabama": The Lynyrd Skynyrd song played to warn everyone in Sanctuary when Acheron comes into the bar.

Sword of Cronus: Julian Alexander's sword. Only those with the blood of Cronus in their veins may touch it without being burned.

Talpinas: At one time, a type of Squire whose sole purpose was to take care of Dark-Hunters' carnal needs. Long since banned by Artemis.

Tartarus: Greek version of hell. The realm where humans are punished for the sins of their lifetimes.

Tessera: A group of four Were-Hunters sent out to hunt others of their kind.

Thanatos: The Greek word for "death." Also, an Apollite to whom Artemis gives special powers and whom he sends to kill rogue Dark-Hunters. Known as the Dayslayer in Apollite mythology. There has been more than one Thanatos over the centuries. See also **Callyx**.

Themis: Redheaded Greek goddess of justice, mother of Astrid and the Fates.

Theodorakopolus, Colt: A Were-Hunter Acadian Sentinel, Colt was orphaned at birth and raised at Sanctuary. Colt hides his Sentinel birthmark.

Theti Squires: The Squire police force that makes sure all Squires obey the laws. Unlike the Blood Rite Squires, they are not allowed to kill.

Thirio: The need Were-Hunters feel when mated to combine their life forces so if one dies, they both die. Can be resisted.

Thrylos: Greek word for "legend."

Tigarian, Wren: A Katagari Were-Hunter who can turn into a white tiger, a snow leopard, or a combination of the two. He has lived at Sanctuary since his parents died mysteriously violent deaths. He busses tables there and is extremely dangerous and withdrawn. He has no prejudice—he hates everyone and everything equally. His only friend is Nick, and he will only interact peacefully with Aimee and Marvin. Hero of *Unleash the Night*.

Tree of Life: Supernatural tree that blooms only in the garden of the Atlantean Destroyer. Its leaves alone can break the ypnsi.

Trelosa: A disease similar to rabies that can strike Were-Hunters at the time of puberty. It causes a madness that leads to the infected Arcadian or Katagarian becoming an indiscriminate killer. There is no cure.

T-Rex: Talon's favorite irreverent nickname for Acheron.

Tryggvason, Erik: Son of Cassandra and Wulf and a direct descendant of Apollo. Guarded carefully and loved by too many protective males: Wulf, Chris, and Urian.

Tryggvason, Wulf: A Dark-Hunter Viking warrior whose recklessness brought him into contact with Morginne, a powerful Dark-Huntress. She tricked him into trading souls with her. He is the only Dark-Hunter who was never granted an Act of Vengeance.

And since he was wrongfully brought over by another Dark-Hunter, his powers are very different from those of the rest of his brethren. The most curious power of all is that of amnesia. No human or animal is capable of remembering him five minutes after they leave his presence. The only exceptions to that are those who bear his blood. Hero of *Kiss of the Night*, husband of Cassandra Peters, and father of Erik Tryggvason. His soul is held by Loki.

Urian: A reincarnated Spathi Daimon, formerly Stryker's eldest and last surviving son, a former member of the Illuminati, and husband to Phoebe Peters. Stryker killed Phoebe and cut Urian's throat for helping Cassandra Peters, and since then, Urian has been an occasional and prickly ally of Acheron and the Dark-Hunters.

V'aiden: A Dream-Hunter who longs to feel. Hero of "Phantom Lover (*Midnight Pleasures*)."

Villkatt: An old Norse endearment meaning "wild cat."

Were-Hunters: An ancient Greek king (Lycaon) unknowingly married an Apollite. She hid what she was from him until her twenty-seventh birthday, when she perished painfully. When the king realized what she was, he also realized that their two sons would follow in their mother's footsteps and die horribly at age twenty-seven.

To prevent this, the king rounded up Apollites and began experimenting on them. He magically spliced their life forces with those of various animals (lions, dragons, birds of prey, tigers, wolves, bears, panthers, jackals, leopards, jaguars, and cheetahs) to create hybrid beings.

The splicing created two classes of beings: Arcadians, those who held human hearts and could shapeshift into animals, and Katagaria, those who had animal hearts and could become human.

Once the king was done experimenting, he chose the two most powerful creatures (wolves and dragons) and merged them with his own children. When the Greek Fates saw this, they were angered that he would dare to try to thwart them. They demanded he kill his sons and all the others he had created.

He refused.

As punishment, the Fates decreed that the two species would always war against each other. The Arcadians and the Katagaria would never know peace. To this day and beyond, they hunt each other and wage their war.

Unlike their Apollite cousins, they live for hundreds of years. They share the same psychic abilities as the Apollites, plus they have a few extra abilities such as time travel and the ability to shapeshift.

Were-Hunter patrias are: Litarian (lions); Drakos (dragons); Gerakian (hawks, falcons, and eagles); Tigarian (tigers); Lykos (wolves); Ursulan (bears); Panthiras (panthers); Tsakalis (jackals); Niphetos Pardalia (snow leopards); Pardalia (leopards); Balios (jaguars); Helikias (cheetahs).

Were-Hunter Mate: Each Were-Hunter has a mate who is chosen, usually against their wills, by the

Fates. Mates are indicated by a special matching tattoo that appears on the hand of both partners a few hours after they have sex. They then have three weeks to accept or reject the pairing. There is no way to force one partner to accept the other. If the mating is mutually accepted, they can have children together. If not, both will be sterile for the rest of their lives. After finding his mate, a male Were-Hunter will never be able to have sex with anyone else again. A female Were-Hunter will be able to have sex, but won't be able to have children with anyone else. (See also **Thirio**.)

Whitethunder, Carson: An Arcadian Were-Hunter who changes into a hawk, Carson is the resident vet and medical doctor at Sanctuary. He goes to Dr. Paul McTierney for advice on particularly tricky animal cases.

Wink: A minor Greek god of sleep, son of Nyx and Erebus. His mist can be used by a Dream-Hunter to make a human drowsy or to exert control over one, V'aiden's great-uncle.

Ydor: Atlantean ocean god.

Ypnsi: Sacred sleep that Orasia had once dispensed from the sacred halls of Katoteros, back in the days when the ancient Atlantean gods ruled the earth.

Zarek of Moesia: A Dark-Hunter who was born the unwanted son of a Greek slave and a Roman senator. Moments after his birth, his mother gave him to a servant with orders to kill the infant. The servant took mercy on the child and took him to his father,

who had no more use for the baby than his mother.
Thus Zarek became the whipping boy of a noble
Roman family. He trusts no one. He seldom inter-
acts with other Dark-Hunters, and when he does, it
is always grudgingly and with the utmost disdain for
them. Because of his steadfast refusal to follow any
orders (even those of Artemis) and his lack of re-
gard for anyone other than himself, he is kept in isolation in Alaska where his activity is seriously
limited and closely monitored. There are many who
fear he will one day unleash his powers against humans as well as Daimons. He is the hero of *Dance
with the Devil* and married to Astrid.

Zurvan: Ancient Persian god of time and space. Also
known as Cas.